Shady City

By the same author

Of This Our Time
Under the Tropic

Shady City

Tom Hopkinson

Hutchinson

London Melbourne Auckland Johannesburg

First published in Great Britain in 1987 by Hutchinson Ltd, an imprint of Century Hutchinson Ltd, Brookmount House, 62–65 Chandos Place, London, WC2N 4NW

Century Hutchinson Australia Pty Ltd
PO Box 496, 16–22 Church Street, Hawthorn, Victoria 3122, Australia

Century Hutchinson New Zealand Limited
PO Box 40–086, Glenfield, Auckland 10, New Zealand

Century Hutchinson South Africa (Pty) Ltd
PO Box 337, Bergvlei, 2012 South Africa

Photoset in 11/11½ pt Bembo by Deltatype, Ellesmere Port
Printed and bound in Great Britain by
Biddles Ltd, Guildford and King's Lynn

ISBN: 0 09 168330 0

To Africa,
the awakening giant

To the Reader

Seeing how many Nigerian novelists, playwrights and journalists of talent write and have written about their country with an intimacy of knowledge no outsider can possess, it may appear wilful – even presumptuous – for an English writer to choose Nigeria as setting for an imaginative work.

But any writer who undertakes the labour involved in a long novel is likely to do so rather as a victim of obsession than guided by the light of reason, and from the day early in 1958 when I first set foot in Lagos I was obsessed by Nigeria and its people. The frequent visits I paid over the next seven years took me into many parts of the country among people at all levels of life. The visits were often short, but they had one common factor: I was in the company of Nigerians rather than of expatriate whites or visitors.

The impressions I took in, to haunt me after I had left, were of men and women with an energy, an openness of feeling, an impulsiveness in action and an exultant enjoyment of life which I encountered nowhere else. The ministers laid down the law, the military men strutted, the market mammies haggled, the taxi drivers blew their horns and drove at pedestrians with cheerful ferocity. The girls in the dance halls jived and pranced with exuberance, and the pimps outside the night clubs extolled what they had to offer with a flow of humour and a rich vocabulary. The very beggars assailed passers-by with an energy that did them credit, and where else but in Lagos have I seen a delivery boy with the cardboard notice 'Future Prime Minister' fastened to his bicycle?

More than twenty years ago, while living in East Africa, I began to write this book and continued to work on it in several continents over the next twelve – only to lay it aside a few years ago when the difficulties of getting it published seemed insuperable.

For the fact that it was ever completed I have to thank my

wife Dorothy, who read the early chapters, urged me to continue, and later gave me the encouragement to rewrite it several times. And for the fact of its appearance now I have to thank Tony Whittome of Century Hutchinson who joyfully accepted the much-rejected manuscript.

A few facts may help the reader find his/her way. Walpole is born about the year 1928, so that he is in his early thirties when his country achieves independence in 1960. For the extraordinary story of the conspiracy of 1962 which comes into the concluding chapters, I have made use of newspaper reports of the subsequent trials, particularly those in the *Daily Times* of Lagos. Two books which proved of special assistance were *The Trial of Obofemi Awolowo* by the distinguished journalist L. K. Jakande and *Fugitive Offender*, the autobiography of Chief Anthony Enahoro, who has recounted the vicissitudes of his life both in Nigeria and Britain with urbanity and humour.

In attempting to pick my way through the maze within mazes of West African names and name systems, I owe much to the pamphlet 'Grammar of African Names' by Increase Coker – a name familiar in the history of Nigerian law, journalism and political life; but the mistakes which will have crept in must be charged to my account, not his. The well-informed reader may also detect that two or three East African proverbs have managed to appear in a West African setting, a transfer I consider legitimate in these days of easy communication.

Contents

1

Beside the Lagoon

At the age of six when his mother died, Walpole Abiose was neither Walpole nor Abiose. His true name was Babarimisa, meaning that his father had vanished as the baby approached. The name probably conveyed a slander, however, since it is unlikely that Walpole's father had the least consciousness of having achieved paternity. Except sometimes crooningly by his mother when she took him in her arms, the name Babarimisa was never spoken, and to the children with whom he played in the cluster of tumbledown shanties on the fringe of Lagos where they had their home, he was known only as 'Wa'poo'. Scuttering around after the bigger children in the mud and dust, sending the seedy hens squawking and the mangy bush-dogs cringing beneath the huts, the boy was always struggling to catch up, and his cries of 'Wa! Wa!' and the puffing noises he let out before he was able to speak clearly, earned him his nickname.

From the time he could walk at all Wa'poo would have nothing to do with small children like himself; the company he sought was that of bigger boys and girls, and particularly of the grown-ups. When the older men sat chatting gravely over the day's events, around a fire made of driftwood and odd pieces of coal washed up along the shores of the lagoon, a flicker of flame would reveal a tiny figure standing solemnly, thumb in mouth, behind the oldest man. Gently rebuked by one of the elders or summoned away by his mother's cry, he would vanish into the darkness only to creep back a few minutes later and resume his watchful, silent stance. With battered trousers trailing below his calves, a string across his shoulders serving as braces, and a vest of indescribable colour hanging loose behind, Wa'poo seemed less a child than a dusty miniature man and his unuttered assumption that he had a right to be present at the men's discussions impressed itself upon them by degrees. Believers in reincarnation, worshippers of those ancestors who might well be living among them now in other bodies, they accepted that some force out of the past was working in the child, a force which it might be unwise to flout, so that by the time he was four years old it aroused no rebuke that, long after other children lay sack-covered in sleeping corners, Wa'poo should stand, gazing with abstracted wonder into the lined faces of his elders as they reminisced.

The world into which Wa'poo had been born consisted of an expanse of sun-baked mud, fringed on one side with palm trees, dissolving on the other by imperceptible degrees into salt-water brown and thick as coffee. During the long dry seasons dust was like a second skin; it filled Wa'poo's eyes, nostrils, mouth and peppercorn knobs of hair, and when the children fought they rubbed handfuls of dust into one another's faces. During the short months of the annual downpour the ground cracked open with fertility, knurls of hairy green thrust up into the light and the thick-leaved plants which came bursting out could almost be seen growing. Sliding and slipping, the barefoot children raced happily around, letting the rain sluice through their rags and almost through their skins, steaming themselves dry in patches of sudden sunlight or around the fires made by the men engaged in caulking their canoes.

The coffee-coloured lagoon was shallow as a bath. In some mysterious way the children did not understand, the water was sometimes near and sometimes further off, but it was never deep. Wading into it with shouts and splashes, the children were tired with the effort long before the level reached their necks. For men who did not work in the city the lagoon was a source of livelihood, and they poled their heavy canoes, axed and burned out of a single tree trunk, far out of sight into the mist or along the shore, casting their circular, light entrapping nets a hundred times to bring home a small basketful of fish. Once, it was said, the lagoons had been full of crocodiles and the men must carry spears with them as well as paddles, but the noise and effluents from the nearby city had driven them all off, so that they survived now only in the children's games and the stories of their elders. On shore the fishermen did little except mend their gear and dry their nets while the women, clothes tucked round their waists, bent forward with straight backs on planted feet to work the precious patches of soil beneath the palms, from which came the yams, cassava, sweet potatoes, plantains and fiery peppers for their cookpots. Centre of all life was the cluster of shacks, precariously perched on piles for protection against flooding, beneath which, among the poles and paddles, nets and fish-traps stored by the fishermen, were a thousand delightful, evil-smelling hideouts for the children in their games.

The thirty or so families living in the village formed a closely-bound community, even their feuds serving to unite them. The grown-ups all ranked as Wa'poo's 'aunts' and 'uncles' and the children he fought with were his 'brothers' and 'sisters'. All uncles and aunts, but particularly the older men, must be obeyed and treated with respect, which they repaid with a benign consideration. No child, whatever his origin or status, was made to feel unwanted or a nuisance; its childish dignity had also to be regarded, and though a blow or an angry shout was not uncommon, rebukes were rare and gentle. By day most of the aunts and uncles went away to work on the lagoon or in the cultivated plots, or else vanished on bicycles into the vast, murmurous city. Of the children no more than a handful attended school, much to the envy of the rest who crowded round when they came back in the afternoon, questioning them eagerly in hope that some of the learning might brush off on to themselves. But few parents had money for school, and most children had chores to keep them occupied.

Small girls of seven or less must take charge of still smaller brothers and sisters. Bound firmly to their backs, with legs stuck wide like tiny jockeys, the babies rode while their sisters carried water, swept out huts, tended cookpot and fire, or visited the shop for a yam or a ha'porth of salt. Small boys cleaned out the boats, washed nets, gutted fish, or wandered far along the shore to gather driftwood or coal spilt overboard as ships unloaded. Occasionally they would come shouting home with treasure such as a plank, a tattered lifebelt or even a case containing tins. Others trudged off into the city to sell goods from head-high trays. During the afternoons the man friends of Wa-poo's mother came to call on her, enormous genial beings who patted the boy's dusty head, laughing far down inside rumbling bellies as they searched their loose robes for copper coins or edible fragments

As evening closed, a roar of traffic rose up from the great road half a mile away along which white men and the more prosperous citizens drove or cycled home into the suburbs,

unaware of the lagoon life which they flashed past twice a day.
By now the uncles and aunts also were returning home, and as
at last the roar of traffic faded, the village took on the ancient
face of Africa, above all on nights when a full moon floated
high over the palms, reflecting itself many times over in
lengthened arcs across the oily waters. Now fires glowed
between the huts, and the men, having eaten the stews served
by their women, would gather in groups with a gourd of palm
wine tapped from the treetops and a little hoarded tobacco, a
cigarette or half a cigarette. It was then that Wa'poo,
irresistibly drawn, would creep out from the sacks under
which he had been put to sleep and stand, like the ambassador
from a state of pygmies, silent with thumb in mouth behind
the oldest man.

It was through this habit of listening to the discussions of
grown-up men that Wa'poo learned, when his mother left
him, what was to be his fate. His mother died without long
sickness from some infection steaming out of the swamp in
which they lived. On the first day of the week she was about
the hut as usual; on the last she lay motionless and silent, and
Wa'poo realized that she would never move or speak again.
His mother had been the condition of Wa'poo's existence
rather than an especially loving being. Though seldom angry
and never harsh, she found a small boy often in her way, and
had built a half-door across the entrance to their hut to prevent
Wa'poo running in when one of her patrons was visiting her.
From very early Wa'poo had thus learned to cope with his
small troubles on his own. Once the visitor had gone,
however, and they did not usually stay long, she would catch
the child up and dust him off, handing him a piece of roasted
yam or plantain, brushing his tears away with real if transient
tenderness.

The night after his mother had been put into the ground,
there was a council to decide what should be done with
Wa'poo. Everyone knew the decision to be reached; both
commonsense and custom pointed the same way, and indeed
the necessary arrangements had already been made. The
council met to let everyone see that the matter had been
thoroughly gone into; to give formal approval to what had
been decided; to express the community's satisfaction that so
proper a solution had been found; and to make sure, if
necessary by a general levy, that Wa'poo was equipped with
clothes and food for the new stage in his life.

Once Wa'poo realized that the discussion concerned himself, he understood that it would not be proper for him to stand listening and accordingly slipped away. He listened indeed, but from the mouldering darkness under a nearby hut whose floorboards creaked over him as the woman went about her evening tasks. In this way Wa'poo learned that he was to be put next day on to a mammy-wagon, or long-distance lorry, and sent in the driver's charge on a two-day trip across country to a relation of his mother. This 'auntie', whom custom made in effect into another mother, had children of her own and when word had been sent a couple of days previously that Wa'poo was about to become an orphan, she had sent a message back accepting the responsibility. One or two of the village families had also offered to take Wa'poo in with their own children, but the elders, after consideration, had decided that it would be in Wa'poo's interest for him to go away.

Wa'poo had no objection to making his home with this distant auntie – how could he have indeed, since he had never met her? He imagined just such another voluble, harassed, laughter-loving but uncertain provider as his mother, and certainly he would not object to going for a ride of two days in a mammy-wagon. But there were two points in the plan now being unfolded in the men's slow talk against which his mind struck in refusal. He had noted many times the pride with which older people spoke of their city life and themselves as men and women of Lagos, one of the mightiest cities in Africa and perhaps in the whole world. A hundred times he had heard them tell how they had left home and come here, venturing out of the unchanging past of Africa into the perils and profits of the modern world. This was a journey across centuries, and each was justifiably proud of having made it, made it once for all for himself, his family and future generations. Wa'poo had heard the contempt with which such men spoke of that vast, indiscriminate countryside, 'the bush' which they had left, and of those 'bush people' who had opposed their leaving or stayed timidly behind.

Wa'poo too in his own way was a city man with the modern world as birthright, and he had no intention of sinking back into a mere 'bush person'. Secondly, though he had nothing against this unknown aunt and uncle, he had no wish to become one of a family of small children in which he must quickly be reduced to the common level. This was asking him to go back to infancy, a condition he had rejected even while still an infant. Crouched in the friendly darkness, secure from discovery as in a treetop, Wa'poo concluded that the plan made by his elders, however well intentioned, was misguided. To oppose their decision openly would be an unthinkable act of rudeness; also it could only end one way – in his being packed up and sent off with an added burden of disgrace.

He was six years old. The time had come to take matters into his own hands. Before morning he must strike out for himself.

2
City Streets

Noiseless, in the half-light before anyone was stirring, Wa'poo flitted around the shack, putting together a small pile of belongings, a tattered vest which did duty whenever his present one was given a wash, some pieces of bread, a small jar of salt, a box of matches and two candle ends. He added his own knife and spoon and the cigarette tin which served him as a cup, wrapping everything together in his stained blanket to make a bundle he could carry on his head. After much hesitation he went over to his mother's bed, climbed slowly up and drew aside a loose piece of corrugated iron covering an opening in the wall. He had seen his mother go there a thousand times and reach her hand inside for money, but he had never in his life moved the piece of metal and almost expected his arm to wither as he touched it. Inside were four shillings and a pile of coppers. Tying the money into a twist of cloth which he hung down inside his trousers, Wa'poo crept to the door, bundle in hand. Nobody was stirring, and in a moment he was gone.

From the settlement where he lived it was a long ride to the city, but Wa'poo knew the look of the bus he had to take. As he crouched by the dusty roadside waiting for it to come nosing round the palm trees at the far-off bend, he felt no fear or apprehension. His only concern was to slip away from his old life undetected and get started on the new. He had a plan as to how he would make his living. All he need do when he reached the city, he believed, was to buy a small packet of cigarettes, put them inside his tin, put the tin on his head and walk about, selling the cigarettes one at a time to workers on sites and buildings, large kindly men like those who used to visit his mother during the long afternoons. Wa'poo had been into Lagos with his mother many times and picked up something of the city's economic life seen from below. Almost everyone, he knew, sold something; and children, like women, have their place in this scheme of things. Market stalls, the selling of vegetables and fruit, of cloth and household goods, is in women's hands. From the imposing market mammy presiding over a row of stalls down to her poor relation crouched over a pan of charcoal selling fried bean cakes far into the night, it is women who meet the million needs of daily life for food and clothing, cleanliness and warmth. But they sell from a fixed spot where clients can always find them, and what children have to sell is their mobility.

Infinite in number and so always on the spot, they save harassed workers the trouble of slipping away to shop or stall, thus earning a percentage on their tiny outlay. Bigger boys and girls, invisible under trays of kola nut, aspirin or chewing gum, throng the bustling pavements. Little ones, their whole stock contained in a cardboard box or cigarette tin, haunt building sites and docks, landing stages, bus stops, factories. Wa'poo had seen all this a hundred times, not as a visitor observes customs but as an apprentice soaks in the craft by which one day he must make his living. There is a difference, however, between a way of life when studied and the same way when one tries to live by it; Wa'poo bought his stock without difficulty, it was when he tried to sell that trouble started. Whenever he picked a likely selling point some established owner would appear and chase him off. Usually it was a bigger boy demanding, 'What person say you come roun' here? Whaffor you take dis place?' as a sharp kick enforced his ownership.

Sometimes it was the beggars who drove him away. Asprawl along every pavement, like lice in the seam of an old garment, they were too lazy to move, but their threats and curses – demanding clear access to passers-by and no childish competition – terrified Wa'poo. Tearful and despairing, he

wandered from one street to the next. The pavement burned
his feet and the string of his bundle cut into his hand. The day
dragged endlessly along, and though he had no idea where or
how he could spend the night, he was almost glad as he felt
darkness closing in to hide him. He had drifted down to the
Marina, the waterfront where great ships from far-off
countries lie anchored only a hundred yards or so offshore.
Wa'poo gazed at them in wonder. Their sounds carried to him
across the water, the shouts of officers and the rattle of
winches mingling with the roar of homebound traffic from
the road. As he stood, staring through the thickening air, the
deck of a ship out in the tide was suddenly lit up, a row of
bright circles marking the saloon. Wa'poo supposed it to be
full of wealthy travellers, feasting to celebrate their arrival in
the capital, and it seemed a sign that he too would one day be a
rich, successful merchant moving freely and powerfully
across the world. He picked up his bundle and moved on.

A woman whom he asked to sell him a pennyworth of food
gave him a lump of roasted yam, a white peeled orange and a
tin of hot, sweet tea. She would take no payment, but pointed
to a spot beside her stall where he could sit. Warmed and a little
comforted, Wa'poo found a cleft for himself in the root of a
palm, wrapped his blanket tightly round him, put his bundle
beneath his head, and fell asleep almost before he had lain
down.

Next morning was like the day before. The kindly food-
seller had gone home, leaving the few planks which formed
her stall padlocked to a palm tree, and Wa'poo was soon once
more being chivvied from place to place. He could walk
unharmed along the pavements, but once he tried to stop and
sell, every pitch in the city belonged to someone and it was late
afternoon before he found a gleam of hope. There was a big
match on the football ground at the far end of the Marina, and
as work finished crowds started to come streaming in along
the pavements, their numbers swelled by the ferries moving in
from Apapa just across the water. Youths hung out along their
decks, vying to be first to leap ashore before the boat touched
land, then darting away through the traffic to secure a good
position for the match. Dodging cars and one another, they
shouted good-humouredly ahead to clear a passage: 'Here
come future Prime Minister – make way dere!' 'Move aside,
mistah, for de Oba hisself!'

Standing in the shelter of an entrance, where he could not

easily be knocked down, Wa'poo had soon sold all his cigarettes. He refilled his tin, and sold again, some of the buyers being too hurried to collect their trifling change. For half an hour he felt his troubles were over – when a sharp push in the back sent him sprawling, his bundle was knocked out of his hand and the last cigarettes scattered underfoot. The child attackers jeered as he struggled to rescue his bundle, and then rushed off when one of the incomers cursed them for getting in his way. Too dispirited to try further, Wa'poo gathered his trampled belongings and crossed to the waterfront to find shelter for the night. Wandering back along the marina, he looked again for his one friendly contact, the woman who had given him yam. She had not come back, and Wa'poo sat down in the cleft of his tree, hoping she might return when darkness fell. But her boards remained padlocked, and when Wa'poo approached another seller to buy food, she took him for a beggar and ordered him away.

Hungry and snivelling, the string of his bundle sharp as a wire, Wa'poo drifted into Lagos Island where the big stores are and the rich firms from overseas have their godowns. In daytime the Island is all bustle, and it is hard to cross a street in safety, but now the traffic had gone and the pavements were clear except for flickering candles where women squatted beside dishes of hot food, still hopeful of a final customer. At first glance these were the only humans, but Wa'poo, making his slow way, could see that in every doorway and corner some beggar had his nightly hideout. Avoiding their cookpots and bed-rags, stepping round their twisted limbs – spectacularly deformed in infancy by parent or guardian seeking to give his charge a good start in life – Wa'poo drifted aimlessly along. Despair invaded him, long resisted but now filling his whole being. He was shut out from life in which everyone in the world had some warm lighted corner of his own, but he had none. No place to go. No cranny to creep into and rest. The loss of his mother, accepted at the time as a natural calamity, now hit him like a blow. There was no knee for him to cling to. No arm to go round his shoulders. No voice to speak comfortingly. He was abandoned and unwanted. After two days of struggling to face the world as a man, he could keep it up no longer. He was lost. He was alone, and he was painfully, humiliatingly small.

After a while this sense of his own helplessness and smallness became a distraction. Drifting and pausing, staring

sightless into darkened windows, he had become an insect
moving across the floor of a huge hut. He could actually see this
insect, to whom every floorboard was a desert, making its
painful way with hesitations and demented wanderings.
Though he had become the insect, he was at the same time also a
child and drew comfort from its being even smaller and more
helpless than himself. The insect stopped, and Wa'poo stopped
as well. He was about to lie down against the wall without even
bothering to seek shelter, when he heard voices. They came
from a flight of steps leading up to some warehouse or store
entrance. He could not see over them, but there was a glow of
light so he began to climb, lifting both feet on to each step before
making his way up to the next. As his eyes came high enough to
peer over the edge, Wa'poo saw what appeared to be a camp of
wanderers settling down for the night.

At the top of the steps immediately in front was an open
space, enclosed by a low wall or balcony. At the back some
heavy doors, now shut, gave access to a building. To one side,
protected from night winds by a tarpaulin carried on poles,
stood the brazier whose glow of light and promise of warmth
had drawn Wa'poo from the pavement, and at ease around it
squatted the four men whose voices he had heard.
Conspicuous among them was one in loose white clothing
with a round white cap, who Wa'poo knew must be a man
from the Northern Region. More than one of his mother's
visitors had been tall, white-clad men like this one. Men from
the North, it was well known, were chosen for such posts as
storekeepers or night watchman, since they were thought to
be more honest and known to enjoy fighting. The group
around the brazier brought back to Wa'poo's mind those
evening councils at which he had stood so often in the
vanished past of two days earlier. Silent inside his thoughts,
the child drew closer, laid down his painful bundle and stood
still, thumb in mouth. The man in white watched for a while,
and then asked: 'Whaffor you come here, picken?'

Wa'poo made no reply. He heard the question, but had
faded too far from himself to frame an answer. He just stood
there gazing into the fire. The man in white seemed about to
speak, but instead beckoned with his finger. It was easier to
move than speak, and Wa'poo drew closer to him.

'Where from you done come, picken?'
No answer.
'You 'lone in city? Where bin you' father an yo' mammy?'

Wa'poo lowered his head.

'You sayin dat you bin orphan chile?'

When this inquiry also got no answer, the man turned to his companions: 'Dis chile bin cold an' wantin' chop.'

At sound of the strong voice and with the promise of warmth and rest, Wa'poo's mind came back to him. He gazed at the white-capped man, gulped, and burst into a storm of tears. Ignoring this outbreak the man got up – he was even taller than Wa'poo had supposed – went over to a corner and pulled out a sack which he handed to the child. On the brazier was a cookpot, and using a cigarette tin as ladle, the tall man filled bowls for himself and his companions, then tipped the rest into the tin which he passed to Wa'poo. By the time he had swallowed his groundnut stew and another tin of sugary tea, Wa'poo could no longer keep awake. Lying down on his sack he tried to undo his bundle. One of the men leaned across and untied it, spread the blanket over the child and put the rest of his belongings by his head.

The men, it seemed, spent most of the night in talk, for hours later when the sound of a passing lorry woke Wa'poo, they were still chatting and drinking tea.

'What you 'tend doin' wid dis picken?' one of the men asked. The tall man waited before answering.

'If picken hones' an' good, him sweep up an' fin' wood for fire. Den I 'low him chop an' place for sleep. But if he go for steal an' talk wid big mouf, I chase um off.'

'Maybe some auntie come seekin' picken for carry um back,' suggested one.

'All same he go or stay,' the tall man replied with dignity. 'But Allah not 'low for chase lost picken away in night time.'

Much comforted, Wa'poo fell asleep. Allah, he supposed, must be the owner of the building where the tall man worked, and if the owner was a kindly man it seemed reasonable to hope that his workers might be kindly too.

3
A Step on the Ladder

When Wa'poo woke again he was no longer on the portico. He lay, with his familiar blanket round him, in the darkness of what seemed a small windowless room or hut. He was still lying there, recalling the dreamlike happenings of the night, when the door opened and a tall figure stood silhouetted against daylight. Gratefully Wa'poo accepted the piece of bread and tin of tea.

'What yo' name, picken?'

'Wa'poo.'

'What kin' of name dat? You want I call you Wa'poo?'

A nod.

'Me – "Mr Ali". You understan' dis?'

Wa'poo nodded, then repeated the name respectfully, 'Mr Ali.'

'Lissen, Wa'poo. Dis now yo' home. You do what I tellin', you stay. You no do what I tellin', you fin' some place else. Understan'?'

Wa'poo nodded.

'Well now, dis mos' important. Any person ask for me, you tell um – "Mr Ali out front", or "Mr Ali jus' go roun' de back." You not say, "Ali go roun' de back", not even if dis person ask for "Ali". You say always "Mr Ali". An' you not shake head and say "no know where bin Mr Ali". *All times* Mr Ali workin' 'bout dis building some place.' He paused. 'You understan' what I tellin' you?'

The boy nodded, wiping crumbs from his mouth as he gazed intently at his benefactor. Mr Ali smiled indulgently. 'Well, Wa'poo, you plan become idle no-good picken? Or you work hard for livin' an' grow up hones' man?'

'Work hard for livin', Mr Ali.'

Wa'poo breathed the words with fervour as if registering some inner vow, as indeed he was, a vow that, if he could only remain in the atmosphere of kindness coming from this tall, white-clad man, he would indeed be diligent and obedient. Over the next few days, partly by Mr Ali's instruction and partly through his own observation, Wa'poo picked up the duties and privileges of his new life.

As night watchman for a big importing firm Mr Ali had a double status. At the beck and call of managers and clerks by day, he became master of the great building from the time the last workers went home, the swing doors were locked and the gates to the yard chained up. At weekends the property was in his hands from midday Saturday till Monday morning. Such was his paid employment, but it was a position in which the perquisites meant much more than the pay for – in the desperate shortage of living space in Lagos to which people from all over Nigeria were crowding in search of work or the good life – Mr Ali was landlord of much-wanted accommodation. The three Wa'poo had seen sitting round the brazier were his tenants; one worked in the docks and one in the railway yards, and the third picked up a living as a carrier in the markets. All paid rent for the right to doss down on Mr Ali's portico. It was part of the bargain that he maintained an evening fire on which they could cook whatever they bought or managed to acquire during the day, or else for a few pence extra they could be served with a plate of chop from Mr Ali's cookpot. A tick was marked on a slate every time one of the men had such a meal, then at the month's end, when everyone in Africa is paid, the ticks were added and accounts squared. Except for the Sunday-morning lie-in, tenants had to be gone by six, so that the place could be cleared and washed down before foremen or office staff started to arrive.

Round at the back, in the outhouse where Wa'poo had awoken, Mr Ali had established the headquarters for his private activities, expelling over the years everything not his and then finally buying and fitting his own padlock. This acquisition, the result of a long and carefully-planned campaign, was invaluable, for here he kept the tarpaulin with its poles, the brazier, cookpot and drinking tins, with the bundles belonging to his tenants, and here Wa'poo too might store his own small bundle. Each morning he would be given a piece of bread and a tin of tea. At night he would have a bowl of Mr Ali's chop and a second tin of tea. He would have his own place by the fire with his sack to lie on. His duties were to wash the place down thoroughly each morning with water from a tap in the yard and a broom kept in the outhouse. During the day he was to collect enough wood and pieces of coal around harbour and beaches to keep the brazier going for a few hours each night. To the tenants he must be respectful even if they shouted at him, since indirectly they supplied his living. As regards the office people he did not exist and ought not to be seen, but if one should notice him and ask his business he must say he had come with a message for Mr Ali. If they ordered him off, he was to vanish till nightfall and come back after they had gone.

Each night as he wriggled down into his sack, drawing the blanket close around his neck, Wa'poo felt deep satisfaction that he had stayed on in the city and not allowed himself to be packed off into the bush. His confidence in himself and in destiny had been justified; the doors of life had opened wide before him, and with satisfaction came a flow of gratitude and love towards the stranger who had given him a home and with it such a promising start to his career.

Now that he had a home it did not take Wa'poo long to become familiar with his surroundings. Once he had picked up the local slang and passwords he was accepted by the packs of prowling boys as one of themselves, and as he got to know the places where men worked and their tidal movements in and out of the island area, he was soon making a shilling or two by selling cigarettes.

When two or three years had passed and he grew stronger, with Mr Ali's full agreement Wa'poo bought a tray which he stocked with a variety of goods, not only cigarettes but chewing gum, matches, kola nut, shoelaces and combs. Quick to adapt, when the season for oranges came round he would leave his general stock in the outhouse and carry round on his head a chipped enamel bowl full of the fruit, white all over with the outer skin deftly sliced away, leaving a protective covering of pith which his customers spat splashily out on to the pavements. On misty mornings or afternoons in the rainy season he carried roast corncobs, plantains or bean cakes, and at times of festival when bush people thronged into the city, he would pack his tray with serried rows of pencils and beads in violent colours. Unlike food and cigarettes, these had no fixed prices known to simple buyers so could be sold for whatever pence they fetched.

On Sundays, with Mr Ali's permission, he would make his way over to Bar Beach, begging a lift on a friend's bicycle – for the bicycle in Africa is a two-person vehicle – and Wa'poo would sit on handlebars or carrier with his legs trailing, shouting and waving to his friends. On the beach he offered

Coke or Fanta Orange; hired out strips of matting to whites who disliked getting sand into their swimsuits, or whose too-sensitive skins needed protection from its heat; or sold fancy hats for shillings, having bought them for as many pence. All this increased his outlay and the risk of theft by the rough youths who lurked beneath the palm trees or among the drawn-up fishing boats, but it also brought bigger profits, so that before long Mr Ali was guardian for some pounds of Wa'poo's savings. The life also developed in Wa'poo the talent to please, shrewd appraisal of an opportunity, quickness of wit and dramatic sense, as he clapped one of his sunhats on his head and shuffled a dance on the sand to draw in customers. Peaceful by nature, he had learned from Mr Ali always, if threatened, to rush in to the attack and strike out fiercely. Also, though eager for profit, he refused to beg and would never, like his companions, conclude a deal with the whining plea: 'An' now, sah, how much master "dash" dis poo'-poo' boy?' Mr Ali noticed this and, realizing perhaps that it was his own manly self-respect which Wa'poo sought to imitate, had remarked more than once, 'So, Wa'poo, now you grow big, I see you becomin' a man an' not a beggar.'

At twelve or thirteen Wa'poo formed one of a gang of boys of his own age. But though the gangs gave themselves fancy names, and made mystery with passwords and secret signs, there was a serious intention underlying their activities – to get money, and one of their small rackets was in car-watching. Through a fight, or through staking their claim when a new building went up, the gang would secure a pitch near a hotel or office block, the best pitches being those where Americans worked since it is known that Americans lack all sense of money values and have forgotten how to walk even short distances. Also they have bigger, newer, more vulnerable cars. The system was that the gang leader must wear a white shirt and look honest, while the rest could be their impudent, dirty selves. When a car drove up the gang swarmed aggressively round it, shouting. The driver, knowing that if he refused protection his car might be scratched with a rusty nail or have its tyres let down, picked what he considered to be 'Honest Joe' as watchdog. Joe would then round on the others and drive them angrily away. At the day's end takings were shared out, with a double share for 'Honest Joe' who had to wash his shirt out every night. Sometimes when they saw an owner coming for his car, the gang would stage a fight so that

Joe earned an extra sixpence for devotion in protecting it.
Car-watching was fun for a while, but gangs never held
together because none trusted for long the honesty of the one
who took the money.

Raiding markets was riskier and so more exciting. Lagos is a
city of markets. There is one for vegetables, another for meat,
a third for household and kitchen goods, separate markets for
different kinds of cloth, even a market for gourds and
calabashes to hold water – nine important markets, with
temporary ones springing up wherever a site was waiting to be
built on. Inside the markets merchants and mammies have
permanent shops, one- or two-storey buildings with roofs of
corrugated iron that echo deafeningly in a cloudburst; petty
traders sell from stalls, and the poorest from planks laid across
piles of bricks or from a tray on a tree stump in the open. Even
the smallest corner serves some commercial end, perhaps for a
barber whose stock in trade is a backless chair, scissors, a
razor, a bowl of slime and a brush long since grown bald, and
the gratified customer can inspect his improved appearance in
a fragment of looking glass tacked against a tree.

When spirits were high and car protection low, the gang
would gather in a market. Peering round corners for their
opportunity, one would dart out, knock over a tray of
vegetables or fruit, then double off round a stall and vanish.
Swooping behind him came the rest to snatch whatever they
could, a couple of corncobs, a handful of fiery capsicums, a
yam or sweet potato – before melting away to meet laughingly
somewhere safe. However, the penalty for being caught was a
ferocious beating in which passers-by, eager to improve their
community's moral tone, joined with fervour, and having
seen one grown-up thief three-quarters killed by market
women, Wa'poo resolved to stick to honest trade. He was
strong enough now to be given an occasional day's work
minding stalls or delivering goods for petty traders, but
meantime continued to wash down the portico and pavement
every morning and to serve Mr Ali in any way required,
though nowadays he often bought driftwood and seacoal
from pickens instead of searching for it along the foreshore.
To the office staff he had long been familiar; they supposed
him to be the night watchman's son or nephew and found him
useful for fetching ice cream or cold drinks. Wa'poo carried
out their orders with a smile or joke, taking care to receive a
tiny commission from the shop in addition to the tips given
him by the office girls.

Though Mr Ali still kept the same modest employment his private business had extended greatly. As the prosperity of Lagos grew, more and more bush people flooded into the capital with nowhere to live or sleep; even clerks on good salaries were lucky to find themselves a tiny room, or half, or a quarter of a room. Mr Ali now had half a dozen tenants on his portico, and to meet growing demands had started to let out the pavement between portico and roadway as a sleeping ground. Once darkness fell there was little traffic through Lagos Island and few walkers on its silent streets. For a space close to the balustrade, with a wall to lean against and some small protection in the rainy season, Mr Ali charged a shilling a month. For the lower row, with risk of a bicycle over-running the feet and occasional splashings from lorries, he took sixpence or whatever he could extract when the month ended and Wa'poo soon learned to keep a sharp eye on sleepers as pay-day neared, and be off up the street shouting after any who had failed to hand over.

For Wa'poo's training and education Mr Ali laid down few and simple rules. He insisted that the boy wash himself thoroughly each morning and again before going to his sacks at night. He had always to wash face and hands before chop, and in his childish days Mr Ali would send him away if he thought the rule had not been kept, nor would he allow Wa'poo to take food until himself and the tenants had been served. He must clean his teeth carefully with a twig or matchsticks. Every Sunday morning he had to show Mr Ali his clothes, neatly washed and mended, and when they became too ragged Mr Ali would order him to use some of his own money and buy new ones. He also taught Wa'poo to recognize numerals and do simple sums in money, instructing him on the slate or on scraps of paper saved from office waste baskets. He demanded prompt obedience to all orders, and further insisted on good temper. He had a way of looking inquiringly at him which the boy instantly recognized. It did not mean, 'Are you going to obey?' for about that there was never any question. It meant, 'Are you going to obey cheerfully or sulk?' and one glance was usually enough to brace Wa'poo into cheerfulness, for there was nothing he feared so much as the loss of Mr Ali's favour. An occasional blow or sharp word he could endure but the feeling which some childish wrongdoing could bring, a feeling of being excluded from acceptance and no longer welcome, left

Wa'poo rudderless and adrift, unable to apply himself to any activity until the cause of his distress had been removed.

Deeply impressed by Mr Ali's dignity and calm, his practical mixture of kindness with keen business sense, and the courage he had once shown when thieves broke into the building, Wa'poo modelled himself on the older man whom he now addressed as 'Baba' – father or master. Wa'poo had realized long since that Allah was not the name of the Swiss proprietor owning the offices and godown where he worked, but was the cause of Mr Ali's withdrawal five times a day into a ritual of prostration with which even the demands of his employers were not allowed to interfere. These withdrawals were connected in Wa'poo's mind with the calm and authority surrounding his Baba, and at last, summoning courage, he asked if he might become a Moslem too and have a share in these devotions. Mr Ali considered the matter carefully before replying that he would be happy if one day Wa'poo chose to adopt his religion, but that the decision should wait until he could decide the matter out of knowledge and not under the influence of an older person like himself. There was no Koran school at hand where Wa'poo could be given instruction, so for the present nothing was done, but Mr Ali from time to time gave the boy lessons in morality which served to counteract those lessons in sharp practice which the world – and indeed Mr Ali himself – were giving Wa'poo every day.

One evening when the boy was about thirteen years old Mr Ali sent him as usual to the market to buy vegetables. There was change of a few pence, and instead of bringing it back Wa'poo bought himself a cold drink, soothing his conscience with the thought that Mr Ali often gave him pennies for a cold drink anyway; conscience, it seemed, did not entirely accept this argument for Wa'poo was troubled in himself on the way back. When he handed the vegetables over, Mr Ali put his hand out for the change.

'Bin no sma'-sma' money, Baba,' Wa'poo replied, adding quickly, 'Yams in market costin' more today.'

'What place you done buy dese yams, Wa'poo?'

'From big mammy, Baba, same place always go.'

Mr Ali rose, seeming taller than usual as he did so. 'Come, Wa'poo! We go spik wid dis mammy one-time.'

Wa'poo hesitated, foresaw the dreadful scene that lay ahead, and broke down, confessing the deception in tears and self-accusings. Sternly Mr Ali turned away to seat himself beside the brazier. The five minutes' silence which followed seemed a full hour of blackest horror to Wa'poo, convinced he was going to be sent away, handed over to a policeman who would carry him off to prison; or perhaps Mr Ali would beat him as he had seen the thief beaten in the market, beaten until his body ceased to twitch. Yet even such a beating would be preferable to the blackness and despair of being sent away. Finally Mr Ali spoke.

'Whaffor you do dis, Wa'poo? Whaffor you make lyin' talk to Baba? Done no person ever teach you what is difference of right from wrong? Is no voice inside yo' own heart tellin' you' what is good or wicked action?'

Wa'poo hung his head. His throat seemed filled with lead and tears of shame burned his eyelids. He wished he could melt into the air or sink beneath the concrete of the portico, so that no such person as the boy Wa'poo, who lied and cheated his benefactor in order to get a cold drink for himself, would ever be seen or heard of in this world again. Only an hour ago he had been a happy carefree being – and now here he was, sunk by his own sin into depths of wretchedness from which he could never rise, and ought never to be allowed to rise, again. He choked and could not answer.

'Bin easy for Baba punish you, Wa'poo. Dis not trouble Baba de smalles' bit. But s'pose punishin' not make you better boy, an' you grow more an' more bad person every day?' He paused, and Wa'poo, appalled at the thought of such increasing degradation, gazed down through misted eyes at his own feet. 'What I askin' you, Wa'poo, is – why you do such wicked act as tellin' lie for cheat yo' Baba?'

But into Wa'poo's distracted mind had crept a slender ray of hope, and after a moment's silence he summoned courage to stammer out his perplexity.

'Baba, I know I mos' bad boy, deserve beatin' with thick stick. I know dis, Baba, but all same. . . .'

'Well, Wa'poo?'

'All same, Baba, dis mornin' in yard, I hear you tell Mr Ogunde you needin' one new broom from stores. Mr Ogunde give um you. I know you not need broom. I know you go sell new broom to market mammy – an' tonight you will tell me scrub ole broom, make look same like new. Den you go use de ole broom maybe one year mo'. Is dis true what I sayin', Baba?'

'Dis mos' true, my son.'

'Well den, Baba . . .' the question failed, and Wa'poo stood unwilling to express his critical thought in words, till compelled by Mr Ali's silence. 'Is dis not lie you tellin' Mr Ogunde?'

Mr Ali smiled and laid a hand on Wa'poo's dusty tight-curled pate.

'You big boy now, Wa'poo. Surely you know difference between frien' an' stranger. You know difference of business deal, from robbin' yo' own Baba or yo' brother?' He looked down into Wa'poo's pleading gaze.

'You plan for sell dis or dat to stranger, den you lie. You say dis fines' comb or fines' chop. Dis yo' *business* for say dat. An' stranger's business is for say dis no-good comb and no-good chop, an' he kin buy better chop up road for half de money. You understandin' dis for sure?' Wapoo nodded; it was indeed as clear as day. 'But after talk, when you done make 'greement wid dis man – "I givin' you plate good chop each evenin' fourpence" – den you keep yo' word. You no give de man dirty chop, an' no tell um yams cost more, so he 'bliged pay you sixpence. For you done 'gree dat he pay you fourpence.' Again Wa'poo nodded acceptance of this basic principle.

'But when' – and Mr Ali's voice took on a sombre tone which drove guilt into Wa'poo's heart like a nail – 'when you deal wid *frien*', wid yo' brother or yo' Baba, den you *never* tell lie nor cheat um. Not even if you lose money, you no cheat um. An' yo' frien' an' yo' Baba no cheat you. An' when yo' frien' say he have no money, den you help um, same as when you done come dis place long while back as sma'-sma' picken an I helpin' you.'

He paused, and for Wa'poo, clinging desperately to Mr Ali's hand as he sobbed agreement, the world stopped spinning and hung suspended as he waited for judgement to be pronounced.

'So now, Wa'poo you get yo' sack an' lie down in yo' corner. You eatin' no chop dis night. 'Stead you thinkin' 'bout what I say, an' you rememberin' dis in yo' heart. To frien' you never tellin' no lies. Not tomorrow. Not nex' day. Not any day at all. An' you never go cheat yo' frien', yo' brother or yo' Baba, for dis mos' wickedest act dat man kin do.'

Wa'poo bowed his head upon Mr. Ali's knee and wept, tears of repentance, tears of gratitude for his guiding wisdom, out of a full to bursting heart.

4

Gates of Manhood

At nineteen Wa'poo was a tall, powerfully-built bold-featured youth, well known around the markets. For the past two years he had given up selling from a tray and now owned his own stall, an arrangement of planks on kerosene cans with a sacking roof which he set up at daybreak every morning alongside the office building where he lived with Mr Ali. Trade prospered, since so many country people continued to flow into the city and most of them felt safer buying from stalls and markets such as they were used to in the villages, rather than venturing into the darkness of shops in which anything might happen to them or their money. Wa'poo still washed the place down each morning, he still served Mr Ali dutifully as assistant and looked up to him as his Baba, but both understood that a time was approaching when Wa'poo would leave home and step out into independent life.

For the last five years or more Wa'poo had been attracted by many of the girls and young women he saw about the streets and markets. Many looked appreciatively at his powerful build and smiled invitingly at his fresh, open face – an interest to which Wa'poo responded eagerly enough, and later, gaining confidence, he was quick to initiate adventures of his own. Wa'poo could not, like most Western boys and girls, remember his initiation into sex, recalling separate stages as momentous experiences; on the contrary, he glided imperceptibly into the exercise of manhood, accepting those easy opportunities which offered themselves by night and day in the crowded alleys and back streets. This was a world in which privacy was scarcely known; where home meant a single room shared by persons of all ages; where few doors existed and fewer still were ever closed, so that birth, death and couplings were visible to all who walked abroad, arousing little interest and no comment. Here the mysteries and secrecies of human life were as public as the open sewers which carried the city's refuse, and much else beside, into the lagoons.

Till now all sexual contacts had been passing alleviations or excitements, matters of the moment from which no conclusions followed. One morning, however, when he had gone into one of the markets to buy stock for his stall, Wa'poo was called over to help unload a mammy-wagon. He walked across unhurried, for he had no need of odd jobs any longer and, being a man in his own right, did not run for anybody's call except his Baba's. Once having started, however, he worked hard, not so much for the shilling or two as out of pride in the exercise of his strength. When they came to the last big crate, with which two shopmen were struggling ineffectually, Wa'poo pushed them aside, braced himself upon powerful legs, wrapped his arms round the crate hugging it close against his chest, then lowered it gently to the ground without a jar. As he rose, tucking his shirt into his shorts, he heard a deep chuckling laugh – 'Dis boy bin worth more dan two men' – and the mammy for whom he had been working beckoned him over to the doorway against which she leaned while keeping her eye on the shop inside as well as on the men unloading.

Madam Abiose was a large woman in a land where size is a valued element of beauty, no longer young but with a youthful air about her; still handsome, with the glossy skin derived from much oiling in a well-cared infancy and childhood, which retains its smoothness far on into age. She wore a buba, a loose-sleeved blouse of plum-coloured velvet, with a lappa or skirt of printed material in white and purple wound tightly up under her vigorous expressive breasts. A violet satin head-tie, fashioned into an enormous bow, gave height and dignity. Her long gold earrings, gold ornaments at neck and wrists, her low neckline and heavily-scented hair and bosom appeared to Wa'poo the extremes of worldly luxury. Beckoning Wa'poo to follow her into the shop, she walked before him with a sensual roll, due partly to her heavy build and partly to the wooden beads strung on a leather thong which she wore over her hips so that her dress would slip and slide seductively at every step.

'Git out!' she ordered the clerk writing on a stool in front of a high desk. 'An' don' you go off talkin' an' chatterin' in de market! Mind what I say! You wait dere in de shop, an' come back de same minute I callin' you.' Nodding submission, the clerk slipped silently away.

'Now, my frien', stan' here an' let me take good look at you. Come now, you kin look into my face! I no bite you – or no bitin' you dis minute. . . . Well now, I see you not boy at all but big, pow'ful man. Why I not seein' you roun' dis market sooner before?'

Wa'poo looked into Madam Abiose's eyes as ordered. They were bright and melting, and he thought them the largest he had ever seen, but their look of humorous appreciation made him feel abashed, more like a small boy than the big powerful man she called him. He managed, however, to reply with firmness.

'I havin' stall of my own, ma'am. Is sma'-sma' stall, but I bin independent petty trader. So I not comin' in de markets, only sometime for buy stock.'

'What is yo' name?'

'Wa'poo, ma'am.'

'Wa'poo! What kin' of name is dat?'

Then catching his expression, she quickly checked herself. 'An' what other names you havin' besides Wa'poo?'

'Wa'poo is all my names, ma'am.'

'What place you livin' den, my frien'? Is yo' mother an' yo' father livin' dere? Have you brothers an' sisters all wantin' you shall care for an' give dem education?'

Wa'poo explained his solitary condition and his life with his patron, Mr Ali. His account seemed to please Madam Abiose, for she smiled once or twice to herself, while continuing to survey him coolly up and down.

'Well, Wa'poo – I think I findin' job for you in my business. Is better you give up yo' stall. You doin' more good for yo'self by comin' here wid me. I inten' teachin' you modern ways for business. How to buy an' sell. How to keep 'counts – not jus' countin' pennies on yo' fingers – so you kin run proper business like big traders. Den one day maybe I help you set up on your own. How you like dat?' She paused. 'I s'pose you hones' boy, willin' for work hard – an' not jus' tell lies an' try for cheat me?'

All softness vanished as she looked into Wa'poo's face and watched his lips as he replied. But Wa'poo gazed steadily back at her. 'Yes, ma'am. I c'siderin' myself hones' man.'

Madam Abiose's look relaxed. 'I givin' you hard-hard life, Wa'poo. But I s'pose you strong enough to stand hard life.'

She gave a chuckle in which Wa'poo hesitated to join. 'But first you takin' me to see yo' Baba. Mr Ali bin good frien' an' father for you, so we fix nothin' till we talk wid him. But I think we make 'greement dat please all three. . . . You goin' to be lucky boy, my frien'. Mos' lucky boy!'

Mr Ali had recognized long since that Wa'poo would leave him on reaching manhood, and Madam Abiose was no unknown figure in the market world; she would make a powerful protector for the youth he regarded as a son. He was happy that such a chance should have come to Wa'poo and had no intention of standing in his way, but equally this was a business opportunity and as such must be dealt with on business lines. He accepted with appreciation the handsome amount – more than twice the sum which had come into his mind while Madam Abiose was outlining her proposition – which was now being offered him for the loss of his young helper's services, and was grateful for her assurances that she wished Wa'poo to continue to visit him regularly, and that he himself, who had done so much for the boy, would always be welcome at her home. Only when all seemed settled and she was about to leave, did he allow it to appear in his manner that some question still was troubling him. Encouraged to speak out, he explained with seeming reluctance that he had over the years naturally come to look on Wa'poo not merely as an active helper – a fact which Madam Abiose had already generously acknowledged – he had also come to count on him as a staff for his old age. He had spent on Wa'poo in one way and another big sums which he would otherwise have saved. He had fed him well and seen that he grew up strong and healthy. He had taught him to be honest and not to cheat those he worked for and who might one day be his benefactors. This being so, and having shown himself a father towards Wa'poo, he had expected that Wa'poo would play the part of a son in due course towards himself. He was now – he looked deprecatingly down at himself – approaching the infirmities of age. He could not expect to work for ever. What was to become of him when he could no longer do all that was required of him by the whitemen, and so was forced to give way to some younger, stronger man? In parting with Wa'poo he was not only parting with a helper in the present, he was losing the support which could provide for his old age.

Madam Abiose smiled appreciatively. 'I kin see you still man of force an' power, Mr Ali. You gittin' yo'self plenty more sons for support yo' ole age. Also I s'pose yo'self big landowner wid plenty huts an' plenty goats up dere in Northern Region.'

Surprised at her penetration, Mr Ali was about to call on heaven to witness his poverty and lack of possessions, but Madam Abiose cut him short: 'All same, Mr Ali, I und'stan' what you tellin' me. So now I givin' you one hundred pouns more for protectin' yo' old age.'

After some half-hour's intensive bargaining, the matter was settled to the satisfaction of both sides. Madam Abiose secured what she wanted and Mr Ali far more than he had dared to expect. His leavetaking from Wa'poo was long and affection-ate. Wa'poo begged Mr Ali to give him a father's blessing and to assure him that, apart from a few lapses, he had shown himself a faithful son. To this Mr Ali warmly assented. He embraced Wa'poo, holding him to his chest, and told him to be a good boy and work hard for Madam Abiose, adding: 'I done de will of Allah, Wa'poo, when I take you in dis long time back. An' Allah done reward me well for my good deed. I bin mos' happy dis day for you, Wa'poo my son, an' I bin happy for myself as well.'

5
Secret Student

For the first few months after Wa'poo found himself installed in Madam Abiose's home and business, he was in confusion. He could not make out what had happened to him nor what his position was supposed to be, and there were times when he wished himself back on the portico with Mr Ali. By night he was a cherished darling sharing Madam Abiose's bed, the first he had ever slept in, a bed huger and softer than he had imagined could exist. Moreover this bed, with its mattresses, pillows, blankets and coverlets, occupied – together with other furniture such as two large wardrobes and several mirrors – a room set apart solely for themselves to sleep in, though it might have been rented out to house two families. Nor was this all, for opening out of this one was a second room, again used only by themselves, and for no other purpose but to wash and bathe in. Its walls were white with shining tiles, except where they were covered with yet more mirrors, and here there was not just a single tap as in Mr Ali's yard, but *four* taps from two of which hot water would flow readily by night as well as day.

In this world of bewildering luxury where he lived from around seven each evening until sharp on six next morning, Wa'poo ate as he had never eaten and drank as he had literally never drunk, for no form of alcohol was allowed by Mr Ali. Before many months had passed he owned a wardrobe of clothes he hardly knew how to put on without Madam Abiose's help and half a dozen pairs of shoes he would never have put on at all but for her insistence. He had – what he had always longed for – a wristwatch, and this one was actually of gold on a gold bracelet; hairbrushes which he knew cost more than the whole contents of his stall; a pigskin wallet with a handful of notes which Madam Abiose had not even counted when she stuffed them in, and a gold signet ring with a real jewel.

But all this glory ended, or at least the enjoyment of it vanished, the moment the day's work began. Once the shutters had gone up and the first van started to unload, Wa'poo was sent off here and there around the town, given orders he could not follow, shouted at by everyone in a senior position including Madam Abiose, with scarcely five minutes to himself till darkness fell. If his patroness had been concerned with only one business or two, he felt he could have mastered their workings easily, for his mind was quick, he was eager to please and not afraid of work. But Madam Abiose was a true mammy with a finger in a dozen – indeed far more than a dozen – commercial pies, and she seemed determined to make Wa'poo familiar with them all at the same time.

In the choice of titles for her enterprises she showed both her love of imagery and a powerful religious streak. Besides her two main stores in the market – The Divine Providence General Supply Association selling household goods of all kinds, and The Universal Peace and Love Drapery Co-operative – she owned a shop in a commanding position near the end of Carter Bridge. This, The Paris Nite-Life Exclusive Fashion Depot, not only did a thriving trade among Lagos ladies such as would have supported a less important mammy, but also provided an outlet for the goods of the Drapery Cooperative. Nor was the cultural side neglected. Among her properties was The Invincible Ajax Literature Bureau which sold office stationery, textbooks and working materials for schools, besides doing good trade in girlie magazines imported from the United States. Since these were old copies coming into the country as ballast in ships or packed around breakables in crates, Madam Abiose bought them by the hundredweight for next to nothing. Smoothed out, ironed where necessary, tidied up and sorted, they could be sold off separately at a rewarding profit. In addition to her shops and stores Madam Abiose ran a mammy-wagon business with a small fleet of lorries and pick-up vans. These did all the collecting and delivery for her enterprises and, when not needed for this purpose, ranged far and wide over the Western Region, transporting market produce, machinery, live animals and human beings in the greatest disorder and enjoyment. Much more than any of the businesses, it was the lorries that made an impression on Wa'poo and he promised himself that, when the time came for him to have a say in his own destiny, he would apply himself to this side of the business, and in this way would also travel and get to know the land in which he lived.

Yet even this was not the end. Madam Abiose, he came gradually to realize, owned property, or shares in property, or was planning to take shares in property, all over Lagos and its neighbourhood; nothing was too small that would bring in profit and few projects so large as to lie outside her scope. To her inner office, reached up a flight of rickety stairs and looking like the cabin of some crazy vessel – but housing three telephones, a modern safe and the latest accounting machinery – climbed labourers, stallholders, herdsmen, petty traders and village headmen. But up the same rickety stairs also came financiers, lawyers, bank directors, managers of national businesses, and politicians renowned throughout the country. For this range of visitors Madam Abiose had many manners, voices, varieties of tone and language; a quiet voice, careful pronunciation and a gracious manner for important customers; a raucous bellow and homely pidgin for the drivers and loading men; a range of friendly vernaculars for the villagers who ventured hesitantly inside her stores. Having seen a well-dressed citizen off with smiles and handshakes, Madam

Abiose, waiting only until he was out of earshot, would whip round to bawl out an assistant: 'Hey you! Whaffor you stackin' dat cloth 'long dose back shelves? You – Joseph – you I talkin' to! Dose new cloths bin lates' fashion! Done you throw 'way all yo' five senses, man? You s'posin' Lagos women all bush persons like yo'self? Ho, Wa'poo! Come help Joseph lay dese new cloths out on front of store!'

Scarcely had Wa'poo got started on the job before she was saying to him, "Nuff of dat, my frien'! Jus' you go over Divine Providence an' tell manager come here spik to me. You stay an' manage store till he git back.'

Exhausted with hurrying from one place to the next and from one task to another, confused by the many people he must deal with at all levels, constantly faced with demands for knowledge he had not got and decisions he did not know how to make, Wa'poo would sink at the week's end into something like despair. But once they had left the store behind, Madam Abiose was another person altogether, and a teasing intimacy, a gentle mockery reserved for him alone, were her answer to these moods.

'So, my frien', you findin' all my businesses too many for you, I see. You wishin' you kin stay one place an' understan' one thing only like some sma'-sma' clerk? Maybe you sorry now you done leave yo' stall, and settle down here with dis woman who is always askin' you do something new? Is dis true? Are you sorry, my young frien', dat you livin' here now wid me?'

Wa'poo sighed. 'I mos' happy with you, ma'am. An' I 'preciate fine opportunity you givin' me. But I bin slow for learn all things you wishin' I shall learn. . . . All dese books of 'counts. . . . Dis telephone too. . . . I find dat mos' hardes' machine for talk into.'

His patroness smiled largely and eased the velvet blouse beneath her arms. 'You learnin' well, my frien'. You make fine progress an' please me much. . . . Hey! Alake!' she shouted across into the kitchen without getting up, 'Whaffor you no bring de master col'-col' beer? You fetch quick-quick, 'fore he done finish all his chop.'

Wa'poo had a secret which he kept from Madam Abiose. It was often difficult to hide, particularly when she gave him a string of complicated messages to be handed on to different agents when he went out in the morning. He was obliged to try to memorize them all, and if he felt uncertain about any message would suggest casually to the clerk that he ring back and check with Madam Abiose to make sure he had understood just what she wanted. Wa'poo's painful secret was that he could neither read nor write. He knew the numbers, could add, subtract and do simple multiplication or division in his head – could reckon while arguing just how much 120 packets of cigarettes at one shilling and elevenpence would cost, less 10 per cent. All this Mr Ali had taught him, spurred on by the painful experience of having been swindled several times by sharp-witted traders when he stocked his tray, but he could not read so much as the headlines in the newspapers. Reading and writing appeared to him deep mysteries, comprehensible to those intended to understand them, but beyond reach of normal people like himself. He was convinced that if his patroness got to know of his ignorance, though she might be too kind-hearted to drive him away, she would certainly despise him and regret her choice; so he maintained a studied pretence of reading, glancing at the newspapers she passed him, leaving books she lent him open about the room, and pretending to follow prayers and hymns in the church to which Madam Abiose took him every Sunday.

One day however Madam Abiose sent Wa'poo to the Invincible Ajax bookshop with a long list of stationery needed for her stores. Wa'poo handed this to the clerk, Thaddeus. Thaddeus, who had to get the various packets down from many shelves, handed the list back.

'Here!' he said. 'You go for read list one by one. I pass things down an' you stack um here on desk.'

Wa'poo hesitated, stammered, and finally took Thaddeus into his confidence. 'I no knowin' how for read an' write.'

Thaddeus gazed back in amazement. 'No kin read an' write? How you manage in business den?'

'Myself, I never 'tend for be in business. Jus' petty trader an' stallholder. . . . You think you kin teach me read an' write if I comin' to you after work?'

'Course I kin teach you, my frien'! Who kin teach you better dan myself?' He waved an arm proudly at the shelves. 'Don' I have teachin' books all roun' my head de whole day long?'

'Okay! I come here three evenins each week one hour, an' I pay you two shillins cash for each lesson you done give me.'

'Dat *okay*, Mr Wa'poo. Dat mos' cert'nly okay!' And, then fearing perhaps that his enthusiasm might have gone beyond a teacher's dignity, he added sternly, 'But you 'bliged for study

hard all evenins you not comin' here if you wishin' for make
progress.'

Wa'poo agreed, but added that the arrangement would end
at once if anyone but their two selves came to hear of it. To
Madam Abiose he explained that he found the Ajax Book
business hardest to follow, so was going round for a few
evenings to learn all about it from Thaddeus. His mistress
looked surprised but made no objection, and so now Wa'poo
under Thaddeus' tuition was ploughing steadily through the
primers used by children in first forms. Once he had mastered
letters and could read short sentences, he was seized with a
passion for study and wanted continually to be reading and
extending his knowledge. He was astonished to discover that
reading was not something confined to books but that the
world was full of it. Indeed the whole of life had been
organized, it seemed, to make things interesting for the literate
few.

Wa'poo now saw writing everywhere. He read the names of
streets, names which had been familiar to him all his life. He
had supposed them to be derived from chiefs, Obas or some
high authority, but he could now see they were taken from a
small notice at each end, and that he could find out where-
abouts he was in Lagos – or perhaps in the whole world –
simply by studying such notices. He read the names of
buildings as he went along, the lists of occupants and tenants,
the notices warning away hawkers and the instructions for the
lift. He would cross the road eagerly to read information
outside police stations and post offices, times of church
services and the name of next Sunday's preacher. The very
packets of cigarettes and sweets he had been selling all
his life carried, he now found, important messages, and the
shop windows were full of announcements, exciting if
misleading, about what was available inside. Most alluring of
all were the posters outside the open-air cinemas, full of
heroism, violence and seduction. The hoardings too, with
those stupendous faces and lettering painted by giants, raised
questions to which reading alone could give an answer.

Many times in the past as he walked the streets Wa'poo had
wondered who that rich chief could be whose laughing eye
and lustful grin beamed out over the hurrying traffic, and had
taken him for some politician seeking votes. But now he
understood the truth, the chief was happy because he had
obtained power through drinking Guinness; 'power' in West

Africa means sexual potency, so no wonder the chief looked more than life-size and grinned jovially round at passers-by. Those young men lounging in academic gowns and mortar-boards were not trying to attract pupils for some famous university, they were smoking Varsity cigarettes, delicious in flavour and long-lasting, which would also calm their nerves and get them through their examinations. That voluptuous girl about whom he had often speculated – lying full-dressed but expectant on a mattress the size of a house roof, each swelling breast the size of a horse's buttock – was a mystery no longer. Her very name was on the poster. YOU WILL FIND COMFORT ON A VONO MATTRESS. For once though, his new ability provoked more questions than it answered. Comfort, like Chastity, was a popular girl's name, he knew. But why did Comfort advertise herself so brazenly? And how did you learn where she and her enormous mattress could be found? For Wa'poo the days now passed in a long dream, reading everything he could see as he went about his day's work, pulling a primer from his pocket when alone, devouring the legends on packets and wrappers, looking at files and records, trying out his own writing in a notebook carried out of sight in an inside pocket.

One evening when Madam Abiose worked late, Wa'poo was walking up and down in the quiet of their bedroom. Traffic had drained away out of town, the night was still and Alake occupied in the kitchen, and there was nothing to distract him. Under Thaddeus' guidance Walpole had progressed to quite difficult readers used by children of ten or eleven. Absorbed in study, exulting in the mastery of each new word and phrase, he was following the lines with his finger and slowly spelling them out aloud. . . .

'On the island the trees and the plants are new, the fr-uits are st-r-ange and cu-cu-curious. . . .'

At that moment the door opened and Madam Abiose stood directly before him. Being tired after a heavy day she had walked upstairs slowly, supporting herself on the handrail. Deep in his book, Wa'poo had heard no sound and now gaped at her open-mouthed. He had not even time to slip his primer out of sight and think up some explanation. Indeed the mere attempt looked so suspicious that she snatched the book out of his hand and ordered: 'Go fetch me col'-col' drink from fridge!'

Wa'poo was back in a moment. Madam Abiose was sitting

on the bed with her head bent over the book. He offered her
the drink on a tray, hoping his reading exercise would not
cause trouble, but recalling that his few evenings with
Thaddeus had somehow extended themselves over months. A
blow on his arm sent drink and tray spinning across the room
as his furious mistress sprang up before him.

'Whaffor you doin' dis thing to me?' she demanded, her
voice thick with anger as she thrust the book into his face.
'Whaffor? Dat what I askin' you? *Whaffor?*'

'But I do nothin' to you, ma'am. . . . I just try for
learn. . . .'

'Den whaffor you no tell me? Answer dat! Whaffor you hide
dis secret in yo'self. Whaffor you no come say – "Madam, I
wishin' for learn read an' write"? Whaffor you no speak out
like a man?'

Wa'poo gaped. In face of this onslaught, he struggled to
recall his wits and to find some explanation which would not
make matters worse.

'Ma'am, I wantin' show you I kin. . . .'

'Ha! I see how 'tis den, Wa'poo. You s'pose I not concerned
for helpin' you – so you doin' all yo'self in yo' own way. How
many times you hear me say – "My frien', I inten' you shall
become great an' famous man"? How many times you hear
me say dese words? Fifty times? One hundred times? Answer
me – Wa'poo! How many times?'

'Many, many times, ma'am.'

'Den you s'posin' I not willin' for help you learn to read?
Don' you know I do everything in my power for help you?
Dat I hire de fines' reading teacher in all Lagos? You make me
into liar? You s'pose I not speak truth when I say I do
everything for help you learn an' make good progress? When I
ever sayin' you somethin' which is not true? When? *Answer
me*, Wa'poo! When I say you thing which is not true?' She
choked with passion.

'No time, ma'am, no time you say lies. . . . But I
wishin. . . .' Wa'poo stumbled, at a loss to anwer reproaches
so bitter and which he felt to be so little deserved. But while he
searched for words the storm broke over him again, convict-
ing him of blacker and still blacker offences.

'De fac' is, Wa'poo, you no trust me! Dat de long an' de
short of everything. You placin' no trust in me. Here we livin'
in dis house side by side, an' I lovin' you more dan any husban'
an' cherishin' you like my own son, an' still you puttin' no

trust in me at all. You fix everything yo' way for yo' own self. Dis not love! Dis not trust! Dis not even hones' frien'ship!'

'Ma'am, I wishin' for show you I kin learn. . . .'

'You *stupid* boy, Wa'poo. . . . You stupid, stupid boy. . . .' And now at last, as Madam Abiose's rage began to spend itself, Wa'poo managed to get in his explanation, and once he started to speak the words poured out.

'I too much 'shamed in my heart, ma'am, dat why I not spikkin' 'bout dis many-many time. I bin 'fraid when you know I kin not read dat you consider me no-good boy an' bin sorry you ever take me in yo' house. So one day I spik to Thaddeus in Ajax Bookshop and he promise he teach me. So I goin' there after work three evenins each week. I make Thaddeus swear to tell no livin' person, an' I pay Thaddeus two shillin' each lesson from all de money you givin' me. . . . I not understandin' I do wrong for try an' git learnin' for myself. I think you mos' happy see me work hard, like you done order me long time back when I first came here, an' I hopin' I kin work better for help you in de business. I mos' cert'nly not wantin' hurt yo' feelings, ma'am, an' 'blige you git so mad at me. . . .'

To Walpole's bewilderment his patroness flung herself full-length on the bed, and burst into a fit of weeping as though she herself were grievously at fault: 'You jus' de mos' foolishes' boy! Dat de one thing I kin say. An' I see you not lovin' nor trustin' me de least bit. You jus' wishin' fix whole life for yo'self widout help from me who lovin' you wid all my heart an' prayin' an' plannin' for you night an' day.'

Regaining confidence from her breakdown, and realizing she needed comfort in her own violence of feeling, Wa'poo dropped on his knees beside the bed.

'Is not true I not lovin' nor trustin' you, ma'am. Dis not true! But true I bin de foolishes' boy, for I not und'stan' an' 'preciate your too-good heart. . . .'

As he talked on, a hand reached out across the coverlet and in a moment they were kissing each other's salty, tear-stained faces with abandon. Later, after they had eaten supper and Alake cleared away the things, Madam Abiose said in an unusually serious voice: 'Wa'poo – der bin somethin' you an' me 'bliged for discuss.'

The boy's heart sank. Was the trouble not over after all? Was his crime worse than he had imagined? Was he going to be sent back to Mr Ali, or perhaps ordered to go away for schooling?

'What dis, ma'am?' he asked tremblingly.

'Dis de question of yo' name.'

'My *name*, ma'am?'

'Yes, my frien', yo' name. How you intend become great an' famous citizen of Nigeria wid name like "Wa'poo"?'

'But Wa'poo bin my name,' he replied with dignity, 'I done carry dis name on me all my life.'

Madam Abiose leaned across and patted his hand tenderly. 'I not plan rob you of yo' name, my frien'! But we mus' look to future times. . . . Wa'poo bin all right for shoutin' after market boy. But you no longer jus' a market boy, an' one day you mixin' wid important persons. How if parliament man, or lawyer, or some of dese rich whitemen come here – are dey goin' speak to you as "Wa'poo"? How you feel when bank director ask you sign yo' name on big loan document – an' you 'bliged for write down "Wa'poo"?'

The boy hung his head. The whole of his life, with its lack of normal family and background, seemed summed up in his haphazard, ridiculous name.

'What you wishin' I shall do 'bout my name, ma'am?' he asked in deep confusion and distress.

Madam Abiose did not reply directly.

'You not thinkin' 'bout dese matters, my frien', because you concerned wid yo' own life in de present. But I 'bliged keep yo' future, an' yo' happiness in de future, always in my mind.'

'So what you wishin', ma'am?'

'S'pose we not give you no new name, but 'spose we changin yo' name sma'-sma' piece? S'pose we go for call you "Walpole"? How you think you will like dat?'

'Walpole. . . Walpole. . .' he tried out hesitantly but with growing satisfaction on his tongue. 'Dis not bad-soundin' name – Walpole! An' dis not mak' too-big change. But where you find dis name Walpole, ma'am?'

'What, my frien'? You tellin' me you not know who is Walpole? De mos' famous man in History of England after King George an' King Henry Eight an' all dem other kings! I promise you, Walpole, 'fore I finish wid yo' education, you going' know all 'bout who Walpole is.'

Walpole was flattered and ready to be convinced. He thought for a moment, and then ventured on a question which had begun to trouble him lately.

'But am I not needin' *two* names, ma'am? Walpole for friens, but some other name for sign on paper? Same as Mr Ali done always write "Ahman Ali" an' you signin' yo'self "Florence Abiose"?'

'Yes indeed, my frien'. An' I fix wid lawyers dis very day dat you shall *have* two names. One name we done 'gree on – Walpole. An' now I givin' you a second name, my own name, Abiose. So from dis day you goin' be "Mr Walpole Abiose". Dat now your rightful, legitimate name. How you like dat?'

Walpole's eyes began to shine. He blinked and could not speak. The conferring on him of his patroness' name meant far more than talk of future greatness. He experienced it both as a gift and an act of faith in him, and also as a powerful incantation performed over his future, transforming him from a market boy whom everyone could shout at into a citizen of dignity and position. Dazzled by his newfound grandeur, he stretched out his hands towards Madam Abiose and tried to utter his thanks, but the tears filling his eyes and pouring down his cheeks prevented him from speaking. Madam Abiose took his head in her arms, kissing his eyes, and in a few minutes they were in bed again.

As those great thighs closed round him, smooth as silk and soft as butter, Walpole felt a surge of power throughout his body, in which passion was reinforced by gratitude and gratitude blended with excitement. The desire of the instant melted into the promise of all the tomorrows opening out before him. Those tomorrows and his sensual, generous mistress became one. Young, strong, confident, avid for life and finding it all around, beneath, ahead of him, Walpole's whole being concentrated itself into a single point and act of penetration. As she twisted and throbbed ecstatically beneath him he went driving on, into her and into his own future. He could, he felt, go driving on like this for ever.

6

Day of Rest

As a cultured Southerner Madam Abiose inherited a way of life which derived partly from West Africa and partly from three or four centuries of European contact. It was a way of life based on a great seaport with worldwide trade and so quite different from the village life of the 'bush' people inland, or from that of dwellers in the Northern Region who – despite the harmless guise in which they appeared as watchmen, cattle-herds bringing meat down to the markets or travelling salesmen – seemed to the Southerners to be still Arab warriors at heart. Easily recognizable by their white robes and tall, lean bodies, they showed in their bearing a discipline based on hardship which to the comfort-loving peoples of the South carried more than a hint of menace.

Part of Madam Abiose's way of life was a staunch Christianity, this being not so much a matter of holding religious beliefs as of maintaining social contacts with her fellow Christians and observing Sunday as a day of rest. 'Six days shalt thou labour,' she told Walpole many times, 'but Sunday bin de day of rest. De Lord hisself never doin' nothin' on dis Holy Day.' On Sunday she would transact no business, and her managers knew better than to telephone her however advantageous the opportunity. But Sunday was more than a rest day, it was also the day of grandeur on which Madam Abiose appeared no longer as the hard-driving market mammy but as a wealthy city lady. Not only did she present herself at her finest, but she liked others to do so as well, and many a clerk or shop assistant, wanting a loan for some private necessity, had secured it with the plea: 'Please, ma'am, I beggin' in name of de Lord, borrow me three-four pouns, ma'am! I got nothin' I kin wear for visitin' my church on de Holy Day.'

Every Sunday morning, arrayed in her finest clothes and jewels, Madam Abiose carried Walpole off to her favourite among the city's fashionable churches. Except in the rainy season she preferred to walk, making her stately way with a smile and a nod for those she recognized, appreciating to the full the effect occasioned. Walpole looked forward to Sunday as eagerly as she did, savouring the freedom from pressure now that the week's work was over. He enjoyed the dressing up, the expansive good temper of his patroness, their impressive entry into the crowded church. Unconsciously he assumed a devout expression and walked more slowly as they moved up the aisle to the places near the front kept for them by a respectful verger.

Once Walpole had become familiar with the pattern of

devotions and no longer feared to be caught by the congregation all sitting down while he remained standing, he
revelled in the long service as an imposing pageant in which all
present had a part to play. He drank in with delight the
language of the psalms and prayers, unintelligible yet the more
impressive for that reason, full of powerful and lofty incantation: 'Prevent us, O Lord, in all our doings with thy most
gracious favour, and further us with thy continual help; that in
all our works begun, continued and ended in thee, we may
glorify thy holy name, and finally by thy mercy obtain
everlasting life. . . .' Magic surely, and potent enough to
charm spirits up out of the black and white squares beneath
their feet – black for the living and white for the ghosts of the
departed ancestors. At times, hearing the glorious promises of
the Bible read out by two heavily-built cloth-covered citizens,
he almost expected the wall behind the altar to split and the
celestial landscape of heaven to be revealed, with serried ranks
of angels kneeling far up into the sky.

He exulted in the preacher's eloquence as he craned far out
above their heads, his passionate appeals to which nobody
responded, lamentations answered with no tears, denunciations which evoked no outcry of repentance – though one
would think even hearts of mahogany must burst. Walpole
did not know which to admire more – the preacher renewing
his useless attack week after week, or the congregation which
received his spiritual broadsides without a murmur, except for
the rustle of dresses and the clink of coins being got ready for
the collection. Above all the hymns delighted Walpole. His
heart expanded and his shoulders swayed, he could hardly
keep his feet from breaking into a shuffle as he raised his strong
voice in those calls to battle, those haughty challenges to Satan
who would surely, if he had any fiendish spirit, leap up
shaking his spear before them in reply.

> 'The Son of God goes forth to war
> A kingly crown to gain;
> His blood-red banner gleams afar:
> Who follows in his train?'

At other times, in the words of a hymn or of some passage
from the Bible, Walpole caught a note of menace, as though
from the depths of the forest some witch doctor or wizard
were crying out warning of disaster.

> 'The world is very evil,
> The times are waxing late;
> Be sober and keep vigil,
> The Judge is at the gate.

The Judge is at the gate! What fearful words. Too late for
repentance now! He is already here – and what can we answer
to the judge? Through the words of such hymns, Walpole
could positively feel calamity approaching like floodwater
down a dried-up river bed, and yet all the minister and
congregation did was to sing of its approach. In his mind he
contrasted the stern ritual and obeisances of Mr Ali, which
meant getting up early, breaking into each day's work and
risking the displeasure of his masters, with the fervent
emotion of his new religion which promised so much but
resulted in so little action. Yet even while he pondered on
God's anger and the judge, the organ had already started to
unfurl a gentler tune, and Madam Abiose, her low notes
melting in intensity, was murmuring beside his ear as though
they were already in bed together.

> 'From heaven he came and sought her
> To be his holy Bride,
> With his own blood he bought her
> And for her life he died.'

Great mysteries indeed – and what did he want to die for at
such a moment, Walpole wondered? Often he longed to
discuss with his patroness the problems raised in his mind by
her religion, but was restrained by a natural tact, feeling she
might have difficulty in answering all he wished to ask. Only
now and then was he provoked into a question. Every year in
the church which they attended, the clergyman, who had been
to a theological college in England, insisted on a 'harvest
festival'. This lacked agricultural logic in Lagos, since there is
no procession of seasons so close to the equator, only long
periods of heat broken by shorter spells of heavy downpour,
bringing not one harvest but a succession as the various crops
ripen – yam harvest, cocoa harvest, sweet potato harvest and
the rest. But this did not deter their pastor who considered the
Harvest Festival an essential highlight of his church's calendar,
so that once a year the church was decorated with fruit,
vegetables and even the supreme extravagance of flowers,
presented by the wealthy congregation and wilting as soon as
put into position, and Walpole found himself singing:

'He sends the snow in winter,
The warmth to swell the grain,
The breezes and the sunshine,
And soft, refreshing rain.'

'Whaffor we sing 'bout snow falling down in winter?' he asked Madam Abiose as they stood waiting for friends in the churchyard. 'Snow not b'long here in Nigeria one bit.'

'No,' she agreed in affable explanation, 'bin no snow fallin' in our country, Walpole. But dis hymn show dat we b'long to great worldwide church. Dis church cover Nigeria and de other African countries, but it also coverin' countries like England where snow fall over de whole land far as eye kin see. So Christianity not small local religion for persons livin' in one district but for peoples over de whole worl'. . . . How you doin' Mr Mensah? Happy to see you an' Mrs Mensah lookin' fine.'

As they stood outside, Walpole exchanged greetings with the important men who came up with wives and families to speak to his patroness and showed themselves friendly to him on her account. While they chatted, he was studying them closely. On Sundays many would wear European suits as he did, and he noted their material and styles and compared them with his own. He studied their ways of standing, how they handled their hats, shook hands with one another, the gesture with which one would bring out a cigarette case, offering them round to relax after the formality of church. He noted their expressions – dignified, humorous, aloof or condescending – and their 'goodbyes' as they turned away for home, all of which he would later practise, observing his own gestures and expressions critically in the mirror.

About his position as Madam Abiose's protégé Walpole felt no awkwardness. On the contrary it was a source of pride to be known as her 'Scholarship Boy', a status between accepted lover and adopted son with the privileges of both. Nor was the difference in age a subject for embarrassment. To have been chosen by a mature woman was tribute to his manhood, and the possession of such a one as Madam Abiose could only be a cause for envy. Walpole, standing by her side as churchgoers paid respects, was equally proud of her wealth and of her voluptuous femininity, smooth-skinned, soft-eyed, with heavy breasts and flanks at which so many desirous glances were directed; and when young girls in silk or muslin shot appreciative looks at him from beneath their long lashes and saucy hats, Walpole knew they were not just responding to his expensive clothes, but paying tribute to him as a man of potency and vigour.

When all the chats with friends were over, a heavy lunch succeeded, a 'Sundays only' feast, for there was little eating before evening during the working week. This they always took alone since it would be followed by slow hours of love-making in their shaded bedroom, hours to which the formality of church-going made decorous prelude. Both were relaxed and tomorrow's work seemed far away. Walpole's mistress was a woman of experienced sensuality, well understanding how to rouse her young lover to a pitch of frenzy, leave him to recover, and then excite him more fiercely than before. As darkness loomed beyond the curtains they would reluctantly rise and dress for the round of social visits which Madam Abiose paid on Sunday evenings. But sometimes she would brush aside her duties, bring food and drink into the bedroom and let the passionate afternoon merge into night.

Once when they were making ready to go out, Walpole, already dressed, sat watching her as she completed her toilet. She had washed and perfumed herself, combed up her mass of hair and put colour on her lips. She slid her arms into her buba and wound one of her bright-patterned lappas tight beneath her breasts. And now, following an intricate pattern of familiar movement, she was knotting her head-tie of gold and violet brocade. Having wound the material round her head, she flung a triangular end over her face as she drew tight the bow which would add twelve majestic inches to her presence. In a moment more he would have lost her, she would be translated from bedroom intimacy into the world of every-day. As she sat with her face hidden behind the triangle Walpole, partly in playfulness and partly out of reviving sensuality, flung himself on his knees in front of her and began covering her throat and breast with kisses.

In a moment Madam Abiose had flung aside her head-tie and slipped out of her buba. She pulled off his coat and forced his mouth passionately against her own, then throwing herself on to the bed she drew him down into her with a moan. But long after the bout was over she continued to moan and sob, clinging to Walpole with a paroxysm of tenderness as though the essential core of her being had melted and she could no longer recover. 'My honey,' she murmured, 'oh my honey

child, never go leave me . . . stay all your life . . . I lovin' an'
carin' for you too-too much. . . . You killin' me, Walpole, if
you leave me now. . . .'

Walpole had meant to arouse her desire, but this was
something altogether different and he trembled at her
intensity. He did love Madam Abiose so far as he understood
the word. He was truly grateful for all she had done and was
doing for him; she had opened the gates of life; she assuaged
his disturbing passions and inspired him with confidence in
himself. But such emotion as she was showing now carried
him far out of his depth, implying demands which he could
never satisfy. His wantonness had exposed what had so far
been concealed, the inequality in their relationship. She loved
him far more than he could ever love her in return, and
Walpole's intuition told him the gap must widen, that she was
bound to suffer deeply and he bound to cause her suffering,
and that she was moaning now in anticipation of this pain.
Slowly they recovered and silently dressed, but memory of
the shock remained with Walpole and since he feared to release
again such tides of feeling, his approach to his mistress began
to be inhibited.

For the moment, however, Madam Abiose restored her
authority with a brisk stroke. She did not always take Walpole
with her on Sunday visits to relatives and friends. Sometimes
she would set off alone in her American car, taking the most
reliable of her drivers in a purple chauffeur's uniform and
packing Walpole off with money in his pocket to amuse
himself. Then he would visit a cinema, a pleasure recently
discovered, have a drink with one of his few acquaintances, or
sometimes go and pay a call on Mr Ali. It was always she who
decided where they visited, and once they arrived, would treat
Walpole with motherly authority, telling him when she
wished to leave, and asking his opinions only when she chose.
But she usually let him know beforehand if he was to go with
her, and for this evening no such warning had been given, so
when she told him to get ready to come out Walpole answered
that he was going with Thaddeus to a film and might he not
come with her next week instead?

'Very well,' Madam Abiose replied coolly, 'you know I
only askin' you when we meet important person kin help wid
yo' career. Tonight I visitin' Chief Julius Ogun. But no
matter! If you wish for go out playin' wid yo' little frien' – den
you go!'

She started for the door. But Walpole, made more sensitive by what they had just been through together, threw himself in front of her.

'No,' he cried, 'you bin de Queen! I do what you say. I bin happy come visitin' wid you – not jus' for de Chief, but because dis bin yo' wish.'

Though deeply gratified Madam Abiose gave no sign of such feeling but surveyed her young man critically. 'Go then, my frien', an' take off dat tie. Not suitable for meet important person. Put on one of yo' plain ties like Mr Chukuma always wearin'. An' yo' new black shoes. Hurry now! You fin' me waitin' for you in de car.'

7

The Doors of Knowledge

Madam Abiose had not forgotten her promise to help Walpole with his education. It was one of her principles in life to have a trusted friend or two in every calling whom she could turn to for advice or help when it was needed, and the person she turned to now was Mr Chebe. Mr Chebe was headmaster of a school in Lagos and ordered all his books through the Ajax Bookshop, for which he received a generous commission which did not appear in the accounts. There was thus a bond of mutual interest between Madam Abiose and himself and he was happy to look in for an evening at her request. After an hour's discussion as to the best way to proceed, Walpole was called in.

The plan proposed by Mr Chebe was that Walpole should work for the business in the mornings and apply himself to study in the afternoons and evenings. As to the plan of study, his advice was to begin at the beginning and take things slowly; Walpole should first learn to read and write English correctly, and he warned that this alone was going to take the best part of a year. Walpole's face fell – his own plan had been to set about education in the way Mr Ali had taught him to set about an opponent, brusquely, with determination, and not leave off until the enemy was beaten. He was in favour of attacking all subjects simultaneously, or at least in groups of half a dozen adversaries at a time. Sensing his disappointment, Madam Abiose put in: 'If it takin' half-year for Walpole spik good English – how many years 'fore he b'come educated man same like yo'self?'

Mr Chebe, who foresaw considerable profit from this young man's education, did not laugh or reply that this was too much to be hoped for. 'It takes a long time, madam, to become well-educated. It requires many years of concentrated effort. But Walpole is young. He has an excellent patron to encourage him, and if he sticks to his task, he may well surprise us all.'

There was no doubt about Walpole sticking to his task. He shared the African conviction that education is the key to success, for which every sacrifice will prove worthwhile. Simply to be in contact with education – through helping a son, a younger brother, even a member of the village or tribe – is good, but to have education brought within one's own reach is the greatest benefit a man can hope for. As little more than an infant playing round the huts, Walpole had gazed with awe at those fortunate village children who went off to school each morning. Later, as a boy of nine or ten selling from his tray, he had been racked with envy over children no cleverer than himself who came back from school in the afternoons wearing clean shirts and shorts, carrying in the two or three books beneath their arms the passport to success. But now his own chance had come, and he seized it with both hands. Mr Chebe saw him for an hour on two afternoons a week, during which he talked with him and made him read aloud from books and newspapers, correcting Walpole's speech and extending his vocabulary. For the other afternoons he set him written tasks, and Walpole's evenings were spent listening to radio and records, or studying the books his teacher recommended. In her eagerness to encourage him, Madam Abiose insisted that after supper Walpole should go over with her whatever he learned during the day, and though he found this tedious he was too grateful for her kindness to object. Patiently he explained correct pronunciation and the use of tenses; Madam Abiose would repeat all after him and then, drowsy from her arduous day's business, instantly forget what she had been repeating. While Walpole sat listening to his radio programmes she would doze off, but found it easy to remain awake when he read aloud, dwelling with fond attention on his voice and the growing correctness of his speech.

'You not sayin' "dis" no more, Walpole,' she noted proudly, 'you say "this" – same like Mr Stanwell, young whiteman from motor company who sellin' me dat new lorry.'

'Is so, madam. Mr Chebe tell me always to say "this" and "that". He also make me say "telling" – not "tellin' " and "doin' ", like we say in market.'

'Dis strange manner for spik English! All same, Walpole, you pay 'tention to Mr Chebe. He knowin' bes' way for educated person spik.'

'For an educated person to speak, madam,' Walpole corrected gently.

Madam Abiose sighed. 'I too-too old, my frien', for learn new ways. If am still smart young girl, den I work hard at learnin' like yo'self. But my life half way finish', and yo' life only jus' begin. . . . I bin too happy for you, Walpole, but sometimes . . . for myself . . . I feelin'. . . .'

Madam Abiose's tears, lately become more frequent, always made Walpole guilty and uneasy, so he changed tack. 'In two weeks, madam, I am facing examination. If I pass I shall be given a certificate.'

'What dis "certif'cate", Walpole?'

'A certificate saying I can speak and write good English, so I am now an educated person in the English language. An' this certificate, Mr Chebe says, is recognized all over the whole world.'

'Is so, my frien'? Dis will be great day for you'n' me. If you winnin' de certificate, I tell Mr Chebe he take what books he like from Ajax Bookshop – an' for yo'self I buyin' fine new suit. But if you not win certif'cate, den I forced find punishment make you work harder . . .' and she hesitated, at a loss how to conclude her threat.

There was no need for Madam Abiose to think up punishment, however, for Walpole passed his examination easily, too easily perhaps since the success flew to his head. He had accepted Mr Chebe's plan and been patient over applying himself to English, recognizing it as the key. But now that he had acquired the key, the doors of the house of knowledge had opened and he meant to take full possession of its contents. Geography, history, astronomy, biology, chemistry, physics, geometry, algebra – the very names only lately learned – lay all before him, and he intended to become their master. And languages; to the one successfully acquired he would add the rest – French, German, Italian, Spanish, Russian, Chinese, Latin, Greek. . . . The world's accumulated knowledge was now an open quarry from which he had only to hew out whatever chunks he chose.

Mr Chebe was due to call in on Madam Abiose at the weekend following Walpole's success, but Walpole could not wait. Having secured his patroness's agreement that he might buy books in place of the suit she promised him, he spent a whole afternoon – and far more than the value of a suit – in an orgy of book-buying. He chose them for their subjects, the pictures on the covers, because their titles sounded familiar, or in mistake for some different book he had been recommended. There were large books on art, thick books on economics, thin books of poetry, forbidding books on mathematics; they ranged from biographies in which no one could be interested to treatises scarcely anyone could comprehend. There were also atlases, dictionaries and books of reference. Even those which seemed to consist solely of diagrams did not terrify Walpole; he had the key and would master the lot of them before long. By the time Mr Chebe arrived for Sunday drinks they were lying scattered over armchairs, tables and the bed, half-open as Walpole had snatched them up and tossed them down. Walpole was elated, Madam Abiose proud but frightened by the storm she had unloosed.

'What is all this?' Mr Chebe began. 'Walpole cannot simply rush ahead in all directions. We need to make a plan. He has taken the first step – good. But now we must think out a second step, and after that a third, and fourth.'

Madam Aboise nodded agreement. 'I tellin' Walpole not to buy too many books before he done ask yo' advice.'

'What is this "second step"?' Walpole asked. Mr Chebe, unaware of Walpole's resistance, unfolded his design. For the next year Walpole should study elementary mathematics, make a start on history and geography, and learn a single other language such as French. That would be quite as much as he could manage for the coming twelve months. 'After that we can think again.' As for all these books lying around the place, they were quite unsuitable and should be sent back. He would send round a suitable reading list in a couple of days.

'You think all I can do in one whole year is *elementary*

mathematics and a little history and French?' Walpole
demanded.

At this tone of voice and the omission of any 'sir' or 'Mr
Chebe', Madam Abiose looked up sharply, but Walpole,
carried away by offended vanity, would not be checked.

'I am telling you I can do more than this,' he insisted. 'I am
not one of your schoolboys. I work hard and can get on fast –
and I am not sending back these books. I shall study them and
see what I can find. If other people can learn from them, then I
can too.'

'My friend,' said Mr Chebe, but in a patronizing tone which
added to Walpole's indignation, 'you have done well so far.
But the step you have taken is a very small one. You speak of
my schoolboys – but the schoolboys at least know that they
must move up from one form to another in a proper progress.
They cannot leap from the bottom to the top in just one
stride.'

'Dat mos' cert'ly bin true,' put in Madam Abiose.

The intervention of his patroness was the last straw for
Walpole. 'I am the one who is having to learn,' he declared, 'so
I am the best judge of how much I can learn. And I say I can go
faster than you allowing me.'

As headmaster of an important school Mr Chebe was
accustomed to dealing with insolence, and it was on the tip of
his tongue to point out that if Walpole had acquired just a little
more knowledge he might better appreciate the difficulties
which lay ahead. But even while framing his retort he
considered that it might suit him better to take Walpole at his
word. The young man had obviously become conceited, and
might well soon become intolerable; he himself had done
handsomely out of the situation so far, but from now on the
difficulties could outweigh the rewards. By staying in the
picture he might cash in for a few more months, but then the
situation would blow up, Madam Abiose would support her
'scholarship boy' and his profitable relationship with her
would be ended. Better to retire now, hand this conceited
youth on to someone else, and later on come in with sage
advice.

'Do you know, madam' – addressing his patroness was the
only rebuke to Walpole he allowed himself – 'I believe your
young man is right. I have the idea that he should walk before
he runs. But someone closer to his own age may think
otherwise – and then they can both run on together.'

Madam Abiose had not liked Walpole's attitude to a man much older than himself whom she respected and had herself chosen as his mentor, and was surprised when Mr Chebe answered with such mildness.

'No one kin do so much for my boy as you, my frien'. If you not wish continue teachin' Walpole, dis becos you havin' too many calls upon yo' time. We both' – and she looked sternly at Walpole until he murmured agreement – '*both* of us bin mos' grateful an' 'bliged for what you done. But if you kin not go on teachin', who you propose for take yo' place?'

'I have a graduate from Cambridge on my staff – a clever young whiteman with excellent degrees. He is gaining experience here before working in his own Ministry of Education. I shall speak to Mr Green. If he will take on Walpole's education, you cannot wish for a better man.'

Madam Abiose was delighted and Walpole flattered by the thought that a scholar from a world-famous university should become his tutor. He shook hands cordially with Mr Chebe, suffered without resentment Madam Abiose's rebuke over his rudeness, and even acted on her instruction – 'Go write nice letter of thanks to Mr Chebe for all de help he givin' in yo' education.'

Since his firmness and initiative had brought such a satisfactory prospect, Walpole felt he could indulge her over a small point like this.

8

Misunderstanding

Mr Green at first sight was not impressive, being short and slightly built, with sandy hair and pink cheeks which flushed easily. He peered through thick lenses and stuttered when he became nervous or was deeply interested. He dressed as though still at Cambridge, in a tweed coat and flannel trousers, seeming hardly to notice that he was living in an altogether different climate. His shoelaces often came undone and he

would tie them up without looking what he was doing but
continuing to address Walpole on the subject in hand, so that
he would be hopping up and down the room on one leg and
when he put his foot down, still arguing, the lace was no more
secure than when he started. However he was an excellent
teacher, sympathetic, adaptable, completely without pom-
posity and with a range of knowledge which surprised his
pupil and a casual attitude towards it which disconcerted him.

Once Walpole, coming in a few minutes late, found Mr
Green reading a book he had himself bought the day before, its
subject was El Greco and it contained a number of illustrations
with a few thousand words of text. Walpole had picked it up
among several others without noticing that the text was in
Spanish and now, finding it useless, meant to take it back. He
glanced sharply at his tutor.

'Why you not tell me you speak Spanish?' he demanded.

'B-b-because I can't!' Mr Green replied, taken aback. 'Who
on earth t-t-told you that I could?'

'But that book's in Spanish – and you're reading it!' Walpole
was indignant as though some deception had been practised on
him.

'Oh g-g-g-ood heavens! I suppose anyone can *read* a bit . . .
that is, make out the meaning. Spanish isn't difficult, if you
happen to know F-F-French and Italian, and remember a bit of
Latin . . . they're all pretty much the same. But *speaking* a
language is altogether different.'

'Why?' Walpole asked. 'Why is it so different? Surely you
either know a language or you don't?'

'Speaking means knowing how to pronounce and to put
sentences together. And it's got to be all there inside you
ready. When someone talks to you you've no time to puzzle
over how to reply. It's got to come straight out of you. No, I
can't *speak* Spanish. Not at all.'

Occasionally while they were talking – for Mr Green turned
many of their sessions into discussions, leaving Walpole to do
the necessary study in his own time – he would sketch
excellent likenesses of his pupil on scraps of paper or the
margin of an exercise book.

'But you can *draw*!' Walpole exclaimed the first time this
happened. 'Why you never tell me about that? You must show
me your pictures.'

'G-g-good God!' Mr Green replied with no sign of affect-
ation. 'You don't call that *drawing*, do you? It just happens to

look like you. Any fool can get a likeness. It's only a question of looking closely and putting down what you see.'

Unlike Mr Chebe, Mr Green carried his learning lightly, and Walpole was quick to realize that this implied deeper learning and a humbler attitude. For Mr Chebe it was something to exploit, but Mr Green was on such familiar terms with scholarship that he could laugh at it. And so now, with Walpole eager to progress and his tutor delighted to have somebody to teach, as well as finding the extra money welcome, the pair got on happily and Walpole was soon making rapid headway. Mr Green decided that he should learn mathematics and French, with the history and geography of Africa for a start, other subjects to be added as he seemed able to take them on. At the outset, to Madam Abiose's relief, Mr Green had discreetly arranged to return most of the books Walpole had bought on the ground that they cumbered the place up and that by the time Walpole wanted them more up-to-date editions or better alternatives might be available.

By the end of eighteen months Walpole spoke some French, understood more mathematics than he would ever need, knew something of the physical nature and history of his own continent, and had acquired – mainly through discussion with his tutor – some rough notion of past civilizations and the course of human development. He had read much poetry, some novels and works of criticism and could hold his own in chat about problems of the day. And yet, despite this progress, there was a snag. Walpole – ambitious, competitive, with a pressing sense of lost years to be made up – was continually comparing himself with Mr Green and becoming first dissatisfied, then angry at what he considered his own slow rate of progress. Had he been one of a class he would have measured himself against the rest and, so long as he was doing better than his fellows, might have been content. But he had no one to measure himself against except his tutor, not much older than himself yet so much further along the road. At first, while there was still some distance between them, Walpole accepted the disparity, but when through familiarity he had lost all fear, he began to feel that Mr Green had enjoyed unfair advantages from his background and to feel sorry for himself. Mr Green's offhand attitude to his acquirements made things worse, for what was Walpole to think of his own situation when one so far ahead of him claimed to be nothing more than a beginner? As months went by, gratitude faded and he began

to compensate for a sense of his own deficiencies by aggress-
ion.

'What about this Italian?' he would demand. 'When am I
going to start on that? This book says Dante is the world's
greatest poet – not Shakespeare or Milton as you are always
telling me. And every poet needs to be studied in his own
language! Translations are nothing but deceptions – you see, I
remember your own words! I can't read Dante until I know
Italian, so what am I waiting for?'

'You can start Italian, Walpole, when you speak French
really well. You still make far too many mistakes – no one
could take you for a Frenchman. And if you try learning two
languages at once, you'll confuse yourself and won't get
anywhere with either.'

Walpole flared up like a can of petrol. 'But you say English
schoolboys are having to learn Latin and Greek – and they are
also learning to speak French at the same time. Isn't that so?'

'W-w-well, yes. S-s-some of them do that.'

'Then either I'm much stupider than English schoolboys –
or you're not such a good teacher as English schoolmasters.'

Mr Green put up with many such attacks. Despite their
increasingly frequent brushes he liked Walpole. He admired
his energy, self-reliance and a candour which was the positive
side of his brashness. He liked Madam Abiose and her
generous cheques, but he also considered that he gave
excellent value, taking pains with his pupil such as few
teachers would and none had ever taken with himself. Walpole
was his first personal pupil, and he was eager that Walpole
should acquire not so much the mass of knowledge he wanted,
as that sense of history and man's place in the world, that
regard for human achievement in every form which, to Mr
Green's mind, was the mark of an educated man. But Mr
Green also had his vanity, and when this was roughly handled,
could hit back.

It was their custom when the afternoon's task was over to
spend half an hour in general talk. At first both men had
looked forward to these periods of easy interchange, but
increasingly of late as work drew to an end they were inwardly
girding themselves for battle. On this particular evening
Walpole could hardly wait for their books to be closed before
bursting out:

'Who is this Sartre? Why have you not told me about him
and given me books of his to read?'

Mr Green blinked through his lenses. 'B-b-but why Sartre in particular? H-h-has someone been talking about him to you?'

'Last night at a party I was with some professors and learned persons from Ibadan' – and as he spoke of 'professors and learned persons' Walpole shot a glance which was not wasted on Mr Green – 'who were talking about Sartre. I am obliged to keep silence because I am not even knowing this man's name. Do *you* know the name of Sartre? Have you read the books he has written? . . . Then why have you not told me about him and his work?'

'Y-y-yes,' Mr Green replied with what Walpole, had he been less occupied with his own state of mind, might have noted as ominous calm. 'Yes, Walpole, I *have* heard of Sartre, and I have read a number of his books. . . .'

'Then why have you not given me these books to read?'

'Because you are not ready for them yet.'

Walpole laughed sarcastically. 'You see – this is the attitude you always take! *You* can read such books. The professors from Ibadan read such books. They expect me to have read them since they tried to talk me about Sartre. But I cannot answer because I know nothing. I am "not ready for them yet". You suppose I am unable to understand any book which is difficult – isn't that so?'

'N-n-not exactly,' Mr Green replied. 'But I *had* supposed you would find Sartre too difficult at present. Indeed it's possible that those "professors and learned persons from Ibadan" also find Sartre difficult. It's possible they have not read much of him, in spite of discussing him so learnedly.'

The irony provoked, as it was meant to do. 'Ha! So it's only *you* who understands philosophy! No one but yourself. Not even Nigerian professors.'

'W-w-whether you are ready for Sartre or not,' Mr Green replied smoothly, 'can easily be tested. Tomorrow I shall bring one or two books of his to leave with you for the weekend. Instead of anything else you will read them and do me a short essay. Just put down in your own words what the books are about, and how far the author succeeds in what he's trying to do.'

'Indeed I will!' Walpole answered, not sure whether to be mollified by this offer, but confident to meet its challenge. 'I shall – *then* you will see!'

Next day Mr Green brought a copy of *La Nausée*. He

explained that he had picked one of Sartre's simpler books, a novel, for Walpole to begin on, but that if he found this easy going there were harder works for him to tackle. Together with *La Nausée* he also left *The Philosophy of Existentialism* by Gabriel Marcel, remarking that if Walpole found any difficulty in following Sartre's thought, he could turn to Marcel's commentary for elucidation.

Eagerly Walpole sat down to his task. He meant the essay he would write to teach his tutor a lesson in respect. After reading some pages of *La Nausée* however, he found he was being forced to go back and cover the same ground again, and yet again, until after a couple of hours' study he had to admit to himself that he had taken in very little. Hopefully he turned to one of the passages marked by his tutor in Gabriel Marcel's essay on 'Existence and Human Freedom'.

to get down to principles, what manner of being should be attributed to a being who exists for himself – that is, to a being who is conscious of his own existence? This kind of being is regarded by Sartre as something altogether different from that of being-in-itself. Being-in-itself, he tells us, is completely full of itself, it is purely and simply what it is; it has no inwardness and, consequently, no potentiality and no future. It can never be in the relation of 'other' to another being; indeed it can have no relationship with Another. It is itself, indefinitely and without any possibility of being anything else. We need not ask at this point if this view of being-in-itself is real or mythical, nor if the author is justified in speaking of positivity in this context. The important point is that, in contrast with being-in-itself, being-for-itself is defined as not being what it is. . . .

Often during the weekend Mr Green's mind turned to his pupil, at first with satisfaction, mentally rubbing his hands as he pictured Walpole wrestling with the difficulty of abstract concepts – a humiliating experience which his insolence had brought on his own head. But as time went by other thoughts came up and his attitude began to change. He felt he had acted out of resentment, Walpole having offended him by questioning his authority so that he wanted to score off him in return. But this, he now realized, was abusing his position as a teacher and he ought to have made allowances for the young man's vanity instead of confronting it with his own. He began to feel ashamed of what he considered his vindictiveness, and though by Monday afternoon when he met Walpole again he had not reached the point of being ready to apologize, he had resolved to make a joke of the whole incident.

'Well, Walpole my friend,' he began with a jauntiness he did not feel, 'how goes the work? Have you brought that essay for me to read?'

But Walpole too had had the whole weekend for reflection. He had spent Friday evening and much of Saturday in an increasingly desperate attempt to write the essay until, after many false starts, he was forced to admit that he was beaten. The defeat had shaken his confidence in himself and the belief that his mind could solve any problem which confronted it. He saw now that this was not so, that there were many problems, indeed whole vast areas of knowledge, which were and would always be beyond the range of his understanding – the fact that they were beyond the range of almost everyone else in the world was no comfort to him at the moment. He considered he must now accept that his mind was inferior, and that his tutor must have been laughing at him all along. Having reached this conclusion, he had all Sunday in which to plan his reply.

'No, sir,' he answered. 'I have written nothing.'

'C-c-come, Walpole, surely Sartre isn't as difficult as all that? What is it that has held you up? Bring the book and let's look at it together.'

'I am not able to understand the books you have given me to read. They are too difficult.'

This was the last answer Mr Green was expecting and he seized on the admission eagerly.

'Why that's very honest of you, Walpole, very honest indeed. I admit I find a great deal of Sartre not at all easy to follow. Sh-sh-shall we take a look at those books together?'

'No thank you, sir,' Walpole replied coldly. 'You have been teaching me now for more than one and a half years. If I am not able to understand a modern novel and a commentary which you told me would make everything plain, then I am wasting my time and Madam Abiose's money. We will end this pretence of education now. It is either beyond my power to learn or yours to teach me.'

This carefully prepared speech hit Mr Green like a blow beneath the heart. He stammered and blushed. His glasses steamed and he started to do up his shoelaces. Finally he suggested that they might both have a word with Madam Abiose; since she was his employer it seemed only right to bring her in on the discussion. But Walpole saw this as yet another insult, implying that he had no right to decide the issue for himself.

'*I* will give Madam Abiose any explanation she wants.'

A stronger man would have insisted on his rights, but Mr Green could find no answer to Walpole's determined insolence. He stood up, and for a moment the two men faced one another. Each was aware that to spite his face he had cut off his own nose and was hoping that the other even now would make some gesture to which he could respond. Walpole had been proud of having the Cambridge man to teach him; he recognized that Mr Green had spared no effort as tutor, and somewhere below the surface was aware, or half-aware – or might, if he allowed himself to, *become* aware – that it was his own competitiveness which had caused this conflict. But he was elated to have turned the tables so dexterously, passing on the humiliation to his rival, and he could not deny himself a triumph prepared with so much calculation. Mr Green's better nature had long since regretted the easy score over his pupil. He could also expect an awkward explanation with Mr Chebe, or perhaps worse a patronizing 'Ha! Well, I always knew that was how it would end. You were expecting too much of this young man.' He knew that he would miss Madam Abiose's generous cheques which had given him for a time the supreme luxury of not having to worry about money. But he had been caught in his own snare; the only way out must be through an apology and the time for that was when he first came into the room. With his hand on the door handle Mr Green looked back, intending to catch Walpole's eye and say at least some friendly word, but Walpole, idly turning the pages of a book until he found himself alone, did not look up, pretending to be absorbed in an illustration which he was examining without seeing.

And so, after a year and a half of almost daily contact, rising at times to friendly intimacy, the black and the white man parted without another word.

9
Back to Work

When Madam Abiose heard what Walpole had done she telephoned Mr Green to hear his side of the story and the fact that he was frank and largely blamed himself added to her anger. She was furious that Walpole had parted with his tutor and doubly furious he should have done so without discussing it with her, yet her anger did not prevent a sense of pride that her boy was becoming a man, and, as she grew calmer, she began to see that this situation, like any other, might with proper handling be turned to her advantage.

But first she intended to tell Walpole what she thought of him, and she ended a dressing down he would remember all his life as painfully as he remembered the one given him by Mr Ali, with the words: 'You done grow too big for yo' boots, Walpole. Dat de fax of dis matter. You blown up wid pride an' importance in yo'self. I try for meet yo' wishes an' help you git de education you want – an' what you done? You bin disrespectful to Mr Chebe, my good frien', an' now you chasin' away Mr Green, de man yo'self choosin' for tutor. You done take too much 'pon yo'self. You forgettin' who you are. You not de Oba of Lagos nor de King of England – you jus' poor boy needin' to earn livin'.' And she presented him with a choice – either to apologize to Mr Green and resume his studies, or else to come back and work whole time with her in the business.

Walpole, greatly chastened, asked for a day to make up his mind, which his patroness granted, and then set himself to do what he had done very seldom in his life before – think over two courses of action and make choice between them. What had shaken him was not so much the force of the telling off Madam Abiose had given, but that he had found himself unable to reply. Despite all his education and the capacity to express himself gained over the past year, he had been incapable of putting up a defence. He had stood in front of her as tongue-tied as any small-time criminal in the dock and now, as he thought the matter over, he was obliged to admit to himself that it was for the same reason. He had nothing to say for himself because there was nothing to be said. He had acted trickily towards Mr Green and ungratefully towards Madam Abiose – who, he was forced to admit, had been generous not to rebuke him more than she had done, and particularly to have made no bitter references to all the money she had spent on his behalf. A few hours ago nothing would have induced him to apologize to Mr Green, since apology would destroy the triumph of which he had been so proud; but that, which had given him so much satisfaction yesterday, looked mean and pitiful today. He was sorry, truly sorry, for his ingratitude to Madam Abiose and would say so. He was willing also to make matters up with Mr Green, which must certainly involve an apology of some kind.

But now another question rose: did he really want to go back to being a student? In argument with his tutor he had belittled all he had learned with him, but to himself he could afford to be honest, and honesty told him he had learned a great deal. How much more did he want to learn? Was not what he had learned already enough for his own purposes in life? What were those purposes?

As a result of his painful wrestling match with Sartre, Walpole had made a discovery – the discovery of limitation. Till now the more he learned the more he felt he could learn; like Napoleon, the further his conquests spread, the further he expected to go on conquering. But over Sartre he had experienced a shock. He had been unable to understand thoughts and expressions which some other people, evidently, must understand quite well. His mind could not be the all-conquering instrument he had supposed, since there were subjects with which it, and he, were unable to cope. Till now he had felt he could become anything he chose, but from this incident he had discovered that there were some things he could never be – a philosopher, a writer, a mathematician, a scientist . . . the list once started seemed endless. What then *could* he be? The answer was ready to hand – he could be a businessman, and the first step to becoming one was to accept the alternative his patroness was offering. Business might not make him famous all over the world as writers and philosophers such as Sartre had made themselves famous, but it was far more likely to make him rich – with all the agreeable consequences of riches which a young man covets.

Madam Abiose was delighted and her broad smile was seen

again when Walpole told her his decision, adding – since he was no grudge-bearer – that though he would not again become Mr Green's pupil he would write and thank him for his help. She enfolded Walpole in her capacious arms, and at once set about planning what tasks he should take on. He should start as her personal assistant, enabling him to pick up the threads of all her interests and then in two or three years he would become her general manager.

Walpole's gradual withdrawal over the past two years had been welcome indeed to the managers and others who rightly saw a rival in him, so that they were correspondingly angry over his return, and Madam Abiose, aware of this, lost little time in showing that she would brook no opposition. As one of his first duties, his patroness sent him to interview a client for her, and when he replied that there were phone calls to make first, she told him to give a list of them to the chief clerk and let him make the calls. Walpole approached the clerk who worked in the office below with hesitation, and was not surprised when the man objected – he had quite enough work to do, and Walpole must make his own telephone calls.

From the top of the stairs came a trumpet blast: 'Git up out dat seat dis minute, Tunde, when Mr Walpole spikkin' to you! Who you t'ink you am? Why you no write down de instructions Mr Walpole givin' you? Have you done fin' yo'self big job wid other market mammy? If not, you better go fin' yo'self one quick-quick!'

Tunde sprang up as if hit by a brick, and began in a fluster to write down Walpole's instructions. When he had recovered and started telephoning, the news that Madam's Scholarship Boy had become 'Mr Walpole' and her chief assistant, went round the network in a morning.

In his earlier years with his patroness Walpole had been little more than an apprentice, yet had managed to acquire a general grasp of her interests. Now, however, he was returning as Madam Abiose's right-hand man. He intended to work himself back into the picture quietly, but once there he had little doubt there would be improvements to be made, and as the months went by he began to feel himself fully qualified to make them. While still a child Walpole had learned about trade not in classes or as a trainee but from the hard school of the streets. There he had learned how to bargain, buy and sell, study the market and take advantage of changing tastes and fashions. He saw what rivals and enemies were up to because he knew what he would be doing in their place. Beneath a friendly manner he was shrewd and sometimes suspicious, but he was the reverse of cynical since he did not expect his fellow men to be other than they are and so no more complained over their dishonesty and greed than he was willing to be defeated by it. In his new position it did not now take him long to realize that in understanding one of Madam Abiose's businesses he had understood the lot; what remained was a matter of personal acquaintance with one or two hundred of his fellow Nigerians, and of appreciating not so much whom his patroness trusted or distrusted, but up to what financial limits she would trust the trustworthy and what methods she employed in keeping the untrustworthy at bay, ranging from the politest of 'postponements for future consideration' to bawling a man out for trying to play 'rascally tricks' on her.

For Madam Abiose's judgement of her fellows Walpole had profound respect, but education had given him a very different attitude to business. In business Madam Abiose was a clever peasant and her method was to keep all her activities separate. If she bought a shop it must pay its way. A house had to bring in rent to cover depreciation, interest on capital, all possible costs, and show a profit. If in any of her concerns the profit dwindled, she fired the manager, and if loss persisted sold off the business. She never retained a loss-maker and was never fully satisfied with a profit, since any increase implied that further increase must be possible. When she lent money the interest was always well above what she paid when she borrowed, and she often used her credit to borrow cheap and lend to traders whose standing was less good than hers, and some of her most profitable businesses had been acquired through foreclosing on mortgages when debtors could not meet their contracts. Madam Abiose's superiority to other mammies was thus a matter of quantity not scale; she owned or had shares in a hundred money-making operations compared to their one or two or twenty, and she spent her life supervising rivulets of trade, which though together amounting to a considerable flow, remained each in its own channel. The key to all operations lay in her own head, and until making Walpole her general assistant she had allowed no employee to know much beyond his immediate duties. She kept her chief clerk, Tunde, in a state of mystification with orders, counter-orders and explanations which only added to his confusion, so that he had long since given up trying to form a general picture and now simply did whatever he was told. When she needed to draw up contracts or assert her rights she employed half a dozen lawyers, so that no one could have a grasp of her interests as a whole.

Walpole, however, was not a peasant. He was a man of the city and the modern world, not by chance but through conscious decision at the age of six. His intuition urged him to combine and structure, and after a few months in his new position he began to do this, creating a bazaar for cheap goods out of five stalls and a shop; employing one capable manager to do the work of four for the salary of two; training three well-armed night watchmen to cover a small area and replace a dozen of the usual doorway slumberers whose jobs were so pitiful they would never fight a thief for their protection. In all he did Walpole took care to move slowly, weeding out weak enterprises but avoiding open threat to powerful managers such as Mallam Ajao of the Divine Providence store. As his arrangements proved effective, Madam Abiose took to relying more and more on her assistant, sending him to act on her behalf while she stayed thankfully in her office, fanning herself with a cardboard folder, telephoning sharp instructions to her managers, exercising her powerful charm on those who were worth charming and paying special attention to small economies.

Only after being back at work for more than a year, and after a number of his ideas had proved successful, did Walpole start to introduce a change which would affect the firm as a whole. From the first he had been interested in transport. He would often drive the various vans and lorries owned by his patroness, and, not content with that, had become familiar with their mechanism and was always happy to take a faulty vehicle on to a patch of waste ground, strip down the engine or back axle, laying the parts out on newspapers and re-assembling them into a working whole. So, being eager to launch some dramatic development, it was to the organization of transport that he now applied his energies.

In line with her policy of subdivision Madam Abiose allowed each manager to buy his own vehicle and hire his driver. Vans and mammy-wagons were of all shapes and sizes, and it was common for several to make the same cross-city journey to deliver small quantities of goods which could easily have been carried in one vehicle. At weekends managers would take the vehicles home on one pretext or another, using the firm's petrol and occasionally ordering tyres or spares which they kept for themselves or sold to friends.

All this Walpole had learned when, for six months with the approval of his patroness, he had worked as driver in some of her businesses, at times when the regular man had a few days off or was absent for some reason.

The plan he now unfolded to Madam Abiose was that, instead of each manager being responsible for his own transport, there would be a pool with a transport manager. The various businesses would send him in every evening a list of their next day's deliveries, and he would work out the most economical way to meet them. A hangar was to be put up near Madam Abiose's office to serve as garage. Vehicles would be standardized to two or three types only, with a range of spares and a mechanic for servicing. Petrol, oil and tyres would be bought in bulk, and no vehicles would be allowed out at weekends.

To support his project Walpole presented two sets of figures, showing how much was being spent at present and what he estimated the firm ought to spend. Madam Abiose spent a whole day studying the figures, and when Walpole got home in the evening she beckoned him to sit beside her at the table.

'What you tellin' me in dese papers is dat I am a t'ief. I rob my own self each year five-six t'ousan' poun'. Is dis what you tellin' me?'

'Yes, madam.'

'An' besides being t'ief, I am a fool also. Because all my managers robbin' me as well. Is dis true?'

'It is indeed true that they rob you.'

Madam Abiose poked her generous pile of hair with the butt end of her pen. 'I no like dis, Walpole. I no like dis idea dat in ten years I done rob myself of sixty t'ousan' poun'.'

'No, madam, I don't like this either.'

'But you understan', Walpole, if I go for make dese changes I havin' much trouble wid my managers. Dey losin' big advantage. Dey lose power an' dey lose cash. Dey lose de power for give drivers' jobs to dere own families. Dey lose de use of vehicles at weekend, an' dey 'bliged for look small to dere own families an' friens.'

'True, madam. They lose the power to take your vans home and wear them out. They lose the power to steal your petrol. So they will be angry. But which do you want – for your managers to be happy, or to save six thousand pounds a year?'

Madam Abiose put her hand on Walpole's knee. 'Only one person in dis world whose happiness worth six t'ousan' poun' to me – dat bin my boy. If de managers not accept dis plan, I go find new managers.'

10
Mallam Ajao

Anticipating trouble over Walpole's project, Madam Abiose called a meeting of her managers, and gathered now into the storeroom used for such discussions were some fifteen men, the more important towards the front with Madam Abiose and Walpole at a table facing them. When all were present she outlined the scheme, which she assured them would result in substantial savings, and promised that if they cooperated in making it a success they would all get a worthwhile bonus at the year's end. By this means she shrewdly split her hearers into two. The smaller men, who had no vans under their control, were heartily in favour, but the bigger well knew that no bonus could make up for the advantage of having free transport over weekends plus the capacity to do small services for relatives and friends.

This was not an argument, however, which could be stated openly and the first two or three managers to speak in opposition stressed probable delays; the indignity of have to beg for vehicles instead of simply giving orders to their drivers; and the special nature of their businesses which no one but themselves could understand, and the likely consequence that important clients would be casually treated or insulted. In short, the scheme would never work and could only cause delay and loss. Madam Abiose sat silent waiting for further comments, and after a moment or two Thaddeus, no longer clerk but now manager of the Invincible Ajax Bookshop, got up and said that as far as his bookshop was concerned he had no doubt the transport pool would work out very well.

Walpole shot him a grateful glance, but all this, as everyone understood, was no more than a preliminary skirmish and what they all, including Madam Abiose herself, were waiting for was to hear how Mallam Ajao would react.

Mallam Ajao, manager of The Divine Providence General Supply Association, largest of Madam's many businesses selling household goods in one of the chief markets, was a slight thin-faced man driven by a burning passion to make money. The Divine Providence vibrated all day long with the intensity of his zeal for selling and with the staff's fear and hatred of their master. The twenty-odd men and women, from under-manager to doorkeeper, lived in terror that his weasel face would come peering round a crate, pop out from behind a pile of pans or emerge from behind a customer's shoulder. Most of them could have picked him up and flung him into a corner without difficulty, but he held them in a grip of fear. When the day ended and workers from other shops had only one thought – to get home quickly – a group from the Divine Providence would gather under a tree or in an open-air bar, unable to leave the place where all their most intense experiences were concentrated. There they exchanged stories of the day's indignities, and threats of what they would do to their tormentor once they had found themselves another job. Mallam Ajao had indeed been beaten up more than once in the dark as he crossed some lonely patch of ground, but he emerged little altered except that any lingering traces of humanity appeared to have been battered out of him. From time to time a deputation of employees, summoning their courage, had visited Madam Abiose to complain, and as a result some immediate cause of resentment might be modified, but the source of all resentments and complaints – Mallam Ajao himself – remained, and since under his demonic governance the profits of the Divine Providence surpassed themselves each year, there was little chance of his removal.

Even his name offended, 'Mallam' being a courtesy title he had acquired as a leader among the community of Moslems living in Lagos. By race he was a Yoruba like his employees and so might be expected to share their ancestral religion or become a Christian, but he had chosen to be a Moslem in order, it was said, to facilitate dealings with the Hausa and other Muslim traders from the North from whom he bought most of his stock.

The room where the discussion was being held had become

by now almost unbearable. It was a typical Lagos evening, moist and sultry, and the sweetish stench of corruption from the open sewers outside added to the reek of human bodies after a hard day's work. Madam Abiose fanned herself continually with a folder and held a heavily-scented handkerchief to her face. For Mallam Ajao rage added to the heat and literally poured off him as sweat. From time to time he snatched off the flop-eared cap he was wearing, mopped face and arms with it vigorously, then dived his hand under his robes to dry his arm-pits out before cramming the cap back on his skull. This he did as he did everything, furtively and fiercely, as if grudging the moments lost from making money, but when Thaddeus rose to give the project his approval, it was too much for Mallam Ajao. Bursting to speak, with bitter phrases souring his tongue and poisoning his breath, he was just able to wait until Thaddeus sat down – and then was on his feet. He repeated all the arguments already uttered but went on to say: 'All of us here, madam, bin managers in our own right. We work hard, an' we make big profits for you. If you plan for make changes in de business set-up, changes dat affec' our lives an' way of workin', den we expec' you shall discuss dese changes wid us – not *after* you make up your mind but in de beginnin' when you still considerin' dem. I say you owin' dis to us, an' dis de least you kin do. Now you done call us here together. But we see from yo' words dat you done already make yo' decision. So I give you solemn warnin' now, madam, dis new system not goin' work – an' when it not work, dis boun' for affect de profits of de businesses. Remember my words! When de year end an' de profits done fall – I don't want you blamin' me or dese other managers for yo' own decision. I know you pow'ful woman an' strong person in runnin' of yo' business. I know you rememberin' well who spik against you now – but I spik out for sake of yo' business an' for all dese other managers same like myself. If you want profits of dis business to go on risin', den de mos' bes' thing you kin do is stop dis plan for transport pool straight'way, because dis pool goin' turn into a transport swamp!'

There were gasps at Mallam Ajao's daring, and even a few handclaps from supporters who felt they could clap in safety behind others' backs. Everyone expected Madam Abiose to spring to her feet and join battle with the Mallam, but instead she continued to fan herself before asking mildly: 'Any person else wishin' for say somethin'?'

There was silence. Mallam Ajao shot a furious glance at his employer, and his anger was not softened when she continued: 'If none of you got more words to say, den I sayin' few words myself. I understan' yo' anger. Some of you losin' advantages for yo'selves over dis transport pool. I already tol' you dat dis pool kin only work if you all cooperatin'. If you cooperatin' an' de scheme bin success, you get good bonus.' She paused before adding in a sharper tone: 'But if you *no* cooperate, if you try for *make* dis scheme break down, if you usin' de scheme for excuse in keepin down yo' profits – and you den blamin' dis loss of profit on de scheme – den *out* you go! Dis go for de highest man here' – and she looked directly at Mallam Ajao – 'as much as for de smallest. De business bin' more important dan each individual person. You done give me a warnin',' and she paused for a full quarter of a minute before adding slowly, 'an' I done give *my* warnin' to each an' every one of you.'

All eyes were on Mallam Ajao. Powerful as he was, he knew very well who had the upper hand. If he had been speaking to Madam Abiose privately he would have backed down, offered to give the scheme a trial, made difficulties for a month or two and then accepted the inevitable, taking out on his workers the rage he could not take out on his employer. But to back down in front of all the others was more than he could stomach. He had been elated by the support he sensed and maddened by the cool tone of his patroness – putting him in his place without allowing him the status of antagonist. He had, however, one final card to play. That he would be far from wise to play the card he had been telling himself all day, ever since he got word of the meeting. But there was a chance that playing it would evoke support from the other managers – and all of them would certainly be astounded at his boldness. In any case Mallam Ajao was not accustomed to curbing his rage even when it was in his own interests to do so, and it was his rage which governed him now as he rose to his feet, declaring:

'Dere bin one more thing, madam, dat I wish to say.'

'You kin spik.'

'You done ask our cooperation in makin' dis transport pool a success. Not so?'

Madam Abiose nodded.

'Den we on our side askin' de same thing of you, we ask *yo*' cooperation for make de pool a success. We ready do our share' – he looked round at the faces concentrated intensely on him – 'so we hab right for demand you do yo' share as well. We ask dat de person operatin' dis pool bin person of experience, trained in de runnin' of transport. Big stores like Kingsway an' Highlife done operate transport pools many-many years. De men runnin' dese pools got de know-how an' de experience for make yo' pool a success. You take a man from dem, or you fin' yo'self retired manager from city bus company. Man like dat kin make success, an' he gettin' full cooperation from yo' managers. But if de scheme goin' be run by boy wid no knowledge an' no experience of transport work – den it one hundred per cent boun' to fail. Boun' to. *Den* don' you blame hard-workin' managers for not cooperatin' an' not increase de profits for you!'

Mallam Ajao sat down in a silence that was as audible as a shout. In sitting down he could not resist a rapid glance round the room, hoping to collect admiring looks from his fellows. He collected nothing. Appalled at the Mallam's daring, fearful of revealing himself an accomplice, each man stared blankly ahead or gazed down at his own feet. One or two, overcome by tension and the room's oven heat, drew the loose sleeves of their robes across dripping brows, but the rest, dreading the attention even such a movement might attract, remained rigid though the sweat was streaming down backs and faces.

For half a minute or more Madam Abiose sat silent facing her audience, then: 'I think bes' plan is for you all judge fo' yo'selves if de man I done appoint transport manager know anythin' or nothin' of de matter.' She turned to Walpole, who had sat silent for the past two hours and added: 'You bin called a boy of no experience. Now show dese managers how much you done learn about de business.'

Walpole stood up. 'Mallam Ajao – you say I got too little experience an' knowledge to run de transport pool. Am I right?'

'Mos' cert'nly I say dis. I not criticizin' you as human person.' He paused and added insolently, 'Dat no concern of mine. But what experience you ever had for runnin' business transport? Dat concern us all. An' dat my question.'

'Mr Ajao,' said Walpole, pointedly leaving out his title and taking care to tone down the newly learned English which his audience would resent, 'at dis moment you yourself organize transport for Divine Providence? Not so?'

Mallam Ajao snorted agreement.

'And since you handle all arrangements yourself – you

know jus' what goes on?'

'In course I knowin' what goes on!'

'And you bin satisfied,' Walpole pursued, 'wid de conduct of de transport? You satisfied dat it bein' run in bes' interest of de store and of Madam?'

A shadow, a faint trace of suspicion, passed over Mallam Ajao's furious face, and he answered in a thinner voice: 'I not und'standin' you, Mr Walpole. Kindly make yo' meanin' clear.'

'If you done handle all transport arrangements for de store, den you kin cert'nly say how many miles yo' van travel in one year.'

Mallam Ajao paused before replying: 'I s'pose 'bout thirty t'ousan' miles.'

'And how many of those miles bin covered in de week on Madam's business – and how many at de weekend on your own?'

Mallam Ajao looked startled, but was not done yet. 'Dat easy matter for answer! Twenty-nine out de thirty t'ousan' mile done in de week for Madam's business.'

'I see,' said Walpole, fishing a small notebook out of his pocket. 'But takin' only de las' two months – an' goin' into de figures for each week, we find. . .'

Hastily Mallam Ajao cut in: 'De only few 'ccasions I done take de store's van home wid me at weekend bin for deliver goods for de firm in my own area. Dat de one sole purpose in my min'.'

As though not having heard the words, Walpole turned over a couple of pages slowly. 'In first two weekends of dis month,' he said, as if puzzling out a difficult problem, 'yo' van covered two hundred mile each weekend – but only three hundred an' fifty mile durin' de whole week. An' it go out full with petrol from de store – an' come back on Monday empty.'

There was a sharp intake of breath. How was Mallam Ajao to answer this? And how would each of them answer such questions if they should be put?

Mallam Ajao darted a dry tongue over his lips as his mind cast this way and that. Meantime Walpole was continuing to read, and with every sentence Mallam Ajao could feel the iron jaws closing round his ankles. He knew it would be fatal to become involved in detailed argument, seeking to explain the inexplicable and to justify, mile by mile and gallon after gallon, what could not possibly be justified. Happily, for such situations there is a sound technique, approved by long experience. As Walpole continued his recital, Mallam Ajao sprang to his feet, tore off his cap, and burst into outraged protestation: 'I pray Allah for strike me dead! Dat what I prayin' for! I call Allah for strike me down dead dis minute in dis room – if ever I done cheat Madam de smalles' piece! If you no s'posin' me hones', Madam, den you not leave me manager one moment mo'. No – nor none of dese men neither! We all hones' men. You send each one home if you got no trust nor confidence in us at all!'

But Madam Abiose had no wish to split her firm in half. She was not deceived for a moment by the protestations, which all present knew were not a cry of defiance but of surrender. The day was gained, and in face of what might lie buried in Walpole's notebook – the record of six months as a working driver for the different businesses – there would be no more opposition to the pool nor to him as manager.

'My friens,' she inquired mildly, 'what all dis uproar? What dis cryin' out? No man here bin accused of nothin'. I understan' dat in de past it bin custom for managers to take vans home after work. Sometimes dis custom bin abused. 'Bout dis matter I say no mo' words. De past now bin a closed book! You all come here tonight for discuss new transport pool dat Mr Walpole done propose. I don' lissen to each an' every word you said. I understan' yo' feelings, but now I askin' you all – give dis new plan fair trial. Give Mr Walpole fair trial. If de plan no good, if de manager I done choose bin no good, I knowin' as well as you de way to act.'

She paused, looking slowly round. Each man, as her gaze rested on him, was impelled to look up, acknowledge her gaze and nod assent. She came last to Mallam Ajao. He too, resist as he might and conscious that the eyes of the whole room were on him, had finally to look up and nod. 'So now, my friens, de hour grow late. Is time for us all have sma'-sma' drink an' say goodnight.'

11
Ambition Calls

The transport pool did not take long to justify itself, being based on common sense and backed by Walpole's drive and youthful vigour. He was ready to work long hours, demanded that his men do the same, and saw they were well paid by the standards of their time and place. More important for rootless city dwellers, they felt they had a place in life and belonged together, so that there was soon eager competition to become one of the drivers, mechanics, clerks – or even a doorman or storekeeper – in the transport group. When one of the drivers sold his spare wheel – their custom in the past, when they would claim to have been robbed and the wheel stolen – Walpole waited only for the month's end to deduct the cost from his pay and sack the driver. His promise to save Madam Abiose 'five to six thousand pounds' a year was easily achieved, and when a handful of disgruntled managers approached her with complaints, they were given short shrift.

'I no see you!' she shouted at them. 'I no hear you spik! You not standin' before me in dis office. What you got say 'bout transport matters – you go spik wid transport manager!' And as she moved threateningly towards them, a bulkier figure now than she had been five years earlier, the group edged round the door and fell over each other down the stairs. Notable about the deputation was that it did not include Mallam Ajao. He, it appeared, had been converted – in the sense that rapacity had carried the day over resentment – for, at the year's end when the accounts of the different stores were presented, he spoke highly of the pool's advantages.

'Dis done lift big weight off all our shoulders,' he asserted. 'I bin wrong, so I bin firs' man sayin' I bin wrong. An' Walpole mos' clever man – sutt'nly de bes' man you kin find for transport job.'

From this first business success Walpole gained much confidence; his intuition had been sound and he had proved his ability to carry through a complicated piece of planning. This very confidence, however, soon started to make him discontented with the limited scale of his activities. Madam Abiose might be elated over a small rise in profit levels, but Walpole longed for achievement on a grander scale, something that would make him famous. He wanted people to look at him and point him out, to be mentioned in the newspaper: 'Walpole Abiose, the man who has done so much towards . . .' this, that or the other. And the direction in which his mind turned was to an extension of what he had already started in transport, but on a far grander scale.

Besides the vans which served her businesses Madam Abiose, like other market-mammies, owned some half-dozen lorries or mammy-wagons, with which she operated as a general carrier in a desultory way. The lorries ran to no schedule, seldom travelling more than a couple of days' journey out of Lagos, and control of their operations had always been haphazard. Everyone throughout the markets knew Madam Abiose, as did the importing firms and the agents who hung around the docks at Apapa. When one had a consignment for delivery up country he would phone her and two or three other mammies, asking each to quote a delivery date and price. Once she secured an order Madam Abiose applied herself to making the trip more profitable, taking on other goods for places along the route and trying to arrange loads for the return.

In his days of learning the business, Walpole had made several cross-country journeys. Travel excited him, the contact with people on the way, his sense of a country waiting to be opened up and brought into contact with the city just as the city itself had been brought in contact with the world. So the idea now filling his mind was to do with the mammy-wagons what he had done for office transport – organize them on a modern basis. This was an altogether bigger project. The first had involved little outlay; it was a matter of reorganization, in which the benefits of change could be costed out. But to reorganize cross-country travel would not only involve much capital, the result was finally incalculable, since no one could tell whether a regular service would catch on.

The present haphazard method operated after a fashion, that is, it brought profit when a trip went well and loss when a driver stole a lorry and its contents, or met with an accident and, as was common practice, vanished into the bush to avoid facing the police. But at least the stakes were known, and the charges allowed for an occasional disaster. There could be no halfway house, however, between the present casual set-up and a regular service, if only on a once-a-day basis, with wagons running to time, fixed charges for goods and passengers, depots for storage and servicing, and inspectors keeping check. To launch such a service would require a daunting feat of organization, and the capital required would strain his patroness's resources to the limit. But the return could be proportionate and the prestige immense.

Madam Abiose listened with patience as Walpole outlined his ideas, not arguing that success was certain, but suggesting she let him look into the matter and find out the facts. Her business understanding however, and her intuition, were both firmly against what he proposed.

'Dis too-too big. Is costin' more money dan I got. An' de whole idea bin more dan I kin handle. Dis bin projec' for big company wid bankers, politicians an' whitemen. Here in Lagos I know all de worl' an' de worl' know me. If trouble come I know de man I mus' spik wid. But if someone make trouble in Ife or Benin, den I not know de man I mus' spik wid – an' I not fit for go racin' off over de countryside. My life bin here, an' my money bin here, an' my business boun' remain here too.'

Walpole argued and pleaded, promised that if there were trouble up country he would go and see to it himself. He was not asking her to launch out into a big organization on her own; to begin with it would only mean putting the service she already provided on to a regular footing. This could be the starting point for something bigger later on, but if that proved to be so she would have a gold mine in possession. It would then be in her power either to float a company – taking in bankers, politicians and the rest on her own terms – or else to sell out for a round sum.

'I don't want to see you work for ever,' he told her. 'In this way you can make yourself a fortune and retire when you wish.'

Madam Abiose looked mournfully at Walpole. 'I see you wantin' I shall retire, my frien'.'

Walpole protested that he hoped she would be in charge for many years, but that she should be free to take life easily as she grew older.

'I kin retire dis same day. But what am I doin' wid myself if I retire?'

Walpole hesitated, and his patroness heaved a sigh.

'I knowin' you done grow up, my frien'. You try an' hold yo'self down to de size of my businesses, but you rarin' for go off into de worl' an' do things yo' own way. Don' s'pose I don' see all dis! I thinkin' 'bout nothin' else de whole day long. . . . I growin' old, my frien', an' you no longer my boy, my Walpole, an' I no longer yo' mammy – an' I too-too old for become yo' wife . . . jus' too-too old. I know what you wantin', my frien'. You wantin' become great an' famous man. Dis bin right, an' you will be famous man. But what becomin' of me, dat I not know or see. An' times I not carin' any more. . . . What de benefit to me of all de money in de worl' if I done lose my boy?'

And to Walpole's dismay his patroness stretched her heavy arms before her on the table, let her head fall upon them, and burst into a storm of tears.

Kneeling beside her, an arm across her shoulders, protesting love and devotion and at times weeping too, Walpole sought to comfort her – but his heart told him plainly that everything she said was true. A thousand times he had said within himself that he must somehow get away to set up on his own, that his patroness's businesses were petty and her methods out of date – and then having allowed such thoughts a foothold, he would be flooded with guilt and reproach himself for ingratitude in view of all she had done for him. Faced with this impasse, he had struggled to settle down, only for something to happen which convinced him over again that he ought to be following his own convictions and ideas. So guilt would start up once more, and with it fear, fear of the scenes to be expected if he should ever seek to venture beyond their business partnership.

What Walpole had never faced, but his patroness had now brought into the open, was the sensual and emotional conflict underlying their clash of interests, and over this she had gone to the point in a way he could never have done. She had become too old for him. It was a cruel truth. Her body was too old; he wanted younger women or at least a younger woman. But emotionally she was too old for him as well since he no longer needed a patroness, a mother, who in the last resort would·issue orders. He wanted a wife, a helper, who in the last resort accepted his decisions. He wanted all this, and since he could not face the head-on conflict which must result from the attempt to liberate himself, continued, man-like, vaguely to hope something would happen that would bring it all about.

But Madam Abiose saw the situation without illusion, and in her heart knew that a break could not be avoided. Walpole's was too active and ambitious a nature to accept a secondary role, but though she could admit to herself that the break was bound to come, she could not face the emptiness of life it would bring and so sought to delay decision and avert conflict, trusting the clash need not prove final when it came.

Underlying every love relationship, except for the very few based on truth and full acceptance, is some disposition of power, not put into words and seldom admitted into conscious thought, but which imperceptibly governs the actions of both parties. The basic truth between Walpole and Madam Abiose had been that in their early years together Walpole understood that if his patroness found him unsatisfactory or he flouted her wishes, he could be turned out. He had never loved her in the way a man may love a wife or mistress to the point of putting her happiness or wishes before his own. But he had felt deep gratitude, admiration and a wholesome respect for her severity, feelings which, while he was still her 'Scholarship Boy', formed a sufficient tie. But now the tide had turned. He was no longer afraid of losing her and all she stood for, since freedom to follow his own path was what he wanted most and his only fear now was of distressing her. Fear, the bitter fear of loss, had now moved over and taken residence inside his patroness's heart, and it was she who dreaded that, if she crossed him or put a barrier in the path of his ambition, he would walk out and leave her. The result for Madam Abiose was a slow loss of confidence. She would decide something in accordance with her sound judgement, but then, fearful of angering her beloved boy, would change her mind. Aware of the whisperings her hesitation aroused among her staff, disconcerted by the loss of assurance and the inability to assert authority, she could now only complain, and found it difficult not to be doing so all day long.

In the end it was Madam Abiose's anxiety and consequent willingness to make concessions against her better judgement which resolved the issue. After days and nights of argument involving scenes that shook them both, she at last consented to his going away for one month to explore the possibilities of his project. Nor was it entirely fear which governed her decision; it owed something also to her generosity of heart. She was proud of her boy's ambition, reluctant to stand in the way of the manhood she had done so much to encourage, so she cried and pleaded, argued, refused a hundred times but finally consented. Walpole thanked her warmly but allowed no visible elation, and began his preparations quietly.

On the evening following their last discussions Madam Abiose was solacing herself by giving one of her rooms a good turn-out with Alake's help. Alake had worked for her ever since she started out in business twenty years earlier on the money left her by a rich protector, and being much older than her mistress had assumed as years went by a confidential, even admonitory, role.

'My boy bein' death of me one day,' Madam Abiose observed, 'leavin' clothes all roun' de place. Never t'ink 'bout gettin' suits cleaned. Never t'ink 'bout gettin' nothin' mended. Never t'ink 'bout all de work we women doin' for kip um fed an' de house clean. He s'posin' all dis happen jus' like rain fallin' out de sky.'

'Men bin beasts of selfish gender,' Alake replied, sorting over a heap of dirty handkerchiefs and socks. 'All de lot of um t'inkin' only of one single t'ing – hisself.'

'When my boy bin aroun',' Madam Abiose remarked musingly, sitting down and letting the shirt she was examining trail idly on the floor, 'I bin angry wid um too-too many times. I done lose my temper an' go shoutin' roun' de house. But now he goin' 'way I t'ink how foolish to grow angry 'gainst de one bein' I love, an' my heart feelin' cold like cookin' stove when flame die out.'

Alake shot her mistress a sharp glance. 'You lovin' dat Walpole too-too much! Walpole bin good boy an' hones' boy, but he only bin man same like de res'. He boun' go bouncin' off down him own track. . . . An' he boun' go hangin' roun' after de fresh young girls. Walpole got gratitude for you, madam, dat true 'nough, but gratitude not same t'ing like love. Dat one of de facks of life. An' yo' bin old enough for 'preciate dese facks.'

12
A Taste of Freedom

Before Walpole set off he received a visit in his office from Mallam Ajao. There is something particularly difficult to resist in the overtures of a disagreeable person; it is flattering to be singled out for consideration by someone who treats others with contempt, and where the effort in making an approach has obviously been great it seems churlish not to respond. Walpole did not like Mallam Ajao, but had to admit that since the day of the meeting, his actions had been guided, if not by goodwill at least by the wish to live on friendly terms. He had supported Walpole more than once in business arguments, praised him to Madam Abiose, and invited him to his home – an invitation Walpole would have refused but which his patroness obliged him to accept. And now here he was, offering advice about parts of the country with which he was familiar, providing names and addresses, and insisting particularly that when Walpole visited the town of Abeokuta – as he was bound to do on his way back – he should stop for a night or two with his brother who, as owner of an important garage, could give him much practical advice and information. Walpole found himself shaking the Mallam by the hand and feeling grateful to him almost against his will.

It was with a feeling of relief that Walpole said goodbye. It was a relief to be away from the business with its trivialities and bitter rivalry, and it was a relief to be away from the emotional claims of his patroness. Added to relief was excitement, the excitement of freedom and of doing what he had longed to do from the time he first pedalled his bicycle on selling forays round the beaches – head off by himself for a long look at his own country.

Once out of Lagos the roads were poor and travelling slow over the dusty laterite in the small delivery van he had borrowed from the pool. The country opened endlessly as he drove north-west in a huge arc by way of Ibadan, Ife and Akure to Benin, and on across the Niger by the Onitsha ferry before turning south through Owerri into the vast Niger delta. A couple of hours after leaving Owerri, Walpole passed out of the familiar world into one such as he had never seen or heard of, a land of steaming swamps compared to which Lagos itself was fresh and cool. Here there was little except mud, heat and sinuous windings as though he had found his way into the intestines of the world. Gulfs, estuaries, lagoons, peninsulas, islands – there was nothing that could be called dry land, and though all was damp and flowing, there was no clear water. What passed for water, oozy and bubbling as if with the exhalations of buried creatures, was brackish and thick as coffee. The very sky, loaded with vapours, seemed to have collapsed on to the earth.

The track Walpole was trying to follow led aimlessly from one cluster of mud huts to the next – if indeed it were not the same cluster to which he had blundered back. As he entered the village the children who shouted in an unknown dialect were mud-bedraggled, like the occasional dog which barked beside them. Even the girls he smiled at and who grinned back and waved, looked muddy, and he imagined that if he found welcome with one of them in her hut it could only be on a couch of mud under a mud-stained covering.

The ghoulish landscape brought back to Walpole a story told him long ago, perhaps as a child on Mr Ali's porch by a worker from this region. These mudlands, it was said, had not been created by the same divine being who fashioned the remainder of our world, a God who took pleasure in creation and, loving order, had allotted to each element its sphere and given every plant its unique form, forbidding ox to mate with deer or fox with rabbit. Instead the mudlands and their inhabitants had been handed over, all unformed, to a malignant godling, who had pounded land, water, air into a steamy mess from which they could never again be separated out. The only creatures at home in this sub-world were the dwellers in two elements – crocodiles, hippos, rats, waterfowl or snakes; and the only humans to survive partook of the crocodile's nature, having crusted skins, cold watchful eyes and opaque souls. Here too dwelt the crocodile priests, both masters and servants of their grisly pets, to whom they would throw live chickens, a sheep when it could be got, and – some said – other food better not mentioned. Properly approached and propitiated with akpeteshie-gin, a chicken or two and a sufficiency of cash, the priest in a fearful ceremony would become the crocodile or the crocodile would become the priest, and when this occurred the man-crocodile or crocodile-man could answer questions, foretell the future, or bring down destruction on a hated enemy.

Walpole would happily have cut short this section of his journey, but felt bound to spend two or three days in survey, buying what food he could, sleeping in his van, and digging the wheels out when they got stuck. For it was here in these abominable swamps, so rumour said, that white prospectors were beginning to find traces of that most precious substance – oil. And oil, turgid, slow-flowing essence of the all-pervading mud, might yet achieve for this region what God and man through all the centuries had failed to do, make the land set solid and the water flow fresh and free. And if before long the wealth of international industry was going to dredge channels and build wharves, lay roads, construct depots, attract thousands of workers and make homes for them to live in, here – for all its present horror – might be the base from which a transport service should be launched.

After a few days in the Delta, Walpole was glad to head north to the pleasant little city of Enugu, set in a bowl of green hills. There were garages here, and he left his van to be hosed down and serviced while he set off around the area by mammy-wagon. Hundreds of these were continually on the move, and it was a matter of waiting at some suitable point by the roadside and signalling to the driver, who stopped or not according to his whim and the state of overcrowding in his vehicle. Few mammy-wagons bore any sign of a destination since they travelled no fixed route. Instead they carried a legend in ornamental lettering along side or tailplate, an expression of the owner's attitude to life or sense of humour – 'More Fish in Ocean', 'Trust No Woman', 'The Lord My Keeper', 'All Not as Seen', 'Seek and Ye Shall Find', 'Even Me', or – more mysterious – 'The Wizard of the Holy Sea.'

Most of the wagons were elderly, exhausted creatures, ill-treated from the day of purchase, recklessly driven and overloaded. To Walpole, standing at some turn in a forest road, the sound of its jangling engine and tormented gears – and at times the squeals of its excited passengers – would be heard before the wagon appeared, swirling crazily down the road followed by a cloud of reddish dust. As one now slowed to a stop the cloud swirled over Walpole while the row of youths clinging to its sides shouted and argued, some telling the driver to keep moving, others demanding to know what

Walpole wanted or where he was going. Inside, the wagon was full to bursting – crates of machinery, sacks of yams and grain, bunches of plantains, half a dozen goats tied in a corner, a sow with its legs lashed and a pole thrust through for easy handling, a netful of squawking hens – with several women packed into what space remained. When Walpole brought out money without haggling over the fare, the driver ordered the youths sharing his seat to move out and hang on with the rest and then slammed the complaining engine into gear.

Once installed, Walpole established fellowship through a cigarette or a piece of kola nut, and was soon learning about the area, the number of travellers at different seasons, the kinds of freight and the extent of competition.

'I drive for rich man, sah, big chief in mah village. He tell me where go and what ah 'bliged for carry. He kippin' check on petrol, oil, tyres – he check everyt'ing each time I take de wagon back in garage.'

'But chief no kin check what you pick up on de way?' Walpole suggested.

The driver laughed. 'De ant walk under de lion paw! Each man make bes' livin' he kin. Dis bin footba' team from nearby village.' He jerked his head back at the youths clinging to the sides. 'Dey wait by roadside an' ah done pick um up. Dey pay half what boss ask an' ah keep de cash. . . . Ah havin' wife an' pickens too.'

'You make a journey many times? Or you take new way each day?'

'Ah jus do what boss say, sah,' the driver answered, cupping both hands to light the cigarette Walpole offered and driving with an elbow through the steering wheel. They had overtaken a small car which was skittering over the deep ruts and bringing a gritty dustfall down on the football players.

'Pass um! Pass um!' they screamed. 'Go for pass – one time!'

The driver took both hands to the bucking wheel, trod the accelerator into the floorboards with his naked foot, then – taking his chance as the car swerved wildly and was forced to slow – began to pressure his way past it inch by inch. The youths yelled with delight and hurled obscenities at the car-owner, who fell back as the dust befouled his windscreen.

'You findin' same persons travel same time, same road, one week an' de next?' Walpole inquired.

'Ah see de same faces too-many time,' the driver admitted.

'Ah hearin' is plan for bus service on dis road,' Walpole

suggested. 'How you t'ink youself? Will farmers go for use bus if it come same time each day?'

The driver pondered. 'In de bush, farmers not knowin' time, so no use bus. But in town an' big village I hear ask many time "Why is no bus?"'

'How long dis wagon go for last?' Walpole asked after a few moments.

The driver shot him a shrewd glance. 'You ask many questions, sah. You t'ink put wagons on de road youself? Den you boun' for need good driver. An know all de roads in dis whole country.'

They were passing through a stretch of forest. Every few miles a rusty steel skeleton showed where some mammy-wagon had dashed headlong from the road into the trees, sometimes with such force as to shoot the heavy engine off its mountings and bury it two feet in the earth.

'You never havin' no crash youself?' Walpole inquired. 'You never done turn wagon over in de road?' A sulky look came over the man's features, and it took much coaxing and further cigarettes before good humour was restored.

After a week waiting by roadsides, taking whatever mammy-wagon stopped and sleeping where he could, Walpole made his way back to Enugu for his van with the feeling of having gained much information.

He made a further trip for a few days into the Northern Region, before realizing that this was another world, indeed another century, which for the time being must be left out of his plans. So too would the Delta, while to the east the Niger stood as a barrier to regular communication. The mighty stream split the country down the middle; even at Onitsha, easiest place for crossing, the ferry boats were unreliable through floods and breakdowns. Huge queues of traffic would build up on either bank, and the delays could make nonsense of all timetables.

The result of all Walpole's inquiries he could put into a few sentences: the new service must be confined to the Western Region, the area they already knew, roughly between Lagos and Ibadan but reaching out into the bush on either side of the main road, where there were many farming communities to which no regular service yet extended.

Before returning to Lagos Walpole had one final task – to call on Mallam Ajao's brother in the town of Abeokuta, where the address proved to be that of the biggest garage and petrol station in the area. Walpole gave his name to the clerk, who had no sooner phoned through than there were roars of welcome down the passage and a tall jovial man, of indeterminate bulk beneath his flowing agbada, stamped into the room with arms extended. Festus Ajao was as different from his brother as a large bouncing dog from a slinking jackal. Whisking Walpole into his inner office, he got out the akpeteshie bottle and sent for cold-cold beers, clearly taking his religion – if it *was* also his religion – a good deal more lightly than the Mallam.

'So my frien', my brother done tell me all yo' plans. Great plans! Fine ideas! You man of future, Walpole. You buildin' Nigeria of tomorrow an' de day after! Dis reason I givin' you all help I kin. I unfoldin' you de secrets of my business.'

He waved his arm largely around the office, which seemed to Walpole to hold little except samples of car fittings and tyres, with a single small filing cabinet. However his host quickly showed that he knew a great deal about Abeokuta, a key area in Walpole's projects, and in a few moments they were deep into discussion. Festus was as forthcoming as he promised, and by the time the beer was drunk, Walpole felt grateful to this jovial being who had provided so much information and was now having his clerk type out a list of acquaintances in various towns who would, on his recommendation, do as much for Walpole in their own districts. When the list was handed over and Walpole thanked him warmly, this new friend made little of it.

'I do dis for you, Walpole, because I likin' you – an' I see you bin man for big-scale job. Sma'-sma' man I no help. You know de sayin' – "Milk lengthen de cat's tail but not de monkey's".'

Walpole laughed. 'I see you have travelled in the North, my friend. You have brought back a Fulani proverb.'

Festus rolled a lascivious eye, reminding Walpole of the posters of that chief who found power by drinking Guinness.

'I done fin' much more dan proverbs in de North, my frien'. I bringin' back mos' happy memories.' He leaned forward confidentially. 'In Kaduna you git youssel Fulani woman' – he outlined her charms with both hands – 'you git nice Fulani woman all night five shillins! Dose Lagos women – what dey give you for five shillins? I pity you, my frien', livin' yo' life in Lagos. Dose Lagos women – dey steal de trousers off a snake!' Festus laughed far down in his *agbada*–covered belly and clapped his hands on his fat thighs. 'Lagos women go steal de trousers off a snake!' and he spat profusely into a carton which had once held sparking plugs.

'But now, Walpole, business done finish! You come home wid me an' eat good dinner. You sleepin' dis night in my house. Jus' me, my wife, de pickens an' my young niece Ngosi stayin' in house wid us. . . . We all intend makin' you mos' welcome an' mos' happy.'

13
The Niece of Festus

At the dinner table Festus was in high spirits, but his wife, a massive woman in black velvet buba and lappa of green silk, gave off an atmosphere of disapproval, causing Walpole to wonder if her husband brought home too many guests too often. His efforts at conversation met with small response; she occupied herself with the food, and under her dignified supervision a child servant no more than ten years old carried round platefuls of groundnut stew, followed by dismembered chickens on a small burial mound of rice. From this Festus picked out the most honoured pieces for his guest, keeping up a continual flow of flattery as though Walpole's project had already proved successful and he were an established, influential citizen. Festus asked his advice on the political situation in the capital, industrial developments in the Western Region, and the likely consequences of Nigeria's future independence. He informed Walpole how much he had heard about him from his brother, who greatly admired his handling of the transport pool, how highly he was regarded throughout the firm and that it was expected he would take over from Madam Abiose before long and bring all aspects of the business up to date.

'Your brother is too-too kind,' Walpole replied, not unwilling to hear praise, but embarrassed by its extent and the apprehension that Mallam Ajao might not be so wholehearted an admirer as his brother's words implied. 'You know Mallam himself is a most important person in the firm – indeed in Lagos.'

'Ah, that brother of mine!' Festus remarked in a tone of patronage verging on contempt. 'He make business his whole life. He t'ink of nothin' else day and night . . . day and night. But *you* won't make the same mistake, I hope, my friend?'

'Me – what? Which mistake? I'm sorry – you were speaking of your brother?' Walpole recovered as best he could. Though hungry after his long day, he had scarcely touched his food, and though anxious to please Festus he found it hard to pay attention to his talk. He had been placed next to the niece Ngosi, and since the meal began their knees had been touching underneath the table, but the table was small and the party packed closely round so that the contact might be accidental, and just at the moment when Festus fired a direct question at him, Walpole was stealing a glance at his companion. To his confusion, Ngosi had chosen the same moment to raise her demurely bent head and glance at him. Walpole's whole being gazed into her eyes and Ngosi responded with a sharp intake of breath.

From the moment she came into the room Walpole had been distracted by Ngosi. She was no beauty but something more disturbing, a conscious object of desire, taut with life and ready with response. She dressed in Western style; a short pleated skirt swelled out over her hips, and her frilly white blouse was pushed into two enchanting points. Black hair, vibrant and electric, framed a pleasure-loving little face. Everything about her was small, except for her huge black eyes and smiling lips. Small in scale but far from fragile, to Walpole, to any man, she was a walking invitation.

Making a conscious effort, Walpole questioned the two boys about their school. He paid compliments to Mrs Festus on her cooking – acknowledged by no more than a slight inclination of her head. At last, when conversation halted, he felt bold enough to address a remark to Ngosi. It was the first since he had greeted her on entry, and a dryness in his throat made his voice sound thin and far away, so that even the children looked up in surprise.

'Do you live in Abeokuta?' What question could be more conventional, and yet the moment Walpole had spoken it seemed charged with meaning, as though he were planning an assignation.

'No . . . in Ibadan,' Ngosi answered almost in a whisper. 'I stay here with my . . .' there was a moment's hesitation which Walpole put down to shyness '. . . my uncle 'n' aunt dese two-three days . . . for look after the children.'

'We don' need no lookin' after,' piped up the eldest, a boy of nine. 'We lookin' after ourselves – don' we, Joseph?'

Joseph's mouth was full of chicken and before he could reply Festus shot a stern look at his sons. 'Ngosi is here to have short holiday an' to help my wife wid dese noisy pickens. My wife mos' busy now because we goin' have big weddin' in dis family.'

Walpole could not help himself: 'Is it *you* who is getting married?' he asked Ngosi. Festus let out a roar, while Mrs Festus scowled as though she found the idea improper or insulting.

'Ngosi not done chose husban' yet. . . . Plenty boys glad for marry her when time come.'

Walpole exchanged a glance with Ngosi which showed what he felt on the matter.

'Hey, pickens!' Festus ordered, 'go get youselves to bed!'

Soon Mrs Festus had vanished into the kitchen, and for Walpole began one of the longest evenings he had ever spent. He had obtained from Festus all the information he wanted, exchanged every scrap of news from Lagos, and now found it painful to keep up the boisterous chatter which served his host for conversation. After a while all sounds from the kitchen ceased, and it appeared Mrs Festus must have retired to bed. Walpole would have been happy to go too, if only he could come to some understanding with Ngosi first. Where and how could they meet again? How could he find her in Ibadan – and how soon? If he waited till morning to ask, she might have taken the boys to school or gone out shopping. Should he plead tiredness from his travels, hoping to catch her for a moment on the way to bed, or sit on in the hope that Festus would go out and leave them? Increasingly distracted, he sat on, giving random answers and trying to look at Ngosi without seeming to.

But at last Festus himself showed signs of weariness. 'I t'ink I climb into my bed. But firs' I showin' you your room. Your bed, my frien', is 'cross de courtyard. You excuse my puttin' you dere, but dis big family an' too-small house.'

A wild hope filled Walpole's hammering heart as Festus led the way. Ngosi came too – but perhaps this was just to say goodnight, and she would follow her host back into the house to be near the children. Through the now empty kitchen and across a small patch of grass Festus led the way to a wooden outbuilding with a verandah reached by a few steps.

'Ngosi, dear chile, you knowin' your own room. Goodnight an' peaceful sleep,' and he gave her what might have been a fatherly hug. In the darkness Walpole managed to catch her hand as she freed herself, and received an answering pressure.

'Goodnight, Ngosi,' he said, scarcely able to control his words.

'Goodnight, Mr Walpole. I see you in mornin' – if you not go away too early. Goodnight, Uncle Festus!' and she ran up the steps and along the verandah till her outline melted through an invisible door.

Festus showed Walpole into his room, but remained standing inside as if reluctant to cross to his own bed. He pointed out that the windows were fitted with mosquito netting, and there were matches beside the candle he had lit. He indicated a cupboard for clothes and the jug of water for washing. He said he would be over in good time to wake his guest for breakfast. . . . Tense, desperate, Walpole stood, his whole being concentrated into the longing for Festus to be gone, a silent determination to eliminate him from the room.

'Yes, yes . . . I understand,' he muttered. 'Yes, yes. Thank you for everything. . . .'

'Well, my friend,' Festus observed at last, 'I leavin' you to your dreams. Happy sleepin'!'

'Goodnight,' Walpole insisted, almost like a threat. 'Goodnight. Goodnight. *Goodnight!*'

As the door closed behind his host, Walpole put both hands up to his forehead. If he'd stayed another second I'd have hit him, he thought, as sick with tension he sat down on the bed, then went over and peered through the mosquito wire towards the house. A bolt grated in the kitchen door, and soon afterwards a light shone from an upstairs room. Softly he turned the handle and stared out into the garden, half expecting to see Festus watching from beneath a tree. But there was nothing. Nothing but a clear sky full of stars, the stirring of a wind in the warm night, and the powerful scent of a frangipani bush. Walpole tiptoed back and tapped three times on the dividing wall.

For a moment, for two whole moments, there was silence,

long enough for Walpole to wonder if his wild longing would be cheated. Then there came a reply, three taps just as he had given. He tapped four times, and four taps came in answer. Elation leapt and he started towards the door, but had not crossed the floor when there came another gentler tap, this time on the door itself. Walpole sprang for the handle, but before he reached it Ngosi was inside. Her feet were bare and she wore nothing but a flimsy nightdress which revealed everything that had been tormenting him for the past four hours.

'No one comin'', she whispered. 'They done shut the house.'

Walpole picked her up and carried her over to his open bed, and as Ngosi pulled the nightdress over her tousled hair, he was already tearing off his clothes. Too keyed up for gentleness after prolonged constraint, he was on top of her and with hardly a preliminary caress had forced his way inside. As he gasped and thrust, Ngosi, far more in command of herself than he was, moved adroitly, leading him on while seeming to elude in the tempestuous game.

Later, resting on his arm, she chattered excitedly while Walpole could only lie there, not so much exhausted as overwhelmed in heart and mind by what had happened.

'I was longing for you, darling. Just longing for you! That moment when we were sitting at table – before you even speak to me – I am just wanting everyone else to drop down dead.'

'Why to drop dead?' Walpole was still bemused.

'So that we would be alone.'

'From the moment you came into the room,' said Walpole slowly, 'I felt as if I were on fire . . . I couldn't talk . . . I didn't want to eat . . . I didn't know where to turn my eyes.'

Ngosi laughed softly. 'Didn' you think I should manage for us to be together?'

But Walpole was following his own train of thought. . . . 'All I was hoping was to get one minute with you alone.'

'One minute! What good would that be?'

'To find out where you live – so I could meet you later. I never dreamed we could be like this . . . I just hoped for long enough to find out your address. I wouldn't need to write it down. . . . Tell me, where in Ibadan *do* you live?'

Ngosi had raised herself on one elbow and was teasing his lips with hers: 'Time to learn that in mornin'. Now I only want. . . .'

But Walpole was eager to fix his new love in his mind. He wanted to know all about her, where she lived, how many brothers and sisters she had, how often she came to see her aunt and uncle, where, when and how he would meet her next. Unless he could weave such a net of circumstance around her, it seemed she might vanish as suddenly as she had come. But Ngosi's replies gave little to build on.

'My fam'ly jus' movin' house. Soon we be in new home an' you come visit me there. Two-three days more I stayin' here with my uncle 'n' aunt – then, jus' as soon as I get home, I send you word.'

'What word?'

'I sendin' you telegram: "Here I am, Walpole – come 'n' catch me!" '

Their laughter led to a new bout of love, longer, slower, more intense.

Afterwards, lying back with her hands behind her head, Ngosi asked him: 'Are you likin' me?'

'Whatever *can* you mean?' Walpole's tone was shocked. 'Like you? – I love you, Ngosi. Don't you feel it?'

'Because if you likin' me, Walpole, we can be always together, an' nobody can't stop us!'

'You mean . . . we can get married?'

'No – I know you can't marry jus' like that. My uncle done tell me 'bout yo' life. But he also say you startin' up new business. You plannin' for open office in Ibadan?'

'Yes . . . I'm hoping to do that, but I don't know when.'

'Maybe nex' month, or month after?'

'Maybe. But I don't know yet.'

'Well – when you start, you give me job in office. I can type, write letters . . . many things. I am knowin' this district well. Find some office place for me – an' I makin' you happiest man in this whole region.'

Walpole hesitated. Jobs were not his to give. But Ngosi was insisting – 'Promise me, darling! Say you do this thing for me.'

Weakly Walpole yielded, paying for favours that were immediate and delicious with the softest of currencies, promises on the future. Through his mind passed the thought that if he could not give Ngosi a job, he could give her the equivalent and more – a flat, a home for love, and an allowance.

'I'll find some place for you,' he murmured, rising to her again. But Ngosi seemed determined on his full consent. 'You

promise me a job?' she asked, not yet yielding herself to him.
'Say you promise!'

'I promise. . . .'

'An' I makin' you the happies' man. . . .'

Towards morning it seemed that Ngosi was asleep. Slipping out of bed, Walpole went over to the window. There was a stirring in the trees and a bird woke overhead; it called twice and then, as if aware of its mistake, fell silent. Walpole waited, and a minute or two later there was a paleness in the sky, and a flush lit the undersides of low clouds. Looking back into the room, Walpole could see Ngosi watching. He went back and sat on the bed beside her – and was suddenly overwhelmed with a bitterness of despair.

'I wish there was no one in the world but us. I wish this was our own little hut a million miles from anywhere – or else I wish we were both dead.'

Ngosi stared as if not believing what she heard. Then an enormous tear rolled down her cheek and burst into a storm of weeping. 'Don' think bad of me! Don't be angry with me! Don't let them make you hate me!'

It was Walpole's turn to be astonished, and he gathered the shaking girl into his arms. He supposed she was uneasy at having given way too readily, and feared that once out of her presence he might turn against her. 'But I *love* you, darling! Don't you understand? I *love* you. How can I ever be angry with you? . . . I'm grateful with all my heart. . . .'

But all his tenderness served only to upset Ngosi more. She pulled his head down against her little pointed breast. He felt the throbbing of her heart, and through the thin wall of flesh came her passionate entreaties: 'Don't think bad of me, darling! Promise you won't never hate me! If you hatin' me, I go kill myself!'

Desperately they clung together, as though he were leaving her on some fated mission. But already daylight had turned the window blue, and in a minute more Ngosi sat up, pressed Walpole to her again, slid inside her nightdress, and was gone.

14
Blow-up

Within a day or two of leaving Abeokuta Walpole had completed his inquiries and was back in Lagos. Madam Abiose was tearfully happy to have her boy home, crying with joy at the presents he brought out. . . . 'So you t'inkin' of me in far-off places' . . . 'I see you not forgettin' me in Enugu.' Alake had prepared a lavish evening meal, and not until this was over did Madam Abiose ask him to tell her about his journey and plans for the new service. Walpole talked for an hour, explaining why he now believed the service should be confined to their own region, and why he was convinced it could be made a success within two or three years. From time to time his patroness broke in with some objection.

'But many times my wagons run half empty when they only makin' journey every two-three week. An' here you tellin' me we kin run service each day an' have wagons full! Dis make no sense to me.'

But Walpole was prepared for patient explanation and went slowly over his arguments again; the need for fixed timetables and routes; the need to keep to them even if buses had to set off empty, since there might be thirty passengers waiting down the road; and the need for inspection to keep check on the drivers.

'You pay dese 'spectors more for doin' nothin',' objected Madam Abiose – who detested all inspectors for the trouble they caused her in the markets – 'dan you pay men for drivin'!'

To every objection he replied, giving her time to grow accustomed to each point, then adding one he had not thought of until the last few days, that the main depot should be not in Lagos but Ibadan, it being more central for their area. In addition land was only half the price and building costs much lower. Walpole was guiltily aware that though his arguments were sound, they masked the true reason why he put them forward.

'But dis too far for you come home each night, not so? You 'bliged for spend half week in Ibadan?'

'At first I may have to be there in the week,' he answered soothingly, 'but always I come home for weekends.'

Towards midnight Madam Abiose appeared to have become reconciled to his proposals, but voiced one last objection.

'How 'bout licences? Dat somethin' you not t'inkin' 'bout, Walpole. But dis mos' important! How you git licence for run service all over de region?'

Walpole laughed. 'That's one thing I am not worried about the least bit. Everyone knows Madam Abiose is the cleverest woman in Lagos. She knows how to use long legs an' go round talking to right people. That's one thing she never failed – to fix licence for anything she wanted. And besides. . .'

'Besides what, my frien'?'

'I see in your mind you planning to ask Chief Julius Ogun to become a director of new transport company.'

Madam Abiose clapped her hands on her thighs and laughed.

'All right, Walpole, I not denyin' you is clever boy. An' I not denyin' time is ripe. An Chief Julius is cert'nly de man for smooth way wid white officials. I done hear all you say. But' – and she took Walpole's hand with a pleading tenderness that cut him to the heart – 'you bin wid me long time, Walpole, an' you understan' my ways. When new idea come, I not say "Yes" an' not say "No". I turn all over in my mind. I t'ink of ways we kin be cheated an' difficulties kin come up. I t'ink of all dese in de night. Den, when I done consider everything, I make up my mind! An' once my mind made, is no turnin' back, an' no disputin'. Is true what I am sayin'?'

'Is most true, madam. Everyone knows this is true.'

Madam Abiose looked at her boy. She had assumed that after his long absence they would go to bed together and make love, but his face looked drawn and heavy; she knew he had driven himself for weeks on end, and when she spoke, other words came to her lips.

'Well, my dear, I see you bin tired. You go to bed now an' have good sleep, den tomorrow I t'ink all over an' we decidin' what to do. I mos' happy woman to have you home wid me again.'

Walpole went to bed. In his heart was relief that all had gone so well; ambition for the project which now seemed certain of success; the wild hope that he might soon be spending half of each week with Ngosi in Ibadan; and shame that he should be responding to Madam Abiose's gentle consideration with deception and the wish to get away.

After a night's sleep, Walpole parted confidently from his patroness. She was to stay at home while he spent the day at the transport pool, straightening out threads which had become entangled in his absence. There were many such threads and he was not back till late. Running upstairs he moved forward for an embrace, but Madam Abiose did not rise from the table where she was sitting with papers spread before her, and as she waved him to a seat he saw her face was set. . . .

'Whaffor you spend so much time in Enugu? I see you done pass five days in de district. You tellin' me las' night you plan service only for Western Region. So whaffor you pass all dat time in de East?'

'But Enugu is the key centre for the East, and the East might have been the best place for the new service. It's only through spending time there that I know it's not.'

Dismissing his reply as though it contained nothing to the purpose, Madam Abiose came back again.

'Whaffor you drive up North? Dis nothin' but waste of time an' money. You t'ink you know all about transport matters – you ought done show more sense.'

Walpole shot her an inquiring glance. Clearly something had upset her, and he supposed her accountant or one of her financial advisers had been complaining of the cost and his absence from the business. Having been annoyed herself, she was now passing the annoyance on to him.

'Yes,' he answered with warmth, 'it's true! I spent five days travelling in mammy-wagons round Enugu, and four days digging the van out of mud in Calabar and sleeping on the seat. I spent a week eating dust on the road to Kano. I did all this for your business. If you think that a holiday, I wish you just half a day of it to see for yourself.'

Madam Abiose gave him a mistrustful glance. 'Why you spendin' all las' week in Ibadan an' Abeokuta – but you never once come home for de night or telephone me?'

Even now the truth had not sunk in. Resentful but still confident, he continued to explain.

'But I *had* to spend time in Ibadan! This the most important place of all – where we must have our depot. In Abeokuta a few hours might have been enough, but I spent a day there because Mallam Ajao asked me to visit his brother Festus.'

A suspicion began to form in Walpole's mind as he was saying the words.

'So in Abeokuta you stay only for one day?' Madam Abiose demanded.

'Yes.'

'But also, I t'ink, one night?'

The trap was sprung, Walpole saw the situation in a flash and was left looking into a bottomless pit. Mallam Ajao had never forgiven him for his humiliation over the office transport. He had pretended reconciliation, planned cunningly, awaited opportunity – and seized it with his brother's help. Granted that Festus despised the Mallam, a brother is still a brother and his fortunes have to be pushed by any means. Ngosi must be Festus' mistress-secretary, or perhaps a good-time girl he had come across in the town and hired – hence the wife's resentment that she had been brought into her home as a pretended children's nurse. He understood now Ngosi's wild pleas to him not to hate her. A hundred hints had been given which should have warned him, but the bait was seductive and he had rushed into the trap.

'I see what you t'inkin' in yo' mind, Walpole.'

'What?'

'You t'ink me bloody fool – dat what you t'ink. I see dis in yo' face. You t'ink you kin roam de country amusin' yo'self, an' all I do is find money for pay bills. Dat what you t'inkin' dis minute. Not so?'

'No, madam.'

'Don' lie to me! I say dat what you are t'inkin'! You t'inkin' me stupid old woman dat you kin cheat an' lie to!'

With an effort Walpole fought his temper, reminding himself of all there was at stake.

'I am often thoughtless and ungrateful, madam, but I have never lacked respect for you. What we are talking of now is a business matter and you are a businesswoman. Put this on one side till the morning. Then ask me what you wish.'

'I askin' you now one simple question. Dat what I askin'! I askin' who dis young girl Ngosi, niece of Festus Ajao? I askin' why you seducin' dis young girl by promisin' job in transport office? Who tellin' you kin have office in Ibadan? Who sayin' you kin hire yo'self girls out of my money?'

Exasperated by her question, furious at his own folly and the net in which he had let himself become entangled, Walpole made one last effort.

'I understand your feelings, madam. Too well I understand. But don't throw everything away because of bad men's gossip. When you know the whole story – then do what you please.'

But business success meant nothing to Madam Abiose compared to Walpole's betrayal of her as a woman. She had been wounded bitterly and publicly, since his escapade must become common knowledge. Only one course might have saved Walpole now – passionate self-accusation, protests that he had been tricked, bitter denunciations of Ngosi, vows of future fidelity – tears and ravings which would involve Madam Abiose in his humiliation, building up a scene so painful she would be forced to raise him up and comfort him simply to put a stop to it. Only by crawling could he have saved his position, and he would not crawl. Madam Abiose, accustomed to lashing those around her, letting her tongue voice whatever came into her head, secure in her power over any who might have shouted back, flung herself now into a flood of denunciation and reproach.

'Who takin' you up when you nothin' more than dirty market boy an' make you fine man of de world? Who educatin' you so you kin talk dis fine way same as whiteman? Who workin' for you all day long, an' plannin' an' schemin' only for yo' future? Who buy all de smart clo'es you wearin' now dis very minute?'

With exasperating patience – with what he knew was exasperating patience and politeness – Walpole replied: 'You did, madam.'

His coolness was more than she could stand, and her voice rose high in fury. 'An' you s'pose I doin' all dis so you kin fool aroun' wid dis Ngosi – dat you give job an' pay my money for sleep wid you? You t'ink I not see through yo' big talk about Ibadan as de "natural centre"? I tell you whose "natural centre" you t'inkin' of – de little whore Ngosi's! You t'ink I don' read yo' mind like book wid pages wide?'

Walpole raised his hands and the gesture silenced his mistress so that there was a second's pause in the torrent sweeping both of them away. But he was torn between anger and guilt so that for a second no words came out and while he was still hesitating Madam Abiose rushed into the gap.

'Whaffor you say nothin'? You 'fraid for answer me, dat's why! You find plenty word for dese young girls dat cheat an' make big fool of you. I tell you once for all you done spik too much! Too much for yo' own good an' for yo' future. Nex' time you better hold tongue an' not make promise you no kin carry out. . . . "Give me nice job in office, Mr Walpole, an' let me be yo' little whore!" Dere's big changes comin' roun' dis place – I warnin' you, Walpole. You goin' find it's not me is bloody fool – is yo'self!'

Walpole bounded to his feet. With a sweep of his arm he hurled her papers to the floor and stood over Madam Abiose as though about to strike her. His mouth twitched and his fists trembled. Then, whirling round, he snatched up a heavy clock of brass and marble, one of her greatest treasures, imported from Europe and a present from her workpeople. Whirling it above his head, he flung it full-face against the wall, where it hung for a moment as if embedded before crashing to the floor in a shower of broken glass and fragments.

'Dis bin end of everyt'ing 'tween you 'n' me!' he shouted, lapsing under emotion into natural speech, and rushed out of the room.

Stunned by what she had brought upon herself, Madam Abiose sat for a while trembling among the wreckage of the room and of her life. Then she got slowly up and went looking in the kitchen for Alake, like a hurt child for consolation. But Walpole had stormed into the bedroom where he began throwing his belongings haphazard into suitcases.

An hour or two later, still in a turmoil of anger and confusion, he heard voices outside his door. Alake, who feared neither man nor devil, was speaking with thin-voiced scorn as though to a snake or insect whose ears were too low to be reached in normal tones.

'Whaffor you creepin' roun' dis place, Mr Ajao? You lookin' like you come for put bush poison in Mr Walpole' chop.'

'No Alake. No need for dat, *Mister* Walpole done put bush in him own chop.'

15
No Return

When Madam Abiose first took her Scholarship Boy in hand he had been a raw youth with strong legs reaching out of his too-short trousers, hard-working, alert, capable of scrambling a living from the city rough-and-tumble, but unable to read or write, speaking only the pidgin English of the markets, his highest ambition to become a successful petty trader owning his own shop. When Walpole rushed out of her house some five and a half years later he was a well-spoken, well-mannered young man, quick to adapt himself to any company. Though he had lost his early enthusiasm for education, he retained – what is of more immediate benefit – the appearance and manner of an educated man. He owned a range of clothes in which he took much interest, and his naturally flamboyant taste had been modified by Madam Abiose's sense of fitness. He had an array of costly personal possessions given him by his loving mistress, and a small collection of books chosen by himself, few of which had he yet found time to read. He enjoyed a wide acquaintance among business people and in many walks of Lagos life, but was aware that it was his connection with his patroness which had brought him such contacts, and that, having broken with her, he could expect no assistance from them until he had established himself in his own right.

Of money Walpole had in the bank around two thousand pounds, representing his salary since he was taken into the business, plus odd sums given him by Madam Abiose during their life together. There was also one other advantage Walpole owed her more valuable than the rest – this was the conviction that he had it in him to become a person of importance. From that early morning when he first set out on his solitary journey to the city, Walpole had seldom doubted ultimate success, but his horizon had been low and kept from rising by his humble life with Mr Ali, to whom a steady job at ten pounds a month with opportunities for adding to it on the side was all a reasonable being can hope for this side of the

grave. But Madam Abiose's loving flattery and her insistence
on his splendid future had impressed themselves on his mind,
increasing confidence and heightening ambition. At this
moment, as he sat in a small room in the back-street hotel
where he had taken refuge, ambition was inflamed by anger
and hurt vanity into a burning desire for quick success. He
intended to show Madam Abiose he was not dependent on her
help, and to exasperate those managers who had got rid of him
by a trick. Plans and ideas chased one another through his
head, all tending in the direction of immediate riches, his two
thousand pounds transformed into twenty-five, fifty, a
hundred thousand by some master stroke. And all dreams
ended with his stepping down from his chauffeur-driven
Mercedes on a visit of kindly recognition to the woman who
had helped him in early days – and who now bitterly regretted
her folly in having let such ability slip out of her grasp.

As Walpole was leaving his hotel to call round on one or two
acquaintances, a letter lay waiting for him in the entrance.
Recognizing her bold sprawl and the heavy mauve notepaper
Madam Abiose used for private correspondence, he went back
to his room to read it. How had she discovered his address? It
was only three days since he had left and he had told no one
where he was living, but the discovery was typical of her and
of her mastery over her environment.

You bad boy, Walpole. You take advantage over two-three angry
words and run out of my house. This show you wishing leave me
long-long time and seizing first chance done come.

You know me, Walpole. You done work more than five year by
my side. Everyone with me know my too-quick temper and my too-
sharp tongue. But they know my temper soon finish and then my
warm heart coming back. Alake know this. The clerks and
messengers know this. So they show patience for me. Only my own
boy show no patience.

Why you not wait just one-two hours? I asking you, Walpole.
Then I come tell you how shamed I am. I cry and kiss your face so we
are friends again. But you are not waiting even one hour. You run out
of my house like thief.

Do not think I am only blaming you. I blaming myself much more.
For I not see how quick my boy done grow into a man, so I get too-mad
over this young girl. But in my heart I know is not just young girls
standing between you and me. It is yourself. You wish manage
things your own way, and I am old woman standing in your path.

Each place I go they asking me – where is Walpole? How is Walpole? Where you hiding that young man of yours? When persons asking so the tears run down. For what am I to say? My boy grow tired of me and leave me. I become an old woman, so he staying no more in my house.

You been like dear dear son to me and like a husband. But now you gone there is no husband for me and no son.

I not caring for the business. Not for friends. For nothing I am caring any more. Walpole, I not asking you will come back in my house because I know too-well you not come back. But when you go from me you take my life. . . .

The letter bore no signature, and nothing could have brought home more painfully to Walpole the blow he had struck his mistress than the absence of that striding signature which she added to every letter with such flourish. It was as if her powerful personality had been dissolved by grief, and her words appeared to end because the paper ended – or perhaps there had been a further sheet which Madam Abiose failed to notice, which in her misery she had torn up or let slip on to the floor to be gathered up later by a distracted Alake.

Walpole read the letter through again slowly, he read it a third time, and a fourth. He saw himself as despicable, a criminal. He had betrayed the woman who loved and trusted him. Her rebuke that he knew her fiery temper, followed by quick recovery and penitence, was justified. He of all people should have given her time. He had done wrong and acted hastily. He was ashamed, and sat for a long time on his bed turning the letter over in his fingers. Ought he to go back, say he was sorry, offer to make things up? But if so, what was he sorry for? It had been thoughtless of him to fall into Mallam Ajao's trap and take a girl in circumstances that would hurt his mistress's pride in addition to the wound to her feelings this was bound to cause – yet it was inevitable he should take a girl, just as it was certain he would one day marry, and as an older woman, a woman of the world, she should surely have foreseen it. She had taken him, a boy of nineteen, to be her lover, and in so doing so must have known that such a life could not go on for ever. She called him her 'dear, dear son' and her 'husband', and tears flooded his eyes as he read the words, but he was not her son and he could not, with so much difference in age, become her husband, and she must have known from the first that he could not.

Moreover, in the business world in which they worked together, they were now at cross-purposes and every week, if not every day, must bring fresh cause for conflict. She would not part with final authority, and Walpole had reached the point every man must reach, where he would rather make mistakes and carry the consequences than be wise with someone else's wisdom. On top of which there was her temper, for which she half apologized, but which she had no idea of giving up or changing. She reproached him for having run out of her house, but it was she who had burst into reproaches no man should endure, for what kind of man would sit listening to such taunts – above all to threats about his future and his livelihood – and assuring himself that she would calm down before long?

Deeply affected by her letter as he was, painfully conscious of his ingratitude, he knew he could not return. They would only have more quarrels until he was forced to leave again, after more bitter reproaches, further agony. The one good result of all this was that he had got away, breaking the tie which bound him to her as her child. He was resolved not to go back – but how was he to answer her letter in which she was so plainly hoping that he would?

Pulling the only chair in the room to a small table, he began to write. At first his sentences seemed inspired, he would compel her to appreciate his point of view by force of words and feelings. Forgetting to go out and eat, switching on the light when daylight faded, he continued writing on and on. After a while he had the impression that he was writing words he had previously put down, so he gathered his letter up – there were ten pages of it already – and began to read it through. He was expecting to be impressed by his own eloquence of conviction, and for a page or two all seemed to be going well. But as he read on, Walpole saw to his disgust that the letter was full of self-justification and reproach, and that, the more he tried to justify himself, the less generous and more small-minded he appeared. He started afresh, then a third and fourth time, but at each attempt his sentences grew longer and his arguments less clear, and now not only was his writing confused but his mind as well till he no longer knew what he was trying to say. What was he to do? Whom could he consult who understood his situation? Thankfully Walpole recalled that, despite other claims and distractions, he had made a point of visiting Mr Ali month by month. He would go to his old benefactor.

Mr Ali greeted Walpole as he always did and they were soon seated beside the familiar fire. But to Walpole's consternation he found Mr Ali's one concern was that he should return to Madam Abiose with no more delay before a rival could be promoted to his position, or perhaps a successor in her favours.

'You bin rash an' foolish boy – dat what you done bin, Wa'poo. Madam Abiose pow'ful mammy, so she 'customed for act like pow'ful mammy. What you 'xpect she say when you go roun' sleepin' wid young girls an' she done hear tell 'bout um? She boun' for bawl you out, but dis no reason for you rush from house. Now Madam done calm herself, so you go back an' tell her you bin sorry – an' you go live wid her same like before.'

Patiently Walpole explained. It was not simply the question of Ngosi. He and his patroness had got on happily so long as their aims did not conflict; then she had wanted to guide his life and he was eager to learn and enjoy the wider opportunity she offered. But now their earlier harmony had been replaced by conflict, caused by a deep difference in their aims. What Madam Abiose wanted from him was that he remain a household pet, trusted and even honoured, but controlled. What he wanted was his manly freedom which her jealousy could not allow, and an authority in business she could not accept because it conflicted with her own. If Madam Abiose had been ten years older and wanting to retire, or if he had really been her son, free to form relationships and live an independent life, all could have been well. But as it was, the only honest course was to get out, and in the long run this would be best for her as well. In this way, step by step, with many analogies and homely images and much repetition, Walpole brought Mr Ali to appreciate why he could never go back to his patroness.

'I bin sad you lose dis chance, Wa'poo. When Madam Abiose done take up up, I t'ink you bin safe for lifetime an' bin glad for you like my own son. But I understan' what you tellin' me. You bin now a man, an' a man kin not pass life ruled by a woman. I 'gree wid you, Wa'poo. You done taken de wises' course.'

Walpole smiled with relief.

'But what you plannin' for do now?' Mr Ali went on. 'How you go live? Have you money for make business by yo'self?' He paused, then added hesitantly, almost shyly, 'If you needin' money, you know I done save. . . .'

Much moved, Walpole pressed the old man's hand and
made clear he was in no need. He now had time and enough
money to look around and think what he should do. He had
come because Mr Ali was his father and his Baba, and he could
not feel happy in his mind till he received his Baba's approval
for the action he was taking. However, there was also a second
reason for his coming, since he had this day received from
Madam Abiose a letter which he had been trying ever since to
answer, but without success. So he had come for his master's
advice as to how he should reply. Pleased and flattered, Mr Ali
made Walpole read the letter over to him slowly, and again a
second time. Then he sat gazing into the burning coals until
Walpole could bear the suspense no longer.

'Well,' he asked. 'What am I to say, Baba? How am I to
answer? I see you find it difficult as I do.'

Mr Ali raised his face and looked at Walpole. It was more
wrinkled than the face at which Walpole had gazed for the first
time many years ago and the hair and beard were grey. It was
the same face, but more calm and dignified, and the black eyes
were those into which Walpole had seemed to sink and lose
himself on that terrible day when he had tried to cheat his Baba
out of fourpence. But then they had been stern and now were
smiling.

'Dis bin de simples' letter in de world for answer, Wa'poo.
You writin' answer five-six minute when you bin back home.'

'But *how*, Baba? What am I to *say*? I've already spent the
whole day writing. . . .'

Mr Ali raised a hand. 'Dis woman bin mos' good to you,
my son, an' you done hurt her woman's feelins. She t'ink you
turn 'gainst her an' dat you hate her in yo' heart, dat why she
say she wishin' she were dead. Is no need for arguin'. No need
for defen' yo'self. You jus' write short-short letter. Tell her
you bin grateful for all de love an' care she givin' you. You
never forget dis all yo' life. You lovin' an' carin' for her too,
an' you mos' sorry all done end dis way. You wishin'
everyt'ing good in dis worl' an' de nex', an' you kin never,
never t'ink of her only wid love an' t'ankfulness. . . . Dat all
you write to Madam Abiose.'

Walpole gazed at Mr Ali as he had gazed at him as a little
boy, as one to whom the most complex of life's problems
present no difficulty because of the goodness of his heart.

A couple of days later there were two letters waiting for

Walpole as he set out in the morning. He tore open the one in the familiar writing.

Thank you, Walpole. You saying me the kindest words you can. I see that though you are selfish boy you are not bad boy. If I want to wish harm for you I can not. It is my own fault for loving you too much.

At the end, Walpole noticed with relief, was the familiar scrawled signature.

The second letter was typewritten on paper with a printed heading EKPE ENTERPRISES and an address in the business quarter.

Dear Mr Abiose,
I learn with regret through a mutual acquaintance that you have recently relinquished your habitual spheres of activity.

It occurs to me you may have found yourself on a loose end. I may possibly be of some service to you which would indeed be cause for gratification to,
Yours faithfully,

Lionel Ekpe

P.S. If you are interested kindly telephone my secretary at above address.

16
A Friend in Need

The name of Lionel Ekpe was not new to Walpole, and it was one which aroused mixed feelings. He had come across him on one of those Sunday evenings when Madam Abiose was paying visits on her own and he had gone into the city to pass time with any casual acquaintance who might be around. It was just such an acquaintance, young Basil Chukuma, who had introduced him to 'my friend Ekpe, the promoter' and then slipped off on his own affairs, leaving Walpole to make

the best of it he could. The man in whose company he found
himself was about thirty years old, slim, almost delicate in
build, too carefully dressed in a light close-fitting suit, yellow
shirt and bow tie with the ends exactly squared. His thin face
wore a look of disgust as he pushed away dirty glasses and
ashtrays and nodded Walpole on to the vacant bar stool.
Meantime the barman had appeared and, as Mr Ekpe seemed
not to have noticed, Walpole asked if he would have a drink.

'Yes. A large Scotch. I detest small drinks.'

Walpole gave the order.

'Well, and what brings you here?' his companion asked
without interest.

'Being bored,' said Walpole. 'Like yourself.'

They exchanged a remark or two and then Mr Ekpe,
annoyed perhaps that the younger man could be as cool and
offhand as himself, began putting questions to cut him down
to size. Having learned that Walpole neither liked nor disliked
air travel, since he had not yet been off the ground, and that he
had no preferences among foreign countries since he had never
visited any, he set him a few tests nearer home.

'Were you at Chief Pontius's party in Ikoyi?'

'No.'

'Everybody in Lagos was there.'

'Well, I was one of the handful who stayed away.'

'Going to the right places,' observed Mr Ekpe, 'is as
important as driving the right car. What *do* you drive?'

'Vans,' said Walpole, tired of being patronized. 'Vans,
lorries, mammy-wagons.'

'Ha! Vans. Why, whatever work d'you do?'

'I work for Madam Abiose, the market trader. I help her run
shops and stalls. She is teaching me the business.'

This reply, Walpole expected, would end the conversation,
for if his companion did not walk away, he would. But its
effect was startling. Mr Ekpe blinked twice, then for the first
time a smile opened his face and he laid a hand on Walpole's
arm.

'But, my *dear* fellow, why on earth didn't you *tell* me this?
Why can't you be more candid and direct? Here have I been
struggling to find something to talk about – and all the time
you were holding this back! Why d'you hide your light under
a bush?'

'What light?' Walpole asked, bewildered.

'That you work for the cleverest woman in Lagos!'

'Then you know Madam Abiose?'

'Why, yes . . . that is, I don't exactly *know* her. But there isn't a woman in Lagos I admire more.'

And Ekpe, who had so far made no movement towards refilling their glasses, crooked his forefinger commandingly at the barman.

During the following month Walpole saw Ekpe twice again – once indeed he had looked in on him at work. He was driving a white Mercedes and on his way, he said, to sign an important contract, but had called in none the less. . . . 'The Chief and his friends can wait. I always put friendship before business.'

Before leaving, Ekpe had suggested that next time he called Walpole might take him along to meet his patroness. Walpole spoke of this to Madam Abiose the same evening, having in mind she might ask his friend to dinner. Madam Abiose, however, whose encyclopedic knowledge of Lagos life included Lionel Ekpe, had answered that she would see him if Walpole insisted but that 'since he comin' for talk business, I spik wid him in my office'.

When the day of the visit came Walpole was not, as he expected, invited to sit down and join in the discussion, and that evening his vanity was further ruffled when he asked his patroness what she thought of Ekpe's proposition – the purchase of a piece of land not far from the Mainland Hotel and likely to be required before long when that hotel needed to expand.

'Dis not bad plan,' she answered without interest.

'You mean you'll take it up?'

'Who sayin' I go for take it up? You s'pose I take leave of my five senses?'

Chagrined, Walpole demanded: 'But if the idea's a good one, why not? You're always looking for ways to invest money.'

But Madam Abiose was ruffled too. She had resented having to spend time listening to Ekpe and did not mean to encourage Walpole to bring in other casual acquaintances.

'Is not a question of "Bin dis projec' good? Will dis land sell for more money in two years?" You not understan' de mos' important point in de whole matter.'

'What point?'

'Dis Ekpe not hones' man,' Madam Abiose declared bluntly. 'He not able to act hones' even if he makin' more money for hisself dat way.'

But Walpole had an answer ready. 'Then why do you do business with Chief Julius and Mr Johnson, the whiteman, though many times you tell me they are thieves and liars?'

Madam Abiose closed the ledger she was examining and pushed it from her. 'I see I done waste time teachin' you 'bout business an' financial matters, my frien'. You no understandin' de firs' thing. I do business wid Chief Julius and Mr Johnson because dese persons bin in my power. . . . I kin cheat dem more dan dey cheatin' me. Dis not because I wishin' for cheat dem, but because I got de power – so dey 'bliged act hones' wid me. Dis Ekpe you done bring is wishin' I shall stick my neck inside his trap. I not stickin' my neck inside no trap. Dat de whole facks of dis matter.'

'But. . . .'

'Don' give me no "buts", Walpole – dis de firs' rule of business! Don' do no business wid crooked persons unless you in de position for control de crookedness. Now go tell Alake bring cold-cold beer out of de fridge for cool yo' hot head. An' don' waste time bringin' no more persons like dat Ekpe in for see me.'

It was this same Lionel Ekpe for whom Walpole was now waiting in a hotel bar a couple of days after receiving his letter. Punctual to the minute, with a sharp glance round the bar as if to make a record of those present and a shooting of his cuffs to display a gold bracelet watch, Ekpe took his seat, patted Walpole on the shoulder, made a quick inventory of all he was wearing and hooked the barman towards him with a forefinger. It was a tribute to Ekpe's personality that he could command the attention of barmen and waiters even when experience must have told them there was little advantage to be gained.

'Well, my friend, sad news indeed! I little thought when we last met. . . . But perhaps the breach can still be healed? If there is anything I can do in that direction. . . .'

Walpole assured him there was going to be no reconciliation, but Ekpe evidently wished to make quite certain.

'So the separation is final? You are not planning any new approach? . . . Do you maintain contact with your old employer?'

Walpole shook his head.

'In that case, my friend, I can speak freely! I will be completely open with you. Your Madam Abiose has made herself a big position. But for a young man like yourself, ambitious, with original ideas, it must have been a frustrating life!'

'It *was* at times a bit frustrating,' Walpole admitted.

'I should think so!' Ekpe took a swallow of whisky. 'Madam Abiose, with all her money, still thinks on the level of a petty trader – that was obvious in the half-hour I spent with her. But *you* . . . well, it's a question of grasp . . . grasp and imagination. What I call "vision".'

Though Walpole liked the idea of being on a grand scale and having vision, he was not willing to join in criticism of his benefactress.

'Madam Abiose may be cautious,' he admitted. 'But she's made a fortune – and she's also done everything for me. . . .'

'No doubt! Your sense of obligation does you credit. But there's another side to that.'

'What side?'

'Why, that Madam Abiose owes much to you. Who brought order into her confused interests? Who introduced the modern note? Who knocked those scheming heads together? . . . I've learned a great deal about you in the last few days.'

'I did try to get the business modernized,' Walpole conceded.

'And every managing director in Lagos knows it! . . . The Chief was only saying to me the other day . . . .'

But what the Chief had been saying never reached Walpole's ears, for Ekpe moved on without finishing his sentence, as he often did. 'So that, I suppose, is how the break finally came? Your wish to modernize – with Madam Abiose determined to keep everything in her own hands?'

Deftly as a furtune teller, posing questions as assertions, ascribing doubtful statements to others, building on what was confirmed and hastily dropping inquiries which led nowhere, Ekpe was soon in possession of the story of Walpole's long association and final quarrel with his patroness.

'. . . So then, of course, you left Madam Abiose's house? What else *could* you do? But she let you take your personal possessions? And by now you have your own bank account? . . . However it's she who'll prove the loser, my friend. You will find others to help you – but where will she find anyone to replace you? And how much you could have done with that business if you'd been given a free hand! Now we must think of the future. . . . Where are you living?'

'I lived for a week or two in a hotel. Now I've taken a room in Ebute Metta.'

'*Ebute Metta*?' Ekpe looked grave. 'You must find some-where better – these first impressions matter. . . . But perhaps you're hard up for the moment? If so, you really must allow me. . . .'

Just what he should be allowed to do if his friend lacked funds Ekpe did not reveal, for he had already learned from Walpole's quick shake of the head that he was not in need. This evidently brought relief to his mind for he caught the barman's eye and ordered two more whiskies.

'My friend' – he raised his glass with solemnity – 'you may wonder at my contacting you the moment I heard of your misfortune. . . . Possibly I was the only one of your friends to do this? Through my contacts in business circles I am often able to help friends in need. I shall be particularly glad to help you since I consider myself your debtor.'

'Your debtor?' Walpole was bewildered by the phrase and his third double whisky. 'In what way?'

'You were good enough,' Ekpe reminded him, 'to intro-duce me to Madam Abiose when her support might have been advantageous. True, she failed to make use of the oppor-tunity, and the Chief, to whom I offered the land next day, was only too happy to purchase it. However, that wasn't your fault. You did what you could for me – and I'm anxious, if opportunity offers, to do you too . . . that is, to do the same for you.'

Walpole grunted an acknowledgement.

'May I take it I am free to talk your situation over with certain of my friends? And that if anything interesting comes up I can get in touch with you?'

Walpole replied that he would indeed be grateful.

'You can count on me, my friend!' Ekpe assured him as he rose to leave. 'I shall be bearing your interests in mind.'

A note a few days later summoned Walpole to a further meeting. Mindful of Madam Abiose's methods, he had spent some of the intervening time learning all he could about the man who was now bearing his interests in mind. There was not a lot to learn and it was hardly reassuring, though neither was it altogether negative. Ekpe, Walpole learned, aroused mistrust but also respect. There was no doubt of his ability, but different opinions as to the use he made of it. Madam

Abiose with her customary bluntness had spoken of him as 'not hones' ', but no one else was prepared to be so outspoken. Ekpe was not known to have been 'in trouble', he had never gone bankrupt or been convicted in the courts, yet there was a general reluctance to become closely involved with him, an impression that he was secretive and perhaps had something he was wise to be secretive about.

The same cloud of uncertainty hung over his personal life. Nobody had met his parents. In a country where family connections are as important as passport and money to a traveller, he seemed to be without brothers or sisters, aunts or uncles. No one had ever heard him talk about his childhood, or the village he came from. No one ever claimed to have been his schoolfellow. He was obviously an educated man, but where and how had he been educated? No one believed his story that he had 'spent a year or two at an English university', yet where had he acquired his whiteman's accent and elevated style of speech? It was rumoured that he had been the prize pupil at a mission school up country, training for the priesthood, but had cleared off before ordination and some missionary funds were missing after his departure. Yet no one could say what mission school, what priesthood or what funds. Was he rich? Did he have money of his own – or did he live from hand to mouth by some sort of never-ending confidence trick? Everyone agreed that he frequented only the best bars, restaurants and night clubs. He was always expensively dressed and drove around in a white Mercedes – hallmark of Lagos high prosperity – but whether it was his own or hired; whether he borrowed it from some rich politician on whom he 'had something'; or whether it was loaned him by a generous mistress, no one could say. Did Ekpe indeed *have* a mistress, generous or otherwise?

A similar haze obscured his livelihood. He used notepaper headed 'From the Managing Director of Ekpe Enterprises', just as did the managing directors of commercial mammoths such as African Importers, Nigerian Timber or the Bight of Benin Steamship Lines. Official records showed a company registered as Ekpe Enterprises, formed 'to acquire land with a view to development and to carry on other activities consonant with the main purposes of the company.' Its capital of £100 was derisory and the names of the other directors unfamiliar. But did not Chief Efunshile, the rising politician, also operate through a company with a capital of £100, and had he not used it to become a dominant figure in the business world? And what has been done once may surely be done again?

'I have decided, my dear Walpole, to take you into partnership.'

Walpole leaned back from the table in astonishment while Ekpe took a couple of slow sips.

'Partnership in what?'

'In the new company I'm forming,' Ekpe glanced round and drew his chair closer. 'Let me begin at the commencement. Two or three years back I lent money to a builder. It was more than I could afford to risk – but the man was in trouble and I wished to help him. Matters dragged on unsatisfactorily for a while, but when that man finally *failed*' – and Walpole was surprised by the contempt his companion put into the word – 'I found myself landed with his building concern.'

Walpole understood enough about business to realize that much here was being slurred over, but Ekpe had already moved on. 'The whole affair involved me in losses and a great deal of trouble which was only sorted out a week or two ago. However, good deeds bring good rewards! The wretched man's equipment couldn't have come to me at a better time.'

'Why?'

'Because we now have the opportunity to put it to good use.'

'How?'

Ekpe flashed a glance over each shoulder before replying: 'I have an option on a piece of land. Just the place to run up a dozen houses for quick sale.'

Walpole knew that at this moment, with independence more than a vague prospect and business rapidly expanding, the housing shortage was critical for the well-off as well as for ordinary mankind.

'Where *is* this land?'

'On the way to the airport. Just off the Ikorodu road.'

'How big?'

'My option's on three acres.'

'What price?'

'Two thousand.'

'But you're not paying two thousand for three acres out there?' Walpole protested.

'Who talked about paying, my friend? I'm talking about

being asked. Wait till you hear the whole story,' and Ekpe
nodded to the barman to refill. It was essential, he explained,
to take up this option straight away. That done, he proposed
to build, not the twelve houses local planning regulations
would allow, but half that number – say six, or even four to
start with. They would be attractive houses. Not needlessly
solid or spacious, but modern in appearance and with those
fashionable accessories – flat roof, patio, air-conditioned
bedroom, outdoor barbecue and garage with sliding doors –
which prove irresistible to white businessmen, half-
established politicians and professional people whose home
serves as their advertisement.

'I sold four houses such as these to a petrol company a
month ago. They snapped them up without bothering to see
them. . . . All I made on those was the commission. It's the
builder who makes *real* money.'

'What about capital?'

'We're coming to that . . . but once the scheme is started we
won't need capital. It finances itself.'

'How can it finance itself?'

'Look. . . . We get three or four houses half built, foundations laid, walls up to the first floor. You follow me?'

'Yes.'

'On the half-built houses we obtain a mortgage. It needn't
be big – say three thousand a house. That gives us money for
completion. Once a couple are up, I sell them for eight or nine
thousand each – and we switch the mortgage to others which
are half built. Once we've sold four or five houses our credit's
established. Next time we get a big loan from the bank and
develop a whole property at one go.'

'But suppose we *don't* sell our first few houses?'

'Come, my friend!' Ekpe rapped out sharply. 'Can you
show me a dozen smart new houses for sale in this city? If you
can, I'll find six purchasers for each.'

'H'm, yes,' Walpole had to assent. 'And when those first
three acres are built up? What then?'

'We get hold of three more – or five – or ten. It's the first step
that counts. Once we're nominated, we're elected. And after
handling a couple of small estates, we go after the big stuff.'

'Big stuff?'

'Offices. That's what the rich men are moving into now.
Offices in Lagos for new government departments and all the
overseas firms waiting to come in. All these years the British

kept everything to themselves. But once Independence opens
the door they'll *all* pour in, Americans, Germans, Japanese –
the lot! They'll all need offices – and there aren't any! In six or
seven years' time we'll be providing them – at a price!'

Walpole sat silent to conceal his rising excitement.

'Even office blocks,' observed Ekpe slowly, 'are only the
thin edge of the wedge.'

'What d'you mean?'

'Where the killing comes,' and he ground his cigarette into
the ashtray as though squeezing its last drop of lifeblood from
it, 'where the *killing* comes is when we float our company off
on to the public, and collect two hundred thousand pounds
apiece. Once over the first hurdle, my friend, it's all as simple
as falling into the lagoon.'

The metaphor sounded ominous to Walpole. 'Then why
isn't everybody doing it?'

'A great many are – or thinking of it. But most people are
frightened by the obstacles.'

'Obstacles?'

'They fear there'll be all kinds of regulations and restric-
tions. They worry over getting roads made . . . drainage and
electricity laid on. . . . The things that can come unstuck.'

'But can't we come unstuck too? How about all the licences
and the help we'll need from various departments?'

Ekpe smiled the thin triumphant smile of a man who has
saved his ace for the last trick. 'The land on which I have an
option forms part of a big estate. A hundred acres altogether.
Guess who's developing the estate?'

'No idea.'

'Chief Julius Ogun – and he's backed by the Holy Life
Insurance Company.'

Against his will Walpole let out a whistle. 'But is he *allowed*
to do that? I mean, isn't he chairman of two committees of the
City Council?'

'Happily for us, he is,' Ekpe agreed, 'so of course he has to
keep in the background. However, he organized the deal and
means to draw the profits. It's his nephew who gave me the
chance to come in, in return for a small favour. . . . And
now,' Ekpe continued, following up his advantage, 'you've
asked me a lot of questions. Suppose I ask one or two?'

'By all means.'

'Well, first things first. How much capital can you put up?'
And without even waiting for Walpole's reply, he pressed on,

'Let's not fence with one another. I expect you to be as candid as myself. I have the option and the building firm. Where there *may* be room for a partner is to put up initial capital. My building firm has to pay cash for materials' (So it *has* been bankrupt, Walpole thought) 'and the men paid their wages month by month. The option has to be taken up and the pump primed till we can take out mortgages. I like you. I admire what you did for Madam Abiose. I never forget a good turn, so I'm giving you first offer. But the point is – *how much cash can you put up?*'

Walpole had inwardly resolved on no account to venture more than half his means, but now found himself calculating what was the utmost he could raise. 'I suppose I might just manage to lay hands on fifteen hundred,' he said lamely.

'Fifteen hundred pounds! Less than two thousand – when I thought you were going to say ten or twelve? What on earth can we do with fifteen hundred? We couldn't even make a start on under five thousand.'

'In that case,' said Walpole, not without relief, 'you can count me out.'

Ekpe flung himself back as if bitten by an insect. 'This is too much, Walpole! From some people, yes! But not from you – a friend!'

'What's the matter? What have I said? I'm only pointing out. . . .'

Ekpe raised a hand. 'No more! You led me to talk about my plans, to unfold a confidential project. You let me offer you partnership – something I've never done in my whole life before. Now you take the first excuse to back out as though I were trying to get money out of you! . . . I never do business with people who don't trust me. It's my *one* condition.'

'But I'm not saying I don't trust you,' Walpole pleaded. 'I just haven't the capital, and I know nothing about building.'

'That's no handicap.' Ekpe assured him, seemingly mollified. 'Some of the people making money out of building know nothing either. We've got a first-class foreman – that's all that matters.'

'But what about the money? I can't make fifteen hundred into five thousand. I only wish I could,' and, feeling he had escaped the danger, Walpole allowed himself to add, 'The whole idea appeals to me very much.'

Ekpe stared hard at Walpole as though engaged in some complicated inner reckoning. 'I'm glad you feel like that,' he said at last. 'but fifteen hundred really is too little.' He thought again. 'Well, I suppose we might start in the very smallest way – provided, that is. . . .'

'Provided what?'

'Provided you can lay hands on just five hundred more. On two thousand . . . I can see the way, I think . . . I believe we might just manage it.'

Walpole gulped; there was something uncanny about Ekpe's estimate of his savings, but if he was going to risk three-quarters of them on a venture, he might just as well risk the lot. 'I might . . . just . . . be able to find another five hundred,' he conceded.

'Good!' and Ekpe flashed another of his high-speed mental photographs as if to record the scene. 'Good, my friend! And now I want you to satisfy yourself completely on all the matters we've discussed. Here's a note of the site. Go out there. Talk to Chief Julius's agent. Check on everything. The option is with my lawyers – let me give you their address. And provided you find everything in order, as you're bound to do, then I suggest. . . .'

'What?'

'I suggest you meet me in three days' time – that's to say Friday afternoon at two o'clock – at the lawyer's. I'll have the deed of partnership prepared. All you need do is sign.'

'Okay,' Walpole assented, with an uneasy sense that he might be fixing the time and place of his own execution. 'Friday afternoon at two o'clock.'

'Shake hands on it, my friend,' said Ekpe, 'and be sure to bring the cheque.'

17
A Fairly Square Deal

The day after his meeting with Ekpe, Walpole went out to look over the estate and found everything much as it had been described. Work was going ahead, roads had been marked out, water mains laid, trenches dug for the electricity cables and the clerk in the contractors' hut confirmed that essential services were being carried over the whole site. At the lawyer's office where he went next to examine the option, Walpole also found everything in order, and so was in good spirits when he set off in the afternoon to inspect the third leg of the stool on which his partnership would rest – the building concern Ekpe had taken over when the man he 'befriended' had been so ungrateful as to go bankrupt.

The site was some miles out of town, and the quarter a poor one in which tumbledown dwellings of wood, corrugated iron and concrete sprawled over waste land among patches scratched up by hens that looked too ill-fed to lay anything but pebbles. The gardens grew only tin cans and prickly cactus and their borders had long since dissolved into the roadway which meandered like a tarmac river between sandy banks. At the address given him Walpole could see nothing except two huts, enclosed by a high wire fence and a spiked gate fitted with a padlock; there was little in the way of building equipment or material, and he supposed he had been misdirected. On inquiry at a petrol station up the road, however, he learned that this was indeed the place he sought: 'De builder dat work dere, he done bankruptured hisself.' The foreman, Kwaku, was likely to be in one of the bars not far away, and when darkness fell a 'watchnight' might be coming on duty who could answer questions. Walpole made his way back and climbed the fence at one corner. The larger hut was presumably the office, and peering through the dirty window he made out a desk, filing cabinet, a couple of chairs and an old calendar; the heaps of sacks in the corner would be the bed on which the watchnight 'watched'. There was another smaller hut on wooden wheels which would serve as headquarters on the building site, also a couple of cement-mixers, a ladder or two, three or four wheelbarrows, some picks, spades and shovels chained together, a pile of wooden poles used for scaffolding, some meagre stocks of bricks, breeze-blocks, sand and other building materials, and an abandoned lorry. He had not expected much, but this was a shock indeed.

Back in his small room overlooking the lagoon Walpole tried to think out his situation. The wretched state of the building concern gave sufficient grounds for backing out; not only was there virtually nothing there, but it was clear that he could not trust his partner. Ekpe must have known how matters stood, but supposed that Walpole would not trouble to go out there or did not know enough to size matters up if he did. In any case, all Walpole had to do now was to write a letter calling off the deal, then carry it round and leave it with Ekpe or his lawyers. He need not even meet his unreliable partner again.

But supposing he broke with Ekpe, where did that leave him? On his two thousand pounds he could live for several years, but where and how would he find a job? And in any case did he want just to find a job? The answer was 'No' – had he merely wanted a job he'd have done better to stay with his patroness. What he was after was not slow achievement, but dramatic success. He longed to poke out his enemie's eye, and confound his former mistress with regret. His aim was to flash up into the business sky like a comet, and to do this he must take a chance. Such a chance was now being offered him by Ekpe, and it was evident there were risks attached. However, a chance of this sort – a chance to make thousands in a year and establish himself as one of the up-and-coming businessmen of Lagos – was not going to be offered without risk. The question he had to decide was whether he could cope with Ekpe. Had he the sharpness of mind and resolution to handle such a man? His mind went back to the warning given by Madam Abiose, and her principle of never doing business with anyone dishonest unless she already held the upper hand. Such a principle might serve Madam Abiose well – though it had cost her at least one good opportunity – but it was inapplicable to someone starting out. And as for Ekpe's trickiness, this was surely something which could prove an asset as well as a danger. Walpole had no doubt about his possible partner's ability; his shrewdness and capacity to see into a proposition were impressive and, allied to his own energy and experience, might make a formidable alliance. So what was he to decide?

Though Walpole had gone through the motions of examining the position and arguing the matter out, at the back of his mind it had been decided from the first. To withdraw was to admit himself inadequate to cope with a tricky customer; to go ahead was to back himself and his capacities. There can be no great gains – at least no quick gains – without risk. Moreover Ekpe's appearance just at the moment when he needed to find some new direction could hardly be mere chance. There was a sense of destiny about it. Even his patroness's warning served as encouragement when he considered how glorious a victory it would be, what a knock-out blow for those who had failed to appreciate his talents, if he should achieve his own success through a man with whom Madam Abiose, despite her long experience and vast resources, had not dared to do business!

'Have you the cheque?' Ekpe's demand, without preliminary greeting, brought home to Walpole how painful his partner's anxiety had been.

'I have.'

'Good! Well – here's the draft agreement. Read it if you want – but let's have everything settled on the spot. The sooner we get things moving, the sooner the money will come in.'

Settling, however, took longer than Ekpe was expecting. He had noted Walpole's eagerness, but was mistaken in supposing this would cause him to leave prudence behind.

'What's this?' Walpole demanded before he had got half way down the page.

'What's what?'

'Why, it says here that you get two-thirds of profit after working expenses are deducted, and I only one-third. What kind of partnership is that?'

'What in God's name d'you expect?' demanded Ekpe. 'I'm putting in the option – worth two thousand if it's worth a penny – *and* the whole building concern. All you're putting in is working capital – and far too little of it! That's *at least* two to one in my favour.' He paused. 'After all, my friend, there *is* such a thing as what the British call "fair play".'

'That building concern of yours. . . .'

'What about it?'

'At first sight, I reckon it's worth. . . .'

'You mean you've seen it?'

'What there *is* of it. It didn't take long. A man up the road told me this was the place I was looking for – otherwise I'd have thought I'd come to the wrong spot.'

'Possibly it doesn't *look* much,' Ekpe conceded. 'Contractors' headquarters never do, even the biggest. But wait till you go inside . . . there's a lot of excellent equipment.'

'Go inside! I've been over every inch. I spent half a day there.'

'But how on earth? . . . '

'You can't understand how I could spend more than five minutes? Then let me tell you what I was doing – making a complete inventory.'

'An inventory?'

'Yes. Surely you did the same before deciding it's worth two thousand pounds?'

For once Ekpe was jolted out of his composure: 'Well, not exactly. . . . I've a fair idea of what's there, of course. But no actual *inventory*.'

'Let me get this clear,' said Walpole. 'You're claiming that set-up is worth two thousand – which entitles you to two-thirds of the profit – and yet you haven't even made out an inventory?'

'At *least* two thousand,' Ekpe asserted. 'That's probably an underestimate.'

'Everything on that site,' Walpole asserted coolly, 'could be replaced *new* for four hundred pounds – apart from the lorry. That's valueless, but it'll cost us a thousand to replace unless I can put it into working order.'

Ekpe gulped, though the implication of Walpole saying "us" was not wasted on him. 'But in any case, Walpole, the option alone. . . .'

'Yes,' Walpole agreed, 'the option's okay, provided we can pay in instalments. But to sum up, my two thousand cash is worth as much as your option and the whole builder's yard together.'

Ekpe argued long and bitterly, but Walpole stood firm, and it was finally agree that their partnership should be on equal terms. However, this was only the first hurdle. Walpole was prepared for a long wrestling match, and the conviction that his opponent wanted it all signed and sealed gave him confidence to prolong the struggle. The next question was working expenses. Until the first two houses had been sold, he argued, neither of them should draw a shilling in salary or expenses. Money should go on nothing except materials, wages and instalments on the option.

'But this is madness!' Ekpe exploded. 'Okay! If you don't want to draw salary, I won't either – though I can't imagine what you're going to live on. But expenses are different. I understand *you* won't have any expenses. You won't be spending much time on the firm's business. You won't be travelling around and interviewing clients. But I have to *sell* the houses. I've got to get about, talk to big firms, entertain the kind of people who are in the market. I'm quite prepared to handle all this – but I can't do it without buying clients a lunch and a couple of whiskies!'

'You can buy all the lunches and whiskies necessary,' Walpole conceded, adding – as Ekpe looked up with relief – 'once the first two houses have been sold.'

'God Almighty! How am I supposed to sell the first two?'

'What did you say to me yourself three days ago?'

'Well – what *did* I say?'

'That if I could show you a dozen houses for sale at reasonable prices, you'd guarantee to find half a dozen buyers for each one. Well? We shall soon have two houses. Only *two*. And we want just one buyer for each. . . .'

At last when they had gone through the whole document line by line and Ekpe was about to sign, Walpole raised his final point.

'By the way, I've sacked your watchnight.'

'Why on earth?'

'He didn't keep watch. Also he was selling our supplies.'

'How d'you know?'

Walpole explained that the discoloured state of the ground showed there had been materials lying there at least until the last few days. When he asked the watchman to explain, the man denied he knew anything. 'I could see he was lying. So I sacked him. If your foreman Kwaku had his eyes open he'd have seen this too. Unless he's in the racket.'

'Surely you're not accusing Kwaku?'

'I've no evidence one way or the other. But if he spends his time in bars he's not keeping his eyes on our property.'

'Kwaku's all right. I'd vouch for Kwaku as myself,' Ekpe protested. 'But since you've already got rid of the night watchman, I accept his dismissal – provided you find someone in his place.'

'I've already done that. A reliable man starts tonight.'

Finally the agreement was signed and the cheque which would provide the new firm's bank account handed over. Cheques on this account, it was agreed, would require both partners' signatures. And now for the first time Ekpe relaxed, proposing they go along to a nearby hotel and celebrate with a bottle of champagne. Walpole agreed and the two men drank and chatted for an hour. Walpole would have enjoyed the drink more but for his feeling that Ekpe regarded the signing of the contract and handing over the cheque as an achievement in itself. He also suspected that, despite their agreement over expenses, the notes with which Ekpe paid for the bottle would be coming out of his own £2,000.

When Walpole told his partner that 'somebody reliable' would be starting straight away as watchnight, Ekpe supposed he had contacted some suitable man, perhaps an ex-employee of Madam Abiose, but the person Walpole had in mind was himself, and it was while lying in the office hut on two or three sacks that he was now planning his next steps.

'You won't be spending much time on the firm's business,' Ekpe had said, evidently anticipating that since they were to draw neither salary nor expenses, Walpole would need to find himself a job, and it was this same question of a job to which he was applying himself, keeping one ear open for sounds from the compound. Though Ekpe was confident of having extracted Walpole's last penny of capital, this was not quite the case, Walpole had still nearly £200 in the bank. So the choice now lay between finding a job, thus keeping his small capital intact – or risking everything to concentrate on the building venture, which would mean eating up his savings week by week. The safer course was tempting. However he had not gone into this business for safety but to make his fortune, and his only hope of doing this lay in the partnership. Since it was plain he could trust neither Ekpe nor the foreman, he ought never to have gone in at all unless prepared to keep watch on them with both eyes. . . . Well, if that was the price he must pay to make his fortune, Walpole was prepared to pay it.

Next morning, on starting to clean the hut and tidy the compound, Walpole soon found there was no broom or bucket and that the telephone, like the water, had been cut off. To get these reconnected he must be mobile, so his first task was to get the broken-down lorry moving. At the garage where he had previously called to make inquiries he bought petrol and oil, with a battery and tools from a wrecked vehicle, got the owner to drive him back and was soon at work. Time passed quickly and it was almost midday when, as he was about to crawl out from beneath and try to crank the engine, Walpole heard a shout.

'Hey you, man! What you doin' down dere?'

A heavy middle-aged man squatted beside Walpole's head, gazing with interest at his struggles.

'What *you* should be doing if your name's Kwaku. Why

weren't you here long since? It's midday now. And who's stolen the oil and petrol – and everything else around this place?' Angrily Walpole scrambled to his feet.

'Ho, sah! You bin new boss – Mr Abiose? Happy for see you, sah! When de ole boss done bankrupted hisself, he take away mos' everytin' roun' dis place, sah.'

'Why weren't you here at eight?'

'Don' git no orders for come here, sah. Nobody don' tell Kwaku nothin'.'

'Well, I tellin' you now. We startin' work. Soonest I get engine goin' I fix for connect telephone and water – see?'

'Yes, sah – very good, sah.'

'An you, Kwaku, wash an' scrub de office.'

'Yes, sah. You done fix cleaner boys, sah?'

'No, Kwaku. No cleaner boys. Only Kwaku. Now – go buy brush, cloth, bucket, An' come back one-time!'

Within a week Walpole had his office functioning, and was staying there all day as well as keeping watch. A little 'dash' in the right quarters had got water and telephone connected, the place had been smartened up with paint, and a sign, knocked up out of old planks and with stencilled lettering, announced that 'Ekpe and Abiose, Builders and Contractors' were in business. Walpole had given some thought to the order of the names: he would naturally have preferred 'Abiose and Ekpe', but he considered he was likely to have rows enough with his partner over serious issues, so would be wise to indulge him over inessentials.

Meantime Kwaku and three newly-hired labourers were busy on the building site. Once on the job Kwaku seemed to know how to get things moving. He had their plots marked out and was clearing away scrub where the first houses would go up. Once this was done he set the men on to digging foundations. And so, despite misgivings, Walpole was in a contented frame of mind when at the end of the first month he went back for a couple of nights' rest to his room in Ebute Metta. He had, he felt, shown Ekpe he was not to be trifled with. He had taken charge of the office, put an end to pilfering, organized a flow of supplies, and got Kwaku and his men working. As he pushed open the plank door of his room he saw on the floor a mauve envelope in Madam Abiose's forceful scrawl. The contents did not take long to read.

Dear Walpole,
When this Ekpe done cheat you out of all you earned with me by your
hard work, you go see Mr Chukuma, lawyer. Give him this note and
he find some way for helping you.

There followed the familiar signature, and there was a sealed
letter for the lawyer enclosed. Walpole was about to tear up
both and throw the pieces into the lagoon. Despite her
affection for him, it was plain that his old patroness resented
his seizing an opportunity she had proved too timid to accept.
Ekpe did indeed need watching, nobody could appreciate that
better than he did. But Ekpe would need to get up very early in
the morning if he intended to cheat his new partner out of
everything he had. At the last moment, about to tear the letter
in half, Walpole hesitated and then slipped it in a drawer. It
was not that he would ever need to make use of her advice, but
the message had been kindly meant and deserved to be treated
with consideration.

18
Heavy Labour

For Walpole there now began the most arduous period of his
life. As watchnight he slept at the yard, lying on sacks and
getting his own food on a stove, and by day drove the lorry to
collect materials needed by the building workers. His back and
legs ached continually and his hands were raw and bleeding, so
that he longed for Sunday as he had not done since the early
days with his old patroness. Even Sunday was no day of rest
since he spent it patching the lorry or checking through bills
and records, but at least he was working to his own time and
could lie on in the morning for a couple of hours.

On all that concerned the day-to-day progress of the job
Walpole took orders from the foreman Kwaku. He had never
liked Kwaku and liked him no better after having known him
for a year, but he saw that Kwaku understood his job; he

worked and kept the others working, though Walpole could see that the labourers no more trusted Kwaku than he did himself. Once when Walpole was driving in to collect wages and explained that he could not get back that evening before dark, Kwaku volunteered to put his bike on the lorry, pick up the men's money at the office and ride back with it. There was an immediate outcry of dissent and the one who seemed to be their leader, Hamisu, grunted: 'Mr Walpole fetch money. . . . He give um to us in mo'ning.' The rest nodded approval.

Walpole had taken to Hamisu from the first. He was an enormous man with strength to match his size and where the other labourers staggered under a sack of cement or hefted it between two, Hamisu would gather a sack under each arm and stalk off to the mixer. He was illiterate, lacking even a smattering of education, but his whole body was full of natural intelligence. Like most of the workmen he employed a single tool, an *ada* or machete, for almost every job. This was a long, heavy knife, curved like a scimitar, with two wooden pieces bolted to it for grip. With this instrument, which needed constant sharpening, he cut grass, cleared scrub, dug channels, smoothed the edges of planks and trimmed bricks or building blocks. To Hamisu his *ada* was an extension of his arm and appeared to be in equally intimate contact with his brain.

And now after twelve months the foundations of three houses were completed and the walls of one beginning to rise. From time to time, however, there had been incidents which prevented Walpole forming exaggerated hopes. The first had been the row they had when Ekpe learned he was working as a driver for the lorry besides acting as night watchman, and flew into one of his rages.

'What are you up to now? I tell you I'm not having this. Kwaku is in charge, not you. He should be left to get on with things.'

'So he is. As regards building, he's the boss. I take orders from him.'

'The men on the job won't like this. Nor Kwaku. They'll look on you as a spy.'

'Quite right. That's what I am.'

'It's absurd! You won't stand it two months. You'll be forced to pack it in. . . . And what do your friends think of you – working as a common labourer?'

'I have no friends. Any I have, I don't care what they think.'

A more serious anxiety for Walpole was the fact that there seemed to be no architect responsible for their part of the site. Ekpe had given him to understand that the architect on the main site would be responsible for their section also, but he, when approached, denied any connection, and when Walpole mentioned this to Ekpe, he brushed the matter aside.

'When I took up the option I got a set of the plans being used on the main development. We're just following those.'

'But what about supervision? A set of plans isn't the same thing as an architect.'

'Hell, Walpole. You're always fussing about something. Kwaku's perfectly capable of putting up houses. He's been doing it for years – whether there was an architect on the job or not.'

The partners now met only once a month for 'board meetings'. Walpole would put on a clean shirt, turn up at the office and report progress. Ekpe would hand him a typed slip showing their position at the bank, and they would jointly sign the necessary cheques. Walpole was always anxious to get as much paid off as they could. Ekpe, like all financiers, wanted to delay every payment to the last minute. In order, he said, to save Walpole needless journeys to their bank on the Marina, he had arranged to collect the money for wages himself, and he would have this made up into packets ready for Walpole to take back and distribute.

One morning in the course of his work Walpole made a call on one of their regular suppliers to pick up cement.

'You here agin?' queried the clerk. 'You comin' here three day back. How many houses you go for build?'

'Only three,' Walpole replied.

'Three!' The man rolled his eyes. 'Dese bin fine houses! I s'pose you buildin' ten!'

His casual remark brought back all Walpole's doubts about the foreman, whose recent amenability had added to Walpole's uneasiness. Kwaku had never shown interest in anything but money, and his pay as a foreman was not high. So what had he to be satisfied about? It was not hard to guess, and Walpole cursed himself that to avoid more rows with his partner he had for weeks been damping down his suspicions. The truth could only be that Kwaku was ordering far more than the necessary supplies and selling the surplus for himself. Once his suspicions were aroused it did not take long for Walpole to find proof of Kwaku's dishonesty. At his next meeting with Ekpe he showed him a set of invoices from their suppliers, compared with the amount Hamisu told him was being used daily on the site.

'We have to get rid of Kwaku,' Walpole concluded. 'It won't be difficult to replace him. I know two or three who could do the job for us. I'll soon get this sorted out.'

But to Walpole's surprise his partner showed unexpected reluctance. He neither agreed nor flew into one of his rages.

'It certainly doesn't look good,' he said. 'And since I, in a sense, appointed Kwaku – that is, I took him on with the concern – I accept some responsibility. But in the situation we're in, I really don't know what course to take.'

His moderate tone impressed Walpole. 'Then what d'you suggest?' he asked.

'Depends how far the matter goes,' Ekpe observed judicially. 'If it's just a question of his stealing a hundred bricks or so and a few bags of cement to floor his kitchen – there's no great harm. Every foreman does the same. The fact that the men dislike him may only be due to his making them work hard. . . . And he's saving us far more than he steals through our not having to employ an architect.'

'I can see there's a "for" and "against",' Walpole admitted, 'and it's possible that anyone else we appoint may also be a crook. But when our resources are so small, it seems madness to keep a man we know is crooked in a key position. If I were sitting on top of him all day I might be able to keep control. But that's out of the question – driving around daytimes and spending all night at the yard.'

A look came into Ekpe's eyes as though an idea had struck him. He started to speak: 'I tell you what . . . the thing to do is. . . .'

'What are you suggesting?'

'Nothing, my dear fellow. Nothing as yet. Well, we'll see. . . .' His voice trailed off, and then recovered. 'Leave it with me, Walpole. *Leave it with me.*'

And with this Walpole had to rest content.

When the weekend came, and Walpole called in at his room for a few hours' quiet and a supper of fried bean cakes bought from a street-seller, he found a letter under the door. The address was typed, giving it a formal look. The notepaper was headed with the firm's name, Ekpe and Abiose.

Dear Walpole,
I have been thinking over what you told me the other day, and the doubts you expressed about the honesty of the foreman, Kwaku. I am glad you brought this matter to my attention and only regret you did not do so the moment your suspicions were aroused.

Since you think it best to discharge this man, I agree on condition that you yourself take sole responsibility for the building side of our operation. Let me say that I have every confidence in your ability and the experience you have acquired, and I am sure this side of our joint activities will be safe in your hands. Since you will now be working all day on the site, I presume you will find someone to take over from you as driver and night watchman.

Meantime I shall continue to apply myself to the financial side of our business and am happy to tell you that I expect shortly to negotiate the sale of the first three houses. The client is a big importing firm which requires them as company houses for their European staff. This firm is prepared, as soon as the main construction work is complete and the roofs are on, to put down £5,000 in part payment on each house, subject to their surveyor's approval.

All I need from you to complete negotiations is a letter confirming that I am entitled to act on behalf of the partnership in all financial matters. Final agreement will of course be subject to your subsequent approval.

If you accept these proposals, in which I have tried to give practical shape to your wishes as expressed at our last meeting, I shall be glad to receive confirmation by return.

 Yours sincerely,

 Lionel Ekpe

For more than an hour Walpole sat turning this letter over in his hands. Only a few months since, when he learned Walpole was working as driver and watchnight, Ekpe had sworn that he would never stand the strain and would break down under it, yet here he was, only a short time later, expressing confidence and suggesting that he take full charge. This was a triumph gained by his own efforts over his partner's distrust, and when he thought back to their last more friendly meeting, and read again the expression of 'confidence in your ability and the experience you have acquired', Walpole felt a glow of satisfaction.

There was also the practical aspect. Five thousand down on each of the houses opened up golden prospects. They had agreed to ask eight thousand five hundred for each house – not unreasonable in view of current demand. Fifteen thousand in hand, with over ten thousand more to follow, meant that three more houses could be started on the present site while they looked around for a larger development. A loan from the bank would now present no problem, and after that . . . well, some of the biggest firms in the country had started in an equally modest way to become national institutions within ten years.

Walpole looked round his tiny room with its walls of battered planking and broken windowpane. He looked at the remains of greasy bean cakes wrapped in soiled paper, and thought over his solitary life during the past year. In a very few weeks, he told himself, he would be dining in hotels and restaurants, going home afterwards to his own house or flat. Beautiful women would be glad to be in his company and console him for past loneliness. He would be written about in the newspapers, telephoned by journalists and his opinion asked on issues of the day, all of which would, of course, get back to Madam Abiose and those small-time intriguers who had tricked him out of his hard-earned position.

Walpole read the letter through again and yet again. As he did so a query came up in his mind as to why his partner had written this formal letter, instead of talking the matter out over a drink. There was also a phrase near the end which aroused momentary suspicion: 'confirming that I am entitled to act on behalf of the partnership in all financial matters'. But this was no more than the equivalent of what he had already conceded to Walpole on the building side, and there was the further admission that 'Final agreement will of course be subject to your subsequent approval.'

What, Walpole asked himself, could he reasonably object to in that?

Next morning he borrowed a typewriter and wrote an acceptance of his partner's proposal.

19

An Issue of Confidence

With such prospects before him, Walpole flung himself into the work with fresh enthusiasm. He promoted one of the labourers to be driver and planned, as soon as he found a clerk and watchnight for the office, to go back to living in Ebute Metta where the driver would call for him with the lorry every morning. But where could he find an honest clerk? Taking an hour off one afternoon, Walpole went to see his old friend and colleague Thaddeus. Thaddeus leaped off the ladder from which he was stacking books on an upper shelf, and rushed across the store to give Walpole an exultant hug. There was no problem about leaving the place, he explained in answer to Walpole's invitation to come out for a drink: 'I now have two-three assistants. . . . Hey, Wilson, you take charge while I go with Mr Abiose.' At his name the assistants looked up and Walpole saw from their expression that echoes of his departure had by no means died away.

Walpole quickly put his friend in the picture over all that had happened during the past year before asking if he could recommend a good man to take charge of what was now a fair quantity of supplies at the yard, and also serve as watchnight. He must be trustworthy, literate enough to keep accounts, and have the strength to load and unload. Thaddeus mentioned a clerk who had formerly worked for him but left to take a job in a firm which failed, leaving him stranded. He would be seeing this man, Akin, in a day or two and, if still unplaced, would send him along.

'Well, an' how you'self gettin' on with this Ekpe?' Thaddeus inquired.

Walpole laughed. 'He's not so bad as they say. Of course, he's tricky – but show him you stand no nonsense and you can handle him okay.'

'I see you still that same Walpole!' declared Thaddeus admiringly, adding after a pause; 'But with a man like Ekpe I guess you boun' to keep watchin' *all* the time. . . . I thought mebbe he would be stickin' one or two of his fingers into that new office block.'

'Which block?'

'Why – the one everyone talk 'bout, that's goin' up near the racecourse.'

'Who's financing it?'

'Oh, the usual – Chief Julius Ogun, Mr Johnson and the rest. But they take no chances. They've brung in three-four top politicians.'

'Why so? Why share with someone else?'

Thaddeus looked at Walpole in surprise: 'Why, to make sure the government buys the building. The block'll be sold before it's up – and for double what it's cost.'

The man Thaddeus recommended proved suitable and was taken on, and when the day for his monthly meeting with Ekpe came round Walpole was already asking as he came into the room:

'What news of the big deal: Is our fifteen thousand banked?'

Ekpe shook his head despondently.

'Why not?'

'I can't get hold of anyone to finalize things.'

'Sounds unlike you,' Walpole remarked.

'What does?'

'Not being able to get hold of someone you want. And not getting money that's been promised.'

Ekpe laughed uneasily. 'What are you suggesting?'

'They may be trying to back out. And if so why not let them? Forget this lot and find someone else. It must be easy with all these new firms coming into the country.'

'Oh, they won't back out – I'm sure of that. They mean to have the houses. It's just getting them to put money down that's difficult.'

'Who *are* these damned people anyway?' Walpole demanded.

Ekpe hesitated. 'I'd rather not say till the deal's complete.'

'Come off it!' Walpole urged. 'We're partners, man. I've as much right to know as you have.'

Ekpe turned thunderous. 'Look, Walpole, am I handling this – or you? I've told you I'd rather say nothing until the agreement is signed. Damn it – I'm entitled to some degree of confidence.'

'Calm down! But I don't see why you can't tell me the firm's *name*.'

'And I'm asking you not to press me for the moment,' Ekpe replied. 'After all, I *am* the financial director.'

Walpole checked the retort springing to his lips. 'Very well,' he conceded. 'Keep your secret for one month. But I'll want to know everything at our next meeting, whether the deal goes through or not.'

'It'll have gone through by then,' Ekpe answered soothingly. 'I promise.'

A couple of times during the next month Walpole phoned Ekpe to see if there was any news. The first time an office girl said he was out, and the second time he replied himself, assuring Walpole everything was in hand and the matter would be settled by the month's end. However, something more than usually evasive in his manner added to Walpole's uneasiness. Partly acting on a hunch and because he had no one else to consult, he phoned Thaddeus suggesting they meet on Sunday, when he explained his anxiety over a drink.

'We've sold three houses to a firm who want them for their staff. They've promised to put down five thousand pounds on each house, but now they're hedging. It's gone on like this six weeks and we badly need the money.'

'What firm is it?'

'That's the trouble. Ekpe won't tell me. He's promised to say at our next meeting.'

'When's that?'

'In a fortnight.'

'Why he not tellin' you now?'

'Makes it a matter of confidence. . . . Says he leaves me to run my side of things, so I should leave him to run his.'

'H'm,' grunted Thaddeus, 'your partner's a fine man to be talkin' 'bout "confidence". You should hear what's said of him in the business world. . . So what he tells you is this firm done buy the houses, but won't pay money over?'

'That's what he says.'

'And meantime he not tellin' you this firm's name?'

'Till the end of the month.'

'But if he can tell you in two weeks – why he not tellin' you now? He got somethin' in mind!'

Walpole considered. 'You mean he's up to some game – which will be completed by the month's end?'

'Which he *hopes* is completed by month's end. . . . But when that day come 'long – maybe he just puttin' you off again.'

'He'd better not try,' said Walpole threateningly.

'He may not *try*. Maybe he just do it.'

'How?'

'By not turning up. . . . By saying he gone sick. Why don't you go find this firm's name in Ekpe's office? Make love to his secretary. Poke around his papers. Look at phone numbers on his blotting pad.'

'I wouldn't learn anything. He's too secretive.'

'Wait a minute!' exclaimed Thaddeus. 'What you know 'bout these clients? What has he told you?'

'They're a big importing firm who need houses for their European staff – that is, if Ekpe's telling truth.'

'About the firm I 'spect he is. It mus' come out in the end, so he get no gain for lying.' He paused. 'There can't be too many firms in Lagos lookin' for three-four houses . . . importers . . . bringing in European staff.'

'You mean we can find the firm's name for ourselves? But how will we be better off if we know?'

Thaddeus opened a wide eye. 'Your troubles done turn yo' head, my friend. If Ekpe hidin' name, he hidin' it for gain something – so it boun' to help if you know what he hidin'.'

'Then how do we find out?'

'I got it!' Thaddeus burst out. 'The Islands Estate Agency. . . . That's where big import firms go for findin' houses.'

'But they won't tell you their client's business.'

'Listen, my friend, I ring from the bookshop makin' appointment. When I see them, I say I've an inquiry from big publishing house in England . . . goin' into partnership with government for print schoolbooks. . . . They sendin' out three-four top executives. . . . I seen your estate, and it look just right. My clients are ready put down money in advance. . . . if houses still available.'

'Good for you, Thaddeus! And if the agent tells you an offer's already made?'

'I ask is it definite? And for sure I gettin' the name of that firm out of him before I leave.'

The double wish – to help a friend who had befriended him, coupled with the masculine desire to show himself sharper than that friend – drove Thaddeus to prompt action, and the very next evening he called in at Walpole's room.

'Good God! Is this where you livin', Walpole?'

'For the last few weeks,' Walpole answered. 'Before that I slept in the builder's yard on sacks.'

The contrast between his friend's grim living space and his

luxurious life with Madam Abiose struck Thaddeus, and he put a kindly arm round Walpole's shoulder.

'Did you learn anything?' Walpole asked.

'I did! The firm after your houses are the Italian contractors, Crespi. Same firm who puttin' up that new block.'

Walpole whistled. 'Anything else?'

'Yes, they done pay seventeen thousand on your houses two week back.'

Walpole's first thought, once he was by himself, was to confront his partner, ram excuses down his throat and demand half the money. However he was dealing with a tricky customer who might well spin him a long story, promise to produce a cheque next day – and meantime, perhaps, leave the country. What puzzled and angered Walpole most was the thought that at this moment their firm was on the verge of a breakthrough and that all Ekpe need do was handle the business honestly. But at this his patroness's description came back into his mind. . . . 'He not able to act hones' even if he makin' more money for hisself dat way.' Ekpe must have seen, or thought he saw, some chance to make more money more quickly than by waiting for honest business to produce a profit. What he was up to Walpole could not even guess. He was out of his depth and must seek help. He thought for a moment of going to his old patroness, but that would involve admitting she had been right all along and that he had acted like a fool in ignoring her advice. Then he remembered Madam Abiose's letter advising him how to act, 'when this Ekpe done cheat you out of all you earned with me by your hard work'.

Walpole had no need to turn up his patroness's letter to recall the name of Mr Chukuma. Mr Chukuma, close friend and confidant of Madam Abiose, whose taste in ties Walpole had once been urged to follow, could be expected to give him a gruelling time, but he would at least advise him what to do. Walpole rang Mr Chukuma's office and arranged an appointment for the earliest moment he could be seen, in a couple of days' time. Then he called round at the bank in the Marina for a statement of the firm's joint account. The clerk did not recognize him, so that he was obliged to produce identification and while waiting for the statement Walpole realized he had never been in the bank before. He cursed his own folly in leaving Ekpe to draw money and obtain their monthly statements. Concentrated on the building, he had been so

careless of his interests that his partner might easily have
withdrawn all their capital and supplied the sums needed for
wages out of some personal account.

After ten minutes of waiting, the slip passed across the
counter showed exactly what Walpole was fearing, a balance
of a hundred pounds or so, the depleted remnant of his own
original investment.

Mr Lawrence Chukuma, as everybody of substance in Lagos
knew, was senior partner in the highly successful firm of
Chukuma and Sule, and his importance shed a glow on
everyone associated with it, so that when Walpole arrived and
asked for Mr Chukuma, the youth at the desk affected not to
see him. When Walpole repeated his request, the youth took a
swig from a bottle of Coke, leafed over the pages of *Drum* and
answered without looking up: 'Mr Chukuma not on seat.'

'But I know he *is* on seat. He made an appointment with me
for two o'clock. Ring his secretary at once and say Mr Abiose
is here.'

'Who makin' dis 'pointmen'?'

'His secretary on the phone.'

'Yo' stay here – I go ask secretary.'

Reluctantly, after inquiring, the youth allowed Walpole
through and, following a quarter of an hour's wait in the
secretary's office, Walpole was summoned inside.

Mr Chukuma was a handsome, florid man of forty-five,
whose bulk indicated self-esteem as did also the quantity of
valuables about him. He wore a gold bracelet watch, several
rings with coloured stones and a diamond tie-pin. A solid gold
pen lay on his blotter and his half-smile of greeting disclosed
another seventy pounds' worth of precious metal. Dangling a
casual hand to Walpole, whom he had met half a dozen times
with his patroness in the old days, he pointed to an upright
chair, settled himself into a revolving one, and gestured to
Walpole to begin.

'Slowly now! I want everything in order. Your full name?'

'Walpole Abiose.'

'Age?.'

'Twenty-five.'

'Where d'you live?'

After a few such questions the lawyer remarked: 'And now
let me establish your business situation. You left Madam

Abiose, I believe, a little over a year ago – following a disagreement?'

'Yes.'

'And almost immediately afterwards, you started in partnership with Ekpe?'

'Yes.'

'In a building enterprise, I think.'

'Yes.'

'Under Madam Abiose you had experience of retail trade and in the management of transport, but I understand you knew nothing about building. What led you to take up a business you were ignorant of – instead of one you knew something about?'

Walpole hesitated, then admitted: 'I was trying to make money quickly.'

'To show people, perhaps, what you could do?'

'Yes.'

Mr Chukuma gave a dry smile as if to imply that Walpole had indeed shown this all too clearly.

'So you went into partnership in a business you did not understand. In which case I presume you knew your partner very well, and that he had knowledge of the building trade to compensate for your . . . inexperience?'

Walpole was becoming increasingly uncomfortable as his follies were demonstrated to him, but he had come here to face reality and was not going to draw back. 'I knew Ekpe very little. He knows no more of building than I do . . .' and Walpole went on to explain how, his partner having acquired a small builder's business and an option on a piece of land, he had put in his £2,000 with the aim of making a quick profit from the building boom.

'The idea was not unreasonable,' Chukuma conceded. 'Provided one of you had knowledge, and both of you were honest – at any rate with each other.'

The lawyer glanced up from his notes. 'When you first thought of going into partnership with Lionel Ekpe, did no one point out to you what kind of reputation he enjoys . . . if that's the correct word?'

'Yes. Madam Abiose warned me twice.'

'Oh, she did – did she? Yet in spite of her warnings you went on with the partnership? Evidently you felt you knew more about business than your former employer? Or possibly you consider yourself a better judge of character?'

Walpole looked at the floor. 'I acted foolishly. I should have listened to what Madam Abiose told me. But I was angry over being dismissed.'

'Oh – so you feel you were dismissed unjustly by Madam Abiose?'

But Walpole had been needled enough. 'Madam Abiose had a right to do as she wished. She had a right to be angry with me.' He paused. 'But if I hadn't walked out, I'd have despised myself. . . . Since I *did* walk out, it was most kind of her to send me warnings.' He stopped. It was impossible to explain what he wanted to say, and he wished now he had not started to say anything.

Mr Chukuma gave a cough. 'Well,' he said, 'let's get back to Lionel Ekpe. Who introduced you to the fellow in the first place?'

'I'm really not sure . . . I don't remember.'

The lawer was on him in a flash. 'Come – *out* with it! I can do nothing for you if you're not open with me.'

'Is it important who introduced him?'

'Look here, young man. If I ask you a question – the answer's important. Out with it.'

'I was introduced to Ekpe in a Lagos bar.'

'Yes. And by whom?'

Oh hell, thought Walpole, the man's asked for it. 'By your son Basil.'

Mr Chukuma gazed blankly at Walpole for a moment, then his face unfolded into an enormous smile. 'My son, eh? And you weren't going to tell me? Good . . . good. Well since the family's partly responsible for your situation, I must certainly do what I can to help you.'

He pushed a heavy silver box across for Walpole to help himself. The cigarettes were twice as thick as those ordinary persons buy in packets, and each one carried 'PERSONALLY MADE FOR LAWRENCE O. CHUKUMA' in gold lettering on the side. A heavy gold lighter sizzled beneath Walpole's nose and the flow of questions began again. Who drew up the partnership agreement? Had Walpole a copy with him? Had any lawyer examined it on his behalf before he signed?

All the time Mr Chukuma was listening, he made copious notes and on any point he had not completely grasped, went on questioning until he did. From the manner in which he concentrated and the sharpness of his questions, Walpole soon understood how this plump, overdressed man had become a

powerful figure in the legal and business world. Now he was
on again; who were the firm's bankers? Had Walpole made a
point of calling on the manager? Why not? How did cheques
have to be signed? Did both partners keep cheque books? Who
examined the returned cheques? If Walpole hadn't done this,
why hadn't he done so? Did he balance the statements given
each month by Ekpe against his own record of payments
made? What was the present state of the account?

Lastly he came to recent events. He read slowly through
Ekpe's letter handing over responsibility for the building side
of the partnership, and requesting a letter in return confirming
his own right to act on the partners' behalf in financial matters.
He then turned to examine Walpole's reply.

Dear Mr Ekpe,
I received your letter dated Tuesday last. I note your agreement that I
should dismiss the foreman, Kwaku, and that I am to take charge of
all building operations for the future, and I confirm that you are
entitled to act for the parnership in all financial matters.

But this arrangement must be subject to my written agreement on
any issue of importance.
       Yours faithfully,

'Well, well . . .' Mr Chukuma admitted, 'this was not
altogether a foolish reply. You corrected his point about the
arrangements he made being "subject to your subsequent
approval" – which was worthless, as you evidently saw. What
could your "subsequent approval" or disapproval matter if he
had already negotiated a deal? And you rightly insisted that
your agreement must be given in writing "on any issue of
importance". That phrase is too vague, of course; it would
have been better to say "on any transaction involving more
than one hundred pounds". All the same, it would be difficult
for Ekpe to argue in court that an issue involving seventeen
thousand pounds is not one of importance. . . . But you made
one serious mistake.'

'What was that?' Walpole asked with sinking heart.

'I suggest you read through your letter again, and note it for
yourself.'

Walpole read the letter through twice, slowly: 'I still don't
see what's wrong.'

'You put that last sentence – which from your point of view
is critical – in a separate paragraph. A lawyer would have
insisted it be typed to run on after the previous sentence.'

'Why is that important?'

'Whether it is – or isn't – important will soon be found out. Why it *may* be important is that you've given our sharp friend the opportunity to exercise dexterity. He could extract that last sentence, cutting or bleaching it out, and closing up the signature.'

'But it would show!'

'Not on a photographed copy. He could write to my old acquaintance Mr Esau – your bank manager down on the Marina, whom you ought long since have got to know – explaining that you are over in Ghana on the firm's affairs. Some business opportunity has come up which you've both been waiting for. Knowing this *was* coming, you'd left him a letter of authorization. The original is with the firm's lawyers, so he is sending the bank a copy. Ekpe could be pretty confident that a customer who's just paid in seventeen thousand pounds isn't going to be questioned too closely over a straightforward letter from his partner.'

'But he hasn't just paid in seventeen thousand.'

'Not into your *joint* account. . . . But I've little doubt it's been paid into his own.'

Walpole sighed: 'Then what can we do about it?'

'Before we do anything else, my young friend, I want you to spend a few minutes thinking over what *he* – Ekpe – is likely to do. . . . It shouldn't be difficult. We know the man and we know his situation, so let us, by way of exercise, put ourselves in that situation. . . . Tell me, from your knowledge of your partner, what will he intend doing with a cheque for seventeen thousand?'

Mr Chukuma took from the pocket of a waistcoat, a garment he always wore despite the heat, a small piece of equipment made of gold like everything else about him. It had a tripod base which opened out and two arms from which depended what looked like a tiny set of gardening tools. Planting this arrangement before him on his blotter, he began using the miniature tools to pare, file, smooth and generally beautify his nails.

'Come, come,' he said sharply. 'Have you *no* suggestions? D'you suppose the man will fly the country?'

'All too likely, I should think,' said Walpole dismally.

Mr Chukuma snorted. 'Ridiculous, my friend! You're not applying yourself. Consider the facts! Your partner has just established with you a most promising business. You've made it clear you're ready to work day and night for nothing. You are diligent – but not acute. For a man of his nature Ekpe has the ideal situation – a thriving enterprise and a docile, hard-working partner. Why, in a couple of years' time, he should be able to make seventeen thousand pounds five times over. . . . Oh, I've no doubt he intends to swindle you out of every penny *in the end*. But it's only common sense to let you earn a great deal more for him first. Ekpe isn't a fool – why on earth should he fly the country?'

Mr Chukuma wrestled with an awkward piece of cuticle which he finally removed with a minute pair of golden shears.

'Come now,' he urged as Walpole remained silent, 'you've talked to Ekpe every month. When he first tried to get you to invest he must have laid some grandiose plans before you. Though he's mean and secretive – he's also boastful. He's bound to have given you clues as to what he'd do if only he got hold of a big lump of money. Cast your mind back! *Think!*'

Walpole struck his head with his closed fist. 'Of course – you're right. He told me long ago what his next step would be. He'd use the money to invest in a big office block . . . some new building going up.' A thought struck him. 'And I know *which* building! It'll be the one being built near the racecourse by that Italian firm Crespi.'

'You see,' remarked Mr Chukuma cheerfully, 'you were angry when I asked you to do a little thinking. But I was right, and our time has not been wasted. So now we begin to see the picture – or at least I begin to. Your friend Ekpe has bought shares in the new block, which he aims to sell for a quick profit as soon as the government agrees to purchase. The decision on that is expected this week. Then he puts back the fifteen thousand and keeps the difference, which might be as much again.'

'And supposing the government doesn't agree to purchase?'

'It will. But in any case the investment's sound, so he can always use it to raise a loan, put the cash back in the joint account – and fob you off with whatever he chooses to think up.'

'So he *is* meaning to pay the money back?' There was relief in Walpole's voice.

'Let's say he hopes to slip it back unnoticed.' Mr Chukuma paused. 'But in case you feel your faith in human nature suddenly restored – note that not *all* the money would come back. He wrote that the firm is putting down five thousand pounds on each house. So even if fifteen thousand finally reaches your account, there'll still be a couple of thousand sticking to his fingers. That is, if all works out the way he wants.'

20
Out of the Meshes

The instruction Mr Chukuma gave Walpole when he left his office was to go back to work, say nothing to anyone and press on with the house-building. If he came back in a week, the lawyer might have news for him.

The week passed anxiously, but Walpole found on his return that no time had been lost. Mr Chukuma had started by visiting Mr Esau, the bank manager. A hint that legal action might be pending; a note of surprise that the bank appeared to have been less than cautious in their dealings with Ekpe . . . 'whose past record is not unfamiliar in financial circles'; a suggestion that cooperation now might make it easier for him to keep the bank's seeming carelessness out of the picture in the event of a court hearing . . . this was the sort of conversation Mr Chukuma relished. He could pressurize and threaten while appearing to offer favours and arrange concessions, and he left the bank manager with the information he was seeking – that Ekpe had received a cheque for £17,000 made out to his firm, and arranged for this to be paid into his own account. Most of the money had then been paid over to the consortium handling the new office block.

To make doubly sure, Mr Chukuma had then dropped in on his 'very good friend' Chief Julius, enjoyed a drink or two and a chat over old times, confirmed the situation as regards Ekpe's investment of £15,000, and learned that the government's decision to purchase would be held up for a month or two. . . . 'Though about the outcome there can be no doubt. . . . The appropriate arrangements have been made. . . . You are already in with us, I believe,' Chief Julius concluded, 'for a good sum. But if anyone offers you the chance to take up as much again – do not refuse! Such opportunities do not grow on palm trees.' Mr Chukuma had shaken hands and withdrawn, stopping on the way home to have one or two bottles of the Chief's favourite brandy sent round with his compliments. Having now put Walpole fully in the picture, he concluded: 'And so, my friend, what do you wish me to do?'

'I thought you were advising me,' said Walpole, 'not I you. What do you suggest I do?'

'And I *can* only advise you when I know what it is you want! D'you want to bring Ekpe before the courts and ruin him? D'you want to extract every penny you can from the situation? D'you want to be free of the partnership on reasonable terms? D'you want to ease out a crooked partner and keep the business for yourself? . . . I don't say all these are on the cards, but if you tell me your wish, I'll see how far it can be realized.'

'What I want,' said Walpole, 'is to end this partnership and get my money back.'

'D'you mean,' Mr Chukuma inquired, 'that you will be happy to wind up the partnership and recover your original two thousand pounds?'

'I should indeed!' said Walpole fervently.

'Well I should *not*. You are now my client, and I could not allow any client of mine to accept such a disadvantageous settlement. Also, apart from my duty as your adviser, it would be a triumph for Ekpe and I am in no mood for giving him easy triumphs. No, my friend, you must think again.'

'What would you do in my place?'

'Rather more than a year ago,' said Mr Chukuma ruminatively, 'you invested your whole capital in an enterprise then worth very little. Today it's difficult to set an exact value on your firm, but with three houses sold and three others on the way it cannot be less than twenty-five thousand pounds. Of that you are entitled to a full half. But this success – and it *is* a success – has been built on your back. For more than a year you worked without drawing a day's wages, and for most of that time you worked by night as well. It does not appear that during this period your partner contributed anything at all. . . . The very least I could accept on your behalf is a half-share of the valuation, plus your wages over the past year, with payment for the loss of your reasonable expectations as manager in the form of salary over the next year or two.'

'You mean – I might get something like fourteen thousand pounds?' asked Walpole, almost aghast at the prospect of such wealth when for weeks past he had been wondering whether anything at all could be rescued from his partner's claws.

'He certainly can't expect to take over your share in the partnership for less. . . . But, of course, there's the other possibility – which I incline to think the better.'

'What possibility?'

'Why – not that he takes *you* over, but you take over Ekpe.'

'You mean – I pay him twelve thousand five hundred pounds?'

'No, no, no, no, no, *no*!' Mr Chukuma exploded with indignation. 'Oh, no indeed! In view of the way he's acted – and the fact that he's in danger of prosecution for fraud – he can't expect to be treated with the consideration owing to a loyal partner. Dear me, no! . . . However, I can imagine that, when Ekpe has put that seventeen thousand pounds back where it belongs, you may go so far as to offer half that amount for his share in the partnership. . . . Yes . . . I do believe I could recommend you to offer him eight and a half thousand pounds.'

'What if he doesn't accept?'

'If he should be so foolish as to refuse your generous offer,' Mr Chukuma observed, 'he is likely to find himself in court. I need hardly say that these will not be presented to him as direct alternatives – but I fancy he will perceive my general drift. . . . And apart from the fact that he has no leg to stand on over his latest activities, I have a file on his past dealings which it would be a real pleasure to delve into in public . . . only where strictly relevant to the matter in hand of course. . . . Yes, I think I could promise two or three enjoyable days in court, with the enjoyment very much on one side. Personally I hope Ekpe *will* refuse your offer – but I cannot think it probable.'

'How do we deal with him over this?' Walpole inquired.

'I shall invite him round. I think that would be polite. . . . But tell me first – do you want to *keep* the business? Or do you want to be bought out?'

Walpole considered. 'I should like to keep it . . . and find someone else to come in with me. . . . I would ask your advice over any possible partner.'

'Very wise of you,' Mr Chukuma conceded. 'Well then, I suggest you write your partner a letter and, if you will allow me, I shall dictate it straight away,' and he rang for his secretary.

'Type this on plain paper from the address Mr Abiose will give you. . . .'

Dear Mr Ekpe,
Certain matters have come to my knowledge in connection with our business interests which disturb me greatly and I have been advised that it is my duty to bring that information to the notice of the police. But since we have been in partnership for more than a year I am unwilling to do this without giving you the opportunity to offer any explanation you may wish. I shall be in the office of my lawyers, Messrs Chukuma and Sule, from two until three p.m. next Monday afternoon. Should you fail to keep this appointment, I shall ask them to take whatever action they think best for the safeguarding of my interests.

'There!' said Mr Chukuma, pressing his palms lightly together. 'There, now! I think that can be expected to give Mr Lionel Ekpe one or two sleepless nights . . . I'm sure I *hope* so. There is one word in this letter which will disturb him more than all the rest. D'you know what that word is?'

'Police,' Walpole suggested.

'I admit that mention of the police is not intended to reassure him,' said the lawyer, 'but that is not what I mean. No, the word which will strike your partner so unpleasantly is my own name – Chukuma! Mr Ekpe is well aware that I have had my eye on him for years. . . . The file I have on him in this office, laid end to end, would go two or three times round Tinabu Square. . . . In the meantime you must on no account see Ekpe or enter into any talk with him. If he comes round and tries to speak to you, simply say the matter is out of your hands and all discussion must be with your lawyers.'

'D'you want me to speak to him when he comes on Monday?'

'I shall want you present in the office. But whether it will be necessary for you to speak to him, I can't say. It may well not be, but I should like you to be here all the same.'

'I'm compelled to admire your friend,' Mr Chukuma told Walpole after Ekpe had gone. . . . 'You know there are certain fish which behave boldly until they are hooked or netted, and there are others which fight the more fiercely for being hooked but are finished when you get them out of

water. And there are a few which continue fighting even when
lying in the bottom of the boat. . . . Your partner has been
detected in a grossly fraudulent action, but so far from asking
mercy he had a good try at putting all the blame on you.'

'On *me*? How on earth?'

'He admits he may have "slightly overstepped the strict
legality of the situation" in paying the firm's cheque into his
private account. But he claims he was buying a share in the
new building not for himself at all, but for the partnership. He
says he had several times discussed with you the idea of the
firm's putting money into a new office block – and in general
you accepted the proposal. He wanted, he says, to talk over
this particular investment with you, but hadn't dared to.'

'Why ever not?'

'Because he was sure you wouldn't have the nerve to go
through with it since it involved an indefinite wait before the
deal could be completed. The tension, he said, would be more
than you could carry. So he decided to act first and explain
afterwards. . . . There could be no risk, he told me, because it
was known the government would buy the building on terms
that allow a handsome profit. But if in the end they failed to
buy it, he meant to raise a mortgage and pay the fifteen
thousand pounds into the firm's account without anyone
being a penny the worse off.'

'What did you say to all this?'

'I said that what he appeared to regard as a defence
amounted to a most damaging admission, but that I need not
waste time arguing points which would be gone into fully in
court. I merely asked him to repeat that the sum he received on
account for the first three houses was – as he had just stated –
fifteen thousand. . . . He seemed, I'm bound to say, rather
taken aback at this, but he finally repeated that the cheque was
for fifteen thousand pounds "to the best of my recollection".'

'So then what?'

'I said nothing at all. I simply sat and looked at him with
what I hoped was an interested expression. . . . After a minute
or two of silence Ekpe asked if it were really necessary to do
something so damaging to the firm and the interests of you
both as to bring "this little difference" up in court? After
fencing on both sides, I told him that you could not possibly
remain in a partnership with someone you couldn't trust and
suggested he might care to buy you out. I proposed an
independent valuation of the firm, plus your wages for the

past year and salary as manager for the next two, and I let him know that only an immediate cash settlement would be acceptable.'

'But I thought we agreed. . . .'

Mr Chukuma raised a hand. 'When your partner objected that he could not find so much money at short notice, I told him that in that case there was no point in further discussion. After a while he asked whether you would be prepared to buy him out instead – and, if so, how much would you offer? I was naturally somewhat surprised, and said I had no idea what you might think of the suggestion. I added that, for the sake of a quick settlement – and to avoid the very disagreeable task of exposing him in court and so making it impossible for him to earn a living – I might be able to recommend your terminating the partnership on the basis of a simple division of all cash in hand. That is, he could keep half the fifteen thousand he said he had received and half of anything to your joint credit in the bank . . . and I told him I should want his answer in two days, since the business has to be carried on without a break.'

It took a further week for negotiations to be completed, but at last it was agreed that Ekpe should receive ten thousand for his half of the firm's assets and goodwill – which meant his restoring seven thousand to the joint account. Just how he raised the money he did not disclose but the result was to leave Walpole in sole charge of his own business with a sufficiency of working capital.

The strain of the last weeks had come on top of a year's exhausting work. Walpole's hopes and fears had fluctuated day after day and he found it difficult to sleep despite being tired out when he got home. At the thought that his troubles were now over, he seized the lawyer's well-manicured hand and shook it warmly. But when he tried to express his thanks in words, the tension in his throat prevented speech and tears he was unable to control ran down his cheeks.

'There, there, my friend,' said Mr Chukuma kindly, 'there's nothing to thank me for. Nothing at all. It's a pleasure to keep my files on Lionel Ekpe up to date.'

He walked over to the window and stood gazing out, allowing Walpole to wipe his eyes surreptitiously and blow his nose. When he felt the young man had recovered, the lawyer turned round and remarked, 'You will allow me, I hope, to give you one word of advice.'

'Indeed,' said Walpole humbly, 'I shall be grateful.'

'Well then, until you know rather more of the world than you do at present, I strongly advise you to confine your business dealings to honest men.'

Walpole shook his head ruefully as one who feels a painful lesson has been learned, then, after thanking the lawyer once more, turned to the door. Before he could leave, however, Mr Chukuma attracted his attention with an impressive cough, and added: 'However, where you will *find* these honest men to do business with, I'm afraid I can offer no suggestion.'

The amount of time and effort the lawyer had spent on helping him, and the smallness of his bill when it came in, showed Walpole that he must owe much to the interest of his former patroness. Though often foolish, and no more willing than another to acknowledge a mistake, Walpole was neither cowardly nor ungrateful. He had no wish for a meeting with Madam Abiose which must be distressing, but having recognized his obligation he resolved to give thanks in person rather than evade such meeting by a letter.

It was the first time for nearly eighteen months that he had been inside her office, and the clerk – the same one whom Madam Abiose had once bellowed at for not showing enough respect to 'Mr Walpole' – looked up with surprise and hostility when he came in. Walpole appeared worn and a good deal thinner, so the clerk at once concluded the former master was in difficulties and seeking to get back his old position.

'Wot you wantin' here? Madam Abiose too busy for spik wid you.'

Walpole walked over and bent forward till he was looking directly into the clerk's face. 'Get up!' he ordered. 'Go tell Madam Abiose Mr Walpole is here to thank her for the great kindness she just done him.'

The clerk's jaw dropped with horror. This could mean that Mr Walpole was on the way back – and if so he had already made a horrible blunder. Backing around his stool, he darted up the stairs, stumbling with anxiety, then reappeared almost immediately on the top step and beckoned Walpole to come up.

As he came into the familiar room Walpole was already speaking the sentences he had prepared. 'I have come, Madam, only to . . .' but before he could complete the words her arms were round his neck and he was enclosed in Madam Abiose's powerful embrace. He kissed her and was still struggling to express his thanks when she silenced him with a torrent of affectionate expostulation.

'You mos' foolish boy – dat what you bin! Mos', mos' foolish boy! *Dear* Walpole! Why you not come ask me if you needin' money for start business? You t'ink I 'low you be robbed by dis rascally Ekpe? I tellin' Mr Chukuma – "You git Walpole out of dis trouble or you never do nothin' for me no more." He bin good man, Mr Chukuma – good man an' clever lawyer. If he no fix Ekpe one way, he soon fixin' um two more ways.' She drew back and looked at him more closely: 'You grow thin like knittin' needle, an' I kin see you not laughed since you done run out of my houe. Tunde!' Her shout fetched the frightened clerk scurrying through the door outside which he had evidently been listening. 'Go fetch Mr Walpole whisky an' some chop, quick-quick!'

The outburst relieved her feelings, and they sat down together like old friends. As they talked Walpole realized with relief that, painfully as she had suffered and affectionate as she still was towards him, his patroness was now reconciled to the fact that he had left her and would not come back. She had thrown herself with renewed energy into her many business interests and Walpole could almost feel pity for the managers on whom the full force of her attention was now turned for sixteen hours a day. It was clear that she watched not only profits but the smallest necessary outlay with a vulture's eye. Reconciled to Walpole for having left her, she was far from reconciled to those who had plotted his removal and in scoring over her protégé had scored so cruelly over herself, so that now these men were paying for their triumph in daily anxiety, hard work and humiliation. She had also taken up the support of her church with double fervour, exercising all her energy and resourcefulness on behalf of some new clergyman.

She was fuller in face, heavier in body, more authoritative in manner – who among all her managers, Walpole wondered, would dare to cross her now? She bothered less about looks and dress and it was plain she had taken that indefinable but crucial step in a woman's life which involves giving up claims to youth, ceasing to compete in physical attraction, and accepting that, in the great game of take-and-give between the sexes, she is henceforth no longer a player but an onlooker and critic.

Some few weeks later Walpole was invited to lunch by Mr Chukuma. There was a young man present whom Walpole had met once or twice but scarcely knew, Stephen Balogun, nephew of a wholesale supplier, Hampson Balogun, with whose firm Walpole had had dealings. Over the meal Mr Chukuma told the two men something of each other's background and explained the purpose of the meeting. Stephen wanted to go into business. Having enjoyed a year or two of social life and travel, he was now tired of doing nothing. His uncle, who was also his guardian since his father had been dead for years, was attracted by the large profits made by speculative builders, but as a supplier of building materials considered it unwise to be in obvious competition with his customers. If, however, his nephew and Walpole cared to go into partnership, he would put up capital and remain as a third partner behind the scenes. Mr Balogun had seen Walpole half a dozen times and liked him. What really impressed him, however, was Walpole's having worked for more than a year as labourer and driver. His nephew, he felt, was too mild-natured to launch out in business on his own, but Walpole's harsher experience and determination would make good what Stephen lacked. He himself, while remaining in the background, could ensure they kept their financial ship on an even keel. The two young men took to one another – as it was much to their advantage that they should – and before long Walpole was once more a partner in a building firm, but this time with Mr Hampson Balogun and his nephew Stephen in the new firm of Balogun and Abiose.

So now Walpole was sitting for the last time in his room in Ebute Metta, hearing the oily lagoon water slapping against the mouldering quayside, the children's screams, the women's arguments with their clients and the shouts of men handling the rafts of timber in the harbour. The room, cramped, uncomfortable, full of noisome smells and angry sounds, had been his home, the only refuge he had for well over a year. In the end his efforts had brought success and he was now on his way to being what he had so longed to be, a successful businessman. Tomorrow, still no more than twenty-five, he would move into his own comfortable flat. Shortly he would buy a car and it would not be long before he found himself a woman. All he had wanted would be his, though not in the way he planned. He had set out on his partnership with Ekpe to 'show them all' what he could do, but what he could do, left to himself, was to lose everything he had – and his old patroness, whom above all he intended to impress, had been the one to save him from the consequence of his folly.

21
Changing Scene

Five years after entering this new alliance Walpole had become what he had long dreamed of being, a successful man of business earning a good many thousand pounds a year. In addition to a high salary and share of profits, he had by the age of thirty enough money in the bank to draw servile smiles from the manager and owned what stockbrokers describe as 'a portfolio of investments', together with one or two small properties and pieces of land around the city. His life was now intensely active, active at work and active for pleasure in evenings and weekends; he belonged to clubs, was known in bars and dance halls, and it was unusual if the day's routine ended without a round of enjoyment mapped out until midnight or early morning.

Business and financial success were his chief interest and love affairs his main distraction, giving whatever direction there was to his personal life. If anyone had asked what he looked forward to in the future, he would have found it difficult to reply, but would probably have said that he would like to see Balogun and Abiose become bigger and more important, with branches throughout the country, and that he hoped one day to settle down into a happy marriage. His chosen way of life, however, though it could well lead to the first result, could hardly be expected to produce the second. Meantime, in the office at least, matters could hardly have gone better. Hampson Balogun was a man of experience and wide acquaintance, rich enough to be looked up to in a society where money was the main source of prestige, but not so conspicuously wealthy as to arouse hostility. He made no display of his riches and in general was a man of modest tastes, controlled in his actions and opinions and tolerant towards those of others. He had recognized from the first that the firm could only grow through the energy of his young partners, so

that his own responsibility would lie in advising them against
rash ventures and ensuring that the business did not, in an era
of easy profits, expand too fast through their taking on more
work than they could handle. Walpole had acquired over the
years much respect for the good sense of his senior partner, but
he was also from time to time exasperated by a tendency on his
part to pious utterances and sententious drawing of conclusions.

Stephen Balogun, son of a wealthy father who died young,
had been brought up by his uncle in an atmosphere of
prosperity and consequently had been slow in development,
so that when he and Walpole became partners the advantage at
first was all on Walpole's side. Stephen admired his friend for
having started out with nothing but the breath inside his body,
and his admiration grew when in the early days Walpole
would snatch up shovel or machete to show one of the men
how to set about his job, or crawl under a van to sort out
mechanical troubles. Never having worked with his hands, he
was ill at ease with the labourers, confining his contacts to
manager and foremen, and he envied Walpole's readiness to
drive a truck into a compound where a crowd of men were
milling about for work, choose three or four and disregard the
pleas, often the angry mutterings and threats, of the remainder. Later when one of those chosen proved idle or dishonest,
Walpole could run him off the place as readily as he had taken
him on. Stephen admired Walpole for being able to do what he
found difficulty in doing, act decisively, and also for having
somehow – without ever having been to school or travelled
outside the country – absorbed the advantages conferred by
his own sheltered upbringing: 'If you'd had the start in life I
had,' Stephen told him, 'you'd be a minister in the federal
government by now.'

Any tendency on Walpole's part to belittle his friend or take
him too much for granted, however, had come up before long
against something solid. Stephen, he learned, made his mind
up slowly, but from a decision once made could not easily be
shifted. He was not given to moralizing like his uncle, but
appeared to live by certain principles. As a rule in office
arguments Walpole could count on his support even against
his uncle, though so far he had taken care never to push him
into any conflict of loyalties, but if such a conflict should one
day come, Stephen would decide his attitude, Walpole
recognized, neither by subjection to his uncle nor in accord-

ance with his friend's influence, but on the merits of the situation as he saw it.

For the last year or two, because of an emotional involvement, Stephen had been at odds with his uncle and family as a whole, and so had inclined more and more towards his friend. Cécile, the girl he wished to marry, was from the family's point of view in many ways a suitable wife. She had been educated overseas, one of the élite known as 'been-to's', who had studied and lived in the UK. She was good-looking, strong-minded and her family prosperous and respected, but against all this was the fact that she was not Nigerian but came from Abidjan on the Ivory Coast, where Stephen had met her on a business visit. After some months of pursuit he had induced Cécile to come and live in Lagos in a flat he provided for her, and he was now engaged in breaking down, with Walpole's backing, the family's opposition to his marriage.

'If I were you,' Walpole had advised him, 'I'd just marry her. What could the family do? They might cut you off with a shilling for the moment, but they'd have to make it up with you before long – particularly if you provided them with a son or two.'

'If you were me, that's what you'd do,' Stephen answered. 'And I dare say if you were Cécile you'd accept my offer. But you aren't Cécile, and she doesn't! She'll only marry me with the agreement of my family – she's not going to have it said she came between me and them.' So there for the moment the matter rested.

As for Walpole, though outwardly everything had gone so well, he had not found in money and position the contentment and peace of mind he was expecting. Five or six years ago he had dreamed of owning a comfortable flat to which he could retire after the day's work, but now if he found himself at home with nowhere special to go, he would look round and wonder how he could possibly fill the empty evening. Apart from newspapers and technical journals connected with his work, he seldom read. He still bought books and meant to read them but since he no longer settled down to any kind of study, they accumulated, demanding attention and creating guilt, until finally he pushed them out of sight on to a shelf. Little disposed to self-examination, Walpole was largely unaware of the changes the last few years had brought about in him. He considered himself the same man he had always been, only more sophisticated and assured, and though at times he would become conscious of emptiness and disappointment, as though life were in some way cheating him or there were some vital ingredient missing from the formula, it never occurred to him to alter the whole manner of his existence.

Prosperity, he was also finding, brings worries of its own – worries he would once have ridiculed, but which now seemed real enough. Would the market for houses and property go booming on, and if so ought he to put everything he had or could borrow into property? The shares in his 'portfolio' were sound, but in a time of soaring values there were others which had risen faster. And, looking further ahead still, was he wise to keep everything inside the country? Walpole loved his country and had faith in its future, but well-to-do men cannot, he considered, afford to take the same chances as those with little to lose. Nigeria was still young, its constitution far from settled; there were tensions between regions, based on tribal and religious antagonisms which might one day flare into hostility or even civil war. Would it not be a wise precaution, almost a duty to his own position, to salt some of his growing fortune away abroad – into English pounds, American dollars, Swiss francs or German marks? Most of the big men in politics, he knew, had been doing this for years so that if a sudden shift of power drove them out, they could start new lives tomorrow in any of half a dozen countries, so ought he not to put himself into the same position? No wonder that from time to time there passed over Walpole's face a shadow of anxiety, as though he were burdened by the weight of his possessions and simultaneously haunted by the possibility of their loss.

Added to all these sources of concern – anxieties of the rich from which the poor are happily exempt – was another, more persistent. During his struggling days Walpole had been free from any problem over women. His life with Madam Abiose had resembled a marriage, passionate at first, later settling down to regularity and quiet satisfaction. In his time as a labourer Walpole had lived a labourer's life. He ate and drank what they did, and loved – if that is the word – in the same way as his unmarried comrades. But what in his labouring days had been so simple had now become involved. Walpole had moved out of the world in which sex is bought and sold as directly as a plate of yams, and though at the level he had now reached it was indeed still sold and bought, the price was not agreed beforehand and the transaction had to be surrounded with pretence.

When he saw a woman he wanted he could not just take her
to his room, but must entertain her once or twice. Then after a
few preliminary skirmishes he would express his desire,
describing it as 'love', deeper and more intense than anything
he had ever felt before. Moved by his persuasions, as a rule she
would consent and her compliance would be rewarded with
'spontaneous generosity' in the form of expensive gifts. Then
if he wished her compliance to continue, spontaneous
generosity and flattery must continue too. Nor was it enough
any longer that he should be attracted by a woman's looks, for
if he were to be seen around with her – at haunts where
nowadays he knew everyone and they knew him – it was
important for his friends to approve her too, and not just her
looks but her clothes, her manner, her way of speaking, her
past, even her husband if she had one.

In every country the sweet life of business prosperity has
given rise to a special display, centring round bars, night
clubs, restaurants, in which it is more important for the bill to
be high and the company modish than for food, drink and
entertainment to be good. In every country too there is a type
of woman who flowers in such setting and is nourished by its
opportunities. Young, pliable, rapacious, continually teased
by glimpses of the golden world but not established in it, she
moves with smiles and sharpened claws from man to man, and
as Walpole came up in the world – vigorous, not ill-looking,
smartly-dressed and above all free with money – he was a
natural target for the pleasure-loving. Office secretaries,
receptionists, nurses, assistants in luxury shops, emancipated
daughters and discontented wives, all rolled their bright eyes
and smiled, eager to exchange whatever they had for whatever
it would fetch. Frequently, at times almost against his will,
Walpole smiled back, and the fatiguing routine began again.

Lagos is not a city of beauty in the ordinary meaning of the
word. It lacks magnificent buildings, has no heart or centre, is
wanting in flowered parks or shady gardens, derives small
splendour from the ocean on which it floats. Most of its vast
acreage is a sprawl of shabby markets, ill-paved streets
running over or alongside drains and sewers, dwellings in
decay without ever having grown old. Most of its shops are
stalls, many of its houses makeshift, their materials mud,
concrete and corrugated iron. Even the towers which now rise
up here and there – hotels, government offices, finance houses
and office blocks – serve to emphasize the prevailing squalor.

Yet in one respect Lagos stands unrivalled. The city, whose atmosphere is that of a Turkish bath, spawns female parasites of unrivalled seduction and variety. Nor are they unappreciated. If the men of the world's capital cities were to compete for ostentatious spending on sexual pleasures, the rich men of Lagos would stand proudly at their head. Here a woman must not only be kept but flaunted; not merely enjoyed but coveted – and not only she but her possessor is esteemed for the money he pours out on her. Elsewhere he might be thought a fool; in Lagos he is appreciated as a man.

What other city boasts a sight such as this of Chief Pontius or Chief Julius, descending a flight of steps from the hotel where he has just entertained fifty guests at a lunch party from which many were carried home two hours since by their drivers and retainers? Behold our Chief, resplendent in embroidered *agbada*, one stout arm bare like a black Jupiter, an *adaduro* of crimson velvet crusted with gold aslant his dripping brow, planting his weight powefully from step to step as if to shatter the stones with every impact. Doormen and waiters flutter and bow. An attendant dashes forward shouting: 'De Chief's car. Go fetchum, boy!' Imperiously the great man rotates his head on bull-like folds and in answer to his snort, dark yards of automobile come gliding from the shadows. But the Chief is not alone. Pendant on either arm are laughing girls, fresh from the beauty parlour, gowned from overseas, flashing challenges at one another across his chest, chattering like children being taken to a treat. The driver snatches the door open, the Chief levers his massy bulk on to the leather and the girls slip silken in on either side. Within seconds they have vanished into the heat of the afternoon, and the lascivious speculation of by-standers follows them out of sight.

Such was the life upon which Walpole had embarked, competing for favours with the sons of wealthy families such as his partner Stephen, his befriender Mr Chukuma and his son Basil, with the crown prince of café society, Duke Ombo, and occasionally challenging even the bull elephants, lords of the swamps and marshes of prosperity, Chief Pontius, Chief Julius and that forceful new contender, Chief Efunshile*.

Walpole had seen Bisi for the first time in the Kingsway store. He had left work earlier than usual to buy a present for his

---

*He pronounced his name to rhyme, not with 'Nile' but with 'freely'.

current woman friend, Ayoka Fashanu. Theirs was not an
ardent relationship, and Walpole thought it likely that one or
two of his friends were enjoying the same favours he did, but
Ayoka was a jolly, friendly girl and even a casual relationship
brings obligations. As Walpole strode through the department, where underwear and nightdresses were arranged on
stands or draped over ridiculous putty-coloured dummies, his
eye was caught by a young girl leaning away from him across
the counter to pick up a box. She wore no uniform and for the
moment he was not sure if she were customer or assistant. As
he drew closer she glanced up.

'Is something I kin show you, sir?'

Walpole looked the speaker appreciatively up and down.
Her dress was sleeveless, close-fitting and brief. He guessed
her to be little more than seventeen.

'I'm sure you can show me a great deal.'

A smile and conscious look told Walpole she understood.

'I shall do my best to help you, sir,' she replied demurely.
'What is you looking for?'

'What I have to buy is a nightdress. Can you show me
some?'

'Mos' certainly, sir. What kind of nightdress is you
wanting?'

'Oh . . . something good. Whatever's newest.'

The girl kept silent, but her glance was mischievous.

'Well – what more do I have to tell you?'

'You haven't told me, sir, what size of lady is to go inside
this nightdress. . . . Is your wife a large lady or a small?'

'I have no wife. This is for a friend.'

'Oh, for a *friend*? Then it mus' be smart. . . . So it will cost a
lot of money. But you won't mind that, I think.'

As she chattered, she was reaching down boxes and
unwrapping tissue paper. Seductive rustlings. Glimpses of
soft colourings . . . pink, primrose, pale green or blue, a
cloudy orange; edgings of white, cream, coffee. Her little
fingers moved among the delicate fabrics with assurance,
deftly extracting a few and laying them to one side.

'You still not tellin' me what size is your lady?'

Looking up, she caught the eagerness of Walpole's gaze and
as if complicity had already been established, chose out the
flimsiest nightdress, tucked the neck under her round chin and
strained the transparent material over her breasts. The
garment was short and ended provocatively at her thighs.

'How you like dis, sir?'

'Wonderful! That looks *wonderful*.'

She leaned across till her face was not far from his. 'You wishin' I show you more, sir?'

'Yes, indeed. But I wish you to tell me something first. What's your name?'

'Bisi. My name is Bisi.'

'And mine's Walpole Abiose. If I call for you when the store closes, will you have dinner with me tonight? If you want to change, I can drive you home. I shall have a car.'

Bisi hesitated, but only for a moment. 'Yes, I come with you. . . . I wait downstairs by the door . . . at half-past six. . . .' Then suddenly recollecting, 'But what about this nightdress?'

'Nightdress? Oh, choose the three you like best in your own size, and take them home. I'll pay for them now. . . . It's all right! Just a little present from a friend,' he added reassuringly.

'But what about your lady, Mr Abiose? What she goin' say when she get no nightdress?'

'I tell you what she said when I see you tonight. Half-past six then. At the main entrance.'

In this casual manner there began for Walpole a period different from any he had known, one of excitement amounting almost to distress. Bisi returned with him to his flat, stayed the night and happily consented to come away with him for the weekend. Indeed they had scarcely got into bed before she was already assuming they would be together for the weekend, the following weekend, and the weekend after that. Over recent years Walpole had developed some skill in self-protection and was accustomed to keeping his women friends at a reasonable distance, but against Bisi's blend of childish confidence with ruthlessness he began before long to find himself powerless; she seemed at the same time to trust him implicitly and to insist on having her own way. In bed she was the same bewildering mixture, sometimes simply offering herself for his enjoyment and at others falling on him as if he were her possession not she his. She had a firm young body which in relaxation was all softness and compliance, but she could also grapple with him as vigorously as an athlete, twining her legs avidly round him as if to drain the last drop of his vitality. Walpole who had gone into the affair expecting a few weeks of indolent enjoyment before moving on to fresh attractions, found himself helpless, as if under the enchantment of a drug.

So far from keeping Bisi at a distance he was continually pursuing her, since away from her he was restless, jealous of he knew not what, impelled to ring up, hear her voice, find out what she was doing. But once in her company he found no peace since they had little to talk about, no shared experiences, no mutual friends. Driven continually to draw closer to the object of his passion, Walpole could only make love, and love again, as though their separate identities could be fused through sheer exhaustion.

'Are you all right, my friend?' Stephen inquired, when a conference which should have clinched a deal petered out indecisively through Walpole's absent-mindedness.

'Of course I'm all right. Why ever not?' he answered sharply.

'You've had an odd expression sometimes lately.'

'What kind of expression?' asked Walpole with a sickening heart.

'As if you were having a twinge of . . . pain, or something. I wondered if you weren't feeling well. Are you sure there's nothing wrong?'

'Yes,' Mr Balogun put in. 'I've noticed it too, Walpole. You're not yourself. In my opinion you've been overdoing it. Everything should be in moderation, otherwise it gets beyond control.' He paused, while Walpole's heart missed a beat or two, and then added, 'Even work.'

'M'm. . . . Well, I *have* been anxious over the new block. We've a lot at stake.' And then, dismayed at his own evasion, he added with more truth: 'I think I haven't been sleeping enough.'

'That's my opinion too, Walpole,' Mr Balogun advised. 'Take a few days off. A change of scene can be beneficial. Go off somewhere – by yourself.'

The last two words, though let fall casually, made Walpole ponder. It was clear he was allowing work to be affected, so it was time to take himself in hand.

22
Nor Peace, Nor Ease

During the week Walpole was away from Lagos he did what he seldom did nowadays except in business matters, thought over the problem of his relationship with Bisi and how he could handle it. It was absurd that he, the older and more experienced, should be at the mercy of her moods and impulses. More than absurd, it was degrading, and he resolved that as soon as he got back he would begin to assert authority and guide this bewitching but wayward child into a calmer manner of life. One way of doing this would be to spend less time alone with her and to introduce her to other aspects of his life, and he began by inviting Stephen and Cécile to spend an evening with them at a night club, the Harmony Cabin, where he was well known. It boasted a Lebanese chef, a fine 'high-life' band, and its owner Freddie Fagbemi was a plump jovial young man who welcomed his guests as though the arrival of each one brought him personal happiness and increased his flow of spirits.

On their arrival Freddie guided the party to a table where the girls at once began to chat, leaving Walpole and Stephen to do what they preferred, continue the business discussion they had not had time to finish in the office.

'They look as if they were planning to bring down the government,' Stephen remarked as the girls whispered eagerly together.

'I don't think that's quite Bisi's line,' Walpole answered. 'She's probably asking Cécile where she buys her shoes.'

When the evening ended they arranged to meet again at the same place in a couple of weeks.

'I like Cécile,' Bisi told him on the way home. 'She mos' interesting for talk to.'

'Interesting?'

'Yes. She's interested in same things I am.'

From this time, some part of Bisi's attention was diverted towards her new friend, and Walpole could feel she had someone to turn to during his absences; moreover Cécile's company had a calming effect. Bisi looked up to Cécile not only as a woman three or four years older than herself, but also because she had travelled, could speak several languages and yet was happy to sit for an evening listening to her Kingsway gossip. Cécile who, like a good Frenchwoman, made many of her clothes herself, even taught Bisi some of her own skill so that at weekends instead of demanding continuous excitement she would occasionally spend an afternoon altering dresses or making something new.

'Cécile not likin' it,' Bisi remarked moodily over some purchase. 'She say I have more money than sense. Why you not stop me buying silly things?'

One evening when the four of them were having drinks at the Harmony Cabin Stephen remarked apologetically: 'Sorry we have to leave early tonight. Cécile and I are going to a party at Duke Ombo's.'

'Won't you take us too?' Bisi pleaded.

'No,' said Walpole firmly. 'They can't. We haven't been asked.'

Bisi was abashed, but Cécile broke in: 'I don't see why not – d'you Stephen? Why shouldn't they come along? There'll be hundreds at the party. Duke won't mind. The more the better, as far as he's concerned.'

'What about Regina?' Stephen asked.

'Regina only wants Duke to be happy. So that's no problem.'

'Oh – can we, *please*?' prayed Bisi fervently, looking at Walpole. 'If Stephen say okay, can we go?'

'If Stephen doesn't mind,' Walpole agreed. 'What d'you think, Stephen, should you ring up and ask?'

'No – just come! Half Lagos will be there – we'll just float in with the tide.'

As they approached the house it was obvious where the party was being held. Cars were parked for a hundred yards in each direction with white-gloved cops directing newcomers.

'First time I've ever seen *them* smile,' Stephen remarked.

'They know when Duke gives a party they'll have something to smile about,' Cécile answered.

Their host was standing at the open door beaming welcome. He towered over Stephen and was half a head taller even than Walpole.

'I know you two rascals,' he roared, 'and my Cécile! But who's the lovely little girl?' He bent down to greet a delighted

Bisi. 'Just follow on in!' he urged. 'Follow on in and get started on the booze. Regina will show you where the bottles are stacked.'

Inside the house the uproar was tremendous. Their host's reputation for hospitality and good humour affected everyone; acquaintances shook hands as friends; friends bellowed affectionately across the throng; even enemies found themselves smiling a greeting as all got down to the task of consuming as much of Duke's drink as they could take in. Along one side of the room was an enormous bar too crowded even to approach; but in the garden were other bars lit by floodlights wired into the palm trees, and white-jacketed barmen scurried around with loaded trays. There was no music indoors and it would have been impossible to hear it if there had been, but outside on the daïs a band was warming up. A marquee – into which a few were already worming their way though its canvas doors had not been opened – contained, as all guests were aware, the most spectacular display of food available this evening in West Africa.

Bisi's eyes lit up as she took in the scene: 'It's heaven! *This* is what heaven must be like?'

'And here's Regina,' said Cécile.

A woman with the figure of a black Venus, looking as though she had just been sewn into her dress, greeted Cécile and Stephen with both hands, smiled appreciatively at Walpole and was introduced to Bisi. She had scarcely greeted them before being summoned away by the headwaiter, and Bisi gazed after her in admiration.

'That lovely dress! It come from Europe. Whatever you pay – you no buy dress like that in Lagos.'

'All Regina's dresses come from Paris,' Cécile told her.

'But how she gettin' them in Lagos?'

'By going to Paris. She goes every year – sometimes to Rome as well.'

'Is she always wearing white?'

'First time I've seen her in white,' answered Cécile. 'But then Regina must have fifty evening dresses. All colours except green – she says that's unlucky.'

'She should wear *always* white.'

Cécile laughed. 'You should see her in yellow, or red, or violet. . . .'

'She looks best in black,' said Stephen. 'You don't know where the dress ends and Regina begins.'

They took drinks from a waiter and went out into the garden while Bisi chattered on.

'*Fifty* evening dresses! What about daytime? How many day dresses she got?'

'None – I imagine,' laughed Cécile. 'What does Regina want with day dresses? She never gets up before afternoon.'

Later as they sat having supper indoors, Duke came over to them.

'Sit down, for God's sake!' Walpole urged. 'You make me uneasy towering up there like a lighthouse.'

'I never eat at my own parties. I get too worked up.'

'Well drink, then! But anyway sit down.'

'Regina looks wonderful,' Cécile told him.

'So she should,' said Duke. 'She's nothing else to do, and she's been at it all day. She actually got up this morning around breakfast time. No one can remember when Regina last did that.'

'Well,' said Walpole, 'she must have done some organizing to get the place looking like this.'

'Regina doesn't organize,' Duke laughed. 'The caterers do all that – and I organize the caterers. *And* the band. *And* the lighting. *And* putting up the marquee. *And* the police. Regina has only one thing to do – to look like Regina. Hi – Peter!' he called out, 'come over here! Stephen Balogun – Walpole Abiose – d'you know Peter Adoo of the *Daily Citizen*?'

'Not "Peeping Peter"?' Stephen asked.

'Of course he's "Peeping Peter",' Duke answered for him. 'Most malicious columnist in Lagos. Do you more harm in a day than all the others put together in a month. *What* was that you wrote about me last Friday?'

'Simple flattery, Chief Playboy! The merest flattery. I never write nothing hostile 'bout you. Never! I admire you too much – and I really appreciate your drink.'

'Flattery!' Duke exploded. 'Is calling me a "social pirate" flattery? But you've gone too far, my peeping friend. Put that drink down! I'm going to make an example of you.'

Catching the little man up in his arms, Duke started to carry him across the room. At the top of the steps leading into the garden, he paused, holding the journalist, kicking and struggling, until guests saw what was happening and gathered round.

'Fellow-citizens!' Duke shouted. 'This is a solemn moment in our country's history. I present you the Freedom of the

Press. He doesn't look much – but he's all we've got. What do you want me to do with "Peeping Peter"?'

'Throw him out, Duke!' 'Drop him on the ground and jump on him!' 'Bury him in the garden!' 'Pitch him into the lagoon!'

'No, No!' Duke bellowed back. 'You can't treat the press like that. . . . I'll present him to the man who gets most drunk – and I mean to win the award myself.' He let the little man down on to his feet, rumpled, indignant, but delighted to have been the centre of attention and given something to fill tomorrow's column.

When their host rejoined the group, Regina was sitting with them.

'You shouldn't have done that, Duke. Now he'll attack you even more.'

'Oh, no he won't,' Duke answered coolly. 'Peter and I understand each other. We're like one of those theatre duels. Nobody gets killed because both have to be back on stage tomorrow.'

'Anyway what he wrote was true,' Regina added, 'so you've no cause to throw him out.'

'What *did* he write?' begged Bisi.

'It started with Duke sending me away to Paris,' Regina explained, draping one elegant leg over the other. 'He'd got some little affair he wanted to attend to' – 'Purely a business matter,' Duke put in – 'and thought he could handle this little business matter more easily with me out of the way. So he bought me an air ticket to Paris and sent me off to the airport in a car.'

'But didn't you *want* to go to Paris?' Bisi asked.

'I *never* mind going to Paris. Duke can always get rid of me that way – for a week or two.'

'Then why did you mind his sending you this time?'

'I didn't mind his sending me. . . .'

Duke began to laugh, so did Regina, and Duke took up the story.

'I didn't want Regina hopping back as soon as she'd spent all her money – which would take her about twenty-four hours. So I bought one of those tickets which mean you *have* to stay in the country for three weeks but can't stay longer than three months. That would give us both a change – without having time to get into mischief. But when Regina walked up to the desk and the clerk showed her the ticket, she just turned round and came home. So when I got back in the evening to pick up my things and head off for a few days with my business partner – there was Regina sitting! "What the hell are *you* doing?" I asked. "You're supposed to be in the Rue de la Paix or somewhere." "Oh," Regina told me, "that ticket you bought me was no good."'

He paused and Stephen asked: 'No *good*? You mean it was a fake? Or made out for the wrong date?'

'Nothing like that,' Regina remarked. 'Myself, I shouldn't have minded using the ticket, but I knew Duke would be furious. It was marked "Economy Class". Imagine travelling "Economy" on a ticket bought by Duke.'

'So what did you do?' Bisi asked through the general laughter.

'Just dropped it on the counter and came back. What else *could* I do?'

'Someone must have told this to Peter,' Duke concluded. 'It was all in the *Daily Citizen* next day – in Peter's column. He called me a "social pirate" and Regina a "gilded parasite". If I'd had a pond in my garden I'd have dropped him in it. Regina! Remind me to have a pond made for Peter. About eight feet deep should be enough.'

'You wouldn't throw him in if you had one,' Regina remarked drily. 'You know you wouldn't. You probably told Peter the whole story.' Then opening her enormous eyes still wider, 'My God, that's it! Of *course* you did! That's the only way he could have got it. "Social pirate" is much too mild for you, my friend. And you probably thought up "gilded parasite" yourself.'

If getting to know Cécile had a calming effect on Bisi, contact with Regina had the opposite.

'Why do I not have twenty evening dresses when Regina having more than fifty?'

'Why do I never go to Paris? Regina is going many times.'

'Duke take Regina out every night dancin'! Why we not go?'

'We've been out dancing twice already this week,' Walpole protested. 'I don't want to go dancing every night. And I have to be up early tomorrow for work.'

'Duke works. He makes more money than you. But he not sittin' round every evening jus' because he work during the day.'

'Duke *work*!' Walpole protested. 'He doesn't know what

work is! He has his "royal procession" once a month and spends half a day each week checking his accounts. The rest of the time he's amusing himself.'

'He is havin' nice time, an' he is givin' nice time to Regina. No wonder they always happy!'

'That's not my idea of happy,' Walpole replied. 'But anyway, we're not going dancing tonight.'

Bisi sulked for a while, but her moods never lasted long and Walpole felt he had gained a modest victory. However, a week or two later when he got home from work, he found Bisi lying on the floor in his living room looking at a magazine. Beside her were a suitcase and some paper bags full of her belongings.

'What's all this?'

'I am turned away from the Kingsway.'

'Turned away – what d'you mean?'

'I finish workin' at the Kingsway. They make it not possible for me to go on workin' there. Whatever I do is wrong, so I am come to be with you.'

'You mean you've given your job up? Why?'

Bisi laid down her magazine. 'Do you not understand? I *hate* that job. I try not to worry you by speakin', but I always hatin' it. You have no idea.'

'What did you hate about it? You always seemed to me to enjoy working there and meeting people.'

'Is easy for you,' Bisi objected. 'Your work is easy . . . sittin' in a big office . . . talkin' all day with Stephen . . . so you think my work easy too. You not understan' what it is like, standin' up all day long, bein' ordered around, havin' to be nice to every person who come in.'

'But why didn't you talk about this to me, Bisi? Why didn't you discuss it? We went out only two days ago and you said nothing. And anyway what are you doing here with all your things?'

'I am not happy livin' with those girls. I never happy there. An' now I not work with them any more, so I not want to go on livin' in same place. So I come here – to live with you.'

'Good God, Bisi! You can't live here. There isn't room.'

'Now you get angry!' Bisi began to cry. 'I come here because I want to be with you. If you love me, you will be happy because I givin' up work an' friends to live with you. But instead of bein' happy, all you doin' is get mad.'

'All right, Bisi, calm down! You don't have to work at the

Kingsway if you don't want to. Maybe we find something else which you like better.'

'Regina is not havin' any job,' Bisi objected, still resentful. 'She not havin' to get up and go to work each day. So why am I forced to go every day to work? You are a rich man – you should not let me work.'

After a few days of having Bisi in his flat with all the chaos this produced, Walpole was obliged to contrive a new arrangement. He rented a small flat for her and made her a regular allowance. The flat was bright and freshly furnished, and having installed her there Walpole indulged the masculine fantasy that in putting her at a little distance from himself he was putting himself at a distance from her demands, and that in making Bisi a fixed allowance he was limiting the expense she would cause him. Her life at the Kingsway, he told himself, had perhaps been harder than he realized. But now, having set her free and provided her with the sort of life and home she wanted, he could expect on the two or three times a week he came round to visit her to find gratitude and good temper.

Such hopes did not long survive experience. Bisi seemed unable to keep her small home in any kind of order so that Walpole was soon driven to fresh expense, a girl to come in every day and clean the place up. The allowance he made had often to be supplemented, usually because Bisi had ordered new clothes for which she could not pay. Each such incident led to a scene, followed by a settlement and seeming harmony, to be followed before long by another incident – with growing resentment on both sides.

One evening when a dispute had finally been resolved through Walpole agreeing to pay a bill he had hitherto refused, he said: 'Well, Bisi, that's settled the way you wanted it. Now make us some supper, and let's go to bed.'

'What am I to get for supper? There is nothing in the flat.'

'But Bisi, we talked about this two days ago. I told you I'd be coming round this evening and wanted to stay in. D'you mean you haven't bought us anything?'

'I forget to buy. I am so worried over this money you makin' so much fuss about, I forgettin' to buy food.'

'Bisi – this is too much! I asked you to get supper – I even gave you extra money to buy food. Now you tell me you forgot. Very well, I'll forget to pay those bills.'

Bisi saw she had gone too far. 'Come Walpole! Don' be

angry with me because I forgettin' to buy food. Come – we go into bed, and then you take me out to dinner.'

Within half an hour, however, and while they were still in bed, the argument broke out afresh.

'Why you not come more often to see me, Walpole? You come maybe two-three times each week, but I am all day by myself.'

'I have to work, Bisi.'

'Work, you say? You enjoyin' yourself all day roun' town, but I am here with no person to speak to but the girl.'

'But it was you who gave up your job, Bisi. I never asked you to give it up. If you don't like being on your own, why did you leave the Kingsway?'

'I give job up to be with you – not to be pushed into corner by myself.'

'I'm not pushing you into a corner, Bisi. You said you didn't want to stay with the other girls – so I find you a place to live in on your own. Now you complain I have "pushed you into a corner". What *do* you want?'

'I want to live with you in a real home,' Bisi wailed, 'like Regina live with Duke and Cécile live with Stephen. Why we not live in that same way?'

'Don't you understand, Bisi?' Walpole was becoming exasperated. 'When you live in my flat you make life impossible. My day's full of appointments. If I miss two because you're sitting in the bath and I can't get ready, I never catch up. At night I bring work home – it's the only chance I have to think. But if you're playing records and telephoning all your friends, I get nothing done.'

'How does Duke manage, then? Or Stephen?'

'Duke has a big house – and anyway he doesn't go to work. He can stay in bed all day if he pleases. And Cécile understands what Stephen wants, and makes things easy for him.'

'What you sayin' is – I not makin' you happy like Cécile is makin' Stephen and Regina is makin' Duke happy – so it is *my* fault you not love me any more. An' my fault you push me out of the way into this flat.'

Bisi's lip trembled in a way that touched Walpole. After all, she was only a child. He ought not to be surprised if she failed to understand the importance of work and the need for some routine. It was natural for her to become bored on her own and eager to be taken out often for the sake of change. He put his arm around her. 'Okay then, Bisi. I see you're wanting to go somewhere lively. We'll go to the Harmony Cabin. Put your new dress on while I get ready.'

23
Uncrowned King

During the next month or two Walpole saw a good deal of Duke Ombo. Duke's manner of life and something of his story were common knowledge since he was a leader of café society, revelled in publicity and would rather see his name in the papers in almost any connection than not see it there at all. 'Peeping Peter', who had built the success of his scandal column round Duke and his friends, had given him the title 'Chief Playboy of the Western World', and now always wrote of him as 'Duke Ombo (C.P.W.W.)', and when he had nothing else to write about would often slip a short paragraph in such as: 'No news for a whole week of the C.P.W.W. Must be up to something, mustn't he, folks? But Peter's watching, folks. Peter's watching. And what Peter sees or hears, Peter tells. That's his one almighty, universal, jet-propelled principle.'

Duke was the only son of a poor market trader who had come into Lagos from the Calabar half a century earlier to make a living selling vegetables. When others who prospered put their savings into fine houses or sent their children overseas, old Mr Ombo, with a peasant's distrust of show, put his into land and bought a tract just beyond the city boundaries, intending to grow produce for the markets. However the city's expansion was so rapid that in a few years he had sold the land for three times what he paid and bought again further out. Realizing by now that there are speedier ways of growing rich than market gardening, he raised a loan to build on it himself, and what he built were not show houses such as Walpole had run up for politicians and executives, but meagre abodes for clerks and petty traders or gaunt tenements in which every room was separately let off, a landlord's gold mine. Though in his later years the old man's dissipations had been on a punishing scale, that merely scattered the surplus among a horde of hangers-on, making no inroad on his estate whose value increased as more and more people crowded into Lagos. So that when the old man died as he would have wished, in a sustained debauch, Duke inherited a whole pullulating section of the city's urgent life, lived in mainly by people from the countryside who had lost contact with their villages and tribal roots, their chiefs and ancestors. Among these lost citizens Duke – with his good looks, expansive manner and lavish way of life – had become a kind of unofficial ruler, so that his monthly visits to supervise the collection of rents and other dues took on the air of a royal procession.

Walpole had heard of these occasions, but one day to his surprise Duke invited him to come on such a tour. 'We start early,' he said, 'so be round my place by six. Leave your car there and pick it up when we get back.'

When Walpole arrived Duke's long white Cadillac was drawn up outside the house together with another car and a van. In the front of the Cadillac sat a chauffeur in uniform with two powerfully-built men beside him, and there were a couple more of the same type in the second car. Duke, smartly dressed and smiling as always, beckoned Walpole into the back of the Cadillac and, once they were seated, the driver set off without waiting for instructions. Traffic was not yet heavy and in half an hour they had crossed Lagos. The car stopped at a small shop and a man who had been waiting in the doorway came out, bowed respectfully to Duke and, seeing Walpole, hesitated.

'Get in, Sunday!' Duke ordered. 'Walpole, this is Sunday Ndu, my chief clerk. Sunday, this is Mr Abiose who comes with us today.'

Sunday's bow to Walpole did not conceal his suspicious glance. He was carrying two worn ledgers, one of which Duke took from his hands and started to look through.

'H'm. You've entered up last month, I see. What about defaulters?'

The clerk opened the other ledger and handed over a list. Looking carefully through it, Duke crossed off a few names and gave it back.

'The men must chase the rest,' he ordered.

'Yes, Mr Ombo. Cert'nly, Mr Ombo. As you sayin', Mr Ombo.'

'Are those your rent books?' Walpole asked.

'In a kind of way,' Duke answered. 'Rent books and general records.'

'Mr Ombo no take no rent from po'-po' persons,' Sunday put in unctuously. 'From rich persons, Mr Ombo takin' rent, an' he takin' rent from rascally persons. But from po' persons he no takin' no rent.'

'You allow people to live on your property for nothing?' Walpole asked. 'That sounds generous.'

'Well, a number of people *do* live rent free,' Duke answered. 'However, it isn't really quite so simple. Most pay the full rent. A few crooks pay more than the full rent. And are glad to because they're safer here.'

'Then who lives free?'

'I decide that,' said Duke. 'They're mostly old people who paid when they could but can't work any more. Some young ones too – a few former girlfriends naturally. . . . But apart from the crooks who are paying for security, they all pay less than they'd pay anywhere else. And they know it!'

The clerk, who had been glancing from one man to the other, trying to make out why this stranger was present, broke in: 'Mr Ombo bin too-too good to persons livin' on his property.'

'Don't take any notice of Sunday,' Duke remarked. 'He acts as my official praise-singer.'

'Well, even praise-singers *can* tell the truth,' Walpole replied. 'And if your tenants pay less than elsewhere, that means you might charge more. So why don't you?'

Duke laughed. 'You know how to get to the point, my friend. My lawyers are always on at me to charge higher rents. So, of course, are the other landlords.'

'Why not, then?'

'In the first place, it wouldn't pay. If I got higher rents, I might have to hand over more to the taxmen.'

'And in the second place?' Walpole asked.

'If I put rents up, I'd have to do something about the condition of the property. People who pay proper rents expect the place to be in a good state. People who are paying too little put up with what they find.'

'But *isn't* it in good condition?'

'Some of it,' Duke laughed, 'is in *terrible* condition. Dogs shouldn't be allowed to live in it – should they, Sunday?'

'De persons dat live on Mr Ombo's prop'ty,' the clerk

explained in his rapid ingratiating patter, 'dey not persons same like you 'n' me, sah, dey bin po' persons an' rascally persons. No good for give fine houses to such persons. Dey jus' smashin' um. Dat all dey do – jus' smashin' um up.'

'They chop pretty well everything wooden into firewood,' Duke agreed. 'Most places only have one door left. Where there are stairs, they burn the handrails. They'd burn the stairs too, if the didn't need them to go up and down.'

'Dey unscrewin' de tap, de tap dat give water for dem all,' Sunday put in. 'Dey unscrew tap – and sell for two-three pence. Den tap stopped up, an' no mo' water.'

'We do have troubles of that sort,' Duke remarked cheerfully. 'But if they paid more, we'd have far more trouble because they'd expect more. In short, if I put up the rents I'd be constantly at war with my subjects – whereas now I live in peace and majesty, as what "Peeping Peter" calls their "uncrowned king".'

'Mr Ombo too-too good to all dese persons,' came the pattering voice. 'Every person in dis whole section of de city – men, women, an' pickens – dey all lovin' an' respectin' Mr Ombo. Mr Ombo bin father to all persons.'

'Not to *all*,' Duke corrected. 'A few here and there perhaps. But not all.'

The white car had drawn up, followed by its escort, in a square with a few trees for shade and in no time a crowd was starting to collect. 'Mr Ombo done come'. . . 'De Oba on seat,' the whisper passed round. People peered into the car seeking to catch Duke's eye and bowing and smiling when they did. After a minute or two, Duke got out, telling Walpole to stay inside. The boot was opened and a chair lifted out. The crowd made space for it under a tree and the heavy men mounted guard on either side as the crowd started to press in.

'Mr Ombo, sah, you help me, sah,' begged one in the poor man's uniform of white shirt, khaki shorts and skinny legs. 'My son mos' clever boy, sah. But he need books for school, need money for bus each day. You know me, sah. I done live here all my life . . . I never askin' nothin', sah, an' I done pay my rent each month. Now I ask yo' help, sah. Not for me but for my son. . . .'

'Sunday,' Duke ordered. 'Take this man's name. Go see his schoolmaster. . . . I am in my office all day Monday,' he told the father. 'Come there after one week. If you speak true, I give you help.'

A woman with a sick husband, asking to be let off rent till he went back to work. . . . A shopkeeper due to be expelled but begging for a second chance. . . . A dispute over stolen clothing. . . . An old man who pleaded he had not eaten for two days . . . for half the morning the session went on. To the old people Duke was free with five- or ten-shilling notes, also with hand-outs to the children from a bag of small coins. Any larger sums he gave were entered in the book, and when any story seemed dubious the man was ordered to report back to the office after inquiries had been made. Duke had a sharp eye for layabouts or cadgers – a nod to one of his attendants, and the man had either vanished in a flash or was rushed through the crowd and out of sight. Meantime a scene of another kind was taking place round the van drawn up behind the Cadillac, and Walpole, hearing the chatter, went to watch. This, it seemed, was the other side of the coin. A line had formed leading to the back of the van where a second clerk stood with his ledger while two strong-armed men kept order. Most of the people brought money, presumably rent, small sums as a rule but occasionally handfuls of notes – everything was counted, put into a metal box chained to the van and the name and amount entered. But some also brought what seemed to be gifts – a skinny white turkey, a bowl of eggs, two bottles of local gin, a roll of cloth, some carved woodwork . . . such 'presents' were also entered up and stowed away.

'What's all this?' Walpole asked the clerk. 'Why do they bring these things?'

'Presents from people livin' on de prop'ty. Dey know dey payin' too little – so dey happy for bring presents. An' some havin' no money bring what dey got.'

He put his hand in the front of his *agbada*, drew out a canvas bag and rolled the contents, small lumps of unworked gold, out on his palm.

'Where does that come from?'

The man laughed. 'Rascals an' bad persons live in dis place. Bad persons pay mo'. If no pay, police soon fin' out where dey livin'.'

The audience continued until the sun started to beat down into the square and the heat came wavering up. Then Duke stood up. 'That's all,' he announced. 'No more today. Sunday – you stay till everyone's paid in. Mr Abiose and I go to my house.'

'Well,' said Walpole once they were settled in the car, 'I see what it means to be an uncrowned king.'

'It's two-way traffic,' Duke replied. 'I'm their one-man welfare state. They're my univeral provider and tax-free levy.'

'Two-way,' Walpole agreed. 'But not, I think, fifty-fifty.'

Duke laughed. 'You mean I take more than I give? All rulers do that, but I also give my "subjects" an invisible asset.'

'What's that?'

'The sense of belonging. That there's someone to appeal to. They'd be exploited a lot worse if I wasn't there.'

'What about the police? Wouldn't they keep order?'

'Police? They never go in except when I send for them. . . .'

In the office during the afternoon Stephen was astonished to learn from his partner how he had spent the morning. 'Everyone's heard about Duke's "Kingdom" – but I believe you're the first outsider he's taken on a visit. . . . I wonder why he did it?'

'You think he must want something?'

'Duke doesn't do anything without reason. There'll be some plan in his mind.'

'You're a suspicious fellow, Stephen. Can't Duke sometimes act without an interested motive?'

'He *could*, I suppose,' Stephen admitted, 'but I'd be surprised if he ever does. Anyway, he must like you, otherwise he'd never have allowed you to look over his kingdom.'

A couple of weeks later Walpole had a call from Duke asking if he could manage to come over for a talk. . . . 'Purely at your convenience, my friend. No hurry whatever. But if you *could* fit in a couple of hours early next week. . . . What d'you say to Thurday morning around ten? Hangover starting to lift . . . daylight becoming bearable to the eyes. . . . Okay? Then ten it is. I've got an idea at the back of my mind – and I think you're the man who can help me knock it into shape. . . . Ah! But I haven't said anything about *where* to meet.'

Walpole answered that he supposed Duke wanted him to come along to his house, or perhaps 'that office you took me to.'

'Ndu's broken-down shop?' Duke exclaimed. 'Shouldn't dream of it. That's only for torturing difficult tenants. And Regina's got troublesome lately about my using the house for work during her normal sleeping hours . . . so I've rented some new offices. Top of a block overlooking the racecourse.

Could follow the races from my desk if there were ever races worth watching. Got a pencil? Then take down the address. . . . *And* the phone number in case you get lost on the way round.'

The offices were imposing; they included a large board-room and three or four smaller rooms. There seemed to be several clerks as well as a Nigerian girl receptionist and a white secretary, a provocative creature on high heels. Duke gave Walpole a wink as she teetered out of the room, then lost no time in getting down to business.

'I've had an idea for some time that I ought to develop my estate. It was all very well for my old father to run the place the way he did, but times have changed, and it doesn't seem right to go on in the old way.'

'What sort of plan have you in mind?'

'I'm thinking of rebuilding the place bit by bit – knock some of the seedier blocks down first and put up something better. If we provide a few blocks where people take pride in their homes and keep them in good order, then it'll be easier with the second lot because they'll follow the example of the first.'

'Sounds practical. Even beneficial.'

'You mean for the tenants?'

'Who else?'

'Who else? Well, how about Balogun and Abiose for a start? If I'm going to rebuild my kingdom, my friends may as well get some advantage. This'll be the biggest contracting job Lagos has ever seen.'

'Very nice if it came along,' Walpole agreed, 'but I'm not counting on it.'

Duke laughed. 'It'll come along all right. And very likely come your way. But d'you think it's a good idea?'

'Indeed I do!'

'And you'd be willing to take a hand?'

'Of course! I can't commit the firm, but for myself. . . .'

'The immediate step isn't a matter for the firm. It's for you personally – if you're interested.'

'What is it you want?'

'To tackle something as big as this, I'd need the best advice in a lot of fields. Commercial and financial I can organize. But it's much wider than that. . . . I want the place to have style. To look good. There'll have to be schools. Maybe a hospital or two. . . .'

'Good God, Duke! You mean this isn't just blocks of houses? It's a complete development – a whole town?'

'And somewhere for the pickens . . . playgrounds . . . a sports field,' Duke went on. 'I haven't worked the details out, but I know pretty well what I want, and I thought you'd help me dress the idea up.'

'If I *can* help I will. But where will you find all this advice – from professional people and so on?'

'The idea is to organize a committee – "Advisory Committee" or some such. Really high-powered. A legal big-wig. Some educational tycoons – if that's the word – a vice-chancellor and a couple of professors. One or two medical men. Maybe a newspaper editor. A couple of independent politicians . . . oh, and we ought to get a woman in somewhere! A committee that really sounds like something. . . .'

'H'm, shouldn't be too difficult. But what's its purpose – the terms of reference?'

'Why, to give the project bona fides, make clear it's for real. I have to face it, Walpole, I'm considered something of a playboy. If I announce Duke Ombo's going to rebuild his kingdom so as to give everyone a better life, you know as well as I do what'll be said. . . . What's he up to? Where's the catch? What's he getting out of it? Am I right?'

'Well, some people always *are* suspicious. . . .'

'And some people are apt to be suspected, and I'm one of them. That's why I'm asking you to organize this committee.'

'Me?'

'Yes – you! You're well known and you know everyone. You're hardworking. And you're honest. Nobody's going to ask what *you'll* be making on the side. So – will you do it?'

Walpole was on the spot. This was something that would take a lot of time – each one of these great men would need to be approached separately and flattered or wheedled into acceptance. He would have to make himself a pest to friends and acquaintances through whom these powerful creatures had to be approached and snared. But Duke's project appealed to him. He felt it to be worthwhile, and that, coming at this moment, it had a particular meaning for himself. He had been growing tired of his empty life but reluctant to give it up. Duke's plan would bring purpose into his existence without requiring that he should alter it too much. He was flattered that Duke should have picked on him to help in developing this more generous aspect of his nature, and understood now why he had been taken on that tour of his 'Kingdom' which had so surprised Stephen and his uncle. It would surprise them still more, and many others as well, if Duke, under Walpole Abiose's guidance and with his help, were to rebuild a whole slice of Lagos slums. . . .

'Okay, Duke. I'll organize the committee. You'll need to get something down on paper. Everyone's going to ask for details. But if you draft a proposal, I'll take it round and find you the support. . . . Just one thing!'

'What's that?'

'This will be moral support . . . sympathy . . . goodwill. I'm not on for a money-raising exercise.'

Duke laughed. 'Don't worry, Walpole. I won't ask that of you. You round up the figureheads – I'll answer for the cash.'

24
Gamblers

Over the next couple of months Walpole flung himself into the task of organizing the Advisory Committee. Matters went slowly for no one was willing to believe in Duke Ombo as an altruist wanting to benefit his fellow citizens, but by degrees Walpole's conviction and determination began to take effect. Most of those he approached knew Duke only by hearsay whereas Walpole, it seemed, knew him intimately. He made no attempt to hide what could not be hidden, but presented Duke as a complex character in whom enjoyment of life and the need to prove himself as good a man of business as his father had always held the upper hand. Change, however, can happen to us all, and change was now happening to Duke. Let them, he urged, give him a chance – if his plans proved less good than they hoped, they need go no further. In his arguments, varied for each case, Walpole had one factor in his favour in that many of those he approached cherished some pet project such as a maternity hospital, a new type of school, a trade fair, sports complex or shopping centre which required a million or two to achieve, and which Duke's scheme might render possible. Moreover Duke – who, Walpole perceived must have other advisers besides himself – had produced an imposing brochure, with enough facts to seem practical, but sufficiently vague in phrasing to let everyone believe his own project could be included.

In addition, 'Peeping Peter' inserted a few paragraphs in his column which – despite being written in language more appealing to layabouts than academics – had considerable effect:

Never lissen, folks, to zoo-men telling you leopards ain't capable of changing spots. Here's our Crown Prince of leopards – Duke Ombo (C.P.W.W.) – planning to forsake night-spots for the spotlights that shine on all do-gooders.

What's our Big Spender's big idea? You asking me? An all-time lash-out. A spend to make Rockefeller look stoney – and all in the service of his fellow men.

Duke's aiming to rebuild those ancestral acres. To plant towers of potent architecture on our swampy shores. Homes for happy families. A market full of honest traders in clean linen. A school for smilin' studious pickens. Shops, offices, sports fields, hospitals. You name it, man!

And to guide this mighty project, and help spend these million-billions, Duke's forming a Committee of Great and Noble Citizens. Those asked to serve will not be just the Tops, but the Topmost of the Tops. In every sphere. Still the same Duke, you see, friends, wanting Nothing but the Best.

A place on this Committee – being got together by young Walpole Abiose – is nothing less than a gold-plated certificate: 'You are the Topmost'. No wonder there's hot competition for a seat . . . well, if they want a Columnist, folks, they know where to find the Topmostest. Any time.

Following the appearance of this column one or two imposing figures who had previously hesitated rang Walpole and accepted. . . . 'My friends tell me that membership of your committee is on a very high level and that in the interests of the university I ought to accept.' Walpole even found courage to approach the President of the Senate, the renowned Father of West African Nationalism, Dr Nnamdi Azikiwe. Though unwilling to commit himself, the great man accepted the brochure, said he found the project worthy of careful consideration and asked to be kept in touch with developments.

Duke was elated when he heard Walpole's account. 'You've done a wonderful job, Walpole. Bring Bisi round on Saturday and we'll make a real party of it. Harmony Cabin, then, any time after nine.'

Walpole had been seeing less of Bisi over the past two months since so much of his time was spent on the committee, so he was glad to tell her about the party and Bisi was happy to spend the next few days planning what to wear and deciding she had nothing suitable. Walpole told her she could buy what she wanted providing she took Cécile with her, and when he called for her on the Saturday was surprised by the result. Instead of a seductive little tease he found an elegant young woman, almost demure in a dress down to her toes. When she bounced into the car, however, it was the same Bisi beside him.

'How you think, Walpole? How you like my new dress? I findin' it myself – but Cécile helpin' me decide. If those girls from the Kingsway see me in this they know I gone up in the world. Not so? Where you think we go tonight?'

'Duke said to meet him at the Cabin.'

'Yes, I know. But Duke an' Regina never stay in one place more'n two-three hours. Then we move on somewhere else. Where will we go? Who goin' see me look this way?'

'Why – whatever's happened to my little girl?' demanded Duke, holding Bisi at arm's length and looking her over with fresh interest. 'This is your fault, Walpole! You weren't buying her enough new clothes. Look what happens when you do – she's a princess!'

Bisi wriggled with satisfaction, and Duke ordered two bottles of champagne while they sat chatting at the bar.

'There's no need to give one of those to Regina,' Duke exclaimed as Freddie Fagbemi, the smiling proprietor, brought menus for the party, now joined by Stephen and Cécile. 'I can tell you now what she'll order.'

'Why? Is Regina always eating same thing?' demanded Bisi. Freddie, seeing nothing would be decided yet, quietly withdrew, and Duke launched into his favourite topic, himself – and Regina in relation to himself.

'Too right, Bisi! *Always* the same thing – an underdone steak and a fresh salad. Boulestin and Escoffier may be queuing in the kitchen. But no! Nothing they thought up would induce Regina to eat anything but steak and salad.'

'I just *like* steak and salad,' said Regina.

'Nothing would make her vary,' Duke went on. 'Just as nothing could get her out of bed before afternoon. She sleeps through the morning until one – you couldn't get her out of bed before that, but equally she'd feel her moral fibres cracking if she stayed till two. Then at one she drinks a cup of coffee, and goes to have her hair done.'

Regina smoothed her black hair, cut and shaped to the fashion of the moment, while Cécile smiled at her: 'Looks wonderful, Regina. I wish I knew where you get it done.'

Duke frowned at the interruption and continued. . . . 'When she gets back, she drinks two cups of tea. From five to seven is culture time and Regina polishes her intellect with fashion magazines . . . *Vogue* and suchlike.'

'I read many more books than you do, Duke. When did you last read a book? You never read anything but your bank statements and "Peeping Peter's" column.'

Regina's retort had a sharp note and Walpole sensed that beneath her cool appearance she was far from enjoying the performance. To divert attention he broke in: 'How d'you answer that, Duke? When *did* you last read a book? I'm sure I can't remember when I did.'

But Duke was not to be diverted and continued imperturbably. 'Now and then, when she feels anxious about the world at large, Regina buys herself something serious – *Newsweek* say, or *Reader's Digest*. It eases her mind to know what *should* be weighing on it, even if it isn't. Also it gives her something to talk about if she meets someone intelligent – like Walpole here. From seven to eight she polishes her nails. At eight she starts getting dressed, and if nothing interrupts her, she can just be ready by ten. At ten I'm standing waiting – refreshed by a drink or two after my arduous day – prepared to escort her for the evening.' He glanced at his watch. 'This is actually *breakfast* she'll be having before long, so she's been coming down to breakfast for the last ten hours. It's her only meal, and it's always the same because everyone always eats the same things for breakfast. After midnight she'll take a couple of hours' exercise – dancing with the three of us – and about four or five she'll be ready for a good night's sleep.'

They had moved over to their table now and were starting on their meal. 'How clever to do always what you want, Regina,' declared Bisi fervently. 'Wouldn't you love to live like that, Cécile?'

'Not at all,' Cécile replied. 'Doing what you want means doing the first thing that comes into your head – which is what *you* do, Bisi! Regina doesn't do what she wants, she leads a most disciplined life. It's like being in the army, or a monastery! It doesn't matter what the hours are or what you do, if you keep to a pattern, that's discipline.'

'You're right, Cécile,' Duke answered, filling all their glasses. 'You've got a thoughtful girl here, Stephen. . . . You must lend her to me some time when I have to do some thinking. So Regina's really in strict training – like an Olympic champion.'

'Training for what?' Stephen asked.

'Training to go on being Regina,' Duke replied.

'It can't be easy,' Walpole murmured, with an admiring glance at her sleek figure and the elegance of her long dress, 'to be a work of art.'

His phrase started Duke off again. 'Work of art indeed! Regina's appearance, here or wherever, is the most important day's event in this whole city. And that means in West Africa! Why, there was a man here last week who'd flown all the way from Lisbon just to see Regina walk into the restaurant . . . simply to gaze at her, hungrily.'

'That's all he got,' Regina said, 'but it wasn't all he wanted.'

'Regina here,' Duke declared in a loud voice, looking round at the other tables for approval of his wit, 'is an institution, a tourist attraction that ought to be supported by the state! She's Nigeria's one and only living national monument. . . .'

'Nice to hear you in such good form, Chief Playboy,' cut in a thin voice. 'Mind if "Peeping Peter" pays respects? And drinks a glass or two with you . . . as proof of respect.'

Duke beckoned a waiter, who was never far away when he was in the place. 'Whisky for my friend here.'

'Thanks, Chief Playboy. Well now – about this national monument?' and he glanced at Regina. 'If the country *does* take over responsibility, what's it going to cost? I'm prepared to recommend it in the *Citizen* – but people will want to know what we're taking on.'

Walpole looked expectantly at Duke. He was hoping he would pick Peter up as he had done at his party, carry him out into the middle of the restaurant and drop him. But Duke's smile was imperturbable as ever.

'Are you inquiring what it costs to maintain Regina in the state to which she's accustomed?'

'That's it, Chief.'

Regina flashed Duke an angry look. 'While you men chat over your financial trifles, I shall dance with Stephen. Goodbye, Mr Peeper. You'll be gone when I come back.'

'You see, you've upset her,' Peter remarked through a swallow of whisky. 'Apologize for me when she gets back, Chief. But anyway, how much *does* she cost?'

'A year? You mean, total net expenditure per annum?'

'Yes.'

Duke paused as if making a calculation while Peter eyed him hopefully, seeing not just a column, but half a page.

'Well now,' remarked Duke at last, 'this really is *extraordinary*!'

'What is?'

'This is the first time I've ever worked out what Regina costs me in a year.'

'Yes? What *does* she cost?'

'Why – absolutely nothing! Just the opposite, she's an economy. I reckon she saves me about twenty thousand pounds a year. I can't possibly afford to let her go – even to the state. If she walks out on me, I'm ruined!'

'How d'you make that out, Chief?' Peter's disappointment was apparent. 'I reckon she's costing you at least ten thousand pounds a year.'

'If I hadn't got Regina,' Duke explained. 'I'd need at least another fifteen or twenty women per annum.'

'Apart from those you have already?'

'Not necessarily apart from – additional to. And it's always the first month that's the most expensive – that's when you have to be twice life-size to make an impression. So let's say fifteen thousand just for getting started. And on top of that there are the fares. . . .'

'Fares?'

'Of course! You don't suppose I'd confine myself to Lagos, do you? I'd be forced into the import-export business right away. Importing from Europe and America. Exporting myself now and then to look after my interests overseas.'

Seeing no point in continuing a conversation which would yield no copy, the journalist was examining the book matches Duke had passed him for his cigarette. The cover was gold with black lettering: 'Duke Ombo (C.P.W.W.)'

'I invented that C.P.W.W.,' he said 'You should pay me royalties every time you use your title.'

'I do,' Duke answered. 'One way and another, you draw full royalties from me. In fact the boot's on the other foot. It's time you did something to earn your weekly bottle.'

'What you're saying, Chief, in your sinister fashion, is that if I don't think up some way to amuse your lordly self and guests this evening, then I can't take home a bottle of Scotch? Is that the threat?'

'Right, Peter. As always.'

'Which – means – O mighty one – if I *do* think up some new thrill in this ancient, evil city, then I take my proper payment? Not so?'

'What's your offer?'

'New gambling club, Chief. The Presidential.'

'Where's this?'

'Basement of the President Hotel. Only opened ten days back. Even our Chief Playboy hasn't been there yet, my spies report.'

'You're right, Peter. He hasn't.'

'Okay then. Do I lead the way?'

Duke looked round at the guests now back from dancing, for approval. 'Yes. It seems you do – when everybody's fed.'

Peter's jackal grin split his thin face. 'Just one preliminary. O Chief of Chiefs!'

'What's that?'

'My bottle of Scotch.'

'It'll be added to the bill,' Duke assured him. 'You can either carry it round with you – or leave it here to grab yourself a swallow when you feel the urge.'

'Tell them to write "P.P." on it, Chief, and hold it here. Then there'll be a drop for me in the watering hole next time I'm on the prowl.'

The basement of the hotel looked strangely unlike a gambling club, consisting of a vast cellar intersected by pillars supporting the building's many storeys. In the middle of this space, which seemed better suited to a car park, a section had been carpeted to form the rooms. Shaded lights shone down on green baize tables, but elsewhere a twilight prevailed in which those not gambling moved around watching or talking quietly, while white-jacketed waiters pushed trolleys with drinks and sandwiches from which guests helped themselves.

Walpole felt his arm tugged by Bisi. 'I want to play!' she urged. 'Give me money. I *must* play!'

'Don't stake till you've some idea what it's all about,'

Walpole advised. 'Watch for a while, then have a try.'

'No, no. I play now. You have to let me!'

Walpole had seldom seen her so excited. 'Here, Peter,' he said. 'You know your way around. Look after Bisi and help her lose ten pounds, will you?'

'Sure, Chief. Anything to oblige. . . . But it's no good starting at chemmy, Bisi. Come over to the blackjack table. You can make ten pounds last at least five minutes there,' and he took Bisi's arm and carried her off.

Before long Stephen made an excuse to take Cécile home. Bisi was still bent over the beginner's table with Peter, and Duke was both winning and losing at chemin-de-fer while Regina looked on with elegant lack of interest. Walpole was wondering how he could get her to himself for a while when a swarthy European in white dinner jacket came up, stood behind Duke till the session ended, then put an arm round his shoulders and greeted him effusively.

'Delighted you're here, Duke. Now we really are established! And so *this* is your lovely lady! She lights up the whole room – just as she lights up all of us. Am I right?'

Walpole recognized the man Duke had introduced him to in his office when he called to bring news of the committee. To Walpole's surprise Duke had told him to stay on and hear what was said, explaining, 'Karybdis and his firm are coming into the scheme on the financial side.' He appeared to be in authority here, for a waiter was by him almost before he looked round. 'Bring a bottle of champagne. And quick!'

'You know my friend Walpole Abiose, I think,' said Duke.

'Why, of course.' Mr Karybdis shook hands with Walpole, and then evidently not wishing to waste his cordiality, turned back to Duke.

'What d'you think of this place? D'you like it? Is there any way we can improve it?'

'Ho, ho! So this is another of your bright ideas. I must say you've a fertile mind. How's the club doing?'

'Business? Fantastic! I never thought Lagos would go gambling mad. We've taken more in a week than I reckoned on in the first month.'

'This lot seem mostly overseas visitors,' Walpole remarked.

'Wherever Duke is – and his friends – that is the real Lagos!' declared Karybdis, pouring champagne and handing round the glasses. 'When you've had a drink, Duke, you might like to look round the whole operation. . . . That is, if your lovely lady will excuse us.'

'I'd certainly like to see it.'

'Come with me then!' and taking Duke's arm, Karybdis carried him off.

'What does that man want with Duke?' Regina asked.

'Karybdis? I suppose he wants him – and you – to come here often. Duke's in the public eye. If he comes, others will.'

Regina looked unconvinced. 'What else might he be wanting?'

'H'm well – I suppose he could want Duke to put money into the club.'

'Karybdis has *heaps* of money. Why should he want more?'

'To bring in a Nigerian interest.'

'It's possible,' said Regina. 'But not enough to explain. . . .'

'To explain what?'

'He's pursuing Duke. He rings him at the house, and constantly sees him in his office.'

'Well, if Karybdis is worked up about his gambling club, that would explain that. . . . Don't you gamble yourself, Regina?'

'Gambling? I loathe it. But what have you done with Bisi?'

'She's all right. "Peeping Peter" is helping her lose ten pounds.'

'You may lose more than ten pounds if you leave Bisi with Peter. Let's go see.'

The couple were bent over the beginners' table; Bisi was absorbed in play, but Peter's roving eye had already seen them coming.

'Extraordinary girl – this Bisi! A natural gambler. She calculates the odds while I'm still picking up my cards. Even the croupier's impressed.'

'D'you mean she's been playing blackjack all evening on ten pounds?'

'Not *quite*, Chief. Not literally so. I did arrange with the bank for a small supplement. . . . I knew that's what you'd wish. All the same, she *is* amazing. Give that talent a bit of training and you can retire on the proceeds.'

A minute or two later Duke rejoined them and they decided to go home. On her last stake Bisi, who had lost thirty pounds during the evening, won back ten.

'What a wonderful place!' she exclaimed, flinging herself back in the car. 'That's been the most exciting evening of my life.'

'D'you know this fellow Karybdis?' Walpole asked Stephen next morning in the office.

'Karybdis of Karybdis-Schiller, the big German-Lebanese importers? Why d'you ask?'

'He came up to Duke after you'd gone last night and carried him off behind the scenes. It seems he's running that gambling set-up at the Presidential.'

Stephen whistled. 'Of course he *would* be! I should have guessed.'

'Well, what d'you know about him?'

'He's the Greatest Fixer of All Time. They say he knows every minister in the government – and has either sold or given a Mercedes to most. A gambling joint would be just his mark. He runs quite a few restaurants, night clubs and so on . . . they allow him to do favours to important people. But he also sees that any place he runs turns in a profit.'

'So he gets his cut both ways?'

'That's right. But why let that worry you?'

'Regina thinks he's very thick with Duke. I had the impression she's frightened of him.'

'H'm. She needn't be. He and Duke would be pretty much of a match, I fancy. But how's your committee going?'

'All organized. First meeting next week. Duke's going to outline his plans to them.'

'Well, you've done a hell a lot of work on his behalf. I only hope he's grateful.'

A few moments later Cécile came into the room. 'I'm taking Stephen to lunch – why don't you join us?'

Walpole excused himself, but Stephen remarked: 'Walpole's asking about Karybdis. He owns the place we were at last night and is making a big play for Duke. Walpole thinks Regina's frightened of him.'

'Poor Regina!' said Cécile. 'If Karybdis were all she had to be frightened of, she'd be a happy girl.'

'But *isn't* Regina happy?' Walpole asked.

Stephen and Cécile exchanged glances.

'She's a beautiful girl,' Stephen declared, 'and the best dressed in Lagos. So I imagine she has the life she wants.'

When the meeting of the committee took place the following week, Duke already knew each one by name and thanked him handsomely for coming. Once all had arrived he lost no time in starting the proceedings. He said he had called them together as people concerned with the new Nigeria in whose creation they had already played a distinguished part. He realized that in the past he had been considered little more than a playboy, but he too wished to do something for his country and its capital city. They probably knew of the estates he had inherited. He now intended these should be developed to provide good accommodation for some thousands of his fellow citizens – plus an important new trading centre for industry and commerce and improved facilities for health and education. Besides its value to the nation, this would be a worthy memorial to his late father. Duke talked fluently. There were maps on the wall to which from time to time he referred. He answered questions skilfully, showing himself fully aware of each one's particular concern and giving the impression it was also of special interest to himself.

To those who asked how the plan was to be financed, Duke replied that a project on this scale was obviously too large to be financed entirely from the private sector. Some part of the money would be privately raised, but some backing also, he hoped, would come from the government and the city authorities. He was in touch with both and hoped to have news to give them at the next meeting, due in six weeks' time.

On the surface all went well, but what made Walpole uneasy was the presence of Karybdis, introduced by Duke as his financial adviser who would be organizing privately raised capital.

Having maintained a discreet silence throughout the meeting, Karybdis remarked as the last visitors went out: '*Very* good, Duke. *Very* good. You put that across first rate.'

'How d'you think they reacted?'

'They liked it, Duke . . . liked everything they heard. But it's the next stage that's the tricky one.'

'What d'you mean by the next stage?' Walpole asked.

But before he could answer, Duke cut in: 'Karybdis here's a bit worried over the fund-raising. Feels the government may not come in as strongly as we've hoped.'

'But you said the whole financial side was taken care of.'

'One way or another it *is* taken care of. But if the government doesn't come in strongly enough, then the private sector has to come in more. That worries Karybdis here.'

'Like hell it does!' Karybdis growled. 'I can raise more money than this job takes just by picking up the phone.'

25
Fall-Back Position

Over the next weeks Walpole found himself thinking more about Regina than he wanted to. He had been attracted from the first, but apart from the fact that she belonged to Duke and he was involved with Bisi, he had seen her as a beautiful object wanting only to be admired and so not altogether human. But the sentence or two Cécile had let fall, the understanding glance she exchanged with Stephen, and Regina's angry reaction when Duke was showing her – or rather himself – off at the Harmony Cabin outlined a different picture, and he found the impression of Regina as vulnerable and not altogether happy, caught in the trap of Duke's money and power, much more appealing than the image of her as a contented clothes-horse. Several times he rang Bisi to suggest taking her out, having in mind that in the course of the evening they might meet up with Regina and Duke, but neither time was there an answer. He supposed she had gone round to see Cécile, or taken up with her former Kingsway friends, and was relieved she should be finding her own interests and becoming less dependent on himself. However, when he called for her as usual at the weekend, she at once attacked him for neglect.

'Oh – so you comin' here at last, are you? I begin to wonder if I ever seein' you again.'

'Sorry, Bisi. I tried to get hold of you during the week, but we've been very busy at work. I expect Cécile has told you.'

'Cécile – yes! If Cécile not tellin' me what happenin', then I never hear nothin'. I tell you I grow tired sittin' here in this room waitin' for when you show up.'

'But you're not *always* sitting waiting for me to show up,' Walpole answered mildly.

'What you say? You accusin' me?'

'I'm not accusing you of anything, Bisi. But twice when I've rung you in the evening there's been no answer.'

Bisi looked taken aback. 'I was visitin' Cécile,' she declared.
Adding after a moment, 'I *must* have been there because that is
only place I ever go. You ask my friends if you not believe me,
Walpole! Not one of them never seein' me no place else.'

'All right, Bisi. No need to get excited. Put on one of your
new dresses and I'll take you out to dinner.'

The Harmony Cabin was full as usual, and though Duke
and Regina were not there yet, they turned up before long and
came over to join their table, Duke collecting smiles and
shouts of welcome as they crossed the floor. Regina was in full
splendour. A long creamy dress swathed her body to the
knees, flaring out below them like a Spanish dancer's; the
women in the room had eyes only for the dress and the men for
the amount of Regina it revealed.

'How's everything going with the project?' Walpole asked
after greetings were exchanged.

'I'm putting off our next committee meeting,' Duke
replied. 'There's no point in having a meeting till I've got
something to tell them – and so far the government hasn't
made up its mind. Or hasn't told us, if it has.'

'Well, don't wait too long,' Walpole advised. 'You don't
want interest to fade.'

'No, no. That won't happen. And meantime they're
serving a useful purpose. . . .'

'What's that?'

'Karybdis tells me that interest overseas is now very strong
– particularly in West Germany. There's a mint of money
from foundations and semi-government agencies for anything
that can be classed as "aid to developing countries". That's
where this committee – and you've really pulled in the top
people – is so valuable. These agencies, international banks
and so on have started to come in in a big way.'

'Then what about the government and the city authorities?
If all these Germans and so on are putting up the money –
where do *they* come in?'

Duke laughed. 'The government had to be given the
chance. If it doesn't take it, that's too bad. But whether it takes
it or not, the offer's already served our turn.'

'How's that?'

'All this stuff in the papers. The Finance Minister's statement in Parliament that "the government is deeply interested
and is giving Mr Duke Ombo's scheme their fullest consideration". That's all added to our build-up. The publicity we've

had one way or another would have cost a bloody fortune in the normal way.'

'Duke,' said Walpole, 'I'm not sure I like the way things are going. It seems this whole scheme of yours is changing shape.'

'Don't worry, my friend! It's essential at this stage to keep options open. Nothing'll be done you don't approve of – I promise you that! But this isn't the place to talk business. I'll ring you in a few days, and you come round and see exactly how it's shaping up. And now, my little Bisi, what about our showing everyone what we can do together in the High Life?'

Walpole turned to Regina: 'At last! I've been wanting to see you all week – and for weeks before that.'

'Well, now I'm here!'

'How's everything with you?'

'As it always is.'

Walpole hesitated. 'I see you so seldom. . . . It's difficult. . . . There are so many things I want to know – but don't know how to ask.'

Regina smiled. 'Begin at the beginning. And use words of one syllable.'

'Do you enjoy your life, Regina?'

She sighed. 'Why d'you ask?'

'Because I'm concerned about you. You make such a wonderful impression – but sometimes I have the feeling . . . well, behind it you're not happy.'

'Who *is* happy? Are you? But that's not answering . . . I suppose the true answer's the usual one.'

'What's that?'

'Yes and no.'

'What's the "yes", then – and what's the "no"?'

'The "yes" is that I chose it. I don't *have* to live the way I do. So if I go on doing it, I must like it. . . .'

'And the "no"?'

'If I live this way, I can't be living in a different way . . . like my sister in the bush, for instance.'

'How does she live?'

'With a husband and pickens – a family together in a home.'

'Is *she* happy?'

Regina laughed. 'She's so busy, she's no time to think. She just looks after them all.'

'Would you like to live like that?'

But by now the other two were back and conversation

ended. Later when the meal was over Walpole asked Regina to
come and dance.

Duke beamed: 'Of course she'll dance! It's time for her
exercise.'

'I'm not asking *you* to dance, Duke, I'm asking Regina.'

He led her out on to the square in the middle of the room and
in a moment they had swirled away into the High Life, a free-
flowing dance to a powerful rhythm and repetitive phrasing,
blared out by the band as if to blast bottles off the tables. The
dancers converged, turned their backs on one another, drifted
off into corners jiving on their own, then rejoined to stamp
and sway with hands on one another's hips. Apart, they
followed each other's movements like a parody, when together they fought it out face to face in a frenzy of knee-
bending and shoulder-shaking. From time to time a sentence
would be thrown over a shoulder or across intervening
couples, to be answered a minute later when the partners came
together.

'Tell me – how did you live before you met Duke?'

'As a model girl. Showing clothes. Posing for pictures.'

They danced away and as they converged again, Walpole
asked, 'Before that? Before you started modelling?'

'I served in a shop, and they chose me to be a model.'

'And before that still?'

'I was at school.'

Once more they separated, danced off and came close
together, swaying with hands on one another's hips.

'Your sister must envy you.'

'She does. But. . . .'

'But what?'

'Sometimes I envy her.'

Walpole's hand slid down that lovely swelling contour.
Regina did not withdraw, but looked him full in the face. Her
eyes were almost black and the whites had a bluish tinge –
Walpole felt he was seeing her for the first time and noticed she
was wearing little make-up, only around her eyes was painted
and her lips touched with colour. The skin of her shoulders
shone as though it had been oiled for years, but the oil had long
since sunk in and become part of her. A wave of perfume
floated up which he could not believe came out of any bottle.

Catching his intense, pained look, Regina laughed. 'Beware,
my friend! That's what I'm saying to you. Beware!' The phrases
floated to and fro with the movements of the dance.

'Beware of what?'

'Beware of me. Beware of you. Beware of Duke.'

'Why should I beware?'

'Duke likes you. You know he does.'

'Well?'

'If he likes you he can do much for you. . . . But if he hates you . . . and he changes very quick. . . .'

'Why? What then?'

'You can suffer much. . . . Then you'll blame. . . .'

'Who will I blame?'

'Not yourself. . . . What man ever does?'

When they came back to the table amid surface smiles and affability, Duke took Walpole's wrist and held it as though he were a doctor checking a patient's pulse. He frowned, drew out a silk handkerchief, soaked it in champagne and pressed it against Walpole's forehead.

'What's that for?'

'To cool you down.'

'But champagne's a stimulant.'

'Then it's to revive your stamina. You'll need it. Dancing High Life with Regina can take years off a man's life. . . . And now I'm going to take a few years off mine!'

Duke caught Regina's hand and carried her back on to the dance floor, where by the energy and inventiveness of his movements he was soon showing Walpole, his partner and everyone in the Harmony Club just how the High Life should be danced. Walpole would have liked to compete, but when in response to Bisi's urging he took her out on to the floor, he felt listless and uninspired and she complained he had nothing to say and wasn't interested in dancing. Towards morning when he drove Bisi back and left her at her flat, he realized this was the first time since he knew her that he hadn't gone up and gone to bed with her. And as he drove on home, thoughtful and disheartened, he found himself wondering how he had ever come to be entangled with this girl at all.

Some four weeks later Walpole received a phone call from Duke. 'I've got Reuben here and I want you in on our discussion. We've had an answer from government and are planning the next moves. Can you come over to my house right away?'

The use of Karybdis's first name and the fact that he should be the first person Duke called in were not lost on Walpole, but

he was surprised on arrival to find his friend in a state of
elation. Motioning Walpole to a chair, he started to stride up
and down the room, mouthing out phrases from the official
letter with relish.

' ". . . given our most careful consideration to your proposals . . . sincerely appreciate the importance of projects
beneficial to our poorer citizens . . . most grateful for
initiative . . . value particularly propositions put forward by
private-spirited public citizens – no! it's the other way round –
public-spirited private citizens . . . certain adverse factors
however . . . must militate heavily . . . essential bear in mind
. . . many calls on national resources . . . however if private
sector decides to go ahead independently . . . every possible
encouragement offered . . ." So! What d'you make of *that*,
Walpole? What *do* you make of that?'

'The British trained your lot well,' Karybdis observed,
rolling his cigar over in his mouth. 'Got all the jargon there.
No imperialist could give a smarter turn-down in the language
of a go-ahead. Well – what matters is, we're free!'

'Free?' Walpole asked. 'Free for what?'

The two men exchanged glances, following which Duke
started to explain. 'Look, Walpole. There's something you
should understand. It's been pretty clear to Reuben and myself
for some time back that the proposals I made in my office six
months ago weren't likely to be accepted. So it seemed only
good sense to work out a contingency plan – what Reuben
calls "a fall-back position" – in case we were given the turn-
down. As we *have* been in this letter.'

'So what fall-back position did you work out?'

'What we've had to face,' Duke explained, 'is this. If the
bulk of our money has to come from overseas, the people
putting it up won't have the same concern for the poorer
citizens that we have. *Their* concern is for their money. They
want, first, to be quite sure of getting it back and, second, to be
sure of getting it back with a big profit. With jam on it, if you
like.'

'Too damned right they will,' remarked Karybdis.

'But is there any chance of banks and private investors
putting up so much money?' Walpole asked.

'Depends what for,' Karybdis grunted.

'Not for the project I envisaged,' said Duke, 'as a means for
getting people rehoused. It's obvious that families whose
earnings are around ten or twenty pounds a month or less,

can't afford decent housing unless some official body
subsidizes it. The official bodies have refused, in appropriate
official language, and so now. . . .'

'Now we get down to nuts and bolts,' Karybdis cut in, 'as
we'd have done six months back if you'd listened to me.'

'No doubt, Reuben,' Duke replied. 'But I had to make my
offer. I owed it to the people on my estates. While there was
any chance of getting them proper housing I had to try. That's
been refused – by the people's own representatives. So now
we must handle things the best way we can.'

'Good on you, Duke.' agreed Karybdis. 'You've done all a
legitimate monarch could for your subjects – legitimate or
illegitimate – and now you must think of Number One. I'm
sure Walpole here understands the situation just as well as you
or I.'

'Not so well as that,' Walpole answered. 'But better than I
did.'

'Before you say any more, Walpole,' Duke broke in, 'I'd
like to explain what we see as the next moves.'

'Go ahead.'

'Since we depend on backing from overseas, we must angle
our scheme to attract their interest. And since no one's going
to put down twenty or thirty million at one go, we have to
tackle one stage at a time. The first will attract money for the
second, the second for the third – and so on. That gives us our
priorities.'

'First things first,' observed Karybdis.

'Which means office blocks to start with. Then a big hotel or
two with a casino – which is where Reuben's recent experience
can help.'

'What you mean is a big casino with a hotel wrapped round
it,' Karybdis put in. 'I've never seen such gamblers as you lot
here! And with a big hotel and the right sort of entertainment,
they can take their women along and spend their winnings
without ever going outside the door.'

'After that,' Duke continued, 'we're planning an industrial
estate for light consumer industries. That's important. It could
mean employment for several thousand people.'

'A couple of hundred more like,' Karybdis corrected.
'These'll be capital intensive, not labour intensive industries.
We've already had approaches. . . . The Japanese want a
factory for plastic souvenirs, and another where they'll print
textbooks in English for the schools. The Americans want a

Coke-bottling plant . . . we could damn nearly let that whole estate off right away.'

'And after that?' Walpole asked.

'That's about as far as we've worked out,' Duke explained. 'We have to keep things fluid. For instance, if the offices are taken up quickly, we build more. Or, if pressure's on from the industrialists, we lay out a second industrial area.'

'What about the people living on your estates now? Where do they go?'

'Well, that's up to them, isn't it?' Duke replied. 'Some'll have to do what we all do from time to time – find some new place to live. Of course they won't all be moved out at once. This scheme'll go on for years – at least ten. They've lots of time – and some may be rehoused as the plan develops.'

Walpole said nothing, and after a moment Duke looked across at him and asked: 'Well, what d'you think of it?'

'I think you – and Karybdis too of course – will make yourselves a packet of money. And I see that was what you were after from the start.'

'And what's wrong with that?' Karybdis asked.

This was all that was needed to make Walpole explode. 'Keep out of this! This is between Duke and me. I understand *you* looking on Nigerians as means for making money. That's the sort of man you are – and I don't give a damn for you one way or the other.'

'Then what the hell's all the fuss about?'

Ignoring him, Walpole went on: 'As for making a packet for yourself, Duke, you're welcome to it. But why all the lies and pretence? Why had I to be led up the garden path? Why not tell me honestly what you were planning – and let me come in on it or not? After all, I'm supposed to be your friend.'

'He's got a point there, Duke,' remarked Karybdis. 'He's got a point. But Duke couldn't let on about his fall-back plan. Someone might have talked, which would've spoiled his whole arrangement. . . . Mind you, I didn't want *all* that pretence myself – but then I'm not in Duke's shoes. I haven't got fifty thousand loving subjects whose lovingness I want to keep. Duke had his image to think of as well as profits.'

'I don't see what cause you have to be upset, Walpole,' Duke remarked. 'I understand you wanting me to do something for the poorer citizens – and I was willing to go along with your wish to be benevolent at my expense. But if the government won't play, that's the end of that. Anyway it's no skin off your nose. You've lost no money by it.'

'What I've lost,' said Walple, 'through trusting you, is to be made to look a bloody fool. Tell me – what are you going to do about the committee?'

'That committee's served its purpose,' Karybdis broke in. 'It's been useful while it lasted – especially with the overseas foundations,'

'*I'll* deal with the committee,' said Duke. 'I shall send a formal letter of thanks to everyone, putting the blame on the government and the city authorities. As for your being made to look a fool, Walpole. I'm sorry you feel like that about it, but really. . . .'

'Finish it!' said Walpole. 'What you're going to say is that I *am* a bloody fool. It's true – and I'll tell you why! Because I didn't believe what my friends told me.'

'What *did* your friends tell you?' Duke asked coolly.

'They told me never to go into any deal with Duke Ombo. That you'd have the hide off your best friend if you could sell it profitably. I've been all over Lagos arguing that you weren't in this to make money but to help people. But the only person you ever meant to help in all this was yourself.'

Walpole jumped up and strode across the room. As he slammed the door behind him and moved to the head of the stairs, he was aware that a torrent of argument, mixed with laughter, had broken out behind him. Steadying himself with one hand on the rail, for he was trembling with rage, he walked slowly down. But even before reaching the bottom his mood had changed from anger to depression. He had allowed himself to be deceived because he wanted to be deceived. He admired Duke for his success and enjoyed his lively company. Wanting to think well of him – and because he felt concern for his fellow men and a wish to help them – he had chosen to believe that Duke shared that concern, although, common sense and his friends assured him this was nonsense. Through Duke's project, deftly angled to attract his interest, he had fancied he might do something for the general good, without too much expenditure of time and effort. For that he deserved to be used as a stooge – and a stooge was exactly what he had been. Worse than that, by getting together the advisory committee he had caused a lot of other people, busy people in important positions, to be turned into stooges too, and they would all naturally conclude he'd been a party from the start to Duke's manoeuvrings.

He felt overwhelmed by inadequacy in face of people who knew what they wanted and applied themselves whole-heartedly to getting it – and what they wanted was always the same, money to win power, or power in order to make money. As for himself, he too wanted money and power but not at any price, and his uncertainty made him a victim for those unhampered by scruples. He had glimpses of ideals which never became more than glimpses because of the demands those ideals would make if they ever became conscious – and of the conflict which would arise if he ever allowed himself to compare the way he lived and the man he was with the way he ought to live and the man he might become.

As he stood by the entrance, too preoccupied to raise his hand and open the door, he felt that his whole life till now had been nothing but a foolish mess. His actions were no more than a succession of responses, his work merely well-paid bustle, his friendships only the pursuit of mutual advantage. As for his 'love'. . . .

There was a small room to one side of the door, and Walpole became aware that somebody was standing in its entrance. He supposed it was a servant and not wishing to be seen in his exposed condition, turned away and put his hand on the doorknob.

'Walpole!'

He turned to face Regina. She was wearing a dressing gown, her face was without make-up, and she was gazing at him with an intense concern which rendered her as exposed and helpless as himself.

'Regina!'

He took two steps towards her, and she pushed the door to behind him. There was such blind eagerness in his seizing of her and such surrender in the way she pressed against him, that they seemed to Walpole in that moment to become one person – or rather as if they had always been one person but failed to know it until now.

'Darling Walpole! I knew you'd be hurt. I couldn't warn you – but I had to see you.'

They clung together. Walpole could not speak, but the knowledge that Regina had risked everything to comfort him filled him with elation. And as they clung to one another, at first in mutual despair and then with growing hope and confidence, he was taking in through bodily contact and without need of words the full sense of Regina's situation, her relationship with Duke and all the frustrations and humiliations of her life.

'What can we do?' he asked, knowing every second they stayed meant danger for her.

'Do nothing!' she whispered. 'Just wait – I'll come to you before long.'

Walpole kissed her face, looked round and picked up the case he had let fall, with an effort managed to unlatch the door, and was outside in the garden just as Duke's bellow for Regina sounded down the stairs.

26
Betrayal

Following the moments spent with Regina, Walpole began to feel over the next few days that the whole picture he had of life was being transformed. In Regina he recognized the woman of his hopes and dreams, and she had responded by recognizing him. It was plain they were destined for each other, and that it was destiny which had brought them together. Through this happening, which some might dismiss as chance or infatuation, Walpole felt he had been given a glimpse into the true nature of life. Those forces – ancestral, spiritual, divine – which govern our existence are, he was now convinced, benevolent. They are continually guiding our affairs in accordance with their infinite wisdom, with which all who seek lasting happiness should align themselves.

Nor was this just an intellectual conviction. The sense that each was the ideal partner for the other, that they both recognized this and would allow no force on earth to come between them, inspired a confidence in Walpole such as he had never known, and a calm which would be proof, he felt, against every setback. Regina had said she would come to

him, and he waited, confident that if he had to wait three
months she would fulfil her promise. Meantime there were
matters to be attended to which his former self might have
shirked, but which now he almost welcomed as tests of his
love and newfound determination.

He wrote to Duke saying he did not want him to approach
the members of the committee. Since it was he, Walpole, who
had persuaded them to belong, it was for him to report the
change of plan which had rendered their work useless. He
could not, he said, explain this change, but it was his
responsibility to inform them of it, and over the next few
weeks Walpole called on all the members he could contact,
apologized for having involved them and suffered their
reproaches and complaints. Though all were angry, several
had the grace to thank him for coming in person instead of
sheltering from their annoyance behind a letter.

His second task would be more difficult, but was even less
to be evaded. On his first free evening he went round to Bisi's
flat. For weeks past he had gone there reluctantly, and with
apologies for not having gone sooner forming in his mind. In
her company he had been hesitant and artificial. But tonight he
had no uncertainty. He was going to wind up the affair. It was
not possible to tell her the full truth which could be disastrous
for Regina. He would simply tell Bisi that his feelings had
changed and that he could not pretend a love he did not feel.
She would certainly reproach him with having done exactly
that over these past few weeks and he would have to endure
her storms. But Bisi's emotions were, he considered, not
deep, and it would not take long for them to attach to someone
else as rapidly as they had to him. Also, given time to look
around, she would quickly find herself a job. Young, attractive and with business experience, she was the kind of girl
most in demand, and if she had not found something in a week
or two, he or one of his friends would find it for her.
Meanwhile he would act generously to provide a home and
money for as long as she might need them.

There was no answer to his knock, so Walpole unlocked the
door and went inside. Her clothes were flung around as they
always were, and there were a couple of used glasses and an
empty whisky bottle in the living room. This was not one of
the evenings on which Walpole usually visited her, yet he had
confidently expected to find her in and wondered now why he
had been so confident. The bedroom door was open and he

looked inside – more clothes thrown about, and the bed
unmade. What about the girl who was supposed to tidy up the
place? Was she ill? Had Bisi sacked her? Was this her day off? It
dawned on Walpole that he had little idea what had been
happening to Bisi over the past month. There was a telephone
in the place and he rang Cécile.

'Looking for Bisi? No. I haven't seen her this week. She's
probably out shopping.'

'It's a bit late in the night for shopping.'

'I mean – been out shopping and not got back yet. Is it
something urgent?' Cécile sounded disconcerted.

'Very.'

'Well, you're sure to find her later at. . . .'

'At where?'

'Well, I suppose by now Bisi must have told you, hasn't
she?'

'I expect so. What about?'

'About starting work at the casino?'

'Oh *that*'s where she'll be! Of course! Sorry to have bothered
you, Cécile.'

It was too early yet for the casino, so he waited till late
evening when the crowd would have gathered then walked in
behind a group of new arrivals. He saw Bisi at once; she was
wearing some kind of uniform and standing beside the
croupier at one of the main tables. Walpole watched for a
while, and then went over to a bar and ordered himself a drink.

'Who's the new girl at the chemmy table?' he asked the
barman.

'Dat Miss Bisi, sah. Very good girl, very nice girl. You
waitin' spik wid Miss Bisi?'

'Later, maybe. Now I just want a drink or two. What about
you? Aren't you having a drink?'

'Thank you, sah!'

'Has Miss Bisi been here long?'

'Nobody don' bin here long, sah. I myself done bin here
mos' six weeks. Mis Bisi done bin here one-two weeks.'

'I've seen her before in one of the stores, and had no idea she
was working here. Did one of the other girls introduce her?'

'Mr "Peepin' Peter" done 'troduce Miss Bisi, sah. You
know Mr "Peepin' Peter" who write de newspaper? He come
roun' dis evenin' for sure.'

'Does Mr Peter work here too?'

'I don' know 'bout *workin*' here, sah. I can't say 'bout

workin' here. Mr Peter frien' of Mr Karybdis dat own de club,
so Mr Peter in-out mos' every evenin'. Den he sit here till Miss
Bisi done finish at de tables.'

'Thank you, my friend,' said Walpole, putting a note down
on the counter. 'Maybe I see Mr Peter when he comes in.'

'Thank you, sah. Thank you indeed, sah! Shall I tell Mr
Peter who ask for him, sah? You want I shall give him yo'
name?'

But Walpole had moved conveniently out of range and did
not reply, then slipping out of the club drove home with relief.
Though prepared to speak to Bisi, he was happy not to have to
do so. Had his news been coming as an unexpected blow, he
would have felt obliged to let her rage on as she wished, but
she had taken on this job without telling him, for which the
obvious reason must be that she was having an affair with
"Peeping Peter". To whom, he remembered, he had handed
her over when they first visited the casino. Theirs must be the
two glasses in the flat, and theirs also no doubt the unmade
bed. She could have no complaint against him now for which
he could not bring the equivalent against her. Walpole felt
some concern in having launched Bisi into a world of casinos,
Karybdises and Peeping Peters, but the concern was much
outweighed by relief as he wrote two lines wishing her luck in
her new life, enclosing his key to her flat with a cheque
covering her rent for the next six months and the allowance he
had been making her for the next three. He had thought of
making that six months too, but changed his mind. Bisi had a
job; she was young and strong; the extra money would only
go on more clothes and Peter's whisky. Having written letter
and cheque and posted both, Walpole sat down at his table and
allowed the tide of happiness to flow over him, for was this not
further proof that the powers which order human life were
conspiring to help Regina and himself?

Two or three evenings later Regina rang as he sat at home,
for he no longer wanted to go out in the evenings.

'Can we meet tomorrow, Walpole?'

'Of course. When?'

'I'll be with you around seven. No more now.' And she
rang off.

Walpole got through the day's work and came home early,
stopping on the way to buy some food. Soon after seven came
a tap on the door – and she was there.

'You see I am not late!'

'Regina! But what happened? What makes you free? I didn't like to ask you on the phone.'

He was stumbling to bring her in, to move a chair out of her way, to close the door behind her. Regina gazed slowly round.

'Just how I thought you'd live. It's all as it ought to be. Oh Walpole!'

'Oh Regina! But tell me first how. . . .'

'Duke's away. He's flown to Germany for a few days with that Karybdis to arrange finance for their new plans.'

'A few days? You mean you're actually free for a few days?'

'I don't know. It depends . . . but I'm free now. And how about you – how long are you free?'

'Till the year two thousand.'

Regina laughed. 'That should be long enough. But how about Bisi? What have you done with her?'

'Started work at the casino two weeks ago. She's learning to be a croupier or something. "Peeping Peter" fixed it – so it seems she now belongs to him.'

'Silly Bisi! But doesn't that upset you?'

'It's taken a ton weight off my neck. After we kissed the other day I decided to break with her – then found she'd done it first.'

'Have you spoken to her?'

'No. I went to her flat to tell her, but she wasn't there. So I rang Cécile who let out that Bisi works at the casino. Later in the evening I called round – and there she was, standing at a table with the croupier. She didn't see me, and I talked to a barman who told me Peter introduced her, and now waits every night to take her home.'

'Peter's no good to Bisi,' stated Regina flatly. 'Peter's only got one love – the bottle. But I think young Bisi can take care of herself.'

Their meal was a pretence of eating, and after a while Regina got up. 'I can't eat, Walpole. You make me nervous. Where do I undress?'

He opened the bedroom door.

'It's not very big,' she said, 'but big enough for us.'

Walpole sat down to wait. The pressure of anticipation through the day and through preceding days had been so heavy that now he did not seem to be feeling anything at all. He was stunned by the thought that Regina was a yard or two away. His throat was dry and he felt sick. When some minutes had passed he opened the bedroom door. Regina was lying naked with her head resting on one arm. She was far more beautiful than he had imagined and he stood in the doorway motionless, drinking in an impression which would last, he felt, for the remainder of his life.

Hours later as he lay on his back beside her, Regina asked: 'How long have you loved me, Walpole?'

'Since we danced together and I put my hand on your hip.'

'M'm, yes . . . I felt that too. . . . But I'd loved you long before that.'

'How long?' asked Walpole sleepily.

'Before I ever knew you. When I was a little girl with my sister in the bush I loved you – but I also wondered what you'd be like. Now you're just what I wanted you to be.'

Towards morning Regina sniffed the coolness of the air. 'I must be going. I have to be home before the girl arrives.'

'What time does she arrive?'

'Before six.'

'I'll take you back. When do I see you again?'

'Tonight if you want.'

For answer Walpole drew her to him in the bed, and then had to drive fast to get her home in time.

'Don't take me in the house. Put me down here. I'll walk the rest.'

She got out of the car, took a few steps, turned the corner and was gone.

For the rest of the day Walpole did not attempt to go to work, but simply sat or moved around his room in a bewilderment of bliss, going to the door of his bedroom from time to time and gazing round. Something had happened that had never happened to him in his whole life before – he and Regina had become one person. He knew her thoughts without being told, and when he put his hand on her breast it was as though he were both the toucher and the touched. When he had first become excited by Regina it was her beauty he thought about; he longed to take possession of her and dwelt in his mind on aspects of her looks and impressions of her body, imagining sensual delights. But looking back on the night they had just spent together, he did not recall how often or in what ways they had made love, whether he had been as virile or Regina as responsive as he hoped. What he remembered was putting his arms round her and her pressing close as if for comfort. More vividly than any intimacy he recalled her saying his name 'Walpole . . . Walpole . . .

Walpole . . .' over and over to herself like a child that has learned a new word, and when he asked what she was doing, her answering in a whisper as though it were a secret . . . 'taking you into my heart'. Once when he asked a question about Duke she put a hand over his mouth. . . . 'No! Some other time, not now,' and when he started to explain something about Bisi and himself, she said: 'But I understand everything about Bisi.'

He had now no doubt at all that Regina and he would soon be together and remain so throughout life, and in his mind was already experiencing the stages of their future . . . marriage . . . settling into a home . . . the birth of children and their growing up. There were, of course, practical problems to decide; how Regina was to get away from Duke; how they would settle down in a city where so many of their friends knew each other and where Duke was a public figure; how they would cope with his attempts to destroy their happiness and perhaps themselves. But these were details to be fixed at their next meeting – from which he intended to ask her never to go back. What things she needed from Duke's house she must bring with her, or he would go round later and collect them.

Some time during the afternoon Walpole lay on his bed and fell into a troubled sleep. He was awakened by the telephone ringing and, stumbling towards it, supposed this was early morning – but who could be ringing before breakfast? Then he saw that he was dressed, caught the full light of afternoon from the window, and remembered.

'Bad news, Walpole. I must leave. I'm calling from the airport. I couldn't from the house – I'm watched the whole time.'

'What's the matter? You're not hurt?'

'Duke's sent for me to join him. A cable from Munich. I'm to get on the next plane.'

'But you can't go to Duke!'

'I have to, Walpole – he's sent for me.'

'But you don't belong to Duke any more, Regina – you belong to me. You mustn't go! You *can't*!'

'I have to go, Walpole.'

'Look, Regina – you are *not* to go to this man! Not after last night. . . . We'll get married! I'll look after you.'

From the other end came a gasp, followed by silence.

'Are you there, Regina? Are you *there*?'

'Yes. I'm here, Walpole, but. . . .'

'Then stay there! I'm coming to the airport to pick up up. Stay where you are!'

'I can't, Walpole. My plane leaves in a few minutes. They're calling the passengers now.'

'Regina – listen to me! You are *not* to get on that plane. I'm coming now to bring you back. Tomorrow we'll be married.'

'It's no good, Walpole darling, I have to leave . . . I shan't be gone long . . . writing soon . . . we'll talk about it all when I get back.'

'Regina! Regina!' The receiver clicked and there was no reply.

After Regina's departure Walpole continued for a while to hope. He would not accept her leaving at its face value, could not believe that after the experience they shared she could go of her own free will to Duke. There must be some reason she could not express – probably her call from the airport was overheard – and before long a letter would arrive explaining everything. Impatiently he waited for each morning's post, and, when nothing came, drove to the office to go through the mail before even the post clerks had arrived, and at intervals throughout the day would demand to know if any letters from overseas had come in late. Back at home he hesitated to go out, convinced that if he left the flat the phone would ring, and during the evening would stand staring at the instrument for minutes at a time, as though the intensity of his gaze could make it ring and a voice utter: 'Is that Mr Walpole Abiose? . . . Hold on! I've a long-distance call for you.' But there was no letter, no cable, no long-distance call.

As weeks went by and still no word came, his impression of what had happened became more bitter. He began to look on Duke and Regina as a pair of confidence tricksters, and himself as the sucker who had fallen for each of them in turn. His reaction to Duke when he first met him had been one of open admiration. Duke seemed what he himself wanted to be, sophisticated, wealthy, enviable. He took what he wanted without inhibition, said what he felt like saying without regard for others' interests or opinions. His energy never flagged and his easy humour overrode all pressures. When Duke showed marks of special friendship, when he took Walpole on a tour of his 'kingdom' and made a confidant of him, he had begun, first to imagine and then to believe in, a more serious Duke who concealed under his jovial extravagance a concern for his fellow men. How ludicrous a self-deception that had been! What really lay beneath Duke's joviality was not an idealist but a ruthless egotist disguising his manoeuvres under a playboy's mask. Moreover, as Walpole now plainly saw, he did not even love Regina, for in all those apparently flattering tirades about her with which he amused gatherings of his friends, ran a streak of cruelty. Under the guise of affectionate banter he was at the same time boasting of his wealth and taunting Regina with being the butterfly he had made of her, while warning other men off with the implication 'Don't imagine you could keep, or afford to keep, a creature like this yourself!'

But his detestation of Duke was nothing compared to the desolation that filled Walpole's heart over Regina. Duke was a friend who had let him down, Regina was something else – a betrayer. The short time they spent together had committed her as deeply as it had him. He had no doubt she loved him, was aware she loved him and did not love Duke. He recalled her saying his name 'Walpole' over and over to herself, 'taking him into her heart', she had called it. That had not been pretence – and yet within a few hours she was at the airport on her way to Duke, refusing to let him come and rescue her. On the spur of the moment and with no chance for premeditation, he had offered her everything he had, to marry, take charge of her and face the consequences from Duke's revengeful nature. He recalled the gasp she gave when she heard his words. He had offered everything but it had not been enough, and there could be no other reason than that she preferred her golden chains, or else simply lacked the courage to oppose her captor.

Images of Duke and Regina together haunted him. In the luxury world of Europe to which she had so readily followed him, Duke would have given her the rewards she sought – armfuls of new clothes, heaps of furs and strings of jewels – the treasures for which she had sacrificed herself and Walpole. By now any difficulties with Duke would have been resolved, gifts on his side matched by compliance on hers, and the two once more in close alliance, partners sexually and in every other way, Regina no doubt laughing dutifully at her lord's sarcastic comments on the man whom inwardly she loved. She was gone for good, he told himself, and her image must be uprooted from his heart. But gone with her too was that new Walpole, confident, determined, able to act decisively and equal to all emergencies, brought into being by Regina and

now destroyed by her. His state of rage and misery could not
pass unnoticed by his friends, and Stephen made several
attempts to learn the cause. Getting no help from Walpole he
evidently worked out what he supposed to be the explanation,
and one afternoon when they were together in the office he
began.

'Look, Walpole, I don't want to interfere – but I'd like you
to know I don't believe any of these stories about you that are
going round.'

Walpole looked dumbfounded. Was it possible that Duke or
Regina had actually written or spoken to his friends in order to
humiliate him further.

'What stories?'

'Why, the things Bisi is saying about you everywhere.'

'Bisi?' Walpole could hardly remember who she was. 'Bisi?
What on earth can *she* be saying?'

'Well, naturally, my friend, there's been talk over your
ending your affair with her. . . . After all, it had gone on some
time and we all knew you both.'

'I understand that. But what does it matter what she says?
What *can* she say in the situation?'

'I don't know what she *can* say, Walpole, but I can tell you
what she *is* saying – to everyone who'll listen, which of course
includes Cécile.'

'What?'

'Why, that you got rid of her because you did not think her
good enough for your fine friends – particularly Duke and
Regina. She tells everyone you walked out without leaving
her a penny – which is why she was forced to take a job in the
casino. And she got that thanks to Peter who's the only person
who's been good to her.'

Walpole gasped: 'But it was only *after* she'd taken the job in
the casino without telling me – and started an affair with Peter
– that I broke off with her. I actually saw her working in the
casino as a croupier, and was told Peter waits every night to
take her home. I went back that same night to my flat and
wrote to Bisi. I sent her six months' rent and a further three
months of her allowance. . . . How *can* she say I left her
without a penny? It's a lie – and she knows it. How could
anyone believe such a story? Above all how could *you* believe
it?'

'Calm down, Walpole! Calm down! I knew you'd have
made proper arrangements for Bisi. But obviously I couldn't

know what you'd done or what had happened since you never told me. . . . Bisi, of course, puts it all the other way round. She only took the casino job, she says, because you'd lost interest in her and hardly ever saw her. . . . I must tell you she's convinced there's another woman in the picture.'

'Oh hell!' exclaimed Walpole. 'But does she claim that's why she took up with Peter – or does she pretend she hasn't.'

'Bisi's line is that she'd never have taken up with Peter if you'd gone on caring for her. . . . And, frankly, my friend, it sounds convincing! I can't imagine any woman taking up with that evil little rascal if she'd any choice – particularly if you were the alternative.'

The two men laughed and tension eased.

'I'll tell all you've said to Cécile,' Stephen assured Walpole, 'I'm sure I can convince her. She knows Bisi's a liar anyway. But now, Walpole, let me tell *you* something.'

'What's that?'

'It's your own fault if people don't back you in a matter like this. You don't give us a chance. You're too secretive. Anyone else would have gone round Lagos denouncing Bisi and complaining of the way she and Peter treated you. That gives your friends something to bite on! They may not believe every word, but at least they can speak up for you if they want, and – as you must know very well – I would always want.'

'Thank you, my friend,' said Walpole gratefully. 'And I know I do shut things up inside myself. I sometimes feel I can endure anything – provided other people don't know I'm having to endure it.'

'That may serve with the outside world,' said Stephen seriously, 'but it doesn't leave much room for friends.'

'Well,' began Walpole with an effort, 'since you accuse me of being secretive, let me tell you this. Everything I've told you is true, but it isn't the whole picture. There's something else . . . something I can't speak about yet. But when I can you'll be the first person I'll tell.'

'Good – and now let me give you a piece of news.'

'What's that?'

'Duke and Regina are back. They got in yesterday.'

Walpole jumped up and walked over to the window, so that his face could not be seen. With an effort he asked in something like a normal voice: 'How d'you know?'

'Regina rang Cécile and asked her to look round and see her. I expect she's with her at this moment.'

'Will Cécile be going back to your house afterwards?'
'Yes, of course.'
'Then d'you mind if I come with you?'

In the car on the way to Stephen's house, Walpole told him
the whole story, and watching his friend's face, saw him look
more and more distressed. But all he said was: 'Now I know
why Regina rang Cécile. We'd better wait till we hear what
she reports.'

The two were sitting over a drink when Cécile came into the
room. On seeing Walpole she at once dropped whatever she
was carrying, ran across the room and threw her arms round
him. Cécile was not a demonstrative woman and both men
looked surprised.

'Thank you, Cécile . . . but . . .' Walpole began.
'What's happened?' Stephen asked.
'Have you told Stephen about Regina, Walpole?'
'Yes – just now on the way round.'
'D'you know, Stephen, that Walpole asked Regina to marry
him to try and stop her going to Duke? Do you know that?'
'But how is she?' Walpole interrupted. 'What's been
happening to her? She promised to write. I've been expecting
every day to hear.'

Cécile flung out her hands. 'She *couldn't* write. She says she
wanted to write desperately, but was watched every moment.
Twice she managed to write letters and give them to people in
hotels to post, but Duke had bribed the maids and waiters to
bring him anything she gave them – so of course that just made
matters worse. . . . She's been through a great deal in these
last weeks.'

'She should never have gone back to Duke,' Walpole
explained. 'I begged her not to. *Why* did she do it?'

There was a long minute's silence, and then Walpole turned
to Cécile. 'Did she say *anything*?'
'For you, you mean? What message for me to give you?'
'Yes.'
Cécile hesitated. 'Well. She did send a message – so I have to
give it you.'
'What is it?'
'She said please don't try to see or get in touch with her.
That's all she asked me to tell you in so many words.
But. . . .'
'But – what?'
'I don't know if it makes it worse for you or better,' said

Cécile. 'But then she just burst into tears and cried and cried.'

In the middle of the next morning at a time when he thought it possible Duke might be out on business, Walpole rang and asked to speak to Regina. There was a delay and then a man's voice asked: 'Who spikkin?'

Walpole gave his name, and there was another delay with what sounded like a whispered conversation. Then the first voice came again: 'She no want spik wid you,' and the receiver was banged down.

That evening after work Walpole drove round to Duke's house. As soon as the door was open he stepped inside and ran straight up to what he knew was Duke's working room, brushing off the man who tried to stop him.

'Mr Duke Ombo wants to see me – urgent business.'

Duke was standing at a small table pouring himself a drink.

'I want to see Regina. Where is she?'

'Regina doesn't want to see you. Nor do I.' He made a rapid movement towards an imposing desk, stooped to press something, and a bell was heard. 'She doesn't want to see you again ever!'

'But. . . .' Walpole began, then seeing Duke glance over his shoulder to the doorway, turned. Three men were standing there.

'Throw this man out!' said Duke. 'And if ever he comes back, throw him out again – *harder.*'

Two of the men seized Walpole's arms and ran him down the stairs, the third pulled the door open sharply and in a moment he was lying on his face in the dust beside his car.

'You hear what de boss say? You come back here – we not ask no one. We just fixin' you one-time!'

27

An Opening Move

Beyond a grazed nose and a sprained wrist Walpole had suffered no bodily harm from the manhandling by Duke's

thugs, but his pride had been hurt and for days he could think
of little but how to avenge himself. Every project foundered
though on the fact that Duke was more powerful, because
far richer, than he was, so that much as he would have liked to
waylay his enemy and beat him up or get the better of him in
some business enterprise, Walpole himself would be the
probable sufferer from any such attempt. Before he could
make Duke bite the dust he must strengthen his position, and
the first thing to concentrate on was becoming rich. With
wealth he would know how to make himself powerful, and,
once powerful, a hundred ways of getting even with Duke
Ombo would present themselves. The obvious way to
become rich was through the expansion of Balogun and
Abiose. Such expansion, however, must involve conflict,
particularly with Mr Balogun, now in his late sixties, whose
own ambitions had been satisfied and who wanted nothing
but to hand on an established business to his nephew.

Mr Balogun could be expected to retire of his own accord in
a couple of years and Walpole had hitherto been content to
wait for this, but such patience would no longer serve his
purpose. Even the most rapid expansion would take time and
he was not willing to let a further two or three years go by
before expansion could begin. He resolved, therefore, to give
Mr Balogun a nudge, a delicate task since it would be
necessary to carry Stephen with him if the firm were not to be
disrupted.

Meantime, it seemed, there were further humiliations to be
experienced, for though Walpole had said nothing about the
incident to anyone but Stephen, Duke had taken care to
circulate his own version. In this there were no strong-arm
men but he himself, exasperated by Walpole's ill-mannered
entrance, had run the intruder downstairs and pitched him
through the door. Walpole had therefore to put up with much
pretended sympathy in the form of inquiries about his health
from malicious acquaintances. Worse still, when going
through the *Citizen* one morning, he found that Duke had his
own means of prosecuting the feud, for at the end of "Peeping
Peter's" gossip column was a photograph headed WHO IS THIS
MAN?

Not many moons ago unknown Walpole Abiose started hitting the
high-spots. None other than superlustrious Duke Ombo
(C.P.W.W.) sheltered him beneath his shady aegis for a spell.

The spell was short. For now our Grand Duke has dropped this Walpole like a scalding cat. Whyso? Did the subject raise his eyes too high? Did he seek to rob his benefactor in some way?

'Hope springs infernal in the human beast,' wrote England's mighty poet Milton. So what infernal hope sprang up in Walpole – compelling his genial patron, not just to drop him, but to drop him face downwards in the dust outside his ducal portal?

These, readers, are the questions asked around the waterholes and oases where the Lords of the Forest congregate at nightfall.

But behind these lies a deeper question. Who is this man, this dust-biter? Whence came he upon our Lagos scene? What were his origins? If any?

That which is unknown, the Good Book saith, must be made manifest. Our many-eyed Argosies are on the prowl. Watch this column, friends. Watch this column!

Walpole was still holding the paper when Stephen came into his office.

'Servile little jackal! I'd like to go round and make him eat it.'

'So would I,' Walpole answered, 'if it would help.'

'I guess how you're feeling. But this can't do you any harm,' Stephen assured him. 'Everyone knows what Peter's like, and that he writes anything to please the man who buys his drinks.'

'True enough – and he'd change sides very quickly if anyone else could buy him more. . . . But what worries me is what he's going to say next.'

'What *can* he say?'

Walpole shrugged. 'There isn't much about me for anyone *to* say. I've got no parents, and I come from nowhere. If Madam Abiose hadn't taken me up, I'd be a petty trader with a couple of market stalls.'

'Well – what the hell? He may get a paragraph out of that, but he can hardly carry on a vendetta with it. And if he starts inventing stories, we'll bung a writ in on the editor.'

'I'd never win a libel case against the *Citizen*.'

'You don't need to – the editor'd take no chances on it. He'd just tell Peter to lay off you and find some safer target. You can see what's caused this – "hell knows no fury . . .".'

'But Duke's not "a woman scorned"?'

'Duke? It's Bisi behind this, in my opinion.'

Walpole whistled. 'I was forgetting Bisi. All the same, I'm certain Duke's the motivater here.'

'Maybe – but Bisi hasn't forgotten you. I'll get Cécile to speak to her if you think it'll do any good.'

'Not a bit, my friend. Thanks all the same. One day I'll screw Peter's head off, and one day I intend to kick Duke in the teeth. But it'll be a while before I get that satisfaction.'

Turning the paper over in his hands when his friend had gone, Walpole reflected that the violence of his rage against Duke was having two contrary effects. It had set fire to his ambition but smothered his feeling for Regina, concerning whom he now experienced only a continuing dull ache, rising to a sickness of despair when he heard her name mentioned or was forced by some accident of association to recall her bodily presence. Unable to endure his flat since she had visited him there, he had given it up and now lived in a hotel.

It was the director's practice to spend two or three hours each Monday morning discussing progress on the various contracts, and considering what fresh work to undertake; the meetings were presided over by Mr Balogun senior who had long since given up other interests to concentrate on the firm. At one such meeting, after normal business was concluded, Walpole asked: 'What about our putting in a tender for the block of government offices to be built off Bamgbose Street?'

Both Stephen and Mr Balogun looked at him in amazement.

'But that's a huge undertaking,' Stephen objected. 'It's going to be a dozen storeys high and cover acres. . . . We couldn't begin to handle it. We haven't the manpower or the equipment.'

'We should beware of overstraining our resources,' said Mr Balogun sententiously. 'No good biting off more than we can chew, you know, Walpole.'

'As regards equipment,' Walpole replied, ignoring the older man's comment, 'there's no problem. We always write the cost into the tender anyway. It just means writing in a bigger sum – and we'll be that much better equipped when we tackle something larger still. . . . The only problem might be finding the capital when we've got the contract.'

'Is it difficult to raise capital at the present time?' Stephen asked his uncle.

Mr Balogun considered, before answering with visible reluctance: 'Well no . . . I can't say it would be. If that's what we really want.'

'If *what's* what we really want?' Walpole asked.

'Expansion of our business on that scale.'

'But why not?'

'Because we're better off as we are.'

'In what way? If we get this contract, it must mean a lot of profit. So financially we'd be better off for taking it on. In what way would we be worse off?'

Stephen glanced across at Walpole in surprise. The senior partner was not usually spoken to so bluntly, and in matters requiring his agreement the two usually acted in concert, securing his consent, where necessary, by degrees.

'Worse off?' Mr Balogun asked. 'Why, a firm's bound to be worse off that expands too rapidly. If we *should* ever decide to go after contracts on this scale . . . we'd require more staff, more equipment, more finance . . . we could be forced to move into larger offices. . . .'

He was visibly playing for time, and Stephen stepped in to help him. 'What makes you think we've a hope of getting the contract if we do put in for it, Walpole? Jobs of this size usually go to British and Italian firms – they're geared up for it. We're not.'

'From what I hear,' said Walpole, 'the overseas firms have been taking too much for granted. There's been a carve-up agreement over tendering. Some ministers are saying they're fed up with it. My guess is that if we *do* put in a tender, it's almost certain to be the lowest. Added to which we're Nigerian.'

Stephen whistled. 'You're saying that if we put in a reasonable tender, it may be difficult for them *not* to give us the contract?'

'That's *just* what I'm saying,' Walpole began, warming to his theme, 'and I'll tell you something more. . . .'

'I suggest, Walpole,' observed Mr Balogun, asserting his chairman's rights, 'that you keep that till our next meeting. You've given us quite enough to think about, and I propose we all do some hard thinking before Monday next.'

Walpole realized very well that Mr Balogun's aim in delaying the discussion was to work on Stephen so as to ensure his backing when the subject came up again. He intended to do some working on Stephen himself, but considered that if he put his arguments to him straight away, Mr Balogun would have ample opportunity to counter them. He therefore avoided talking about it until the Sunday evening, when he rang Stephen to say he was bored in his hotel and ask if he might call in for a drink.

'I hope I didn't upset your uncle last Monday,' he began when they had settled into their chairs. 'It was a bit tactless of me to bring the matter up like that – but I happened to be hearing about this Bamgbose Street redevelopment . . . and it seems just the right size as a first step.'

'As a first step to what?'

'As a first step to building Balogun and Abiose up into a great national company.'

'Is that what you have in mind?'

'Yes. Isn't it in your mind as well? Or d'you want us to stay always a small family business?'

'I think that's what my uncle wants.'

'No doubt. But I'm asking what *you* want?'

'I know what I *don't* want – which is a head-on clash with him. He's been very good to me all my life and I owe him a great deal.'

'I understand that,' said Walpole. 'You have family ties here which I don't. But putting those on one side, if you *hadn't* got your uncle's feelings to consider, would you support our expanding into an important firm?'

Stephen considered a moment. 'I can see difficulties – apart from wanting to avoid a clash. But on the whole I'd support it.'

'I'm glad. Because, you know, this *has* to come.'

'What has to?'

'Nigeria having its own great contracting firms – just as we have to have our own doctors, lawyers, accountants. And for the same reason – because the country'll be swindled if we don't. God knows what these overseas giants cost the state, cornering all the work, bringing in overseas staff, employing only rough labour locally – and then taking the profits back overseas. Someone has to prove we're capable of doing things ourselves. I want that someone to be Balogun and Abiose.'

'Sounds good,' said Stephen thoughtfully. 'But you know, Walpole, it's a pretty tall order for a firm like ours to start with a twelve-storey block in the centre of the city.'

'We have to start somewhere. What's more we have to start now!'

'Why? Why not wait a year ot two . . . take on one or two new people, build the workforce up. . . . Perhaps take a few months travelling around and looking at what's being done overseas?'

Walpole recognized in Stephen's voice the words of Mr Balogun. 'Why *not*? Because in that couple of years, while we sit on our behinds and scratch our heads, all the work we might be doing gets snapped up. Not just Bamgbose Street and a dozen more like it. But all the new government buildings for the regional capitals, besides airfields, bridges, hospitals, barracks, schools. If we don't jump in now – someone's going to seize the opportunity and jump in first. It's true we're only a small firm, but we're a lot bigger than the firms which haven't started yet. Waste two years looking around – and they bloody well will have started!'

'God, Walpole – I see *you've* been doing some thinking. . . . But why didn't you talk to me about this before. Give us a chance to work out strategy – put it up to the old man a bit subtly? Now, I'm afraid, he's shut his mind against expansion before he really knows what it's about.'

'Look, Stephen,' said Walpole, who had been waiting for this to come up, 'I don't know your uncle as well as you do, but I've known him quite a while and my impression of him is that he likes everything straightforward. Put something to him direct and he may disagree, but there's no ill feeling. Whereas if he feels he's being ganged up on or got round, he doesn't like it. I didn't bring you in on this before because the last thing I want is to cause trouble between you and your uncle. Naturally, I hope that tomorrow you'll go along with me because I'm certain that's what's best for the firm and the country. And if you *do*, you can truthfully say we'd never discussed the matter before that last board meeting – and you were as astonished as he was when I brought it up.'

'That's just like you, Walpole – and I appreciate it.'

Walpole was well aware that his argument had been devious. His intention was to split uncle and nephew, not to keep them happily united, and when Stephen praised him and looked at him with real affection, he experienced a pang of guilt and half wished he had indeed talked his ideas out openly with his friend. But his aim was money and power and when great prizes are to be won, some small misrepresentations are, he assured himself, inevitable.

'There's something you won't have thought of, Walpole,' Stephen was continuing, 'which you ought to know.'

'What's that?'

'If you and I stand together on this tomorrow, I've an idea my uncle will resign. And that could land us in a difficult position.'

This was the result Walpole was hoping for but had expected to achieve only after long and bitter confrontation. Now, it seemed, the old man might actually walk into the trap of his own accord – with a little help.

'You surprise me, Stephen,' he said. 'I never imagined the chairman would threaten us like that – why, we haven't even seriously discussed the proposal yet. Tomorrow's meeting's supposed to be for the purpose of hearing what each other thinks. Yet here he is threatening to resign before we've even started talking.'

'I'm sorry, Walpole. I shouldn't have mentioned this. No doubt my uncle meant it to be confidential, but it seemed only fair to let you know.'

'It *was* only fair, and I'm grateful. But now that you've brought the matter up, let me say a word about it.'

'Please do.'

'I'm one hundred per cent sure our firm should expand. I'm one hundred per cent sure the country needs us to expand – and one hundred per cent certain we'll be successful if we do. Above all, I'm a hundred per cent sure that *now* – Independence Time – is the moment to act. I know as well as you do all your uncle's done for the firm. But if he can't see the opportunity and he's too old to adjust himself – then, honestly, Stephen, the best thing all round is for him to retire.'

'But what about the chairmanship? You don't suggest we can manage without him?'

'Of course we can, if we have to – just as we'd have to manage if he died.'

'But who would we have as chairman?'

Walpole laughed. 'I tell you one thing, my friend – you won't find me wanting to be chairman. So if you feel like taking on the job yourself, I'll vote for you any day. But if you're asking me what I advise, supposing your uncle carries out his threat. . . .'

'I *do* ask you.'

'I think we should look around for an older man we both of us like and trust, someone sharp and tough – with good political connections. Our firm has a great deal to offer, and I don't think it'll be hard to find the man we want.'

Stephen looked reassured. 'How d'you intend to handle things tomorrow?' he asked.

Walpole got up. 'I shall say my say as briefly as I can, and no doubt your uncle will say his. And then, necessarily, you'll have to say yours. Whatever you say won't make the slightest difference to my friendship for you – or to my liking for your uncle. Thanks for the drink . . . I've talked enough. I'm off!'

At next day's meeting when the usual routine had been cleared out of the way, Mr Balogun looked expectantly at Walpole.

'Well now, Walpole, suppose you state your case.'

'I propose,' said Walpole, 'that we put in a tender for the new block of offices in Bamgbose Street.'

There was a moment's silence, and then Mr Balogun inquired: 'But is that all you want to say?'

'Yes. I can see, of course, that if we're successful we must expand – raise capital and take on staff. But it's time we did that anyway. And with the amount of work there is around, there'll never be a better chance of doing it. So I propose we tender.'

Mr Balogun, who had clearly been counting on a carefully-argued speech, looked taken aback, but recovered and launched into his own course of argument. There was no point in going to the trouble and expense of tendering unless they meant to win the contract, and no point in winning it unless they meant to secure other, bigger ones to follow. What they were discussing therefore was the whole question of growth and the future of the company.

'The logical end of expansion – as I'm sure Walpole knows – is that we become a public company. Properly handled, with sufficient caution, this can be profitable for all of us. But what we should lose would be important too – the right to run things our own way. At present we're answerable to no one. If we choose we take on work that doesn't pay in order to keep workpeople employed, we can. If we want to turn down a contract because we don't like the way a man does business, we turn it down. It's our loss and no one can complain. But as a public company we must have a number of new directors, with some of whom we shan't see eye to eye – and who may outvote us. We're also answerable to shareholders for making maximum profits on their behalf.'

'You mean,' said Stephen, 'that we lose a certain amount of control over our own business?'

'Yes, indeed,' Mr Balogun remarked, 'and that's not all. Remember that once you've started on expansion, there's no going back. You've taken on new partners, new staff, new workers and you have to keep them employed. The staff expect bigger salaries and the shareholders look for large dividends, and you've got much more capital to pay dividends on. All very well while orders roll in, but what happens when they start drying up? That's what you ought to consider before getting worked up over the idea of a bit more profit. . . . Walpole is counting on Independence to keep orders flowing in, but Independence is a once-only activity which may produce work for two or three years. Then the various departments have worked through their programmes, and there's a slump. . . . That's when we're in real trouble, like so many firms when the World War ended and demand fell flat. . . . We have to look ahead, you see, my friends, we have to look a bit further than the ends of our noses, otherwise. . . .'

It was time, Walpole saw, to stop this monologue, particularly as there was some degree of sense in it all which might have an effect on Stephen.

'In and around Lagos,' he stated flatly, 'there will be seven years' expansion for certain. It'll go on longer in the regions because they're slower getting started. After that further new regions are likely to be created. We've got a minimum of ten years' uninterrupted growth – what business really expects to see more than ten years ahead? To pass up this opportunity because there's some doubt about the future would be mad – unless we intend to remain a small family set-up till the end of time.'

There was an assertiveness in Walpole's tone which irritated Mr Balogun, as it was meant to do.

'I don't think you've got anything to complain of in the way this "family set-up", as you call it, has been run,' he replied sharply. 'You've done pretty well out of it.'

'I'm not complaining,' said Walpole. 'I just mean us to do better. I suggest it's time the firm grew up, and that it's in the country's interest for us to grow up. So I propose we tender for the Bamgbose Street block.'

'It isn't in the country's interest, or ours, to act hastily and land ourselves in trouble,' Mr Balogun said reprovingly. 'This is a situation which demands foresight . . . calls for long heads on wise shoulders . . . looking before taking a leap we may afterwards regret . . . for. . . .'

'But the difficulties you've described don't necessarily follow from our tendering for Bamgbose Street, surely?' Stephen urged. 'We could take on a job that size without too much expansion, then, if it turned out badly, go no further. If we take a step at a time and keep our eyes open, I can't see why we shouldn't be successful. Lots of firms expand successfully, so why not us?'

'*Exactly!*' put in Walpole.

Mr Balogun was watching Stephen with anxiety. He had counted on his nephew's support which was now, it seemed, uncertain, and he was casting round in his mind for further arguments when Walpole's interjection, uttered sarcastically with his face buried in his hands, exasperated him beyond restraint.

'What I've been trying all this time to make you both realize,' he explained heavily, 'is that taking one step and drawing back is "exactly" what you cannot do. Bamgbose Street is the thin end of the wedge, the first step on the slippery slope, and if you take that step. . . .'

'I propose,' Walpole cut in, 'that we tender for the Bamgbose Street offices. Can we take a vote on it?'

Deeply offended, Mr Balogun drew himself up and looked at each of his partners in turn. His manner suggested that they'd asked for what was coming to them and now would get it.

'Before I put this to the vote as Walpole insists, there's one thing you must both realize. If you go ahead on this against everything I've been saying' – he paused – 'you may make it impossible for me to continue as your chairman.'

Before he could continue or Stephen utter a word, Walpole seized his chance. 'I hope you don't mean that seriously, Mr Chairman. And if you don't, I ask you to take it back now. I'm sure I speak for both of us in saying that we don't want you to take such a decision just because you are angry over our discussion.'

'What do you mean?'

'I mean that if that threat wasn't seriously meant it should be withdrawn.'

Mr Balogun got up, gathered his papers together, uttered the words 'I resign as chairman' in a choking voice, and stalked out of the room.

Walpole buried his face on his arm, filled with an exultation he must conceal from his partner at all costs. Stephen waited a

few seconds and then, upset over what seemed to be his
friend's distress, began to reassure him.

'You mustn't blame yourself, Walpole. You did everything
you could. Even at the last moment you gave him a chance to
withdraw. If he chooses to go now – that's *his* decision.'

28
Political Business

Though Walpole felt exultant over the chairman's resignation
and had drunk a bottle of wine to his own future when he got
back to the hotel, he knew Mr Balogun had resigned only
because he could not bring himself to back down openly, and
that in one way or another he would attempt to come back
before long. So he was not surprised a few days later when
Stephen came into his office and said: 'You know, Walpole, I
think we should *do* something about my uncle.'

'What is there to do? I asked him to stay on and he refused.'

'I have a feeling that if we were to ask him back he'd be
willing to meet us halfway. Agree to some expansion –
providing it's not too rapid.'

'Look, Stephen, I appreciate he's your uncle and been good
to you. He also helped us a great deal in the early stages. But
you and I have to be practical about this firm. It affects us more
than it does him because there are two of us, and we're likely to
be around the place a lot longer than he is.'

'All the same, Walpole, just for a year or two. . . .'

'Let me finish what I'm saying. Your uncle didn't resign
because he took offence, he resigned over a basic difference
about our future. In my opinion he was right to resign,
because from now on this firm will become a different place –
less cosy and a bloody sight more effective. If he comes back
now – that is, if you and I are so foolish as to invite him back –
two things will happen. First there'll be endless rows, because
he hasn't changed his outlook. Secondly, the firm will never
get anywhere because we'll waste our energy discussing

where we want to get. We'll have made the worst of both worlds – and the old man himself won't really be any happier.'

'There's something in what you're saying, Walpole – but I *do* think we might take him back for, say, twelve months. That's not asking much!'

'It's asking everything,' Walpole replied. 'Twelve months from now, if the old man stays as chairman, this firm will be just where it is today – and the chance of a lifetime will have gone.'

'Well, I see your point – but for myself. . . .'

'Stephen!' said Walpole sternly. 'If you're thinking of voting with your old man to have his resignation cancelled, let me tell you something straight. I'd no intention of saying this if you hadn't forced it on me. But I'm not willing to be blackmailed twice – once by Balogun senior and again by both Baloguns together. Your uncle resigned of his own accord. If he *was* prepared to compromise, then was the time to say so. If with your help he comes back now – I go!'

'But you *can't*! You *wouldn't*.'

'I most certainly will! I shan't leave you in the lurch, or walk out with work unfinished – but from the day he comes back my mind's made up. I look for a new job, or I start up a new firm. As far as Balogun and Abiose is concerned, I'm through.'

Stephen sat silent for a while and then, in a matter-of-fact tone of voice, asked: 'Who d'you think we should invite to become chairman?'

'Chukuma. He's extremely able. Has very good political contacts. Knows the law – which is sure to come in handy in future. Also he brought us all together in the first place.'

Stephen smiled with satisfaction. 'He'd be the very man! What's more, he's about the most acceptable to my uncle we could think of – they've known each other years and years.'

Walpole had an inspiration. 'When you've got your old man to accept it's really best for him to stay retired, why not suggest *he* goes to see Chukuma? Tell Chukuma he's retiring so we need an older head to keep us out of trouble – and so on. Get him to feel it's his own arrangement. . . .'

'I'll see him at once!' said Stephen with delight.

'I shouldn't if I were you.' Walpole suggested. 'Wait till you're having a chat then drop a hint that when he goes, Chukuma would make a good successor. If he's pleased with the idea, tell your uncle he's the one person who could fix it

because of the regard Chukuma's always had for him. Pile it
on a bit, if you don't mind my saying so. And whatever you
do don't let him know that I suggested Chukuma in the first
place.'

A few days later Walpole and Stephen sat in Mr Chukuma's
office smoking two of his hand-made cigarettes. Mr Balogun
had already made a preliminary visit and persuaded his old
friend, without great difficulty, to step into his shoes. Mr
Chukuma listened with attention to Walpole and Stephen
going over the same ground.

'I'm involved in a good many activities already, as you
know,' he told them, 'but there's no reason why they need
conflict with this one. You're not asking me to run the
business – you two are doing that already. You'll expect me to
take charge of board meetings, be available to give advice on
problems – particularly their legal aspects, I imagine. Also, to
make use of such contacts as I have to promote the firm's
interests, particularly in the matter of new business. Is that
how you both see it?'

Both agreed.

'All right, my friends. I'm happy to accept. But before I do'
– and he held a hand up to anticipate their congratulations –
'there's one thing we must discuss, and later a condition I wish
to make. I understand from Mr Balogun that the firm is going
to expand, take on bigger contracts, start working for the
federal and perhaps regional governments. Is that the picture?'

Both nodded.

'Let me say, first, that I think you're absolutely right. This is
where the big money's to be made – and the present is the
moment to get moving.'

Walpole's smile told Mr Chukuma what he had already
guessed, that young Abiose was the prime mover in expansion. He went on: 'But I want you both to understand what
you're doing. You aren't just planning to grow bigger. You're
moving out of an area in which everything is reasonably
straightforward and above board, into one where contracts are
settled differently. We could call this area "political business"
since politicians on the whole decide the way things go, and
politicians must be handled in accordance with their own
customs and conventions.'

'I'm not sure I know what you mean,' said Stephen.

'Then let me put you a question. Suppose you get the
contract in Bamgbose Street which you plan to tender for, and

suppose you're doubly lucky and get another one after that –
how d'you keep up the flow of orders? You've expanded the
firm to three times its present size. You're having to turn over
several million pounds a year, just to pay wages and dividends
and continue the momentum. How d'you make sure of getting
fuel for the engine – the continuous flow of business you need?'

'Walpole thinks there's going to be ten years of expansion
because of Independence.'

'He's probably right. But how d'you make sure you get
your share in that expansion?'

'Surely,' said Stephen, 'it's an advantage that we're a
Nigerian company? The government's bound to favour a
Nigerian contractor over foreigners, and that must go for the
provisional governments as well.'

'Not necessarily. A government can usually justify its
actions since its explanation always gets publicity. If it accepts
the lowest tender, there's no problem. But if not, then it
"chose the firm with specialized experience" . . . it "followed
the advice of its own experts" . . . "factors have emerged
which no one could anticipate" . . . there are a dozen ways to
justify itself. Remember, too, all these foreign firms will soon
be establishing local subsidiaries with Nigerian directors. . . .
So I shouldn't count on nationality as a trump card for long.
What I'm talking about is something different.'

'What I think we're talking about,' said Walpole, 'is making
friends in the right places – and keeping them happy when
we've made them.'

'Exactly!' said Mr Chukuma with relief. 'The rules of
political business require dash, hand-outs, percentages and so
on. The way all this is to be handled we can talk about later –
but it's essential you both recognize what's involved. I can talk
to you two openly in a way I couldn't to your uncle,
Stephen. . . . He's a man of principle, and all honour to him
for it! But principle will take no one anywhere in "political
business". If you prefer keeping your idea of how things
ought to be intact, rather than coping with them as they are,
then stay out of "political business".'

'It's our intention to go ahead,' said Walpole.

Mr Chukuma looked at Stephen, who hesitated. 'Well,' he
said after a moment or two, 'we didn't invent the rules of
"political business". The system's there – so we must go along
with it. Personally I don't like it, but it's evident we won't get
contracts if we don't.'

'One must understand the politicians' point of view,' Mr Chukuma remarked expansively. 'On government contracts the profits made can be enormous because no one's really concerned to watch the cost – at least not in the way a private firm or person has to do. So politicians, who hand out the contracts that produce these profits, naturally think they should have a cut themselves. Also they're only in office a short time, so they're men in a hurry with both eyes on the main chance. If your firm goes into political business, who's going to handle this side of things for you? Will you hire someone? Or does one of you two take it on?'

'I couldn't,' said Stephen, 'I'd be useless. But what about yourself?'

'I can advise,' said Mr Chukuma, 'and I hope to some purpose. But as a lawyer I must watch my step. . . . What about you, Walpole? D'you feel you could handle such matters? Or are you planning to leave them to an inter-mediary, such as . . . let's name no names, but say Chief Judas or Dr Iscariot? There are plenty of them about – full of experience and highly placed.'

'No intermediaries for us,' said Walpole.

'Why d'you say that?' Mr Chukuma inquired in a tone suggesting disagreement.

'First,' said Walpole, 'since bribing to get contracts is illegal, the fewer people involved, the better. We three trust each other – but how should we feel about a fourth party?'

'H'm . . . and secondly?'

'Anyone we bring in for this purpose will be crooked. That's what we'd hire him for. If he were straight he'd be no use. But if he's crooked with others he can be crooked with us too.'

'You've got a point there. But how could he swindle us – we'd be watching him all the time?'

'The ways are endless,' said Walpole, well aware he was being closely scrutinized by the future chairman. 'He can tell us he's got to hand over five thousand, and keep one. He can offer a contact more than necessary, and split the difference. All the time he can play both sides against each other. Meantime he'll be lashing out our money for so-called expenses to buy goodwill in case we find him out. . . . And even if he were straight with us – which isn't likely – there are other problems. . . .'

'Such as?'

'Suppose he's a politician – as most top fixers are since it's mainly their fellow-politicians to be fixed – his party may go out of office, which makes him a dead loss. Then if we drop him, he starts blackmailing . . . "You led me astray. Now you can pay my keep – or else!" '

'Enough!' cried Mr Chukuma, throwing up both arms, 'enough, Walpole, my friend! I just wanted to be sure you'd thought the situation out. I needn't have worried. Shall I put the matter in a nutshell? Nobody likes doing dirty work, but if dirty work has to be done, it's cheaper and safer to do it yourself. I consider that the basic principle of political business. Are we agreed?'

Both men murmured acceptance.

'And now,' asked Stephen, 'what's that condition you spoke about?'

'I want you to take my son Basil on the board.'

Walpole and Stephen looked at one another blankly, but Walpole felt he must give a lead.

'Mr Chukuma – we both like Basil. But he's had no experience in our kind of business – and frankly his record isn't convincing. . . . You must let Stephen and me talk this over.'

There was a moment's silence, and then in a voice unlike his full-throated boom and with a manner almost humble, 'That's all I can ask,' said Mr Chukuma. 'I think there's more in the boy than has appeared, and I'm sure he'll gain from working with you both . . . Basil's weak but he's not dishonest. . . . However, as regards financial matters, I shall give you my personal guarantee in writing.'

Both Walpole and Stephen made deprecatory noises, implying that such guarantees were unnecessary, though it might be in the general interest for them to be accepted, and Mr Chukuma held his hand out to each in turn.

'However you decide, I'm honoured to have been approached. . . . I shall expect to hear from you in a few days. Meantime, Stephen, if I were you I would say nothing to your uncle about the matters we've discussed. It'll only disturb him without doing any good. Is that agreed?'

'That's a hell of a one to be landed with,' said Stephen as they sat over whiskies in a nearby bar. 'The sensible thing is to refuse. But I'd be sorry to hurt Chukuma's feelings. . . . What's your view?'

'I think we should accept.'

'But for God's sake! We don't want to be landed with a wet like Basil.'

'Look, Stephen, I don't know what you got from that interview, but what I got is that we *have* to have Chukuma! It isn't just that he knows the law – plenty of people know that. But he knows the edges round the outside, what you might call the "legal outskirts", the no-man's-land between legal and illegal in which most profitable activity takes place.'

'Yes,' said Stephen, 'and he knows the track record of the people we'll be dealing with.'

'Right. Now if we take Basil, we put old man Chukuma in our debt. He's not going to forget it – and he's bound to do everything he can to make the firm successful since not only his reputation but his beloved son is involved as well. We shall accept his offer of a financial guarantee in writing – which means there's really no risk. But we also make our own conditions.'

'What conditions?'

'Basil has to work his way up the firm for at least two years before coming on the board.'

'Good,' said Stephen. 'I go along with that. But you said "conditions" – what are the others?'

'That's the only condition so far as our chairman is concerned. But there's another that concerns you and me.'

'Which is?'

'Suppose Basil sticks it out – which he just might – we don't want a board in three years' time controlled by the Chukuma family. Their two votes against ours – with a casting vote for the chairman.'

'Walpole,' Stephen declared, 'you've got eyes all round your head. So what d'you propose?'

'Before your uncle finally packs up and Chukuma takes over, we appoint a couple more directors we can depend on. *Our* men, in short. Who would you nominate?'

'The company secretary – Adaji. He was my uncle's clerk for fifteen years. And maybe someone from our accountants. I'll talk it over with my uncle, but subject to that, we take on Basil?'

'Yes,' said Walpole, 'and he can start where I started – carrying bricks.'

A plan for his son's employment with a view to becoming a director was soon agreed with Mr Chukuma, and it was not long before he was presiding at his first board meeting. On resigning the chairmanship, Mr Balogun had also decided to resign his directorship, and a letter to this effect was read out, and an appropriate resolution of thanks and appreciation passed.

Mr Chukuma raised no objection when told about the additional directors, though the reason for their appointment could hardly, thought Walpole, have escaped him. When 'Any Other Business' came up at the end of the meeting, Stephen raised a point about political business.

'Granted we must compete and that this means hand-outs and backhanders, I propose we don't initiate offers but wait until we're asked. I don't want us responsible for corrupting someone who may have been honest up till now.'

'That's a point,' Mr Chukuma observed. 'At least it could sometimes be a point – because actually, you know, these matters are seldom so straightforward. It's not a clear-cut offer and acceptance – it's a vague allusion, followed by a hint. Nobody really makes the first advance, but both sides soon know where they stand.'

'Let's accept Stephen's point in principle,' Walpole suggested.

'I can see I'm being rather simple,' said Stephen. 'However my second suggestion is easier, because it's in our control.'

'What's that?'

'We don't depreciate materials or workmanship in order to find money for dash. It'll have to be added to the tender or taken out of profit, not screwed out of the work.'

'Agreed,' said Walpole.

'Agreed,' added Mr Chukuma. 'And I must say, Stephen, that, as rules for honest corruption, yours take a lot of beating! But now, you've told me how the plans for Bamgbose Street are going – d'you know who's giving out the contract?'

'The Board of Public Construction,' said Stephen, 'they're supposed to handle all building contracts for the different ministries.'

'Except when the ministries insist on doing that themselves, as most of them are already insisting,' Mr Chukuma remarked. 'But who's chairman of the board?'

'He's not appointed yet,' said Walpole. 'It's to be announced next week. But they say it's to be Chief Efunshile.'

'You get around, Walpole, I must say,' said Mr Chukuma. 'I was intending to surprise you both with that piece of information.'

'But I thought Efunshile was to have a post in the regional government?' objected Stephen.

'So he was – until last week,' Mr Chukuma answered. 'He's standing down so that a man thirty years older than himself can become a minister in time to join his ancestors.'

'Very obliging,' Stephen remarked.

'Very far-sighted,' suggested Walpole. 'The man he stood down for has more cash than he knows what to do with. What he badly needs is a little prestige – which he's now got, at least until he loses it. Whereas Chief Efunshile. . . .'

'Efunshile's a spendthrift,' said Mr Chukuma, 'even by Lagos standards. What *he* badly needs is to make two or three hundred thousand pounds quickly. At the moment he would count for little in government. But if he makes a fortune to match his colleagues' – it'll be another story. He's young, ambitious and unscrupulous.'

'So where does all this lead us?' Walpole asked.

'Nowhere – for the moment,' replied Mr Chukuma. 'But if Efunshile's the man I think he is, and we put in a strong tender, we'll be hearing from him before long.'

Assured that matters inside the firm were going the way he wanted, Walpole applied himself to making life more comfortable by finding somewhere appropriate to live. Out beyond Yaba, some half-mile off the road leading to the airport, Balogun and Abiose were developing a new estate. It was no great distance from the one on which Walpole had toiled as a labourer in his days with Mr Ekpe, but since then the city had expanded and a whole new suburb grown up beyond what had lately been the city's outskirts. The area now being exploited had been farmland, the existing trees had been preserved and the houses going up were expensive, well-built dwellings, each in its own well-shaded garden. Some, already completed, had been sold to prosperous members of the community, both Nigerian and expatriate, and it seemed to Walpole that he could not do better than settle himself here.

While his house was being finished, Walpole would run out in the evening in the car to make sure everything was going as he wished. On one such evening he noticed, standing under a tree, a man of medium height but thickset and powerful, wearing a dark robe and a flop-eared cap. The man said nothing, and Walpole drove off. But two evenings later when he visited the house again the man was standing there, and this time came forward.

'You needin' watchnight, sah, for protec' yo' house 'gainst bad persons.' He did not ask, but stated the position. He spoke respectfully, but his eye had a sardonic, almost challenging look, as though defying Walpole not to take him on.

Walpole *had* considered employing a night watchman and, having checked the man's papers, agreed to give him a month's trial, warning him that if there was any trouble or any of the building materials were missing, he would throw him out at once. He had also to keep the garden tidy as well as keeping watch.

'Master take Kalio for watchnight,' the man answered, 'nothin' go missin' from dis place no-time.'

A month later Walpole moved in. He had suffered many pangs over the past weeks from the thought, which came up chokingly whenever some decision about the house had to be made, that this was what he had dreamed of doing with Regina when she left Duke to settle down with him. How different that would have been, and how happily they would have talked over every detail of their new home! In the effort to banish such thoughts, Walpole called in an architect friend and got him to organize everything for a fee.

So now here he was sitting down in his own house to a dinner prepared by his cook and served by his houseboy. After dinner he went to his elegant study and flung himself down into one of his white leather armchairs. He had taken his first step along the road he meant to follow. In a matter of months he had provided himself with the prospect of wealth and a basis for power. He had achieved this by deciding what he wanted, thinking out the means for getting it, and allowing no scruples about ethics or the demands of friendship to stand in his way.

Once, not long ago, he had believed that the forces, ancestral and divine, which guide human destiny are concerned to make us happy. He could see more clearly now. The ancestors are not interested in our happiness, and about our ideas of right and wrong they are completely neutral. What they appreciate is effort and determination. Go for what you want, and the ancestors join in to push you on your way. It's not, as he had supposed, that they 'have their hearts in the right place'. Hearts are not their concern, nor the concern of any sensible human being either. But they have their heads screwed on the right way, as he meant his own to be in future.

29
Bones

Preparing the tender for the new government building put the office in turmoil for a couple of months. This was the first time proposals on such a scale had ever been submitted, moreover the multi-storey building was different in character from anything the firm had handled hitherto so that there was much preliminary investigation to be made. As the day for submission drew near, Walpole and Stephen went over their tender clause by clause, trying to save a few thousand pounds wherever they could.

'D'you suppose we stand any chance of getting it?' Stephen asked during a pause in the morning's labour.

'I didn't think so when we started, but after all the effort we've put in, I've come to believe we'll land it. If we don't, we'll have lost a lot of money. . . .'

'Well, all except one of the other firms will have lost as much – or more.'

'Not necessarily,' said Walpole. 'There are only four or five contractors big enough to handle jobs like this, so it's likely they carve the work up among themselves.'

'How?'

'Agree what each job's worth and all tender around the same amount, but with one a hundred thousand or so lower than the rest, taking it in turns to make the lowest bid. . . . Even if they really *are* in competition, they're sure to have spies in one another's offices – some clerk or secretary with access to the files.'

'D'you suppose there's a spy in our office?'

Walpole laughed. 'Not yet. I don't suppose the big firms even know we're tendering, or would take us seriously if they did. That's where they could be in for a big shock.'

'You mean. . . .'

'If they've been carving things up for the past year or two, they'll have pushed prices beyond what's reasonable. But we're not in the ring. We've just looked at what's wanted and tried to see how we can provide it. So we could be half a million or more below the next-lowest tender.'

Stephen whistled. 'My God! You've convinced me. I believe we're going to land the big one!'

On the evening the tender was handed in to the Board of Public Construction, Walpole drove home late and, seeing a light in Kalio's outhouse, went across. Once or twice recently he had found himself looking in on the watchnight in this way. There was nobody in the house for him to talk to and Kalio's sardonic attitude to life and contempt for his fellow men gave spice to his conversation. There was also a kind of dark authority about the man, as though he understood the world better than anyone about him but found it not worthwhile to express what others would fail to understand. Though Walpole enjoyed Kalio's dry talk he experienced some guilt over the association, as though he were acting against his better judgement and somehow walking into danger; and the fact that his conscious mind dismissed this idea as absurd did not remove a sense of apprehension each time he approached the outhouse. As regards the work for which he was employed, Kalio did exactly what was required of him and no more. He kept guard at night and by day would sweep up rubbish, chopping the grass back roughly with a matchete and trimming trees and shrubs, but he planted and grew nothing. He had a number of visitors both men and women, particularly in the evening and at weekends. Walpole noticed that they arrived singly, and that Kalio always closed the door when he had a visitor as though some kind of consultation was going on.

As Walpole entered the outhouse Kalio stood up, grunted what might have been a greeting, offered the one chair on which he had been sitting and himself sat down on the corner of his bed.

'Well, how is everything with you?'

Kalio nodded, as though to imply acquiescence but by no means satisfaction in his lot.

'An' master?' he inquired. 'Master too-too tired workin' for big-money contrac'?'

'Who the devil told you about a big contract?'

Kalio uttered his brusque laugh, which was more of a rebuff than a sharing of enjoyment. 'I see master workin' late each night. . . . I read in paper 'bout new office bein' built.'

'You read newspapers a lot, Kalio.'

'I wish for know what go happen in dis country. . . .
Also. . . .'

'Also what?'

'Also nothing, master. Has no importance.'

'Then let me tell, Kalio. You read newspapers to learn new
words and expressions. You are doing this because you are
ambitious. One day you intend to go into politics – to become
a leader.'

Kalio bowed his head. The gesture was humble, but his
expression haughty.

'Master seein' everything.'

'I wish I could see one thing – whether we shall get this
contract.'

'Master wishin' know if his firm git gov'ment contrac'?'
Kalio inquired.

'I most certainly do.'

Kalio retired to the back of his outhouse, where he appeared
to open a box and take out various objects. When he came back
into the light he was holding a bundle of rags which he
unfolded with solemnity; in the middle were half a dozen
squarish bones not unlike large dice which Walpole guessed
must be either human knucklebones or the vertebrae of some
animal. From under the bed Kalio drew out a wooden box on
which he seated himself. He planted a candle on the ground to
one side, moving himself and the box about until the light fell
as he wished. He had also, Walpole noticed, put on a leopard-
skin hat with a tail which hung down his back and swathed his
powerful shoulders in some kind of skin wrap. Having
arranged everything to his satisfaction, he sat silent for several
minutes during which Walpole was conscious, first of
embarrassment, then of curiosity and finally of awe. His
whole attention had become concentrated on Kalio and the
bones he was holding loosely in his hand; meantime the silence
intensified like an oven growing hotter. This intensity of
silence sealed off the two men as though they were crouched in
the depths of a forest, and the occasional sound from the
outside world seemed to filter in from a distance. Walpole
could feel the sweat creeping on his skin. Kalio had started to
mutter what Walpole supposed were incantations. After a
while he stopped, listened with head on one side, and then
resumed the incantations as though they had not yet achieved

their purpose. Finally he uttered a loud 'Ha!' and rolled the bones out on to the close-packed earth.

As they came to a standstill he got down on his knees to peer closely at them from all aspects. He appeared to Walpole to take note of how far they had rolled, where they lay in relation to each other and which face was uppermost. Having rolled and examined the bones three or four times in quick succession, Kalio picked up each one carefully, as though in some order of seniority, and wrapped them all away in his bundle. Only after another silence did he remark in a matter-of-fact tone: 'Master no git contrac'.'

'What d'you mean? Why shouldn't we get the contract? How can you tell?'

'Master no git contrac'. Contrac' done bin fix. Big firm from overseas git um. Not British firm. Firm from other whiteman country.'

'How d'you know?'

'Bones done show,' said Kalio with complete assurance. 'But dey also show much good for master.'

'What is that?'

'Dey say master go for meet mos' pow'ful man – oba or big chief. Dis chief 'n' master grow close. Like dese two fingers,' holding up his hand. 'Through dis chief, spirits plannin' make master pow'ful an' rich . . . money, women, place in gov'ment . . . all things master wantin' in his heart.' He paused, before adding sombrely: 'Only master 'bliged take notice what Kalio tell um. No lissen Kalio, master sink down' – he glowered and spat into his cooking fire – 'like no-good person.'

Deeply disturbed by these mixed promises and admonitions, Walpole sat silent. His fingers and toes were numb. His hands trembled. To cover this he put on a joviality he was far from feeling.

'I see, Kalio. So I must always do what you tell me. If I don't the spirits will be angry with me. Is that it?'

'Master make joke,' Kalio replied grimly. 'But spirits no laff.' The tone in which he spoke made it clear not only that master's 'joke' was far from funny but that the interview was over.

From the house Walpole, who knew that spirits do not reveal for nothing, sent over a bottle of gin and a piece of meat.

Some three or four weeks later when Walpole reached the office he found a copy of the *Daily Citizen* lying on his desk.

Blue-pencilled was a paragraph saying that the contract for the new block of offices in Bamgbose Street had been won by the Italian firm of Crespi. He and Stephen commiserated with one another over all the time and money laid out to no purpose and then applied themselves to other work with a view to making up what had been lost.

Late in the afternoon, when Walpole was starting to think about going home, there was a telephone call. It was Chief Efunshile's secretary asking whether it would be convenient for Mr Abiose to call round one morning in the following week for half an hour's talk with the Chairman of the Board of Public Construction.

Walpole had not forgotten the lesson learned from his first business employer, Madam Abiose, so before visiting Chief Efunshile he took the trouble to learn all he could about him and his position as Chairman of the Board.

Chief Samwell Efunshile was a man of forty-five, a lawyer by profession, who had spent some years qualifying in London before returning to practise in Lagos with notable success. His specialization was the profitable one of company law and, being recognized as a skilled negotiator, he had been much in demand by overseas companies. As Independence approached, the Chief had noted the attractions of public service, offered himself for election and been returned to the Western Regional Assembly. His ability, carefully-fostered connections with the ruling coalition, and success as a public speaker – the combination of cynical humour with moral principles being much to the taste of Lagos audiences – would have secured him a ministerial post in his own region. That he should have stood down in favour of an older man had seemed to Walpole a quixotic act until he began to study the board's constitution and the powers which, though not precisely vested in the chairman, were at any rate lying about within his grasp.

It had apparently been the colonial power's intention that the board, which came under the federal government, should handle all important construction work for the various ministries, but the inevitable battle for power had produced the usual compromise. Since the ministries were not pre-cluded from handling their own building programmes within the limits of their departmental budgets, some had already announced their intention to do this. Others with smaller programmes had – according to the press cuttings – simply notified the board of their requirements and left it to make arrangements. In the in-fighting which followed, the board had managed to assert its position as a repository of knowledge and experience, able to ensure that standards were maintained and costs controlled. As a result even those ministries operating on their own had to obtain its general approval for their plans. The Chief's master stroke, however, had been to secure for his board an independent budget, and the block in Bamgbose Street was being put up on his initiative to meet the needs of ministries which, as Independence approached, had taken on staff for whom they had no accommodation.

Having studied the material Walpole summed up the situation. Providing he could keep his board members docile and contented, the chairman must be happily placed to benefit in three directions. He had offices to dispose of for which a number of departments must compete. Ministries planning to do their own construction must obtain his agreement and, while it might be unwise to refuse this outright, it would surely be possible to withhold approval until the right kind of approach was made. But all this would be small change. The solid benefit was to be expected from the construction firms to whom the board itself awarded contracts. Having started his study with the impression that Chief Efunshile had been overgenerous in turning down ministerial office, Walpole ended with the conviction that if the Chief's aim was to make a rapid fortune, no lesser post than that of Finance Minister or Minister for Trade offered opportunities approaching those he had secured by his self-sacrifice.

At the Chief's office Walpole was not kept waiting long, and an attractive secretary made the ten minutes pass rapidly enough. On being admitted he was welcomed by the Chief as though they were old friends.

'Come on in, Mr Abiose! Come in! So good of you to call round when you are such a busy man. I ought, of course, to have asked your chairman. But I am hearing so much about you lately and wished to make your acquaintance. Be seated!'

Walpole replied in suitably flattering terms, and after a few minutes of general talk the chief remarked: 'So now, Mr Abiose, let us cut the cackle and come to the cloth! I have asked you here because I feel it my duty to explain why the board has not accepted your firm's tender for our new block in Bamgbose Street.'

Surprised by this direct approach, Walpole made one or two deprecatory rumblings intended to convey that no explanation was required, his directors being only too confident in Chief Efunshile's wisdom and impartiality. But the Chief was already continuing: 'Let me say first how happy I am we now have a Nigerian firm with the money and resources to compete against these big overseas outfits. They've had all their own way far too long. I can tell you, Mr Abiose, they have positively held our country to ransom. Positively done so!'

Walpole expressed patriotic horror and disgust, and the Chief continued: 'This recent contract – I think it only right to tell you, Mr Abiose – was a close-run thing. An exceedingly damned close-run thing. Some of my board were in favour of giving you the contract. . . . Particularly since your tender was actually the lowest – I tell you this in strictest confidence, of course. In *strictest* confidence.'

'Very good of you, Chief,' Walpole answered. 'But tell me, is there no obligation on the board to accept the lowest tender?'

'No obligation,' the Chief replied urbanely. 'No obligation at all. *In general*, of course, it's expected that the lowest tender gains the day. That's the rule – and a very good rule too. But in any individual case a great deal of discretion – and a great deal of responsibility also – is vested in the chairman. . . . That is to say, of course, in the board, whose decision the chairman must convey.'

'And that leaves you free to take all relevant factors into account.' Walpole spoke with studied smoothness, but the chief shot him a sharp glance, and he thought it wiser to add: 'And I can assure you, Chief, my board appreciates how important such factors must often be . . . technical know-how, experience and . . . er . . . so on.'

'Yes indeed,' the Chief replied, 'and as these were precisely the sort of factors which influenced our decision in the present case, I'm glad to find you so understanding.'

'Please go on. . . .'

'In early days under the British,' the Chief explained, picking up an ivory paper knife and bending it between his fingers as he talked, 'it was an axiom that nothing was ever built more than four storeys high. They were convinced our whole city rests on mud – which it probably does. And in early days, I suppose, this hardly mattered, land was cheap and they

simply spread their buildings over it. But in recent years, with
the expansion of trade and people crowding into the city,
those old-fashioned methods no longer fit the ticket. We can't
afford to waste land, and we can't afford to have clerks and
messengers spending hours every day doing nothing but walk
round delivering letters all over the place. . . .'

Walpole was watching the Chief closely as he talked. He
was a man of medium height, dressed in spotlessly white robes
with a cap of dark red velvet, heavily braided. His face, though
well-proportioned and even handsome when he set himself to
interest, lapsed quickly into brooding. His ready smile and
courteous welcome were impressive, but it was plain from his
brusque answers to phone calls and sharp dismissal of an
official – clearly a senior man wanting advice on something
urgent – that charm and good temper were qualities the Chief
husbanded, to be laid out only to advantage.

'. . . Well, that might have gone on for ever if the British
had remained for ever. Happily they didn't, and as soon as
Independence was assured, the big Italian firms came over
here looking for business. They'd been putting up blocks
fifteen storeys high out in the Pontine marshes ever since
Mussolini's day so they just laughed when we told them about
our famous mud. Their mud, they said, was much worse than
ours and there was no reason why Lagos shouldn't support
fifteen storeys too, if we went about it in the right way.
Know-how, you see, Mr Abiose! Know-how and experience.
Incidentally they were good enough to take me for a delightful
holiday in Rome to show their various building techniques
. . . driving in concrete piles . . . pouring rafts of concrete . . .
and so on.'

The Italians, Walpole agreed, had indeed shown skill at this
type of building. However there was nothing secret about
their methods, and he was sure that whatever Italians had
done, Nigerians could do before long.

'Exactly, my friend! *Exactly* what I have told my board. For
the moment the Italians have the advantage of experience, and
in this case we were obliged to take that into account – which is
why we finally settled on the firm of Crespi.'

The Chief looked across as though expecting some comment from Walpole, who remarked: 'For the moment, Chief.
But only for the moment. Experience is a commodity which
can be rapidly acquired.'

The Chief smiled. 'Undoubtedly! And though your firm

has not been successful on what is – I believe – only its *first*
tender for a government contract, I can give you the board's,
and indeed my own, encouragement to try again. You may be
sure, Mr Abiose, that any tender put in by your firm is going
to receive our most careful consideration.'

'And I can assure you, Chief,' Walpole replied, rising to his
feet as he noticed the Chief glancing at his gold bracelet watch,
'I can assure you that you will find us by no means an . . .
ungrateful . . . firm.'

As they walked towards the door it was clear the Chief had
recovered his good humour. 'I am happy to have met you, Mr
Abiose! I trust you and I will get to know each other really well
. . . I intend to keep in touch. "Gradual by gradual", as we
used to say in the Inns of Court, Mr Abiose. "Gradual by
gradual" will bring everything you wish for.'

And so, after a pat on the shoulder and a further handshake,
Walpole found himself on the landing waiting for the lift.

'You sound rather taken with Chief Efunshile,' Stephen
remarked when Walpole recounted his experience. 'Were you
impressed by the celebrated charm?'

'Considerably – when he turned it on. But he doesn't waste
it. I should think he'd be hell to work for.'

'What was the purpose of asking you along? Pure benevo-
lence?'

'To divert criticism, I imagine. . . . My guess is that he had
quite a struggle with his board *not* to give us this contract – the
lowest tender and the only Nigerian firm. One or two of the
members perhaps argued hard. Having got his way, he
doesn't want us making a fuss – putting up someone to ask
questions in the Assembly, or getting ourselves interviewed in
the press.'

'In fact, why *haven't* we got it?'

'Presumably because he'd already promised it to the
Italians. So they had to have this one – and their experience
gives him a fair get-out.'

'Why send for you instead of for the chairman? Or me, if it
comes to that?'

'My guess is that he didn't ask Chukuma because he didn't
want any witness-box cross-questioning.'

'If he took you for a soft option,' said Stephen reflectively,
'he possibly knows better now. . . . But how *did* you react?'

'Like a soft option – how else? No point in being nasty when the contract's gone. . . . As it is, we're well placed for next time round. Before I left he practically promised us something if we keep on tendering. "Gradual by gradual" is his advice.'

'All this makes it easy for you to look in for a bit of guidance and elucidation before we put our tender in next time. I suppose he didn't bring up what you might call the "personal" side of things?'

'Our whole conversation could have been taped and broadcast nationally.'

'Ah – so he *did* bring it up!'

'Not at all. He merely said what a delightful holiday he'd had in Rome at the expense of the Italians who wanted to show him their building techniques.'

'How did you answer that?'

'I assured him that he would not find Balogun and Abiose an ungrateful firm.'

Stephen laughed. 'You covered the essentials. Next time, I dare say, he'll get down to facts and figures.'

Walpole was already leaving the room when Stephen called him back. 'I've got a piece of news for you. . . . I don't know how you'll take it, but any way you'd be bound to hear it before long.'

'What's that?'

'Regina has left Duke.'

'Good God! But why on earth?'

'You should know . . . if anyone.'

'What's it to do with me?'

'She loved you, Walpole. You know that.'

'Not so much as she loved the life she led with Duke . . . and you know *that*! Regina went back to Duke and then perhaps was sorry she'd lost me. But I see now that if she had come to me, she'd have regretted her diamonds and evening dresses before long. But where has she gone?'

'No one knows. Cécile thinks she's probably gone to Europe. Months ago she told Cécile she'd had offers to become a model. . . . She just walked out of the house two days ago and vanished. If she took a plane it wasn't from this airport . . . you can imagine Duke made all inquiries.'

'How's Duke taking it?'

'Out of his mind with rage. Particularly because she left all her belongings behind – so he can't even accuse her of having plundered him. It's more humiliating almost than if she'd gone to someone else.'

'How's that?'

'Because it's plain she just couldn't endure Duke any longer.'

Walpole shrugged.

'Don't you care any more what happens to Regina?' Stephen asked with exasperation.

For a moment or two Walpole did not answer. Then he opened his mouth as if to speak, stopped himself, and finally sat silent.

'Well, *don't* you?' persisted Stephen.

'I consider I'm well out of it.'

'There are times, Walpole,' Stephen remarked, 'when you seem to me an unforgiving sod. I think I liked you better as you were when I first knew you.'

30
Flesh

Before six months had passed Chief Efunshile proved as good as his half-promise; Balogun and Abiose were given their first government contract and the firm expanded to meet the situation. Other benefits soon followed. National pride ensured that a Nigerian firm's success in competition with overseas giants was acclaimed in the press and the publicity brought further business, not only in Lagos but remoter parts of the country, so that one or two sub-offices were opened before long in provincial capitals. As business boomed Mr Chukuma, who had intended only to preside at monthly board meetings and give advice when asked, spent more and more of each day in the office, finding it, he said, more stimulating as well as more profitable than his other work. His son Basil was now away in Enugu, driving a heavy lorry and enjoying his new way of life. Walpole, who had always spent much time on the sites overseeing work in progress, was increasingly drawn into keeping contacts sweet and looking for new business. He led the luxurious, enervating life of the executive which is the same all over the world, those on opposite sides eating and drinking themselves into agreement with great cordiality but small goodwill.

The keystone of the firm's new prosperity was his relationship with Chief Efunshile, which had procured the original breakthrough and now ensured a flow of less conspicuous activity – such as extensions and alterations to existing buildings – too small in the chairman's view to be worth putting out to tender, and all the more profitable on that account. An understanding had grown up between Walpole and the Chief, nowhere stated but effective, that the Chief should receive 10 per cent on the final cost of all work for the board handled by Balogun and Abiose. As a result he had a direct interest in putting up costs, and even Walpole – whose conscience had stretched from firm to pliable, and over the last months from pliable to elastic – was made uneasy by such easy money. He spoke of this to Mr Chukuma.

'I understand your feelings, Walpole. To some extent I share them. But what can we do? We're in the big league now.'

'How d'you mean?'

'Our country is now part of the world, and the rules of the outside world apply. They apply to Nigeria and to any firms like ours which compete for international business. We can't create a new code of behaviour for ourselves.'

'No – I recognize that, but all the same. . . .'

'Legally,' said Mr Chukuma reassuringly, 'you know you can rely on me. Every stroke we do for the board is covered by official orders. From time to time I even query some addition to a job and get confirmation back in writing. I could go into court tomorrow and show that Balogun and Abiose have been fighting to save public money which an extravagant board insists on spending.'

'I hope you won't ever have to do that,' said Walpole fervently. 'But it isn't the legal aspect worries me, that's in your hands which is the best place for it to be. . . . What I don't like is that nowadays everything's too easy. No fun when there's no fighting.'

'H'm. You may be getting all the fighting you want before long.'

'How's that? Who's to be the enemy?'

'The name may be familiar . . . Karybdis-Schiller.'

'But surely they've got all they can handle over Duke's big project?'

'Duke's let them down,' Mr Chukuma explained. 'It was all lined up, but something made him change his mind. His accountants told him all along that he'd make more money by doing nothing and collecting tribute from his subjects than he could hope to get out of development – at any rate for the next five years, during which the value of his land is certain to increase.'

'So what's happening?'

'He's told Karybdis that the time is not yet ripe . . . political climate too uncertain . . . not sure it would prove in the best interests of "my people". You can imagine his line.'

'I can indeed! So Karybdis-Schiller got themselves all geared up for a big job which hasn't happened? They must be spitting blood.'

'They'll waste very little time spitting anything,' observed Mr Chukuma. 'They're taking the obvious step – going after government business too.'

'Well, we were in the field before them and we've still got our advantage, we're Nigerian and they're what? Lebanese-German, I suppose.'

'They've a plan for getting over that.'

'How?'

'The obvious way. They've appointed a couple of Nigerian directors and shoved a few Nigerians into key positions.'

'Who, for instance?'

'Chief Pontius.'

Walpole whistled. 'As what?'

'As contact man, particularly with government departments. He's been given a few shares – and an unlimited expense account.'

'That'll sink the firm,' remarked Stephen who had come in part way through the conversation. 'There's never been a business yet could pay Pontius's "unlimited expenses".'

'The agreement's only for twelve months, I understand,' said Mr Chukuma, 'after that the firm can renew or not.'

'So he'll be stirring that vast bulk of his into activity,' said Stephen. 'Better watch out, Walpole!'

'I'll be happy to try a fall with the fat Chief,' Walpole replied. 'But as I was saying before you came in, that doesn't altogether reconcile me to the carve-up.'

'What carve-up?'

'Why, what else can you call it when the client who spends the money, and so ought to be watching us and querying accounts, is actually trying to push up costs?. . . . It's as if the herdsman agreed to share the goat with the hyena.'

Mr Chukuma chuckled: 'Well if we're the hyena we can't be blamed for eating what the herdsman gives us, can we? Especially as the party won't be going on for long.'

'What party's that?' asked Stephen.

'The Independence party,' answered Mr Chukuma easily. 'Why, it's only a few months since the British were here. They never spent money and the country was governed from a lot of old army huts and run-down offices. But when Independence came the government obviously had to put on a show. After all if a farmer from Abakiliki visits the federal capital he doesn't want to look at a lot of old huts. He wants to see buildings bigger and higher than he's ever seen before – something to talk about when he gets home.'

'Well, the people are certainly getting fine new buildings,' said Stephen, 'and we're certainly helping them to get them.'

'True,' Walpole agreed. 'But in five years' time when all the fine buildings are going at the corners, the people are going to start asking what they personally got out of Independence.'

'And what *have* they got?' asked Stephen.

'Nothing,' remarked Mr Chukuma blandly. 'In nine cases out of ten, nothing at all. No government can do much for fifty million people in five years, so in five years the political climate may feel very different. But meanwhile this is expansion time . . . and frankly, I'm an expansion man!'

'What d'*you* think will happen in five years' time?' Stephen asked.

'In five years' time,' said Walpole seriously, 'the great friendly populace will be wanting to see politicians' heads rolling in the gutters.'

'Do the politicians realize this?' Stephen asked.

'The ones who aren't fools do,' said Mr Chukuma. 'Take Walpole's friend Efunshile. I don't know him, beyond shaking hands with him from time to time, but I can read his mind as well as I can yours.'

'And what d'you see?'

'A man in a hurry. He can count on three years, possibly five. It's just possible, if he's been very cunning, that after that he may move on to higher things . . . federal Minister of Finance will be his dream. Three numbered bank accounts in Switzerland, with a steady rivulet flowing into each from the national resources. What more could any man want? But it's

much more likely, in my opinion, that by then this coalition
will have cracked and our Chief will be out on his ear . . . and
lucky if he's got two ears, and a head between them.'

'So he means to cash in heavily for the short time he's got?'

'He *is* doing. It's his only certainty, for which he's given up a
highly profitable – and safe – career in law. He can argue that
the state owes him his plate of chop, and his constituents
expect him to keep it pretty full. You can be sure he won't let
opportunity slip, and I don't mean us to let ours slip either. I'll
see we keep the right side of the law, and, Walpole, you sit on
your conscience for the next five years.' Then – Stephen by
now having gone back to his own office – he added, 'After that
you can indulge it if you want to, just as old Mr Balogun
indulges his. He's got enough put by to keep him and his
conscience in comfort for the remainder of their days.'

As it happened Walpole had an appointment that same
evening with Chief Efunshile, who had asked him to call in for
a drink on his way home from work. Walpole had assumed
this was to discuss business matters; possibly, he thought, his
host wanted an advance on money that would be due to him
before long.

'Walpole,' the Chief began once they were installed in his
book-lined study with a whisky, 'you must know by now that
I look on you as my friend. These are not empty words . . .
I meet and entertain many people. I admit I give many the
impression that they are my friends. . . . But in fact there are
very few I really wish to see, and you are one of those few.'

Walpole gave an appreciative grunt.

'You come here often,' the Chief went on, 'and you will, I
hope, be coming here more often, so there's something about
my personal life I want to tell you. It's bound to become public
knowledge before long, and I'd rather you hear it direct from
me.'

What on earth, Walpole wondered, could be coming?

'You must know that I've been living for some months with
a girl. . . . I've become extremely fond of her and intend to
make her my wife. But the fact is this decision has caused a lot
of trouble in my family . . . particularly with my children.'

'What is it they object to?'

'Oh, they naturally take the side of my present wife – after
all she's their mother. The don't object to Pearl being my
mistress, but they want me to keep her in the background, and
I wish her to live with me in this house as my wife. I shall not

divorce my present wife – unless she compels me to. I'm prepared to give her a house and a good allowance, but she *has* to go away. I can't have two women here, both receiving guests as my wife, and I intend to have the one I want.'

Walpole sat silent for a minute, and the Chief with a note of exasperation demanded: 'Well – aren't you going to say something?'

'Forgive me, Chief! I appreciate your confidence. But as I've not met either of the ladies, I can have no opinion – I can only promise you my goodwill and support. How do things stand now?'

'My first wife has left my house. I at last induced her go to to the place I bought for her. But now the children are giving me hell! You'd think I wanted to have their mother executed from the fuss they're kicking up.'

'What sort of fuss?'

'My two sons abused me as if I were a good-for-nothing debauchee. . . . I can't even tell you all they said . . . enough to make a worm turn in its grave. However, I've got the better of those two young men, I fancy.'

'How did you manage that, Chief?'

'The elder one's in the army, and the War Minister is my good friend, so he's kindly sent him out of the country on a long promotion course. The other wants to practise law – so I'm packing him off to London to cool his head in chambers. If he doesn't go, he gets no allowance. So he's going.'

'You've solved your problem then, Chief. Congratulations!'

'No! All I've done is to clear the air a bit. The worst problem remains – my daughter Alicia. She's always been my favourite, and she knows it. The boys could be a nuisance, but Alicia can make my life hell. And she *is* doing.'

'How does she behave?'

'She sets out to make me mad. She's always going out and coming back late. When I shout at her she just says, "I'm following my father's example." When we're alone together she scarcely speaks a word. . . . It gets me down.'

'What d'you want her to do?'

'I want her to live with her mother. Go overseas and study. Anything – provided she gets off my back!'

'Can't you send her to study overseas?'

'Only with her consent. I'd gladly pay for her to study in London near her brother. In Paris – anywhere! But I can't just throw her out, and Pearl refuses to live here while Alicia's in the house.'

'Most girls would jump at the chance of going overseas. So if Alicia's so determined to stay here,' Walpole suggested, 'isn't it possible she has some reason, some emotional interest perhaps, that's keeping her?'

'Could be. . .' said the Chief musingly. 'She has a young cousin she's been fond of – a good looking, useless youth. . . . But talking of emotional interests, my friend, let me show you my own secret.'

And in a moment, having seemingly forgotten the problem about which he wanted his friend's opinion, the volatile Chief had crossed the room and opened a door disguised behind rows of false leather binding as though it formed part of a bookcase. Inside was a smaller study, windowless and with no access except by the concealed door through which he now led the way, and containing little but a divan, drinks cabinet and wardrobe. The Chief took a key from his robe. As the wardrobe door swung back, Walpole was expecting to see a mirror on the inside, but instead found himself face-to-face and almost touching a realistic life-size painting of a naked woman.

Walpole blinked. Then looked again. 'Yes,' he said. 'I *do* see why you want to have her around. She's a knock-out. But. . . .'

'But what?'

'But isn't she *white*?'

The Chief laughed. 'No – thank God! I've enough trouble without *that*. But she's certainly pale. . . . She's an Ethiopian, from a very high family. She came here with a team of state dancers for the Independence celebrations. We met . . . and I persuaded her to stay on when the rest went back. Now she's willing to marry me, if only. . . .'

There were sounds of raised voices from the entrance hall. 'Oh, hell!' the Chief exclaimed. 'That sounds like some of my damned colleagues in the government. Why the devil must they come round now? Don't we see enough of each other at work? I'll take them into another room, and you slip out quietly when the door's closed. . . . Thanks, my friend, for coming round. It's done me good talking to you.'

While speaking he had slammed the wardrobe and swung the protecting bookcase into place, crossed the room and opened the study door. Walpole could almost see the practised

smile and glow of welcome in his words. 'My *dear* ministers!
What a pleasant surprise! How very good of you to call round
and see me! Come this way, and let's all have a drink or two
together.'

Walpole drove home in a state of excitement. The sight,
amounting almost to contact, with the Chief's mistress had
aroused him sexually. It was a long time since he had had
anything to do with women for the shock over Regina's
rejection had gone deep. But the fact that he now considered
love to be a sham was no reason – he told himself – for giving
up sex. As he drove he was hesitating whether to ring up his
former girlfrield Ayoka Fashanu and offer to take her out, or
go into the town and find himself a free woman. If she were
not already spending the evening with someone, he could
sleep with Ayoka with a minimum of explanation and
pretence, but he could get into bed with a free woman without
any pretence at all, and he had just decided to find himself a
free woman for tonight when, as he drove up to his house
before going into town, he saw Kalio talking to a strange and
striking-looking woman. This brought back something Kalio
had told him a few days earlier. They had been talking of other
matters and then, as Walpole rose to go, Kalio remarked that a
woman he knew and whose honesty he vouched for had seen
the master several times as he went in and out and asked if she
could come and meet him. Walpole had answered non-
committally, but that seemed to have been enough assent for
Kalio, for as the car stopped he came forward with the
woman. She appeared to be about thirty, with a round face
and a mass of jet-black wiry hair. Her lips wore an ingratiating
smile, but her manner conveyed an assurance, even an
effrontery of confidence in her power to please. Elegantly
dressed in a *lappa* and head-tie of silk, she was clearly no
common person. Her low-cut *buba* disclosed breasts of
inviting fullness, and arms, bare to the shoulders, showed the
smoothness of a well-tended childhood.

'This woman' – Kalio enunciated the words carefully – 'is
wishing to spik with master.'

Walpole smiled. 'Then please say whatever you wish to
say. . . .'

'I speak with master inside house,' she declared.

Walpole led the way to the front door, pushed it open and
was about to show her into the living room, but she was

already mounting the stairs and went directly to his bedroom.
It was the houseboy's evening out, and it was plain she had
already learned her way around. Once inside the room she
took off her head-tie, unwound her *lappa*, slipped out of her
buba and presented her powerful nakedness to Walpole. Not
troubling to look what effect this had on him, she was already
starting to undo his clothes. Her naked flesh, bold movements, and the scent from her skin excited him. He had
intended to question her but when, without a word spoken,
she lay down on the bed and proffered her breasts to him with
both hands, he flung himself over her and with no preliminary
play forced himself into her. The pain of sharp teeth in his neck
and two strong hands gripping his buttocks was all the
resistance he met, and when after furious minutes he lay
panting back, the woman remained silent as before. Turning
to look at her, Walpole saw that she was smiling. It was not a
smile of merriment, still less of affection, but it was assured
and enigmatic as though she knew quite well what she was
about.

After a minute or two, she rose and went over to a table on
which stood drinks she had evidently put there previously.
She brought one for him and poured another for herself which
she drank slowly, not swallowing the gin but savouring it on
her tongue. After finishing it she held the glass up to Walpole by
way of inquiring if he wanted more. Walpole shook his head.

'Now,' he said, 'suppose you tell me why you wanted to
come and see me?'

The woman gave a short laugh. 'So master not know why I
want for see him? Tell me then something.'

'What?'

'Are you glad I come here for see you?'

'Well yes, I am – but. . . .'

'No "but". Master is glad and so am I. That is enough.'

And without more ado she sat down on the bed and applied
herself with dexterous fingers to bringing Walpole back to
sensual life. This time it was clear she intended to obtain her
own satisfaction. The game she directed was prolonged and
when Walpole finally lay back on the pillow he felt as though
not only all vitality but all power of independent thought and
action were drained out of him, leaving a hollow shell.

After a while the woman got up and poured them each
another drink. This time she did not come back to the bed but
went over to the window and sat down. Gazing out over the

darkened garden she began to mutter. It was not singing and not talking but a kind of crooning chant as though addressed to something inside herself, as though summoning up something not easy to be reached. As she chanted she appeared less womanly and more animal; indeed from the line of her neck and shoulder, from the arm stretched carelessly along the back of a settee, Walpole had the impression of an enormous cat. She did not speak. She had given no name. She was an elemental force which he – or possibly Kalio – had conjured up from the devil knew where. While he pondered, the woman stretched herself sensually, got up and came over to the bed where she stood looking down not at his face but at his thighs and loins. She regarded these with no excitement but with a cool professional eye as a doctor might look at a patient to estimate his progress, then she went back, sat down and continued her crooning chant, but this time she seemed not to be discoursing but repeating some order or instruction.

After about a quarter of an hour Walpole was beginning to regain self-possession. It was time for him to assert himself, he felt, and he raised himself on one elbow intending to question her firmly and take charge of the situation. The woman looked up and then came over, rearranged his pillow for comfort, pushed him back on it, knelt down and began slowly to lick his body, starting at the knees. Her tongue had the practised strength of a masseur's hands and as she started to move rhythmically up his legs and thighs Walpole found himself succumbing to a series of hallucinations more vivid and real than any dream. He was a baby caressed by its mother, a mother he was far from trusting but whom he lacked the willpower to defy, and who caressed him not out of tenderness but with sensuality in order to keep him in her power. Again, he was a newborn animal being freed of its caul and licked literally into shape, her own shape, by its dam, a lioness or leopard. And now he was some creature newly killed or almost killed, being coated with saliva by a monstrous reptile which, once the process was complete, would engorge him slowly into its distended throat.

As the rasping tongue caressed closer and closer, Walpole felt his sexual force flow back and as she mounted and lowered her body on to his, there began a see-saw struggle which, after racking him for what seemed like minutes, worked up into a shudder of mutual violence which went on and on, and in

which pleasure and agony were so blended that it could almost
have been his death throes.

With eyes shut, heaving chest and saliva running down his
face, Walpole lay back exhausted, but the short rest he had
intended passed into a troubled sleep in which, half aware that
he was sleeping, he was struggling to wake from a nightmare
of oppression. When at last he did wake, the room was dark
and the woman gone. Looking at his watch he realized that
she had probably been gone for several hours.

Later, having bathed and got something to eat, Walpole
went over to Kalio's outhouse. Handing him a sum of money,
he ordered: 'Give this to . . . your sister.'

The two men looked at one another in astonishment.
Walpole had not intended to utter the two last words, which
appeared to have come out of him of their own accord.

After a moment Kalio grinned sarcastically, but pocketed
the notes with satisfaction. 'My sister,' he said, 'done thank
master. Master too-too kind. Sister visit master one-time
when master tell Kalio he want spik wid her.'

31
Chief Pontius

Among Chief Efunshile's qualities was a love of lavish
entertainment. He enjoyed playing the host and his manner of
doing so was to give his guests as much to eat and drink as they
could carry, with as much more on top of that as they could be
persuaded to take in. If you dined with the Chief there was no
need to fortify yourself beforehand with a snack, and if when
you got home you could steer between the doorposts it would
certainly not be your host's fault. At larger parties attended by
wives and daughters restraint had to be observed, but when
the Chief gave one of his 'special' parties for a dozen political
or business cronies, each man on arrival would be asked to
name his drink and a fresh bottle of whisky, gin or brandy was
then put beside his place which, with any other drink he

fancied, he would be expected to finish before leaving – which might be at any time before next midday.

'I don't know what you're complaining about,' said Stephen when Walpole objected to too frequent invitations to these entertainments. 'You've got an infernally strong head and a crocodile stomach – they're our company's chief invisible assets. If it weren't for these parties they'd be wasting away for lack of use.'

'Just the opposite. My assets are being exhausted by reckless exploitation. A party every six weeks I might survive, but they're running at one a fortnight now.'

'We all have to make sacrifices,' said Stephen, 'for the general good. Think of Chukuma and myself reduced to poverty, and force down two more tumblers of gin.'

'If we must all make sacrifices, then it's time *you* went to one of his parties.'

'No go, my friend! It's you the Chief likes, not me. Also I've got no head in his sense of the word. You must carry the firm's party-going on your own broad shoulders.'

'If I could drink with my shoulders,' said Walpole, 'I'd face parties twice a week.'

It was at one such party a couple of weeks later that Walpole came face to face with his antagonist. He had been asked to come round early for a quiet drink and chat and was now watching with admiration as the Chief received his guests. His family, he had disclosed, were continuing to give him trouble and only a few minutes earlier his brow had been thunderous and voice harsh when he spoke about them, but as host he seemed able to lay personal problems on one side, making each successive arrival the focus of his interest. Friends responded with boisterous affection and opponents found it hard to remain hostile in face of his flattering attentions. Among these last, much to Walpole's surprise since he knew his host detested him, was Chief Pontius, a shambling bear of a man whose manner of entry, at the same time arrogant and furtive, suggested insistence on the limelight counterbalanced by a fear of being seen through. For him, as he stood blinking in the doorway and shaking out his robes, the host found instantly the right approach. Too much warmth would have seemed insincere and instead the Chief invested his manner with a manly deference; any smaller person than himself, Chief Pontius was given to understand, would have re-membered how often they had been on opposite sides and stayed away. Having arrived with apprehension and full of readiness to take offence, Chief Pontius was gratified to find it had been magnanimous of him to appear at all.

The banquet proved a steamy affair, hotter and noisier even than the run of Chief Efunshile's private dinners. Emphasis this evening was on drink. Often such feasts ended in debauch when some of the younger 'free women' of the city – freshly dressed and coached beforehand – were brought in as the night wore on. But out of respect for his new romance, which was common knowledge though his intention of remarrying was still secret, there would be no 'free women' tonight, consequently no guest had any reason to drink less than he could force himself to hold. Anything like serious discussion would have been impossible in that atmosphere, and even intrigue difficult. Little passed but jovial inanities and bellowed leg-pulling. From time to time the Chief shifted his guests around, each carrying his bottle of spirits with him, and in one such move Walpole found himself next to Chief Pontius. Following his host's good-humoured example, Walpole remarked that he had heard Chief Pontius speak at a recent political meeting and congratulated him on a favourable reception.

The Chief glared suspiciously over his spectacles. 'May I ask what party you belong to?'

'I'm not a member of any party,' Walpole replied.

'Why not? Aren't you interested in politics?'

'Very much. But not in parties.'

'That doesn't make sense,' said Chief Pontius brusquely. 'Interest in politics means being interested in parties. What did you say your name is?'

'I didn't say my name. It's Walpole Abiose.'

The Chief levered his bulk around to stare more closely. 'Ha! So you're Walpole Abiose. I've heard a lot about you from my friend Duke Ombo.'

'No doubt. And you probably heard a lot about Duke from your friend Reuben Karybdis – though *their* beautiful friendship seems to have cooled off recently.'

Chief Pontius tossed his head like a bull uncertain if it was being attacked or not. 'Duke Ombo tells me you landed him in a heap of trouble – some crazy idea for building cheap houses all over his estates.'

'If Duke ever thought of building houses it was because he expected to make more money that way,' Walpole replied. 'He planned to put up hotels with your present firm for the same reason. And he gave *that* up because he makes still more by doing nothing.'

Chief Pontius swallowed angrily. 'I understand *your* firm's managing to make a great deal of money at the present time.'

'We are doing well,' Walpole admitted. 'Mainly because we're Nigerian.'

'Calling a firm "Nigerian" means nothing. A lot of people make profits out of Independence who did nothing to help gain it. It's a disgrace!'

But Walpole, like the Chief, had had more than his share of drink and was conscious of those around them listening.

'Tell us, Chief,' he said loudly enough for half the table to overhear, 'about your part in the national struggle. Have your sacrifices for the cause been rewarded? If not, isn't it time they were?'

Chief Pontius, whose sacrifices had consisted in making all he could out of cooperating with the colonial power, and now all he could out of the new regime, snorted indignantly: 'You'll learn, young man, that it does not pay to be insolent with me! Let me tell you this. . . .'

But before Walpole could learn what it was the Chief meant to tell him, their ever-watchful host had slipped between: 'My *dear* Pontius – come over here a moment – there's an admirer of yours been trying to get a few words with you all evening.'

Conscious of having made an enemy, Walpole spent the next hour cementing a few friendly relationships against the hour when he might need them. At last, well after midnight and with swimming head, he slipped out into the garden where the night air was at least fresher than indoors. But around the house, owing to the presence of two or three ministers and an ambassador among the guests, stood armed police, so that it was not long before he retired indoors again. Reluctant to face the party's noise and fumes he sat down part way up some stairs, held his head in his hands and resolved, as often before, to give up attending Chief Efunshile's banquets.

Walpole had been sitting for no more than a few minutes when the front door moved, was opened cautiously some inches, and a young woman's head peered into the hall. Seeing no one, she slipped inside and closed the door. She was slight, no beauty but with the attractiveness of youth, and expensively dressed. Running with a light step across the hall, she reached the stairs with visible relief, but her hand went to her throat as she saw Walpole seated in her way.

'Sorry if I frightened you,' he said soothingly, 'I'm harmless. My name's Abiose, Walpole Abiose. One of your father's guests.' She gasped and to give her time to recover he went on: 'It got hot and noisy in the dining room, so I went into the garden, but that's full of police. I don't enjoy the company of police, so I came here and sat down on the stairs. Hope you don't mind?'

'Of course not,' she said, now in control of herself. 'I'm Alicia Efunshile. I've heard my father speak of you.'

'Your father's been a good friend to me,' Walpole replied. 'However I see from your cautious entry that he doesn't know you were out – so if you want to vanish while you can, please do.'

She looked at him doubtfully. 'Well no. As a matter of fact I *hadn't* told him. So please, when you see him, say nothing about it.'

But at this moment the dining-room door opened, letting a gust of noise and smoke into the hall as the Chief ushered out two guests about to leave. Walpole put up a hand and pulled the girl down on to the stairs.

'Good God!' exclaimed the Chief, glancing up and catching sight of them. 'What on earth are you two doing up there? I thought you were in bed hours ago, Alicia.'

'All my fault, Chief,' Walpole answered easily. 'Your daughter came downstairs to find a book – and nearly trod on me. I was cooling my head after enough of your gin to drown an elephant. I told her who I was, and persuaded her to sit down and talk about her father.'

'Ha! So how long have you been sitting there gossiping?'

'Time passes quickly in agreeable company, Chief, and with such an absorbing subject! I dare say half an hour or so. But why? Have you been looking for me? Are there bottles that still need emptying?'

Reassured, the Chief turned to speed his guests and Alicia, as she slipped upstairs, shot Walpole a grateful smile. She has a defenceless look, he thought, proud of his presence of mind in affording her protection. She's got good eyes, too, and a reasonable figure – too bad she isn't pretty.

'That was tactless of you, Walpole,' the Chief reproved him over a final drink after the rest of his guests had staggered off into their cars, 'to get into a row with Pontius. It's the first time he's been to my house. He's a detestable man – but you must have seen I tried to make him welcome. Why didn't you follow my example?'

'I'm truly sorry, Chief. It *was* wrong of me, I admit. I started trying to be agreeable, but he seemed set on needling me from the start. Then after he learned my name he became worse. I stood all I could and then started to jab him back. I don't know what I've ever done to annoy him.'

'Old man jealous of a young one, I should think,' the Chief replied. 'He's probably heard tales of your amorous successes. The fact that he's past all that himself would only make him angrier. . . . By the way, Walpole, before you go – some good news for your firm. You remember the big contract for police barracks I spoke about?'

'Yes?'

'Well, it's coming your way. The other tenders are in, and if you cut a hundred thousand or so off here and there, it'll be yours . . .' and the Chief went into details which the two men discussed for a further quarter of an hour.

Over lunch next day Walpole passed on to his partners his news about the barracks contract.

'Looks like the biggest job we've ever handled,' Stephen said. 'There must be two or three years' work there.'

'And that's only the beginning,' Walpole answered. 'The first building is a prototype – there could be a dozen more on the same lines up and down the country over the next ten years.'

'If there's one thing all governments are happy to spend money on,' observed Mr Chukuma, 'it's the police. They feel it's so much life insurance. But I don't suppose we'll get the lot. The government will want to spread the work around.'

'The government may want to,' Stephen said, 'but our good friend Efunshile may not. There can be half a million in it for him if the whole lot goes through us.'

'More than that, I fancy,' Mr Chukuma put in.

'Well, at any rate we're sure of the first stage,' said Walpole. 'But even this sets quite a problem.'

'What problem?'

'Heavy equipment, bulldozers, earth-movers and the rest. . . . We'll need a lot of new gear – and it's becoming harder to get hold of.'

'Why?' asked Stephen.

'Import licences – only a couple of firms bring stuff of this kind into the country, and they're only allowed to bring in so much.'

'Efunshile can fix that,' said Mr Chukuma.

'He can drop a hint to the right minister, no doubt, but he may not want to. None of them likes interfering in one another's little arrangements.'

'So what d'you propose?' Stephen asked.

'Give a firm order now for what we need, though it means putting down a big advance.'

'Is that wise before the contract's signed?' Mr Chukuma queried.

'Not altogether, but afterwards could be too late. This isn't the only important contract going, and with Karybdis-Schiller chasing work through Pontius, we may find we've landed the contract but can't carry it out. Or that we take it on and are involved in a time penalty.'

'Walpole's right,' Stephen agreed. 'We ought to push our order through now.'

'Agreed, then,' said Mr Chukuma. 'But I hope Walpole was sober when he heard Efunshile give that promise.'

The first barracks were to be built outside Enugu, capital of the Eastern Region, where the firm was already planning to open a branch office. Mr Chukuma, anxious to visit his son Basil who was working on a minor development there, offered to go and make necessary arrangements. He returned after a week, saying he had to pay far higher rent than expected and sign a lease for four years instead of two, because of the demand for office space since Independence. 'However, our friend Efunshile will no doubt foot the bill in one way or another.' Meantime Walpole had been busy chasing up suppliers, and after four weeks' effort the partners could congratulate themselves they were well placed to handle the coming contract.

During the past month the Chief, surprisingly, had given no more parties and Walpole had several times thought of ringing him or dropping in on him for a chat, but Stephen counselled patience. Though Walpole could not disagree, he became restless at hearing nothing and it occurred to him to ring the daughter Alicia and see if he could pick up any information from her. Alicia who sounded pleasantly surprised, assured him that she and her father were well, then was clearly waiting to learn what the call was all about. Walpole, who had not thought how to handle this situation before ringing her, found himself asking if she would have dinner with him one evening – an invitation which, after some hesitation, she accepted.

'Damn it!' Walpole said to himself as he put the receiver down. 'That's an evening wasted. But if I'm to keep in with the Chief, it can't do any harm to get to know his daughter.'

Walpole had offered to call for Alicia at her home, but she preferred to meet outside and said she would arrive at the imposing hotel to which he had invited her in her own car. He was waiting on the steps when she drove up, dressed in European style and looking as if she had just visited the hairdresser. They had a couple of drinks before going in to dinner over which they discussed whatever friends they had in common, and such subjects as people talk over when they are trying to learn each other's likes and dislikes, tempers, backgrounds, tastes. At the back of Walpole's mind was the idea that, if the conversation could be led round to the subject of the Chief's remarriage, he might put in a few words on his behalf. He would be glad to do this out of friendship, but he also calculated that such intervention, reaching the Chief's ears in due course, might yield dividends for Balogun and Abiose. To bring the subject up directly had to be avoided, but when Alicia started to speak of past holiday trips to Europe, the door seemed open.

'Both your brothers, I understand are overseas. I suppose they enjoy travelling more than you do?'

'Men do enjoy travelling more than women, I suppose. But my brothers haven't gone abroad for pleasure. They've gone because my father sent them.'

Walpole was about to ask, disingenuously, why the Chief had done this, when Alicia added: 'I suppose my father told you of his intention to remarry?'

'He did. He also told me that you oppose the plan – as I imagine your brothers do as well?'

'Indeed we all do. But I don't have to explain why children don't like to see their mother pushed into the background in favour of a stranger. How would you like it if *your* father treated your mother in that way?'

'I haven't either parent. I only just knew my mother, and my father not at all.'

'Oh? Anyway you can understand how we feel – even though it can't happen to you.'

Walpole was not expecting sympathy, but the girl's manner was a little too offhand. 'Your feelings are natural,' he agreed.

'But it's also natural for your father – who is now an important public figure – to want a wife who can entertain for him and run his home the way he wants. I've never met your mother, so I'm not in any way criticizing her. What I'm saying is that your father may have a point of view as well.'

'He not only has one – he insists on it. Possibly my mother – who came from a village and married young – hasn't progressed as rapidly as he has. But that's no reason why she should be pushed out of the way. And as regards running his house and entertaining, I've looked after that for the past two years, and he's had no cause to complain. I'm sure his new wife can't do any better.'

'I don't suppose she can do half as well,' Walpole replied, while a waiter removed dishes and plates. 'But a man of your father's position has the right to order things as he wishes, even if what he wants seems irrational to you.'

'If what he wants is irrational – which in this case it *is* – then his family must oppose it. My mother's too docile. Both my brothers have been sent away, so it's up to me to act for all of us.'

Walpole smiled. 'I see you're opposing your father out of family duty. However, you've made your protest. Have you thought what happens next?'

'What d'you mean?'

'How are you going to live? Are you planning to settle down with your mother?'

'I'm fond of my mother,' Alicia answered coolly. 'So I *could* go and live with her if I had to.'

'But?'

'Well, for one thing I enjoy social life. I like visiting, going to parties, meeting people. I don't see why I have to give up living as I like because my father wants to have his mistress in the house. I'm his daughter, I'm as entitled to my way of life as he is to his.'

Once more the waiter was fluttering around with food, and while it was served Walpole looked at the slight, demure figure in front of him and realized with surprise that the Chief had a battle on his hands. This was the girl he had thought of as defenceless.

'I understand your feelings,' he remarked as the waiter withdrew. 'However, not everyone will see your situation in that light.'

'How will "everyone" see it?'

'Most people would say that a daughter of . . . what, twenty-two or three?' (Alicia nodded: 'Near enough') 'ought to do what her father wants. He *is* your father and head of the family. Also, I imagine, he makes the money on which you all live.'

Alicia tossed her head. 'I know all about the conventional view – it's been explained to me often enough. But if we all accepted it, Nigerian women would still be carrying tree trunks and planting yams. I don't accept these out-of-date ideas! And I notice those who do – my father, for instance – only accept them when it suits. My father thinks his children should obey him, in accordance with tradition. But he doesn't go off and sacrifice a goat to his ancestors every time he has to reach some decision. He settles such matters for himself – regardless of what his ancestors are thinking.'

Admiration was growing in Walpole for this girl's spirit, but some concern also for the outcome of her conflict. 'What I'm trying to make you see, Alicia, is that in the last resort your father will decide this matter also for himself.'

'Tell me,' asked Alicia, 'have you met my father's future wife – Pearl, or whatever her name is?'

For a moment Walpole found himself confused. He had indeed seen the Chief's future wife; in a sense he could be said to have 'met' her more than many people who knew her better. But he had never spoken to her and had no idea what kind of a person she might be, and he was still constructing some reply when Alicia answered for him.

'I see my father *has* introduced you to her. That's a mark of favour. Not many of his friends have met her. I shan't ask if you like her – I don't. What's more I don't intend to like her.'

'And I shan't try to persuade you to like someone you've decided to dislike,' said Walpole. 'But since I like your father – and am beginning to like you – perhaps you'll let me give you a small piece of advice?'

She gave an encouraging smile.

'Try to avoid a head-on battle over Pearl. What you think of her is your affair, but don't let her cause a final breach between your father and yourself.'

'How can I stop there being a final breach? If he goes ahead and does something against the interests of us all, that's not my responsibility. It's his.'

'Look,' said Walpole, 'your father means to marry this woman. In my opinion you can't stop it. He's prepared to treat

your mother generously. No – don't interrupt me for a
moment! Your brothers and yourself oppose the marriage.
Very naturally. But your brothers and yourself are not in the
same situation.'

'Why aren't we?'

'For two reasons. Your father loves you much more than he
does them.'

'How d'you know?'

'From what he's said.'

'*Said*!'

'And from the facts. He's sent the two of them away, but he
hasn't sent you away.'

'He would if he could.'

'You mean – he *could* do if he would. In his position nothing
would be easier than to insist on your going abroad to a
university – or God knows where. If he determined on it, he
could simply hire people to take you overseas. So if he doesn't,
it's because he doesn't want to.'

Alicia considered. 'Well – and what's the second reason?'

'It concerns yourself. You *need* your father, and your
brothers don't. They can make their own way in the world.
Oh, of course you can earn some sort of living if you have to,
but that's very different from being the daughter of Chief
Efunshile. You talk of enjoying social life – how much social
life will you get if you're working in an office and living in one
room?'

'Are you suggesting I go on living at home after my father
marries this woman? I wouldn't dream of it!'

'Well then, have you thought where you'll live when he *does*
marry this woman?'

'I don't mean him to marry her!'

'But *he* means to and if you force a head-on fight, you'll
lose.'

'He'll get tired of her before long.'

'Maybe he will, Alicia, or maybe he won't. *You* don't
know. *I* don't know. Even they can't know. But if he *does* get
tired of her in a year or two, then all the more reason why you
should avoid breaking with him now. And if he doesn't get
tired, it will be fatal to have made enemies of them both.'

Walpole had put his whole heart into trying to persuade this
girl. Having started the discussion with his own interest in
mind, he had carried it on out of a wish to help her, surprising
himself by the trouble he was taking. He watched her now as

she weighed up what had been said, hoping she would recognize and accept reality. For a moment he thought he had succeeded, then: 'So all you suggest is that I knuckle under and let my father do exactly as he pleases?'

'No,' said Walpole with despairing patience. 'What I'm saying is that your father *will* do as he pleases. So don't lose all the advantages of being his daughter – that is, his favourite child – when you can't affect the situation one way or the other.'

Quick to appreciate his changed tone of voice if not the force of his argument, Alicia replied: 'Well anyway, I can see you've been trying to help me.' She flashed him an appealing smile. 'Whether I take your advice or not I hope I can think of you as my friend?'

Walpole, easy to placate, assured her of his goodwill and, as they walked over to her car, put his hand through her arm. 'I've enjoyed meeting you. It's been a pleasant evening.'

She looked up at him with the large eyes which were her best feature. 'Oh yes,' she said, '*do* let's meet again soon.'

'I'll be in touch.'

'Well, you know where to find me – at least for the present! And thanks for dinner. And the good advice!'

During the next few weeks Walpole took Alicia out a couple of times more. This was partly due to his wish to maintain even an indirect contact with the Chief, and partly to a growing interest in Alicia herself who seemed unlike any girl he had had to deal with. She showed an assurance over her intentions, and a confidence in her power to make events turn out the way she wished, which both attracted and alarmed him. Having listened to all he said about her father's marriage, she remained, so far as he could tell, quite unaffected and in no way less determined to have her own way in the matter, which was now evidently coming to a climax. It was not a problem of choice the Chief faced, since he had no doubt about what he wanted. His problem lay in knowing how to silence or put out of the way a rebellious daughter he had hitherto made much of, without causing a scandal damaging to his political prospects and his hopes of wealth. He had got rid of his wife without much difficulty; she had kept always in the background and been easy to intimidate. But Alicia – as well-educated as himself, familiar with many of his political business secrets, and with friends in the dangerous world of newspapers and radio – was another proposition altogether.

Walpole had spoken as though it were an easy matter for her father to send her out of the country even without her consent, but it was by no means so simple as he had made out.

Meantime something like a brother and sisterly relationship was developing between Walpole and Alicia. He found himself looking forward to their meetings, and though she aroused no sexual interest in him, he was beginning to consider her attractive. On her side, though she seemed flattered by the attention of a somewhat older man, not ill-looking and of standing in the world, she maintained a reserve which could indicate a calculating nature. In the struggle she was waging, Walpole, as a close friend of her father, must represent a valuable ally or a danger in the camp. She was aware, he knew, of his firm's close relationship with the Chief, though perhaps not altogether of its nature, and it could well be from a wish to gain information rather than convey it that she mentioned one day 'that fat Chief Pontius who is always hanging round my father'.

The remark put Walpole on his guard, and he had made up his mind to wait no longer before approaching the Chief direct, when he received a phone call from his secretary, asking if he could manage to call round at the office for an hour or so during the next few days.

32
Touch and Go

'Come in, my friend, come in! It's far too long since I've seen you. One has no right to be too busy to see friends.' The Chief came forward with arms outstretched and the resonance of welcome in his voice; his smile was sweet as ever, but Walpole fancied he saw signs of apprehension in the eyes which rested on him. The two men sat down at a small table to avoid the formality of a desk, and after offering cigarettes and wondering if his guest would like anything to drink, the Chief arranged his snowy draperies over his knees: 'I have first to thank you, Walpole. Before we get to business I must express my gratitude. You've been kind to my daughter in taking her out recently – and I think there was some kindness to myself in your intentions. I appreciate this.'

'I took Alicia out because I enjoy her company. It's true I had hoped to persuade her to be more amenable towards her father's plans. . . . However that's not easy! Alicia isn't only delightful – she's strong-willed. I don't know who you can blame for that?'

The Chief smiled. 'Your kindness in personal matters, Walpole, makes my task much harder. I'd hoped to be able to give you good news at this meeting – indeed I was hoping to give it you long before now. But my position has been difficult. . . . *Very* difficult indeed. . . . I've been faced with a lot of opposition . . . I'm afraid what I have to tell you will be far from welcome.'

Walpole remained silent. He was sufficiently experienced a negotiator not to help his opposite number get off hooks until there might be benefit in doing so, and with a sigh the Chief continued: 'It's about this contract. As I say, I'd hoped it would have been settled before now in a manner favourable to Balogun and Abiose. . . . Indeed I fancy that when we last met I may have given you some hint . . . in confidence . . . that it *had* already been so settled.'

'You did, Chief. Not the *whole* contract. But the first part – the barracks at Enugu – you definitely told me we should get.'

'Ah well – you see how it is! Even about that I was premature – led away by my usual weakness, trying to oblige my friends. . . . I spoke too soon, Walpole, that's the short and long of the matter. I spoke too soon.'

This was far worse than Walpole had been fearing. He had realized there had been some bar to the smooth progress of events, but this was an actual recantation.

'So what exactly is the situation?'

But the Chief had no intention of being cornered into a factual discussion. The more airy and vague he could keep the talk, the better his hopes of somehow slipping through the net of obligation, and so, waving his arms like an enormous butterfly, he started to weave about the room.

'The situation? Life must be simple indeed for you business-men if you can talk in terms of "situations" – particularly "exact situations"! I hope you never find yourself in public service, Walpole. Pressures, my friend! The object of ceaseless pressures, night and day, from every quarter. That's *my* situation.'

'You've had no pressure from me to complain of, Chief.'

'Indeed not – that's another cause for me to be grateful! No, it isn't you – it's the fellow members of my board. They're complaining of the amount of work we give your firm. They've actually added up the value of your contracts over these past twelve months and presented me with the statistics! They're positively insisting the board's work be distributed more widely.'

Walpole had a sharp impression that any adding up had been done at the Chief's own request, and any statistics had been prepared for the purpose of this meeting. All he said, however, was: 'That's odd!'

'What is?'

'The other member of your board with whom I have any contact gave me the opposite impression.'

'What opposite impression?'

'Why, that the members are happy to have a Nigerian firm in a position to take on so much.'

In fact Walpole knew no other member of the Construction Board, but if the Chief was prepared to invent 'pressure' from his colleagues to suit his book, Walpole was equally ready to invent support for his own standpoint.

'In general, no doubt, that has been true till now. But over the issue of the barracks there's been stiff opposition. . . . But which of my colleagues are you speaking of?'

'You'll excuse me, Chief, I'm sure. Whatever my acquaintance said was certainly meant as confidential.'

'As you please. . . . But pressures from inside the board are not the only ones. Ministers in the federal government have wishes too – which they've not been slow to impress on me.'

This required a height of invention to which Walpole thought it better not to rise. 'Indeed, Chief, I realize that as chairman you're subject to every kind of pressure, and I sympathize. But one of the qualities I most admire in you is your ability to ride pressure. You may appear yielding, but in the end, I think, you seldom act except in the way you always intended.'

The Chief sat silent for a moment, then flung up his arms with a despairing gesture. 'How I wish I could tell you everything! There's nothing I'd like better than to lay the whole problem before you. But our meetings, you know, are secret. All I tell you is the conclusion.'

'Which is, Chief?'

'That I'm unable to give you the contract I hoped and which – I admit – I hinted you would have. It's true I'm chairman, but *decision* rests with the board and over this business I've failed to carry them with me.'

'May I ask who *will* be getting the contract?'

'For the moment that's confidential. But it'll be announced within a week.'

'I understand,' Walpole replied. 'However if I were a betting man I'd stake a few pounds on the well-known "Nigerian" firm of Karybdis-Schiller.'

The Chief looked at him sharply. 'Karybdis-Schiller have a great deal of experience of this type of work. Not only in Nigeria, but all over the world.'

'And in their new representative, Chief Pontius,' Walpole suggested, 'they have a capable negotiator.'

Chief Efunshile seemed about to protest, but Walpole anticipated him. The reaction to his remark told him all he needed, but it was essential for the firm's future that he keep his head. Their only hold on the Chief was his sense of obligation, and if he were given the opportunity to become angry that small hold could be lost.

'Let me reassure you, Chief! You and I have always been good friends. It won't be my fault if we don't continue that way. It was my mistake to have taken your general impression of goodwill as a promise. There's no more to be said!'

The Chief seized Walpole's hand in both of his. 'I'm grateful indeed for your taking it this way, Walpole. I too want us to remain good friends, and it would upset me very much if I felt I had let you down.'

'We agree you haven't done so,' said Walpole. 'However for myself the reality is almost worse than if you had.'

'What reality?'

'I've let down my partners – who are also, as you know, my friends.'

'In what way?'

'I passed on to them my mistaken impression that we would receive the Enugu contract. On that assurance we've bought machinery and equipment for a good many tens of thousands.'

'But why buy now?'

'There's a shortage – as you know. If we hadn't bought we'd have been unable to carry out the contract. We've also taken offices in Enugu to supervise the work. . . . Now I must explain to my partners how I came to make so foolish a mistake.'

The Chief looked genuinely concerned. 'My friend – I'd no idea! I appreciate your absolving me from responsibility, but now I fear you yourself will carry the burden. What can I do? Suppose I ask Karybdis . . . that is, if I find another firm to take the equipment off your hands? Would that get you out of the jam?'

'I don't think my partners will want that,' said Walpole.

'Then what *can* I do? There will no doubt be other opportunities, other contracts, before long. . . . I can truly promise you a share.'

Walpole pondered for a moment. 'Is the present contract actually signed?'

'No. But it will be shortly.'

'Have you told the members of the board of your decision?'

'Not yet,' the Chief answered, evidently overlooking what he had been saying earlier. 'I intend to call a meeting in three days' time.'

'Can you leave matters as they stand for those three days – and give me a chance to talk things over with my colleagues?'

'Certainly. It's the least I can do.'

'Thank you, Chief,' said Walpole cheerfully. 'And now would you be willing to declare this meeting informal?'

'As informal as you please. But what d'you want? Drinks, entertainment, beautiful women?'

'Not at the moment. I want you and me to talk openly for two minutes. Is this permissible?'

The Chief looked disconcerted, but recovered himself with a laugh. 'It isn't quite my normal way of doing business, Walpole, and I doubt very much if it's yours either. However, there's a time for everything – so presumably for candour too. . . . What d'you want to know?'

'I want to know if we can still match the offer made you by Chief Pontius. . . So I'm asking what that offer is. You receive ten per cent from Balogun and Abiose – so it must be more. But how much more?'

The Chief took a turn across the room. 'There are some words,' he said, 'which have never been spoken. It is the whistling of the wind which appears to form the sound of words.'

'I'm familiar with that occurrence,' Walpole assured him. 'It applies to everything said in this room from now on.'

'The undertaking is that I receive twelve and a half per cent on costs – with fifty thousand as immediate down payment.'

'And very good terms too. . . . Only one more question.'

'Which is?'

'If my firm matches that offer, can we still have the first contract? I ask in view of all my partners stand to lose by my mistake. . . . I suggest. . . . But have I your permission to make a suggestion?'

'Of course you have, Walpole. What is it?'

'I suggest Karybdis-Schiller might be satisfied with the second stage of the contract – or even two more stages. We'll be willing not to tender – or to tender above them – if you so advise.'

The Chief thought for a minute, seemed about to speak, and thought again. 'It *could* be. . . . It could just be that something on those lines might be worked out. . . . But are you *sure* your firm will match the offer?'

'No,' said Walpole, 'not at all sure. But give us three days, and I'll have the answer. . . . And now let's end our informal meeting and have two minutes' personal chat – if you can spare the time.'

'Indeed.'

'Then let me ask – how are the plans for your marriage? You've a determined young woman for a daughter, but I trust you're getting your way in spite of her.'

The Chief shook his head. 'Far from it, my friend. You know the saying, "One who rides two horses at the same time will be split in half" – I am that unhappy rider. I'm resolved to marry Pearl, but what to do with Alicia I don't know. You called her determined, but she's much more than that, she's damned obstinate. If I don't marry Pearl soon, she'll go back to Ethiopia. But if I marry her without my daughter's agreement, the girl's capable of ruining me. She knows too much – and she knows too many people. That comes of my having been an indulgent father. Truly I'm at my wits' ends. . . . All this, Walpole, has been worrying me far more than business affairs, though they're bad enough.' He glanced at his watch. 'But I'm behind with my appointments. A drink before you go?'

'It's a disaster!' Mr Chukuma declared. 'The worst we've ever had. All that money tied up in equipment we don't want, and a longish lease on an office we've no use for. . . . I *did* query,

Walpole, whether it was wise to trust the Chief's assurance?'

'You did. And you were right. *I* got us into this mess.'

'No recriminations,' said Stephen firmly. 'I backed the decision to buy equipment. In fact' – looking at Mr Chukuma – 'the decision is down in the minutes as unanimous. But what d'you suggest, Walpole? Can we hang on for the second stage in the contract? Would he undertake to give us that?'

'And would his undertaking be worth much if he did?' Mr Chukuma asked.

'I'm not sure the first stage is altogether lost,' said Walpole slowly.

'But I thought he told you we shouldn't get it?' queried Stephen.

'He did. However you haven't heard all yet. Before I tell you, I want a promise that nothing goes outside this building. No word of any kind. No hint to anyone. And this isn't a formality – it's a promise between friends. Is that agreed?'

Both men assented.

'The reason Karybdis-Schiller are getting the job instead of us is the terms they've offered the Chief. They're giving him twelve and half per cent instead of ten. With an advance on account of fifty thousand pounds.'

Mr Chukuma whistled.

'Why did he tell you this?' Stephen asked. 'Is he trying to screw more out of us?'

'No. I screwed it out of him against his will.'

'How?'

'By not reproaching him for having let us down. When I saw there was nothing to be gained by getting angry, I thought we'd better make sure of his goodwill. So I said I must have misunderstood what he told me. Since he knows very well that's not true, he was correspondingly grateful – and could hardly refuse to answer a few questions off the record. He's also promised to make no final decision for three days.'

'What's the use of that?' Mr Chukuma asked.

'I'm not sure. . . . But I thought it wise to obtain all I could. At least it'll annoy Chief Pontius – who was just going in to see him as I came out. . . . If we do match Karybdis's offer, we *might* even now just get the contract.'

'What about his promise to them?' Stephen asked.

'How he gets out of that's his own affair!' Mr Chukuma broke in. 'If Efunshile can wriggle out of his promise to Walpole, he can wriggle out of another to Pontius. But the question is – do we *want* to match their offer?'

Stephen thought for a minute. 'No. In my opinion we shouldn't compete.'

'Why not?' Mr Chukuma asked.

'When we went into "political business",' Stephen reminded his partners, 'we agreed to fall in with "the custom of the trade" because we'll get no business if we don't. But it's one thing to pay what we're compelled to – and a worse one to get involved in a bribery competition. I'm against it.'

'Well, yes,' said Mr Chukuma after some deliberation, 'I'm against it too. Not because I draw any fine moral distinction such as Stephen mentions, but because such bargaining's endless. Efunshile can come back and tell us Pontius is upping his cut to fifteen per cent and seventy thousand down. . . . Do we compete with that, or don't we? We shouldn't even know if it were true! *We* could be bidding against ourselves.'

'What d'you say, Walpole?' Stephen asked.

'I agree with you both. We shouldn't take part in any auction.'

'So what? Do we just withdraw and look round for whatever else we can pick up?'

'Not yet! Not for two days. We need this contract – not the next one, *this* one! And I'd give anything to stop Pontius getting away with it. . . . Let me have one more go at Efunshile.'

'But what have you to offer?' Mr Chukuma inquired, surprised at Walpole's insistence.

For a moment Walpole did not answer, then: 'I know him pretty well. . . . There are ways of working on him. . . . Anyway we've agreed not to offer above ten per cent – but can I take it that the fifty thousand down is okay if it will turn the scale?'

'You can offer him a hundred thousand if it's any help,' said Mr Chukuma. 'The bank will advance what we ask on a contract of this size. But if you can persuade Efunshile to accept ten per cent when he's been offered twelve and half – you're wasting your time in this business. You should be federal Prime Minister.'

'I've missed you,' Walpole told Alicia as they sat at dinner in the night club to which he had taken her. 'I didn't expect to, but I have.'

'Is that a compliment? It sounds two-edged.'

'If it's two edged, it cuts me not you. I'm so involved with business I'm surprised to find myself thinking about anything else – about you for instance.'

'What were you thinking about me?'

'That I look forward to our meetings.'

'Did you say anything about me to my father?'

'Yes. I told him you were a determined young woman.'

Alicia laughed. 'What did he say to that?'

'He says you're not just determined – you're obstinate.'

'D'you agree?'

'I think you're being obstinate over his marriage.'

Alicia sat silent for a moment before answering: 'You may be right. I've been thinking over what you said. . . . I may be being too obstinate towards my father.'

Few things are more softening to a man than to be told his words have had effect, and it was in gentle tones that Walpole asked: 'D'you mean, Alicia, that you might be willing to accept your father's marriage?'

'You've certainly made me see it in a new light. . . . I don't *want* to be obstinate or ungrateful. But if I accept this new arrangement, I have a difficulty of my own.'

'What's that?'

'What to do with myself?' She gave him a look that was half humorous, half appealing. 'It's one thing to stop opposing my father's marriage – which perhaps I might bring myself to accept. But I couldn't go on living in his house when his "Pearl" is mistress of it.'

'No. I can see that,' Walpole agreed.

'So he – my father, that is – solves *his* problem at my expense.'

'And you don't want to live with your mother?'

'No. I don't.'

'Why not? It seems the obvious thing to do. At least for a short time.'

'My mother's a dependent person and dependent people can be very exacting. I know what'll happen if I go to live with her. She'll cling to me, just as she's been clinging to my father all these years. Then if ever I want to leave I must fight to get away. I don't want to spend my life fighting people . . . whatever you may think of my nature.'

'What is your nature, Alicia?'

'Friendly and companionable – in my opinion.'

Walpole smiled. 'In that case what about sharing with a friend?'

'There's no one I care to live wth. I have girlfriends, of course, but none I specially want to share my home. And living on my own doesn't excite me. I told you I'm companionable! I'm appreciative too.'

'You struck me as independent when I met you first.'

'When you met me first – you mean on the stairs at my father's?'

'As a matter of fact,' said Walpole after a moment's thought, 'you didn't strike me as independent then at all. You seemed to me defenceless. But that was probably because you were afraid of being caught coming in late.'

Alicia laughed. 'You were certainly protective. As well as quick-witted. So when *did* you find me independent?'

'In the way you've stood up to your father. I think it's a mistake – but you've been independent and courageous.'

'Well – I suppose one changes,' said Alicia, with what might have been a sigh. 'I don't feel very independent and courageous now.'

After the waiter had been and gone, Walpole looked Alicia in the eyes and said: 'D'you mind if I ask you something? Something personal?'

'What is it you want to know?' she asked defensively.

'Are you in love with anyone?'

The question brought a gasp, and a quick lowering of her eyes before she answered. 'I have been, of course. Who hasn't – at twenty-three years old?'

They both laughed to ease the tension.

'Are you in love with anyone at present?'

'Well no. I've been in love with one man or another ever since I was twelve. But at this moment – no!'

'Can I ask . . .' but before Walpole could voice his question, Alicia rapped his hand with her finger.

'It's my turn now! How about yourself? Everyone knows Walpole Abiose has had more love affairs than there are fish in the lagoon. When was the last? And is it over yet?'

'More than a year ago – and very much over.'

'Don't tell me you've lived a year in total solitude?'

'No, not total solitude. But without emotional excitement – until the last few days.'

'I won't pretend not to understand you,' said Alicia. 'But I don't entirely believe you either.'

The hotel stood on a spit of land between sea and lagoon, and there was a welcome puff of cool wind in the darkness of the car park. Alicia bent down to unlock the door of her car, and when she stood up to say good night, Walpole took her in his arms. He was expecting mild resistance, what he got was a passionate response which left him aroused and frustrated as she disentangled herself, slipped into the car and drove away.

Kalio's fire was still burning and he was sitting outside his hut when Walpole reached home. He went into the house, picked up the gin bottle, came out again and sat down.

'Master wish for somethin'?' Kalio asked, eyeing the bottle with anticipation.

Walpole half-filled the two mugs which had appeared out of the darkness.

'Master wishin' Kalio roll bones?'

Walpole, who had many times resolved not to let Kalio roll the bones for him since it could only add to the influence of this man whom he distrusted, nodded agreement.

'Yes, Kalio. Roll the bones.'

Kalio slowly sipped his mug to the last drop before retiring to the back of the outhouse, to emerge after a minute or two with his bundle of rags.

There was always something obscene about the look of Kalio's bundle, but more so tonight than ever, and Walpole half expected some horror to emerge from it, a severed hand or a dead foetus. Kalio's appearance had also altered for the worse. He had become squat and heavy, toadlike in his movements, and his features had assumed a blankness as though he had laid aside his own personality in order that whatever directed him could take control. He shook the bony dice for a long time before rolling them out, and after rolling them for the third time, spent longer than ever examining them from every angle. At last he seated himself on his box and drew his robe magisterially about him.

'Fat man bin enemy for master.'

'Yes. I know that fat man.'

Kalio sat in silence for a further minute.

'Dis fat man pow'ful . . . maybe, oba, maybe gov'ment minister.'

Walpole nodded and Kalio made a see-saw movement with his hands: 'Luck of master, luck of fat man, dey balancin' like so! One go up – de oder 'bliged for come down.'

'But which one will go up?'

'Depen' on master hisself. Master keep close to big chief – den all well. Master help chief, chief help master – fat man hurt no one but hisself. But dis same fat man' – and Kalio leaned forward and darted his forked hand in Walpole's face, giving so exactly the impression of a snake that he recoiled – 'he got sharp teeth. Kin bite!'

Walpole poured two more half mugs of gin which the two men drank in silence, and after a while Kalio asked, as he had asked from time to time: 'Master wish Kalio send for sister?'

Walpole felt a strong urge for dissipation, all the more since Alicia had aroused and then deserted him. 'Yes, Kalio. Send for your sister.'

Kalio grinned triumphantly. 'Master wait house. Sister comin' one-time.'

While waiting for the woman Walpole had ample time for thought. She was visiting him now every week and sometimes more often. Since his early days as a youth with Madam Abiose he had experienced no such sensual excitement as he found with her. Moreover through this relationship, if one could call it such, he felt he had solved the problem that besets many men and which in the past had caused him distress, the problem of obtaining sexual satisfaction without emotional involvement, and solved it in the simplest manner, by separating sex from human feeling. Having no love for the woman and no concern for her satisfaction, he could concentrate solely on his own enjoyment, and it seemed to him that, by recognizing lust for what it is and not confusing it with love, he had achieved freedom. Half the human race, he told himself, suffers from the failure to separate affection from desire. If there really is such an emotion as disinterested love he would no doubt experience it one day; but meanwhile through the woman he looked on as Kalio's sister – a priestess of sensuality who might have been inhabiting his body for the knowledge she showed of what at any moment he was experiencing – he could reach peaks of excitement amounting almost to delirium.

But enjoyment unfortunately brings fear, and during recent weeks Walpole had begun to be haunted by contradictory fears. There was first the fear that something might deprive him of his pleasure. He might fall ill, or the woman might leave Lagos or refuse to visit him any more. But at times an opposite fear came up, that he might become over-dependent on her potions and manipulations, pour all his energy into her and forget or fail to do his work – for how much consideration could he expect if ever the money should stop flowing? It disturbed him, too, in rare moments of self-examination, to recognize how far his whole life was revolving round this woman's visits. He counted the days from one appearance to another and then, when that was over, found himself living over again the details of their last encounter till it was time to anticipate the next. More than once he had excused himself from business meetings of importance which happened to conflict with an appointment made with her, and he dreaded the thought of having to undertake a long journey involving an absence of some weeks. Despite his claim to have found freedom, Walpole wondered whether one could live in such dependence and still call himself a man.

But now there was a firm footstep on the stair and he found himself already rising in anticipation.

After their first encounter the woman had asked that the money should be handed over to her instead of through Kalio, and this Walpole had always done. Tonight – perhaps because, regardless of his theory, he was hoping for some human contact, some flicker of warmth from his partner even if it were only purchased gratitude – Walpole slipped a few more notes than usual into the fistful he passed across as she prepared to leave. The woman assessed the amount at a glance, smiled triumphantly, muttered a few words of thanks, and pushed the packet hastily inside her *buba*.

A moment later, turning to collect some garment, Walpole happened to glance into the mirror. At that angle the woman was out of his direct vision, and unaware of being seen, was looking at his back with a glare of malevolent contempt as though he were a scorpion she would be glad to trample underfoot.

He waited in silence for her to go, and then lapsed heavily down onto the bed. He felt sick, as though he had actually been poisoned by her look, and the contact he had anticipated with so much satisfaction now seemed a piece of folly, amounting almost to – perhaps actually threatening – madness.

33
Trump Card

The incident with Kalio's supposed sister shook Walpole, making him feel the situation he imagined to be under control had slipped out of his grip. His sexual philosophy had been that sex is most enjoyable and pleasure keenest when there is no emotional contact. What the face in the mirror had shown was that, though he might be detached she certainly was not; and that the alternative to love might be not indifference but blazing hatred and contempt – aroused, it seemed, by his having given the woman more money than she expected. But why should generosity provoke contempt? Clearly because it revealed weakness and dependence.

At a deeper level he experienced something like terror, and several times in the night woke in a sweat as if from fever or a nightmare. Once he got up and searched the house all through, not only to make sure she was not still lurking round but to be certain that no belonging of hers, no malevolent charm or fetish, had been concealed in some corner or hung up outside his door. Intuition tells us that in love-making we are all defenceless, men as well as women, and that in even the most casual or brutal contact one is open, through the act of penetration and receiving, to take in something of a partner's inner nature. What then had he been taking in through regular contact with a witch? She had given him the answer when, relying on the fact that his back was turned, she had allowed what she felt about him to appear. While flattering himself that he was avoiding the distraction of emotion he had actually been absorbing the poison of her loathing and contempt. It would not have been long, he realized now, before the loathing this 'sister' felt was trans-ferred to him, so that, fastened to her by bonds which would become increasingly difficult to break, he loathed himself more and more for his dependence on her. Already, not out of moral feeling but from sheer self-preservation, he was re-solved never to summon or allow this woman inside his house again.

So deeply had the incident disturbed him that he spoke about it next day, not to Stephen whose honest nature would never have fathomed such a situation, but to Mr Chukuma whom Walpole looked on as the epitome of worldly wisdom. Ashamed to relate his story frankly and ask advice openly, Walpole set it in the past, stressing the aspect of mystery and passing it all off as an interesting anecdote. According to this version, the woman, attractive and seemingly rich, had seen him going about Lagos, written a provocative letter and later visited him at his flat. From that point on he told the story much as it had happened, and when he finished Mr Chukuma looked at him inquiringly.

'It seems something puzzles you about the affair, Walpole, What is it?'

'The woman's action. I've thought about it often. Why, when I gave her a handsome present, did she hate – even despise – me for doing so?'

'I presume you've finished with her altogether? This happened a while ago, you say, so you won't be seeing her again?'

'*Never!*' Walpole answered with intensity.

'In that case, my friend, I can speak frankly. Despite her elegance and what you describe as her wealthy background, it's plain she was nothing but a whore.'

'You mean a free woman,' Walpole protested.

'I do *not* mean a free woman. Of course a free woman lives by whoring, but she may have taken to it for a dozen reasons, possibly out of distress – death of her husband, being stranded in the city. . . . No! By whore I mean a woman with a whore's nature.'

'Which is what?'

'Which is that her chosen way of life is to sell her body for money – incidentally, of course, she may be a respectable married woman or a "good time" secretary, but that's beside the point. In her eyes money is more valuable than her . . . than what she has to offer – otherwise she wouldn't do it. Naturally then, she thinks men fools who give what she finds valuable for what she considers worthless – and any man who gives more than he's obliged must be a double fool. Hence the contempt you aroused in her. . . . Why did you do it, anyway? Probably because you wanted her goodwill – you were actually trying to buy goodwill from a whore! My poor friend, you must have been very young at the time.'

'Yes, I must have been,' Walpole admitted. 'But what about the hatred? I hadn't done her any harm. Why did she have to hate me?'

'Out of disgust at her occupation. She knows she's destroying herself by what she does, but she doesn't blame herself, she blames the men she goes with. If it weren't for their "bestial natures" she'd be . . . what we all feel we'd be if we had half a chance, noble souls living in purity and light. Why, I sometimes feel as if I could be like that myself – if it weren't for the need to get the better of people like Chief Pontius!'

Walpole thought a moment. 'Well, I think I understand it now – but it's a problem, isn't it?'

'What's a problem?'

'We all need a sex life. But then you either get entangled with love, devotion and all the rest of it, till you don't know where you are. Or else you go with whores and receive their hatred and contempt.'

'Just as they receive ours. Fair's fair! We despise them for selling themselves for cash, just as they despise us for giving cash for what they consider worthless. But all this is in the past. Whores are for old men or frightened boys. Or maybe perverts. A fine young fellow like you can always find plenty of loving, grateful girls.'

'But what about the emotional entanglement?'

'Damn it, Walpole!' said Mr Chukuma, looking at him over the top of his gold spectacles, 'emotions are what make us human, aren't they? Different from dogs – or pigs. Why grudge a girl a bit of tenderness? But you don't need me to read you lessons in love, I'm well aware. . . . Whatever brought this youthful experience of yours up at this moment?' And, without waiting for an answer to what he evidently thought to be a trifling question, he went on: 'When are you seeing Efunshile? I'm afraid it's not going to be a very pleasant interview.'

Next morning when he went round to see the Chief, Walpole had still not made up his mind how he would act. He was determined not to let the contract go if he could help it and had a scheme in mind which might achieve this end, but he had not brought himself to face what would be involved in carrying it out. He would, he told himself, 'play it by ear', which meant that if what he was half envisaging should come about, it would be in response to the situation that arose and not from conscious calculation.

'Sorry, Walpole, I'm truly sorry,' said Chief Efunshile after Walpole had set out the firm's offer and urged him to accept the ten per cent of Balogun and Abiose in place of the twelve and a half offered by Karybdis-Schiller. 'You're my friend and I'd like to oblige you. But we must be realistic. I naturally supposed, after our chat the other day, that your directors would at least match their rival's offer. I'm truly surprised they haven't done so, and I don't mind telling you – of course in confidence – that if they *had* done so, I should have sought means for giving you the contract, despite the difficulties this would have landed me in. But every door has its key, and that of friendship must be kept well oiled. Why should I land myself in difficulties in order to sustain a loss? I ask you, Walpole. Put yourself in my shoes and be reasonable. I don't doubt you did your utmost, but you can tell your fellow directors I'm not living in their pockets. . . .'

Seeing signs that the Chief was working up to some degree of anger, Walpole interposed: 'Indeed, Chief, I understand your position and I warned my directors how you'd feel. They weren't willing to increase the percentage, so I was obliged to bring you their offer – but I felt sure you'd turn it down. What reason could you have for accepting it?'

'In any normal time,' the Chief explained, his temper vanishing as quickly as it had appeared, 'I'd be willing even to accept some financial loss for the sake of friendship. But these are not normal times, Walpole, and at this moment I need every penny I can get. I'm having to provide for my former wife. I've got two extravagant sons living overseas – and I must meet debts of my own before I can remarry.'

Walpole murmured his comprehension and then asked: 'How about your remarriage? I trust all goes well.'

'Very badly,' the Chief answered. 'I've landed myself on the horns of a cleft stick.'

'I'm truly sorry,' Walpole said sympathetically. 'From some words your daughter let fall the other evening I hoped she was becoming . . . well . . . less obstinate.'

'If so, she hasn't shown it. She won't live with her mother. She refuses to stay in this house if Pearl comes here. She won't take a flat with a friend, something most girls of her age would jump at. Between board work and my family, Walpole, I'm a harassed man. But I don't want to worry you with personal troubles – will you have a drink before you go?'

Walpole accepted and, as they sat over the whisky,

remarked: 'I too have had a disappointment in my personal life.'

'My dear friend,' said the Chief with ready concern, 'tell me your trouble. If there's anything I can do to help, be assured. . . .'

'My trouble resembles your own, Chief. I'd been hoping to get married.'

The Chief looked at him with amazement. '*Marry*, Walpole? You? What on earth d'you want to do that for?' He paused. 'But forgive me, perhaps like myself you've met someone. . . .' His voice petered out. Suddenly he set his drink down and put his hand on Walpole's knee, 'Walpole! You're *not* trying to tell me? . . . '

'Indeed, Chief, I am. I'd been hoping – had my directors made you a reasonable offer so that I could see my way clear over the next couple of years – to ask your permission. But like you, I have debts to clear off. . . . And with the difficulty the firm's in now, we shall need to throw all we've got into the struggle to survive. I must put such ideas on one side for the present. . . . Perhaps I ought never to have spoken.'

The Chief was still gazing at him incredulously: 'You mean you want to marry Alicia?'

'I do indeed.'

The Chief sprang to his feet and enfolded Walpole in his flowing *agbada*. 'My dear boy! My *dear* friend – the best news I've ever had.' He disentangled himself and sat down before Walpole with a beaming smile. 'But this is wonderful! There's no one I'd rather have for son-in-law. You and I are alike in all respects. . . . In family alliance we'll be invincible. . . . *Of course* you must marry Alicia. . . . The contract's nothing! Business difficulties must not interfere with happiness. I'll soon fix that. And with you marrying Alicia, there's nothing to prevent my marrying Pearl. Just wait till I tell her – she'll be mad with joy!' He paused. 'I suppose you've talked this over with Alicia?'

'No indeed – how could I? I can't ask the daughter of Chief Efunshile to marry me till I see my future settled, and till I know the great man himself approves the marriage.'

'Go and see Alicia at once! Tell her "the great man himself" not only approves the marriage but is mad with joy! Tell her all is forgiven, and she shall have the most splendid wedding in Lagos for five years. Tell her to buy all the clothes she wants, furniture, everything. . . .' And he embraced Walpole yet again.

'Well now,' the Chief continued more calmly, after seating himself and filling up their glasses, 'the contract's yours. I accept your firm's offer – or rather I accept *your* offer. Pontius I shall fix. I know too much about him for him to cause trouble, and there's plenty of other work I can put his way over the next few months. . . . Off you go, then! Waste no time! Talk to Alicia and then get in touch with me. . . . This is the happiest day of my whole life!'

Though Walpole had spoken as if Alicia's consent was certain, he was not entirely confident. He had little doubt she would accept him, given time. But there was no time, and there had been an element of bargaining underlying his arrangements with the Chief which would have to be kept out of the picture. No girl wants to be married as part of a financial deal, and though Walpole assured himself he was not marrying Alicia for business reasons, his actions could well be interpreted in that light. Happily when he called on her that afternoon and said what he had to say, Alicia did not seem inclined to probe into his motives.

'*Dear* Walpole!' she said, and happiness made her look prettier than he had ever seen her. 'I'll be delighted to marry you. You're the nicest man I ever met – and much the cleverest. I shall do my best to make you happy.'

'You'll have no difficulty about that!' said Walpole, his thoughts turning to their kiss and all it promised.

'Have you spoken to my father?'

'I felt I had to. I didn't want to land you in another struggle with him when you're already in conflict over his marriage.'

'No conflict at all!' Alicia declared, flinging her arms round his neck. 'He can marry anyone he wants for all I care.'

'But you haven't heard what he said to me!'

'I know perfectly well what he'd say. For once he and I are in full agreement.' And she looked joyfully and possessively at Walpole.

They chatted affectionately for a few minutes, and then Walpole remarked: 'Your father still doesn't know you've accepted me. He asked me to let him know at once. D'you mind if I go and phone him?'

Alicia looked surprised. 'Of *course* I mind! I won't let you out of my sight. Besides I mean to tell him myself. I don't have the chance to bring him good news every day – and I've hated opposing him all this while.'

After half an hour Walpole managed to disengage himself on the plea of having to call in at the office and Alicia, eager to telephone round to all her friends, let him go on his promise to take her out to dinner. Walpole left her with mixed feelings. Everything had gone as he wished, but there had been a warmth in Alicia's response which both touched and made him feel guilty. Alicia, it was plain, had no idea of strings to his proposal. Once they had been married a few months and mutual confidence established, the fact that becoming his wife had brought practical advantages could only be a cause of satisfaction to her, but till then it was a positive duty to keep such knowledge from her.

Mr Chukuma's delight and enthusiasm knew no bounds. 'You amazing fellow, Walpole! I said you should be made federal Prime Minister – now I'm sure one day you will be. . . . How sick that fellow Pontius must feel! He supposed everything was in the bag when he went up to twelve and a half – and now we've won out on the ten per cent we originally offered. . . . Nobody but you could have pulled that one off, Walpole!. . . However, it's a trick you can't use a second time – you realize that? That wouldn't do at all, ha! ha! . . . Oh, and heartiest congratulations on your marriage! The wedding's bound to be colossal.'

'Oh, no!' pleaded Walpole, 'surely not? It doesn't have to be a big occasion. . . . I've thought about marrying, of course, but the actual wedding. . . .'

'Ask Efunshile! Why, it's as good as a personal advertising campaign for him. The papers'll make a meal of it – just think of all the free publicity he'll get!'

'You'd better submit with a good grace, Walpole,' Stephen advised, 'since you have to submit in any case.'

Later, after Mr Chukuma had left, Stephen came into Walpole's office. He fidgeted about the room, stared at objects with which he was familiar, stubbed his cigarette out as soon as he had lit it.

'Well, Stephen – what's the matter? Aren't you going to congratulate me?'

'M'm, yes . . . that is, I'm not sure.'

Visibly bracing himself, Stephen pulled up a chair and sat down facing Walpole. 'I'm going to say something and you *have* to listen. I'm only saying this because you're my friend – and I've liked and admired you more than any man I know.'

'You've been the best of friends,' said Walpole with

foreboding. 'If *you* can't say what you want to me – who can?'

'Answer me truly then, Walpole. D'you really *want* this marriage?'

This was much more direct than Walpole had anticipated, and he could not repress a gasp of surprise. 'Why yes . . . that is I feel . . . in all the circumstances. . . .'

Both were aware how much the half-sentences conveyed, and Walpole was about to try to correct the impression with assurances when Stephen went on: 'Because if you don't, I beg you to give it up. It's all very well for Chukuma – he's only concerned about the firm. But I'm concerned about you – Walpole, my friend. For God's sake, for your *own* sake, don't involve yourself in marriage for any reason but the real one.'

'What's that?'

'That you're determined to live your life out with this woman and no one else.'

Walpole looked at Stephen with a new respect, but all he said was: 'I don't think many men have the luck to feel like that about their marriage.'

'Well – they should have! Or else they shouldn't marry. It's no joke, Walpole, sharing your life. You know I love Cécile – I married her against my family's wishes. It's the best thing I ever did, and I'd do it again every day for a year on end. But we've had some painful times. . . . You don't just face another person when you marry – you're compelled to face yourself. That's *hell*! And if you don't truly love each other, it's hell twice over.'

For one moment Walpole forgot himself and his defences, even his resentment at the criticism his friend's words implied. 'Dear Stephen! It may have been hell – but it's made you a man. I used to take you for granted. No one can do that now, not even me. If that's what comes of marriage, every man should marry.'

Stephen shook his head. 'Thank you, Walpole. But it isn't me we're talking of. I realize what you'll face if you back out now, but it's nothing – understand me, Walpole, *nothing*! – to what you'll land yourself in if you marry this girl without loving her. And what you'll land her in as well. Back down now, and it's a couple of bad months for you both. Go ahead – and your troubles will be endless.'

'But what makes you think I don't love Alicia?'

'Walpole! For God's sake be honest! You *know* what love is. You loved Regina.'

For a second the floor seemed to open up in front of him and Walpole's confidence and self-possession drained away. He looked aghast, and Stephen, distressed himself, began to cover his friend's confusion with a flow of talk. 'Of course I'm not suggesting you'd marry Efunshile's daughter to secure the contract. . . . You wouldn't do anything so foolish or so mean. Not consciously – you *couldn't*. But I'm suggesting you haven't properly thought this out. . . . You've been set on getting this contract for all our sakes. We're at fault too . . . Chukuma and I have egged you on. You've been determined to do down that rascal Pontius . . . and to kill a snake one lays hold of the first stick. But marriage is too important to be confused with business, and if you're doing this even in a small degree for advantage, you can be paying for it all your life!'

For once Walpole said nothing. The mention of Regina had been a stab to the heart, and he was regaining possession of himself only with difficulty.

'I can't say more,' Stephen concluded. 'I never meant to say as much. I leave it to you. But if you decide to back down, I support you with everything I have.'

Walpole, whose determination to go through with the marriage had returned all the stronger for the shock he had been given, saw with surprise that there were tears in Stephen's eyes.

'Thank you, my friend. . . . Thank you. I shall think over everything you've said.'

His tone was cool. The moment for truth had passed, and it already seemed something of a liberty that Stephen should have spoken to him as he had.

After discussion between Walpole, Alicia and her father, it was decided that the wedding should take place in two months' time. 'The sooner the quicker' was the Chief's advice, and two months was the least Alicia asked for all the preparations. His marriage to Pearl, the Chief ruled, would take place after his daughter's, which was to be a public occasion from which nothing must detract, while his own, as a second marriage, would be a modest affair for friends and family. Pearl, happy that the obstacle to her peace of mind had been cleared out of the way, made no difficulty, and Walpole – who already knew she was beautiful – considered, when at last he met her, that she was intelligent as well, but wondered whether she realized all she was taking on in marrying the

Chief. When he gave a hint of this thought to Alicia, she answered drily that Pearl had had ample opportunity to get to know her father, and that if she still planned to marry him she must either love him enough to make everything worthwhile or be a lot less intelligent than Walpole gave her credit for. Either way, it was plain, she took little further interest in the matter.

Over the next weeks, as Walpole got to know Alicia better, he was surprised at the number of activities and the range of people in which she took no interest. She had none in any form of art and appeared to read no books. She was not interested in politics or what was happening in the country, though she had a shrewd sense of individual importance. Her mind was set, Walpole saw, on becoming a hostess and she was already equipped – no doubt from her experience in acting for her father – with that social thermometer which records who should be asked and who left out from any gathering. Perhaps because of her upbringing she showed less than the normal family feeling, though her love-hatred for her father was central to her life and she admired her lively self-indulgent brothers, both of whom she intended to have home for her wedding. The Chief refused at first but finally relented, and when Walpole asked privately how he could ensure their going overseas again afterwards, replied that he had sent 'the boys' their air tickets and a hundred pounds each for a one-week visit – with a warning that he would dock a month's allowance for every day they overstayed their leave.

Towards her mother Alicia offered no more than convention demanded and Walpole had to ask several times before being taken to visit her. She looked much older than her age, and her talk was limited to complaints over her husband's neglect and to asking Alicia when she had last seen relatives whom Alicia was plainly not interested to see at all. Walpole, who had come with the idea that he might make friendly, even affectionate, contact and perhaps do something to lighten what he supposed must be her dismal lot, left with relief that he was unlikely to see much of the Chief's 'number one wife' and considered – as did the Chief himself – that he was likely to find Pearl a great deal easier to get on with. On the way back the question of where Alicia and he were to live came up, for two weeks had gone by already with no decision.

'My father's going to give us a house,' Alicia explained. 'He has a number of houses around Lagos, but neither of those he

wants for us is free. They have government people living in
them he doesn't want to turn out.'

'If he doesn't want to turn them out, how will we get the
house?'

'He says that if neither of them moves, then he'll buy
another for us later.'

'Did he say what he means by "later"?'

'In a little while – when his affairs are straight again. At the
moment he's got our wedding to pay for . . . and my clothes.
Then there's his own wedding, and debts to be cleared up
first.'

Alicia spoke easily and it was plain to Walpole that father
and daughter had recovered their old intimacy, all the stronger
perhaps for the breach which had occurred.

'So how d'we manage meantime?'

'Just as you suggested – we'll live in your house for the
present. Then when my father finds another, we sell yours and
use the money to fix the new one how we want it.'

'Supposing he doesn't find us a new house?'

'He will!' Alicia replied in a tone which made clear this was
one promise the Chief would not easily evade.

Alicia had dealt with the question of their home in a
common-sense manner, but into the elaborate preparations
for the wedding she flung herself with passion. It was to take
place not at any of the Lagos churches but some sixty miles out
at a small town called Ijebu-Ode where there was a vast,
imposing church, and where the Chief had a country estate
and a large house for the reception. To make sure everything
would be just as she wished, Alicia made almost daily journeys
in her car, explaining that she had the clergy to arrange for, the
music to select, the form of service to agree, and complicated
seating arrangements to work out. Then there were brides-
maids to choose and their dresses to order, invitations to send
out – the Chief himself was involved in two days of discussion
before the list was finally agreed – photographers to be
summoned and the press to be informed. The subsequent
party which would go on all night involved not only catering
and drink arrangements on a lavish scale, with the hire of
tables, chairs, cutlery and glasses, but – even more important
for prestige – the booking of well-known singers and enter-
tainers as well as three of the best dance bands in the capital. All
this Alicia saw to. Nothing was too small or tiresome for her
attention, and she would jump up from lunch or dinner with

Walpole to make notes of some detail that had been over-
looked.

'Don't you want me to see to *anything*?' Walpole asked more
than once.

'All *you* have to do is be there,' she assured him.

Only in one respect did Walpole have his own way during
these weeks. Alicia, he saw, did not intend to sleep with him
before their marriage. This was not a matter of principle, he
well knew, nor was she innocent and bashful. She enjoyed
kissing and caressing, would press herself against him when he
left her at her home after they had been out, yet always
contrived at the last moment to slip away. It was as if she were
determined to keep him interested but to concede him
nothing. After this had happened two or three times Walpole
asserted himself.

'You remember what you said about our wedding?'

'What did I say?'

'That all I have to do is to be there.'

Alicia laughed. 'Of course I remember – and you *will* be
there, won't you?'

'On one condition.'

She looked up with apprehension. 'Whatever *do* you mean?'

'If I'm to be at the wedding, you're to sleep with me now.
I'm not having you vanish just when I want you. I've had
enough of that.'

Alicia considered as though weighing pros and cons of some
inner argument. 'All right,' she said at last. 'I'll come home
with you next time we go out. But you'll have to get me back
well before morning.'

This further postponement and the implication that love-
making was a concession exasperated Walpole, and when he
finally got her into bed he went directly to the point with few
preliminaries. At the back of his mind he was dimly aware that
her dallying and flirtatiousness might have causes he did not
understand and that his insensitivity could be harmful for their
future, but resentment drove out tenderness. He was determined to have his way and did. When, however, he tried to
approach her a second time, intending to meet her wishes with
more gentleness, Alicia turned away and would not speak. He
put his arm over her and tried with affectionate banter to
appease, but she still would not answer and when he leaned
over saw that she was crying.

Now genuinely distressed, he began reasoning with her as if

she were a child and at last, after a mixture of coaxing and apology, she turned towards him and buried her face in his shoulder. From her confused half-sentences he could not make out why she was upset, and she even appeared to be blaming herself for some unexpressed reason as though it were he who had been cheated and not her. At last their shared distress drew them together in a second love-making more harmonious than the first, and when after a further hour or two he drove her home, they parted with affection. On both sides, however, there was now reserve and hesitation and though they continued to make love almost whenever they went out together, Walpole was left with the feeling that Alicia was unresponsive and since masculine vanity would not let him suppose her unresponsive only to himself, he concluded that her love-nature was unawakened and would need time before it could be naturally expressed. Meanwhile, he was glad to have some womanly figure in his life round whom desire and affection could be centred, and though recognizing that Alicia's concern was more with having a husband than with him, he assured himself that everything would work out happily before long.

34
The Wedding

The church was packed. It had been full a quarter of an hour ago when Walpole, supported by Stephen as best man, walked up the aisle and took his place in the front pew. Only the half-dozen rows behind them were still empty, reserved for the mighty by a named card on every seat. . . . federal ministers and deputy ministers, MPs, judges, civil dignitaries, business tycoons, Chief Pontius and Chief Julius with their wives, who had all accepted the invitation to see the daughter of their friend Chief Efunshile married. The press had named this 'the wedding of the year'; hundreds had been standing outside to watch the guests arrive, and at the porch Walpole and Stephen had been obliged to push their way through a cloud of reporters and photographers.

Behind the rows set aside for notables, the crowd had begun to fan themselves with prayer leaflets and to mop their necks with handkerchiefs. Except for a sprinkling, mostly from embassies, who wore Western suits, the men were in national dress, mainly flowing *agbadas* whose sleeves required constantly to be gathered up and hitched over one shoulder, leaving an arm free and letting air circulate around the body. Dark colours predominated, grey, chocolate, olive; rich embroidery at neck and shoulders and in a panel down the chest made visible the wearer's wealth and status. In contrast to the men's sobriety, the women dazzled, favouring blue; blue *lappas* swathed over powerful hips; white *bubas* crossed with blue lines and patterns as if reinforced to contain those mighty breasts. Contrasting with the blue glowed combinations of grey with purple, sand with pinkish beige, while here and there flashed out a vivid green, a lilac or a pink.

Looking back over his shoulder, Walpole noticed a small group of women moving up the aisle to reserved seats, all dressed identically in gold and coffee-coloured splendour. There were other such groups throughout the church, half a dozen former schoolfriends or wives of high officials who had agreed, following the custom known as *Aso-Ebi*, to dress alike for the occasion. Having chosen a costly fabric and argued for days over head-ties, shoes and handbags, they would wear the outfit only once after which, the great day over, it would be given away or altered beyond recognition. Elderly as they were, the women moved with elegance and swimming grace, and Walpole recognized with a shock that one of the heaviest of the figures was that of his old patroness, Madam Abiose. She, with some few dozen present-day acquaintances, made up his small contribution to this crowded church; the rest were here as friends of Alicia and her father.

Glancing round after a minute, Walpole tried to catch his patroness's eye, but she had bent forward whispering, and this tiny incident, his failure to exchange a friendly smile with one of the few people here he knew and trusted, gave him a catch of panic. Over the last weeks of wedding preparations he had been surprised by his own confidence. Following his disturbing talk with Stephen, he had regained his calm and had experienced no breakdown of assurance, no overmastering impulse to cut free from the net he had woven round himself.

But now a desperate desire to get out before it was too late
came up like nausea in his throat. Dizzy, he closed his eyes,
struggling to regain control, but when he opened them again
and saw that the rows immediately behind were full and the
aisle blocked by fresh arrivals, he felt terror as though the
church were burning. Again he looked round, not this time to
exchange smiles with his patroness but measuring the distance
to the door and wondering whether a determined dash might
still carry him through, and he had indeed half risen to his feet
when he felt a firm hand on his arm. Stephen, watching him
closely, had been ready to help while help was possible but he
did not mean to let Walpole disgrace himself, his bride, his
best man and all present, after it was too late.

'Not long now,' he said wilfully misinterpreting Walpole's
movement, 'Alicia will be here in a moment.' Walpole
nodded. Since escape was impossible, he must go through
with it, and in face of acceptance panic faded, leaving his
mind blank. The organ was playing and – as his eyes wandered
over the carved choir stalls, the altar with its silver candlesticks
and embroidered coverings, as he caught the murmurs of the
congregation and the rustle of expensive clothing – he was
once more at Sunday church-going with his warm-hearted
patroness. What he was experiencing now was not just
memory but a passionate longing to be back in the past as he
once had been, a hopeful youth with everything before him,
not yet engulfed by the tide of his own ambition, greed and
folly.

The music stopped. There was a pause, and then by the
crash of familiar chords he knew Alicia had entered. The
congregation scrambled to its feet and when after some
seconds he looked round, she was already within yards of him.
In her long white dress she appeared slender and walked with
dignity. Her face lacked beauty, but she had the freshness of
youth and a glow, if not of happiness at least of satisfaction,
and though she looked directly ahead of her Walpole knew she
was missing little in that crowded building. By her side the
Chief, arrayed in a new *agbada* and with much flashing gold
about his person, nodded and smiled, mouthing greetings to
the greatest of his guests. At a nudge from Stephen, Walpole
moved out into the aisle to take his place beside Alicia and the
service started to roll its majestic course. God and the Church
had done Chief Efunshile proud. There were no fewer than
sixteen clergy present with three bishops – two Nigerian and

one white. What was *he* doing here, Walpole wondered –
cementing a political alliance? Making sure his religious
traditions were upheld? Or had the Chief secured him, as the
final seal of grandeur on his daughter's wedding, for an
enormous fee? The heat had become intense as the morning
started to wear on, and though the church was lofty and every
door and window open, the crowd outside, packing into the
doorways and peering through every window, prevented air
from circulating so that the thousand overdressed guests felt
they were slowly stewing in a deep stone pan.

But now Walpole was summoned to play his part. He could
no longer stand like a disembodied presence but must speak
out before them all and declare that he took this woman Alicia
to be his wedded wife, 'for better for worse, for richer for
poorer' and till death should them part. The ring passed to him
by Stephen slid over Alicia's finger, and for the first time she
looked up at him with a smile. But at this moment his own
mind was far away pondering the implications of those words
'for richer, for poorer', which sounded almost as though the
framers of the service long ago had his own case in mind, and
before he could fix an answering smile, Alicia had looked
away.

Out in the vestry there were handshakes, embraces and
relief that it was over. Alicia was in her element, all gracious-
ness and modest charm, with her father beside her making
everyone welcome and important. Stephen, seeing Walpole
trying to merge into the background, took his arm and began
leading him round with whispered instructions. . . . 'The
bishop . . . praise his voice . . . he's proud of it . . . and thank
him for having come so far'. . . 'Minister for Trade – you met
him last week at the Chief's'. . . 'Finance – a top civil servant –
could be useful' . . . and taking him up to a commanding
figure wearing a flat bulbous crown like some Eastern
potentate, he muttered: 'Paramount Chief . . . heap on the
flattery.' Walpole did as he was told and the great man smiled
graciously.

In the course of his tour Walpole felt his sleeve plucked, and
there beaming up at him was the loving face of his old
patroness: 'I bin mos' proud of my boy today,' she whispered.
'Mos' proud an' mos' happy for him!' Walpole, who would
dearly have loved to bury his face in that ample bosom and
confess the truth, gave her a hug and she slipped back into the
throng.

Before long the gathering began to thin; the road outside the church was narrow and guests had been forced to park their cars long distances away. The party would not start till dark and most would be going back to Lagos to bathe and rest beforehand.

Alicia pressed close to Walpole with a confiding smile. 'Happy?'

'Yes, of course. Aren't you?'

She nodded gaily, but before he could say more both were being marshalled by her father to form part of a group which he led down to the church door, where the photographers waited to line them up for execution by twos and fours and eights and finally in mass.

The churchyard on to which they faced wore the air of a nomads' camping ground. Palm fibre mats strung on poles over school benches gave shelter from the sun, and among the hundreds of onlookers who had been here since dawn the sellers of drinks, peeled oranges and kola nut slid purposefully in and out, as Walpole himself had done so often twenty years ago. The uproar was such that the photographers had to bellow their instructions, but it was only when the wedding party walked down the path to the church gate that the full storm broke. The roadway was a seething, gyrating mass. Only the bridal cars had been permitted to approach and around them rival bands fantastically dressed competed for attention and reward. The nearest group, wearing striped football shirts, crashed out a High Life into clouds of dust from the stamping, shuffling dancers; behind them were the talking drums, sounding out a special message for every notable but most powerfully for the married couple. Cords depended from their sides and by pulling on these the drummers raised and lowered the pitch so that to the by-standers, whose language was one of pitch, the drums seemed literally to talk. Reward for the sweating musicians was direct, paper money plastered on dripping brows and shoulders by the guests and now most lavishly by Stephen on his friend's behalf. Police in fresh uniforms were everywhere, wheeling off white-gauntleted on motorcycles to escort ministers through narrow streets, volleying exhausts to carve a passage, while in and out of the throng photographers dived like porpoises, aiming flashes at every well-known or pretty face.

Out at the Chief's country mansion Alicia hugged Walpole and then slipped away to change, and Walpole was taken to a bedroom where fresh clothes were laid out. It would be hours before guests started to return, and Alicia had said she intended to rest before the party, so that for the first time he felt free from pressure as he stood gazing from the window. Out in the garden rose a huge marquee and on the grass stood tables already piled with plates and glasses. Chairs were dotted around in groups, there were floodlights and loudspeakers in the trees, and festoons of coloured lights led up to a daïs for the bands and singers. By custom his own family ought now to be laying on another entertainment as lavish as the Chief's and all night long the guests would dash wildly from one mansion to the other, sampling the food and drink, dancing to hot jazz and High Life bands and then racing off to catch a popular performer at the other house. But Walpole had no family and had firmly refused the offer of Mr Chukuma and Stephen to act as such on his behalf, so the Chief had had everything his own way, and the entertainment which would be taking place before long was the most spectacular his guests could ever hope to see.

Walpole lay down on the bed with the idea of getting an hour's sleep so as to be fresh for the festivities. He seldom had difficulty in sleeping so was surprised when after ten minutes he was still awake, much more awake than he had felt on lying down. His mind went back to his moment of panic in church – what was it all about, and why had he been frightened? Evidently of marriage. Of marriage itself then, or of marriage to Alicia? The answer was all too plain. Had the bride been Regina their marriage would have been the most joyful occasion of his life even if they had been marrying in secret to live in poverty or exile. If years ago he had married his patroness, the marriage would have been foolish but it would have been a generous foolishness, with love on one side and on the other respect and gratitude; though it must have ended in disaster, it would not have been contemptible. If in the early days with Bisi he had married her out of lust, that too would have been absurd, but a natural absurdity since we are all betrayed by bodily desires. It was worse, far worse, to do as he had done and marry for advantage – no wonder nausea had risen in his throat. Yet even that word 'advantage' was too smooth. He had married for a contract worth two million pounds from which he might benefit to the extent of an extra twenty thousand, and for this twenty thousand, plus some steps on the ladder to future prosperity and in order to triumph over a cunning rival, he had tied himself for life to a woman he did not love. So that even if, through some unbelievable circumstance, Regina should one day come back to him, it would be in vain – and this time by his own choice and through his own action.

What value, he asked himself, did he really put on love? Less, evidently, than twenty thousand pounds. Or had he simply acted out of ignorance? Did he at all know the nature of love or was it, like death, something he had still to experience? Madam Abiose had loved him long ago but he had not loved her. He had loved Regina, but if he had loved her enough then surely they would have come together again and he would have pardoned her weakness in going back to Duke. Love must include tolerance and patience, and the fact that she had in the end left Duke of her own accord meant that if he had endured the pain of waiting she would have come back and begged forgiveness. Certainly he did not love Alicia, his wife of two hours, and he doubted very much if she loved him. She had accepted him to get away from home and to achieve the status of married woman, he being the most presentable suitor at a moment when marriage was desirable. And if later on love should come to one or other of them from a different quarter, what would become of a marriage based on twenty thousand pounds on one side and a wish for status on the other? Walpole closed his eyes and fell into a troubled sleep.

He dreamed he was walking through the forest and came into a glade where everything was fresh and green. Two children, a boy and a girl, were walking ahead of him hand in hand. He came up to them and tried to speak, but no words came out and it was as if they did not see him. They just looked into one another's eyes and went on walking till at last they were out of sight. The sky grew dark and heavy rain began to fall. . . . Walpole half sat up, thought it was night time, fell back and went to sleep again. Now he was climbing an enormous mountain, carrying an armchair. He did not know why he had the armchair with him but supposed it was so that he could be comfortable when he reached the top. He climbed a considerable distance and now at last could see the summit, remote and awe-inspiring. He stood gazing at it for a while and then decided it was too far and difficult for him and started to descend, still carrying his chair. At the bottom was a bar full of noise and singing, and when he entered two women took his arms and brought him a bottle and glass. He picked up the

bottle to pour himself a drink and saw that the label on the
bottle read Hoare's Beer. . . . Again he struggled out of his
dream state and sat up. Through the window came the sound
of cars arriving. Walpole remembered where he was and
realized it was time for him to get dressed and play the part of
happy husband.

Walpole and Alicia had agreed that around three in the
morning – the earliest they could hope to slip away – they
would drive out to the house which was now to be their home,
but at three Alicia was still dancing gaily and it was five before
she could tear herself away from the festivities, and dawn
when they reached home. Walpole left Alicia to get into bed
and went to his study, intending to join her in a few minutes,
but as he threw off his coat and loosened the knot of his tie he
was overcome with memory of the night when Regina had
come to him in his flat and he had stood in a tremble of desire
and happiness waiting to join her in his bed.

He sat down at his desk, laid his head on the confusion of
papers, and wished with his whole heart that he were dead or
that the earth would open and swallow him up, just as he had
wished long ago when he stood covered in guilt before Mr Ali
after cheating him of a few pence for a cold drink. He sat for as
long as he dared and, wretched though he was, would have
been glad to remain sitting here all night, but it was necessary
for him to join his bride and he went into the bathroom to
finish undressing and put on the new dressing gown, bought
only a day or two ago, whose expensive jauntiness seemed
now the final mockery.

As he stood there, delaying if only for a few seconds the
moment when he must take his place beside Alicia, he realized
with cold horror that it would be impossible for him to make
love to his expectant bride. For the first time in his life he had
been overcome by impotence, and could recognize the reason
– his body, more truthful than himself, was refusing the
pretence of passion he demanded of it. Some other day or
night no doubt, in easier circumstances, he would manage to
go through the familiar routine, and probably through many
days and nights to come, but tonight his physical nature had
deserted him, leaving him to get out of the mess into which he
had landed both of them as best he could.

In a sweat of apprehension he approached the bedroom,
meaning to plead tiredness, headache, the long day, knowing
well that excuses could only emphasize, not hide, the painful

truth. But to his infinite relief he saw that excuses were not needed, for Alicia was already fast asleep.

35
Marriage

After his marriage Walpole made a conscious effort to conform to Alicia's way of life and to meet her requirements in a husband; it was his fault rather than hers that they found themselves in this situation and he determined to make the best of it he could. As the months went by they did indeed begin to attain some equilibrium of content if not of happiness, and to their friends it appeared that they had settled down and become a married couple much like any other in their circle, the man occupied with his work and making money and his wife busy with the home and social life.

The Chief had not yet carried out his promise to give them a house, but in view of all the expenses of the wedding – which was still being talked about and whose extravagance would have ruined most businessmen and even many politicians – Alicia did not press the matter and contented herself with making changes in their household. She had demoted Walpole's houseboy, Kumle, to keeping the house clean and tidy under her sharp eye and introduced a well-qualified cook into the kitchen. She chased Kalio to make the garden look like one and, not caring for his sardonic stare and off-hand manner, would have got rid of him altogether if Walpole had not intervened, saying he had obligations to the man and wished him to remain.

'Well, he can stay for the time being,' Alicia conceded, 'though I don't know what you see in him. He grows nothing and he hardly answers when I speak to him.'

Alicia had by no means given up her ambition to become a social and political hostess and soon began organizing dinners and parties for the successful and the up and coming. She had a sharp eye as to who these were and, though in general an economical person, was willing to lay out time and money to achieve her aim. Walpole saw to it that the drink was lavish since this was something he appreciated; he also liked people to enjoy themselves and wanted to do what he could to further Alicia's ambition. At first all went well since people were interested to visit the new couple, but after one or two visits based on curiosity those who were invited simply suited themselves, as they did with any other invitations. Some accepted and appeared, others declined on the grounds that they were already engaged, or else – a practice acceptable by local custom – wrote thanking for the invitation in order to show politeness but failed to turn up on the appointed day.

All this seemed natural enough to Walpole, but Alicia, accustomed to her father's household to which any invitation was accepted with enthusiasm, found it distressing, even insulting, that her own efforts were less successful. One evening when elaborate preparations had been made and only two out of six expected guests arrived, Walpole watched her mounting anger with concern. She complained to the two present of the 'bad manners' shown by the absentees and made her disappointment felt throughout the meal. As soon as it was over, their two guests drove off, and when they did it was a question of whether Walpole or she exploded first.

'That's four out of six who didn't trouble to turn up for my party!' Alicia began. 'Didn't turn up and didn't ring up. . . . Those Bakares might at least have let me know they weren't coming.'

'And the two who did come won't be coming to your next party,' Walpole answered grimly. 'How can you be so foolish? Don't you know they're friends of the Bakares and are bound to tell them everything you said?'

'I just hope they will! Let them tell them what they like. What d'you expect me to do? Smile and pretend not to notice when people treat me badly?'

'That depends on you.'

'What depends on me?'

'It depends how much you want to be a hostess. That sort of success has to be built up, like every other. It means putting up with setbacks and wooing people to come here. When only two turn up you have to make them feel they're the only ones who matter, and so long as they're here you don't give a damn about the rest. Then when the Bakares or Olobisis ask what kind of a time they had, they'll say it was great and make them feel fools for not having come. But *now* what d'you suppose they'll tell them? "Lucky for you that you stayed away – Alicia was in a rage all evening." And the wife will chip in with – "But if you *had* come, dears, you'd have heard a few things about yourselves!" Then she'll repeat everything you said, with her own additions.'

'It's easy for you to criticize, Walpole, you don't care if people come here or not. You're not interested in what I'm trying to do. . . . No wonder people find it boring.'

'It's true I'm not interested in turning our home into a centre of culture and influence – but I *do* want you to have what you want, and I've done my best to help you get it.'

The aggrieved note in Walpole's voice exasperated his wife. 'They're *your* friends – those Bakares and Olobisis. You ought to make certain they show up.'

'How the hell can I "make certain"? I can't drag them here if they don't want to come. What d'you expect me to do – drive round in the car and fetch them?'

'I expect you to protect your wife and not let her be insulted. I expect you to speak up and tell them what you think. Go on now – ring them up and tell them off! Don't let them get away with it!'

Wrangling went on till they were too tired to quarrel further, but as they were getting into bed Alicia asked plaintively: 'Why do people always go to my father's parties but don't come to mine?'

The answer to Walpole was only too plain. The Chief had a warmth and effusiveness which made his guests feel more alive for being there. Each one was given the impression the party had been organized specially for him, with the host present to see his guests got everything they wanted plus a lot more besides. Whereas with Alicia it was obvious that her parties had been planned to further her ambitions and enhance her picture of herself. If Walpole had been candid he would have told her this, and if he had been more sympathetic he would have suggested that they talk it over in the morning and then tried to help her see the futility of her ambition. As it was he evaded the question: 'Your father's an important man. Guests come to keep in favour and because they're hoping he'll do something for them.'

'There, you see, that's what I told you,' Alicia replied. 'It's *your* fault people don't come here for my parties – if you were important enough they'd have to come.'

The fact that Alicia's parties were not the success she hoped
might have been got over, but the two had other problems, in
particular because both had expected much more happiness
than they found in one another sexually. In marrying Alicia,
Walpole considered he was giving her the status of a married
woman, which she wanted and no one else seemed eager to
confer. He was also sacrificing his bachelor freedom to sleep
with anyone he pleased, and expected in return a grateful – and
before long responsive – wife. But Alicia, it soon appeared,
saw their marriage differently, and to her the advantage lay
much more on Walpole's side than hers. She was the daughter
of an important public figure and might, in her opinion, 'have
married anyone I pleased', and she soon made it plain that she
expected to be wooed and courted as though he were the
admiring young lover of a celebrated beauty. Both parties, in
short, were counting on being loved, cherished and made
happy by the other, and neither expected to make efforts and
sacrifices to meet the partner's inclinations.

Disappointment over sex life is a feature of most marriages,
but some degree of harmony is generally reached on a basis of
mutual interest and joint concern over their children. But no
children were in sight for Walpole and Alicia, for whom a further
cause of conflict now came up. One evening as they were having
a drink before dinner Alicia said: 'Walpole, I'm going to ask you
something – and I want you to tell me the truth.'

Ominous words. But in addition Alicia spoke in a choking
voice as though tightening her throat to keep down anger,
which was a sign Walpole had learned to recognize.

'I always tell the truth.'

'I'm not sure – but this time you will.'

'Go on.'

'Did you marry me in order to get a contract for your firm?'

This was a moment Walpole had long dreaded, but was no
better prepared for on that account. 'What on earth are you
talking about . . .' he began, but realized while words were
still leaving his mouth that this would not do. Alicia knew
something, and the more he tried to cover up the less
conviction his words would carry, so rapidly changing course:
'Well, yes, there *was* a contract negotiated at that time, the
time when I first got to know you. That's true – and it's also
true that our firm got the contract, which some people didn't
like since they wanted it themselves. We owed our getting it to
your father, as chairman of the board.'

'And what had this to do with your marrying me?'

'Nothing at all, directly. I was wanting to marry you in any case.'

'Indirectly what had it to do?'

'When your father told me we would get the contract, I said that our winning it made things a lot easier for the firm. I added that it also made things easier for me, since now I could see my situation clear over the next few years. Then I asked if I might ask you to marry me. . . . He said he'd be delighted, providing you agreed. So then I came to see you.'

'Let me get this clear! The two things happened together – the contract and my father's agreement. Right? But there wasn't any bargain? No "if you do this then I'll do that"? Nothing of that sort?'

'Certainly not.'

'You swear it?'

'Yes. I swear.'

'Well – thank God!' said Alicia, looking at him with more kindness than she'd shown for weeks. 'I can't tell you how relieved I am . . . and I'm sorry for seeming so suspicious. But I *do* know my father, and I'd hate to have formed part of some package deal. . . . Get me another drink, darling. I need it.'

Walpole poured the drinks. 'And now – what was all this about?'

Alicia took a long swallow before answering almost gaily: 'It's that little bitch, Asabi, Chief Pontius's daughter. She turned up today when I was lunching with two of my friends. She's a hateful girl – and I suppose I may have annoyed her in some way because she asked out of the blue: "How's your husband, Alicia?" ' Alicia, who was a good mimic, put on a kind of haughty squeak. ' "How is he since the wedding?" I told her you were well enough, only a bit tired. Asabi said she could well understand your being tired. . . .' "But it isn't Walpole's stamina I'm asking after, Alicia, it's his happiness." I was just going to tell her that was no business of hers when she jumped up to go. "Give Walpole my love," she said, "and tell him I suppose having got that contract compensates for everything," – and off she went.'

'I haven't met Asabi twice in my life,' Walpole protested.

'That's okay! It wasn't love for you that made her speak. It was the wish to score off me.'

'You certainly must have annoyed her,' Walpole answered. 'D'you remember what you said?'

'I remember well enough . . . though it was just a passing remark. . . . Nothing for her to get in a state about.'

'What was it anyway?'

'Asabi came in full of herself. . . smiling and all dressed up. We all knew why – she's just taken a man away from another girl we know – Ayoka Fashanu. Ayoka's nice, but she's always losing men. . . . So I said to Asabi that I'd seen Ayoka the day before and asked why she looked so happy. She said it was because she'd just got rid of something she'd been wanting to lose for a long time. . . . Well, naturally the other girls laughed, and Asabi looked as though she'd swallowed a spoonful of hot yam. . . . Then after a minute she started on about you.'

'And *had* you just seen Ayoka?'

'No – haven't seen her for months! But I like her a lot better than I do Asabi, and I thought I'd bring Asabi down a bit. Anyway what does it matter now? . . . But what d'you suppose made her talk about contracts anyway?'

'She'd heard her father talk,' said Walpole easily. 'Chief Pontius tried to get the contract for a firm which made him their agent – Karybdis-Schiller. But we put in the lower tender and your father gave the work to us. . . . It was a long and complicated story – but that's the essence of it.'

'Just wait,' exclaimed Alicia, 'till I meet that Asabi again!'

The danger had passed, but the conversation left Walpole apprehensive. Asabi would go on talking, and no doubt others were talking too. It couldn't be long before some new remark was made to Alicia or reported to her by a 'friend'. Though there was little he could do, Walpole thought it at least worthwhile to call on Chief Efunshile and tell him what had happened. The Chief laughed uproariously and made Walpole repeat all the two girls had said to one another.

'I must tell that to Pearl. . . . Women's gossip, women's friendship! God – they do know how to stick the knife in. But don't worry about this, Walpole. We'll see it through between us. Remember exactly what you tell Alicia and let me know. Whatever you say I'll back a hundred per cent . . . of course there's bound to be talk and chit-chat! How much chit-chat d'you suppose there's been over my marrying Pearl? But what does it all amount to? Nothing! the fact is you've got your contract – and Alicia's got a husband. . . . Well, well, so Ayoka Fashanu comes into the picture? I had her for a time – and I dare say you did too. You couldn't really help having

Ayoka. . . . A nice enough girl – but what's the good of being nice in a world like the one we're living in? I *ask* you? . . . Well now, Walpole, to come to serious matters, the barracks at Enugu. Now that the main job's finished, I'm fixing with the regional government to add an extra wing, accommodation for another fifty men. The way things are looking in the East, they're going to need those extra police, so they're going to want that wing to put them in. . . . Well, you and I are going to give it to them . . . at a price, a "reasonable" price. As they're in such a hurry, of course it won't be quite so reasonable as if there were time to put the job out to tender. I've explained all that to them and they understand it. There'll be no need to pass this through the board, I'll just mention it to them afterwards. The authority comes from regional government direct. . . .' And for the next hour or so Walpole was able to forget his own problems in the easier world of business negotiations.

As he was leaving, however, the Chief called him back. 'I think I can say that at last my family troubles are finally over – and it's thanks to you, Walpole.'

'How's that? What's happened?'

'Alicia rang Pearl last night and said it was surely time they buried the hatchet and became friends. They've met, as you know, at my parties and elsewhere – but this is the first time Alicia's made a genuinely friendly move. So naturally I'm delighted.'

'What did Alicia suggest?'

'That the two girls had lunch together today. They'll be somewhere or other at this moment, I imagine.'

Walpole did not have long to wait for the consequences of their meeting. That same evening after dinner, Alicia began again.

'That contract you got from my father – was it going to your firm in any case?'

'No. It was going to Chief Pontius, through a dishonest trick.'

'Never mind *his* dishonesty – that's common knowledge. I'm asking about you. If the contract was going to his firm, how did you manage to get it for yours?'

He was now, Walpole realized, on the spot on which all concealment puts one. If he said less than Alicia knew, he would have the truth wrung out of him and have lost credibility by the deception, but if he told more than he need, he could give away his whole delicately-balanced case.

'The contract had originally been promised to our firm.'

'By my father?'

'By someone in authority.'

'Ha! *Men*! How you all stick together! "Someone in authority" indeed! It's my father we're talking about – right?'

'On the strength of that promise, our firm bought heavily . . . big equipment. We were forced to take a chance because the stuff's in short supply. Just at this time Chief Pontius came on the scene. He'd been at that party of your father's where I first met you, and afterwards must have gone along to his office. You remember telling me once that he was always hanging round your father.'

Alicia nodded.

'I don't know, of course, what arguments he used – something about his firm's overseas experience perhaps – but he convinced your father that his firm, not ours, should be given the contract. . . Your father sent for me and told me his decision.'

'So what did you say?'

'Well, that my firm would be disappointed. . . . We'd laid out a lot of money which was now wasted. I asked him to delay the decision and think again.'

'What did he say to that?'

'Well, finally he agreed – and gave us two or three more days.'

'What was the point of that?'

'Look, Alicia – these are business matters. They're not the sort of thing you're used to dealing with, and anyway they're confidential. If you want to know the details of the agreement – ask your father.'

'I already know the details. I know Chief Pontius offered my father two and a half per cent more than your firm did. What I'm asking you is why his firm didn't get the contract – and yours did? Why my father went round to Pearl and told her everything had turned out wonderfully – you were taking me off his hands, and as soon as you'd married me, he and she could get married too? How did *that* happen – that's what I'm asking you?'

'I don't know what you've been told, Alicia – but I can tell you this. Contract or no contract, I intended to marry you.'

'Why?'

'Because I was in love with you.'

Alicia laughed. 'What you were in love with wasn't me – it was the contract! It's all as plain as that bitch Asabi's face. . . . And there was I like a bloody fool thinking you loved me.'

Her last words touched Walpole – even through his barriers of defensiveness and fear. He reached to take her hand. 'But I *do* love you, Alicia. Truly I do. I really wanted to marry you.'

Alicia sprang up with something like a howl. She was shaking with rage and her words seemed to be strangling her. 'Love! You – Walpole Abiose? *Love*? You don't know the meaning of the word.'

'But I *do* love you, Alicia. . . . It's not true – there wasn't any bargain. Ask your father! It was just. . . .'

'Love *me*? You love money, Walpole. You love your-self. . . . But love a woman? Don't make me sick.'

'I swear to you, Alicia. . . .'

'Who the hell believes anything you swear?' And as if his words were the last straw, Alicia sprang at him and struck him in the face. In a mixture of rage and horror at having provoked this slight woman to such frenzy, Walpole seized her wrists. She twisted violently to get free but he held on.

'Lies – lies – lies!' she screamed. 'You've taken lots of girls in with your lies – and you took me in too. No longer! Not another minute!'

Walpole pushed her into a chair, standing over her to see whether she sprang up and went for him again. But she was looking at him now with a coldness of hatred worse than rage.

'You make me sick, Walpole. Literally *sick*. I wish to God I'd never seen you.'

36
Too Late

Alicia as well as Walpole had been shocked by their clash and frightened of its consequences, so that for a day or two truce was observed. Walpole went to work early and came back as late as he could and their conversation was confined to

practical matters. At the end of two days, eager to find
something that would please Alicia and over which they
might cooperate, Walpole suggested they give a party – in
about a month so as to allow time for preparation. This would
not be a dinner where a few absentees could ruin everything,
but a larger affair with a band for those who liked to dance,
bars indoors and out, and a marquee in the garden for supper.
They would invite up to a hundred of their friends and count
on sixty or seventy turning up, Walpole promising to get in
touch with as many as he could beforehand to make sure of a
good attendance. Alicia's anger melted as he unfolded the
details of his plan and before long she had thrown herself into
preparations almost as enthusiastically as for her wedding, and
Walpole could hope that no more would be heard of his
offence at least for the time being.

In all the complicated arrangements for his marriage six
months earlier Walpole had neglected one important duty – he
had failed to visit and inform his earliest friend and benefactor,
Mr Ali. When the list of guests was being draw up in
discussion wth Alicia and the Chief, Walpole put forward the
names of Madam Abiose and Mr Ali and explained the
importance to him of them both. Over Madam Abiose there
had been no question, the Chief being well aware of the
influence wielded by the great market mammies, but he
suggested that instead of inviting Mr Ali – who would be
bound to feel lost in such company – Walpole should visit him,
explain that the marriage would take place a long way from
Lagos and dissuade him from wishing to be present. Walpole
had not liked the proposal though weakly assenting to it. He
had not, however, been to see Mr Ali. During the past years
his visits to the old man had become fewer and, fearing
reproaches, he put off the task from one week to another until
at last when the wedding morning dawned the visit had still
not been made.

Afterwards, realizing Mr Ali could not fail to hear about the
wedding, Walpole made the long-overdue effort and went to
see him. He was living where he had always lived, but told
Walpole he had been sick and could see the firm was going to
dismiss him before long. Applicants had been coming to see
the manager and he could tell from their appearance –
Northerners like himself, only young and strong – that it was
his job the firm planned to fill. Walpole asked his Baba
whether he now wished to go home to the Northern Region

where, as he knew, the old man had land, wives, a flock of goats and half a dozen gaunt ghost-coloured cattle. No, he replied, he had not at present strength for such a journey, and when turned out of home and job together – which was likely to happen in a week or two – he would find a room in the city where he could recover his health before returning. Walpole made sure Mr Ali had his phone numbers and addresses and urged him to send word if he needed help. As soon as the old man felt ready to go North he intended either to drive him there himself or send Hamisu with the van, and he also insisted on giving him a sum of money in case he should need it for his stay in Lagos. The old man refused this more than once, but finally accepted with a look that went like an arrow into Walpole's heart, for it said with no words spoken, 'I accept this money if it's any comfort to you to give it, but I would much rather have had a little kindness and attention over the past months.'

Walpole left with a deep sense of guilt, determined to come back in a few days and do all he could to help his benefactor. But the week went by, and another week. The end of the month came and the end of a second month. As each new week began Walpole made a mental note to look in on the firm where Mr Ali had worked and learn where he had gone. Once he did actually drive round there but had forgotten that, as this was a Saturday afternoon, there would be no one who could tell him. There was a new watchnight at the place, middle-aged with scowling look and surly manner, who knew nothing of what had happened to his predecessor and made it plain that he cared less. All this had happened weeks ago, but Walpole had not written to the firm nor sent any servant round to make inquiries, and only now when he got back from his office to make final arrangements for the party, was he handed by the houseboy a message scrawled on a scrap of paper by someone evidently unused to writing. It said only "Mr Ali say come", with an address, and had been left by a youth on a bicycle who rushed off before he could be questioned.

'Ah! There you are at last, Walpole,' exclaimed Alicia. 'And about time! You promised to be back early today – have you forgotten it's our party? People will be here in a couple of hours and the drinks aren't put out. Get Kumle to arrange the glasses on the bars – but see to the bottles yourself. If I'd let the hired staff do it, there'd have been no drink left by now.'

'Look, Alicia, there's something I must speak to you about.'

'Not now! Put the drink out first. When that's done we can talk.'

Well, Walpole thought, drinks have to be put out, and if there's to be no host when guests arrive that makes it all the more necessary for there to be drink. He bustled around putting everything in place, appointing a man in charge of each of the bars, warning him he knew exactly how many bottles there were of each sort of drink, and then went to find Alicia who was dressing.

'I'm sorry, Alicia, but I must go out. I've had an urgent call from Mr Ali, the old man who took care of me as a child. He may be dying – he wouldn't have sent for me if things weren't desperate. I *must* go to him now – but I'll be back the first moment I can.'

Alicia held her hand out for the scrap of paper, read and turned it over. 'There's nothing about dying here. It doesn't even say he's sick. You can't possibly go – your guests'll be here any minute.'

'I'm sorry about the guests. It's the worst time this could have happened. But everything's ready – and now I must go to my friend.'

Alicia had been putting final touches to her hair and make-up in the mirror while talking to him. Now she faced him squarely. 'Walpole! If you leave this house after everything I've done to make this party a success – and after all your promises to help – you might just as well not come back. You're proving what I always told you – you don't *want* to help me and don't take the least interest in anything I do. . . . If you *must* go and visit this old man – who probably only wants to ask for money – go in the morning on your way to work. Give up some of your precious office time. But don't come and tell me you're going out just when you've invited a hundred guests to the house . . . I won't have it!'

In face of her onslaught Walpole gave way and went to dress himself. Thanks to the efforts both had made almost all those who were asked turned up, ate and drank heartily, laughed and chatted loud enough to hear nothing one another said, danced to the High Life band and were all gone by three o'clock next morning.

'Well, that really *was* a success, 'Alicia declared, 'though you looked like a sick dog all evening. Come on now, let's go to bed – and in the morning you can call round and visit your old man.'

'It *is* morning,' Walpole answered, 'and I'm going now. I don't know what time I'll be back.'

'Do as you please,' said Alicia, turning away.

It was little more than ten years since Walpole himself had been living in Ebute Metta as a labourer, but despite his knowledge of the area, its narrow streets and battered houses, it was not easy to find the address he wanted in the dark. It proved to be a rooming house not far from the waterfront. The door was locked, or rather what remained of the door was padlocked to a battered doorpost, and Walpole had to hammer and shout until a woman put her head out of a window.

'Na whatee dis palaver? Whaffor you come here night time? You no fit catch girl dis hour. Girls all done sleep.'

Walpole took out two notes and waved them. 'For you, missis. Come spik one minute at door – I dash you two poun'.'

The woman came down grumbling. She evidently expected something more than conversation was required because she looked him over carefully before unfastening the padlock. Once inside, Walpole pushed the notes into her hand and said: 'Tell me, sister, you know old man here, Mr Ali? Come live here maybe one-two month?'

'Dat ole sick man? Deed I know um. Po' man – he too-too sick long time.'

'Mr Ali done bin good frien' for me. You takin' me see um one-time – savvay?'

'I savvay, sah,' the woman answered and led the way upstairs. Walpole followed, having remembered to bring torch and matches he was able to avoid the filth on stairs and landings. The woman tapped on a door and getting no reply pushed till it stuck against a broken floorboard. Against one wall on a plank bed lay Mr Ali on his back under a heap of sacks, so silent and motionless that Walpole, on his knees beside him, thought he was already dead and said so to the woman. She came over, peered into his face, licked the back of her hand which she held under his nose and shook her head. By the bed was a packing case and on it a piece of lighted candle and a mug. The woman looked into the mug, saw it was empty and went off, returning after a while with a pitcher of water and another piece of candle. She straightened the coverings, laid her hand on the old man's forehead, said, 'Mornin' I come, sah,' and went out.

Walpole looked round the room with mounting dismay. In one corner were three or four cardboard boxes tied with rope,

Mr Ali's possessions which had been standing there since he arrived. Nearer the bed was a battered tin trunk which must serve as seat for anyone who sat here – if anyone ever came to sit. On the wall was an iron hook from which clothes were hanging. They hung much as clothes always hang, yet gave Walpole the impression they had been hung up for the last time, and would remain hanging till either they dropped off the hook or the hook fell out of the wall. He drew the trunk closer to the bed and sat down to keep watch. The room smelt foul and he wondered if he should try to wash Mr Ali and rearrange the sacks spread over him, but decided it would be better not to disturb his sleep. When morning came he would find a doctor and have his friend moved to hospital. He started to try to open the only window to let in some air, but the old man stirred uneasily so he gave up and sat down to spend the rest of the night beside him. One of Mr Ali's arms lay along the bed and Walpole took the hand in his. For an hour he sat, and for another hour, seeing nothing but Mr Ali's sunken cheeks, the deep hollows over his brows, the gaunt and wasted neck. Only the nose, a powerful bony beak, seemed still to contain life as though it were the last room in this bodily tenement to be vacated, and through it his breath, scarcely detectable a few hours earlier, was now sounding laboured and distressed.

Walpole thought, in an agony of shame, of all Mr Ali had done for him in his childish years and of all he might have done to make the old man's last days easy. In his mind he called round to visit him, sat by his bedside, fetched doctors and carried him off to his own house, slept in the same room to meet his needs. In the intensity of reliving what might and should have been, he became lost to the present and seemed to have been sitting here for days and weeks in patient service to his benefactor. A change in the breathing recalled him to the present. It was too late now for such attentions since plainly his old friend was dying, and even the doctor he would summon first thing in the morning could do nothing. But though, through selfishness and weakness, he had got here too late to be of help, at least he was not too late to declare his gratitude, pour out his regrets with tears, and undertake whatever last wishes Mr Ali might entrust to him . . . perhaps that he take charge of and educate some promising child or grandchild – and happy indeed would he be to take on such a burden. It was something at least that before he finally left this earth Mr Ali would open his eyes, turn his head, and recognizing that his erring son had come back, would smile and say some word of blessing – at which Walpole, flinging himself on his knees, would bury his face in the sacks, knowing that all the love he felt but failed to show must convey itself somehow to the dying man.

As Walpole sat on, holding the bony hand and seeking atonement for his long neglect, what he took to be a sound caused him to look up. It was not a sound, however, but the absence of sound. Mr Ali had stopped breathing, and as Walpole gazed in terror that his old friend might be leaving him with no sign of recognition and therefore with no hope of forgiveness, the jaw dropped and the eyes turned upwards in the skull.

Next morning Walpole found a mullah and made arrangements for Mr Ali's funeral. He would have to be buried in Lagos since it would be impossible to transport his body on a journey lasting several days. A van from the firm carried the corded boxes and tin trunk for safety to the office, and when the funeral was over Walpole set out with Hamisu – who came from the far north-west – as driver, to convey Mr Ali's belongings back to his family.

It was an arduous journey, allowing little time for speculation or regrets. After the first day they were travelling over dust tracks during the dry season so that their Land-Rover moved in a blinding cloud. Dust seemed to float up from the track some yards ahead of them and the few other vehicles on the road could be seen from miles away by their accompanying swirl. In places where the dust of the laterite roads was especially fine, it would steam up through the floor as though the vehicle were on fire, and Walpole could scarcely make out Hamisu's huge form beside him on the seat. From time to time they would stop to beat the dust out of their clothes and wipe it from eyes and faces. They ate at chop bars and slept as best they could. Throughout the journey Walpole had only one thought, that he ought to have made it many times over while his friend was still alive.

In Sokoto they obtained directions for the village they were seeking and found it before dark next day. Mr Ali's eldest son, a black-bearded man in his forties, took charge of the belongings, cleared a room for his guests and ordered the women to prepare a meal. He told Walpole the family had

been expecting a visit from the old man for a long while, and
when he did not come had concluded he was sick. Neither side
wrote letters, but word would reach them occasionally from a
mammy-wagon driver or through some Hausa trader who
had been to the city peddling his goods. No such message had
come, however, over the past two years. As they sat at the
meal Walpole told the son the little he could of Mr Ali's recent
life and was thanked gravely for his kindness by the new head
of the family, his guilty disclaimers that he ought to have done
far more being treated as routine politeness. The family now
were prosperous, owning more goats and cattle than anyone
around and it was evident that, though Mr Ali had continued
to have part of his salary paid into a bank in Sokoto for his
wives and children, they could far more easily have contributed to his support than he to theirs.

So long as there were duties to attend to Walpole managed
to keep the events of the last few days at bay, but once he set off
for home he could no longer postpone facing them, and as the
miles went by and they drew nearer to Lagos and his home,
distress flowed over him until it became impossible to speak or
think. At last, in a large village on the road some hundred
miles from the city, Hamisu, who had cast many anxious
glances at his master, suggested they pull aside for a drink.
Sitting in a roadside shack with an untouched Coke before
him, an idea which had been forming in Walpole's mind for
the past few hours hardened into resolve.

'You go on back, Hamisu. I stay here. I don't want to go
home yet.'

'Master sick?' Hamisu asked.

'No. Not sick. Just not wanting to go back. I stay here
two-three days.'

Hamisu did his utmost to dissuade Walpole, saying he could
lie in the back of the Land-Rover with a blanket over him
while Hamisu drove quickly home. When Walpole shook his
head, he proposed to push on only a few miles till they reached
some better place. At last, meeting no response, Hamisu
found the owner of the chop bar, told him that his master, an
important man, wished to remain here alone for a few days
and asked what accommodation there was, saying his master
would pay well for his keep. The first Walpole knew of this
talk was when the owner, a grizzled man with a wife grey and
elderly as himself, led him apologetically to an outhouse
containing a chair and a plank bed, and explained that this was

all they had to offer: He could have his meals in the chop bar where the wife would do the best for him she could.

This would serve very well, Walpole brought himself to say, and he hastily scribbled two notes, one to Alicia and the other to Stephen, saying only that he had stopped off on the road for a few days but would be home before long. Having thanked Hamisu and waited at the door while he drove off, Walpole went back into the outhouse, closed the door, sat down on the plank bed, and burst into a storm of tears.

How long he remained in the village Walpole was never afterwards sure. He was not always sure whether it was night or day, since there was only one small window high up in the wall and he would sometimes fall asleep for an hour or two by day and remain awake all night. At first the old man or his wife came to call Walpole at mealtimes, then, since he took no notice of the summons, they started bringing food and placing it beside him, but all he did was to drink some tea. He had a pitcher of water and a cup, a candle and matches, and these for the time were his only wants.

By the death of Mr Ali and his failure to help the old man when needed, Walpole had been dealt a shattering blow, a blow so heavy that he had ceased to care whether he recovered from it or not. It seemed to him that the whole of his life since he left Madam Abiose had been one long trail of selfishness and greed in which he had lived without thought for anyone but himself. He had gone on pursuing success in the belief that money, power and pleasure would bring happiness if only he obtained enough of them. He had continued on his way despite every warning, deaf to all who tried to help him. Stephen had wanted to prevent his idiotic marriage. Even Mr Chukuma, worldliest of men, had been shocked by his philosophy of self-concern as the guiding principle in 'love', and the word 'pig' still echoed in his ears. He had shown himself a pig indeed, and a pig he would have gone on being had he not been brought up sharply where each one of us is finally brought up sharp, by death. Only in his case it had not been his own death, but the death of his beloved Baba.

Hitherto Walpole had been able to find excuse and justification for his pursuit of money, his loveless sensuality, the endless lies and deceptions in which he had involved himself. But the one thing he knew he would never be able to excuse was the failure to be with Mr Ali when he needed help, and he now realized and accepted to the bottom of his heart that this failure was not the result of chance but the inevitable consequence of his way of life, in which he had established no values and recognized no duties, but simply did whatever seemed most pleasant from one day to the next.

From time to time fresh storms of weeping shook him. Sometimes he wept aloud, calling on Mr Ali's name and begging his forgiveness. Sometimes, when he seemed to have shed all the tears his body could produce he sat sobbing with dry eyes. Sometimes, when his mind became too exhausted even for reproaches, he sat staring vacantly before him, until the sense of abhorrence overwhelmed him and he began to weep afresh.

At last, towards evening on what was perhaps the third day of his stay, the grey-haired woman, whom he had scarcely seen till now, opened the door. She did not speak or offer anything, but sat down beside him on the bed, pulled his head against her breast and sat holding him as if he were a child. Walpole continued to sob but gradually it became difficult for him to breathe, so closely was he held against her ragged dress. He disengaged himself and sat back, giving her a faint smile by way of thanks. From somewhere about her the old woman fished out a rag, dried his eyes, patted his face and went away. Within a minute or two she came back with tea and a piece of bread, and sat beside him till he had eaten it. After she left Walpole got to his feet, looked round the room, and for the first time wondered what he was going to do.

Till this moment he had had no thought about the future except to hope there would never be one. He had felt unfit to live and unequal to the burden of trying to think ahead. But the old woman's silent embrace had said more plainly than any words that we all of us suffer but have all to go on living. What had she and her old husband been through, he asked himself, to be able to recognize the sufferings of a stranger instead of merely thinking he was mad? Whatever it was, they had survived, and he must make up his mind to do the same. But where and how was he to live? The repulsion and horror he felt towards himself extended to his whole way of life, and he turned over in his mind all manner of ideas for becoming immediately and visibly a different person. Could he become a Moslem, as Mr Ali had been, seek out some sect or group devoted to helping others, qualify as a member of it and devote his life to service?

Could he discover in Madam Abiose's Christianity an answer to his needs? He had hoped, as he sat by Mr Ali's deathbed, that the old man might commit to his care some favourite child, perhaps a grandson whom he could bring up. This had not happened, but there were other children in the world, lost and helpless as he had been. Should he become a teacher? He had no qualifications but might obtain these, or he might serve in some humbler capacity, as doorkeeper or attendant. He turned such possibilities over in his mind, but none seemed to offer the answer to his need, and since it was himself he had to change, he could begin to do this as well where he was as elsewhere, and in the work he was doing as in other ways of life. Moreover he had responsibilities, to Alicia and his firm, which he could not disregard.

That evening Walpole asked for some warm water, washed and shaved himself and took a clean shirt out of the case he had not opened since Hamisu left. In shaving he was obliged to look into the fragment of mirror the old woman brought him with the water. The sight of his face made him shudder, not because he was gaunt, unshaven and red-eyed, but because it was the face of the man he no longer wished to be. At last, however, washed and in control, he walked through into the chop bar and for the first time ate a meal.

Tomorrow, he told the old couple, he would find a bus or mammy-wagon and return to Lagos.

37
A Certain Distance

'Good God! Walpole,' Alicia exclaimed, 'what's happened to you? I thought you'd stopped off to amuse yourself – but you don't look as if you'd done much amusing. . . . You haven't been *really* ill have you?' she asked in a more kindly tone.

'No, not ill. Distressed.'

'You mean over your old man?'

'Yes.'

'That *was* unfortunate,' Alicia conceded. 'But it wouldn't have done to let everybody down. Did you see his family?'

'Yes. I saw them.'

'Well, they must have been grateful for all your trouble – weren't they?'

'Yes.'

'*That's* all right then. Now you'll need to look after yourself for a few days. . . .' and she went on to discuss her social engagements and a coming dinner party with the Chief.

At the office the first person he came across was Mr Chukuma. He was bustling down the passage with a sheaf of papers, but stopped dead in his tracks.

'Walpole! Is it really *you*? You look as if you'd seen a ghost! My goodness – Hamisu told us you were ill and that he was going to drive up there and bring you back. But we'd no idea it was so bad. You've had fever, I see, and a stomach upset too, no doubt. That's what comes of eating in those damned roadside chop bars. Never do it myself – sooner go without. Well, and now you'll need feeding up! Have lunch with me in town today. No,' hastily turning the pages of his diary, 'can't be today. Let's say tomorrow. How will that be?' and Mr Chukuma bustled on to give orders to the accountant.

Walpole went on into Stephen's office. Stephen, who was writing, did not immediately look up, but when he did he sprang to his feet and taking Walpole by the shoulders stared intently at him for a second or two, then pulled a chair forward and pushed him into it.

'You've been through it, I see. You shouldn't be around. You've no business in the office.'

'Perhaps – but I'd sooner be here.'

'I knew you'd stopped on the way back from the north, and Hamisu said you were ill. At least he didn't quite say that, he said, "Something done happen to master." So what *did* happen – or don't you want to talk?'

'I don't mind talking to you. It started the night of our party – the one you and Cécile came to. I had a note from my old man and wanted to go to him at once, but I . . . we . . . thought I should wait till everyone had gone . . .' and Walpole went on to tell Stephen briefly about Mr Ali's death, his journey north to see the family, and the distress that had overcome him on the way back.

'Does Alicia understand this?'

'I told her what I could.'

'I see. . . . All the same you ought not to be at work.'

'But as I *am* at work, Stephen, I want your help. I mean to make one or two changes.'

'What sort of changes?'

'Changes in what I do. I can't take any more of this "nice time" life. I feel I've done nothing for the past six months but eat and drink. . . . I want to get out on site and work the way I used to before we got involved with this top-level stuff . . . "political business" and the rest.'

'That's not going to be easy to arrange,' objected Stephen. 'Our whole position's altered since you were wheeling barrows. The company's differently geared up – with us in the centre and managers out on the separate jobs.'

'Well, I'll be a super-manager and go round seeing that the managers manage.'

Stephen laughed. 'All the same, Walpole. . . .'

'If we *don't* make this change,' Walpole said firmly, 'I just can't carry on.'

Stephen sat up. 'Why, in that case it must be done. But how d'you see the change operating? Who's to look after clients?'

'With contracts coming in the way they are, we don't need a full-time fixer and back-slapper. After all most firms manage with about one-tenth of the time of a professional crook like Pontius. I can keep in touch with our clients for one week every month, do another week here at my desk, and get out and around for the remaining fortnight.'

'H'm, yes. I see the point of that. But have you thought what this'll mean for you? It's the work in Enugu and the Eastern Region that matters most at present. . . . You're going to be away from Lagos half your time.'

'I *have* thought about that.'

Stephen sat silent for a moment and then asked: 'Have you spoken to Chukuma?'

'Not yet. Why?'

'I suggest you leave him to me. Let me put it as something good for the company we might persuade you to accept. I'll tell him it may benefit your health as well. He's fond of you. On both counts I think he'll go for it. What d'you say?'

Walpole smiled for the first time. 'I say "thanks, my friend". And incidentally. . . .'

'Incidentally what?'

'We can pass on a lot of the contact work to Chukuma

himself – why not? He likes eating and drinking, and he's good at both.'

They laughed. 'I knew you'd help,' said Walpole.

'But there's one thing I can't help you over.'

'Which is?'

'You can't pass on the client who matters most. You *must* go on handling the Chief. You're the one he trusts, and we'll be sunk if the flow of new orders is cut off – at any rate for the next twelve months. . . . By the way, your father-in-law must have been patting himself on the back these last few days.'

'Why? What d'you mean?'

'I forgot you'd been away. . . . There's been quite a bit of rioting in the Western Region. Looks as though it might spread. Not being a Minister, the Chief can stay on the sidelines, out of the line of fire.'

'Where's the trouble been?'

'So far in country areas. . . . Stoning police . . . burning the huts of unpopular chiefs . . . refusing to pay taxes. But I shouldn't be surprised if trouble doesn't start up nearer the capital before long.'

'I haven't seen anything in the papers.'

'No – and you won't see anything either. Nor on the radio. They say it's being fixed behind the scenes. Discreet silence in the national interest.'

'Then how do people know what goes on?'

'Those who travel around keep their eyes open and bring back word.'

'Okay, Stephen. I'll keep mine open too.'

When everything at the office had been arranged, Walpole told Alicia.

'What's the meaning of this?' she asked sharply.

'The meaning as regards the firm is that I'm wanted in Enugu. The meaning for you and me is that we need a little distance between us. I haven't got over Mr Ali's death – I'm not going to talk about that, but it's affected me a lot. I need to think, and I want to spend time by myself.'

Alicia gathered herself up in the way he now knew well, but it no longer caused him apprehension.

'Look, Alicia – if you're planning to make a row, then *don't!* I won't be answerable if you make rows. Accept what I'm telling you. If in two months' time you want to talk things over, say so and I'll listen.'

She looked at him in astonishment, and for a moment did not answer. Then all she said was: 'Please yourself, Walpole. You always do anyway. But I expect you to let me know which days you'll be away – and I shall want you here for any parties I arrange, or those we should attend together.'

Walpole accepted readily. Having expected angry opposition, he was agreeably surprised by her compliance. However, a couple of weeks later when he called in on her father there was a more frank discussion.

'I won't pretend not to see what this implies, Walpole. I understand your wanting to get around the country and I don't doubt what you say about the need for air and exercise. . . . All the same, newly married husbands don't stay away from home for weeks when all is well. . . . I've been a newly-married husband myself from time to time – or the equivalent. . . .' He laughed. 'You and Alicia have your problems, no doubt. You're both strong-willed, and both – if you don't mind my saying so – used to getting your own way. Oh, I know what my daughter's like. She's a slight little thing, looks easy to handle, and I dare say you didn't realize all you were taking on. However, Walpole, you *did* take it on, and there you are! Luckily you're a man of the world, and luckily for you, you've a father-in-law who's a man of the world too.'

Though it was only mid-morning the Chief went to his locked cupboard and got out the whisky. 'My rule is "never before midday" – but this is the exception which improves the rule. Good health, my friend!'

They drank in silence for a minute before the Chief asked: 'D'you want a piece of advice, Walpole, or d'you prefer to be guided by inner illumination?'

'I'll take the advice.'

'It sounds easy, but isn't altogether. . . . *Don't worry!* Don't take things to heart. I suspect, Walpole, there's an idealist buried in you. If so, keep him in his place – which is where he can't affect your actions. Once he takes control, you'll never achieve anything. *Never!* It's fatal in politics. And in marriage it's the recipe for certain misery.'

'How d'you make that out?'

'Through expecting the impossible and refusing to be content with the available. Idealists look for hundred per cent harmony in marriage – "two minds without a single thought" and so on – and when they don't find it blame each other, so there are endless rows. It's rows which make marriage hell –

but why blame one another over the fact that you're different people? Let Alicia have her social life, parties and the rest. You won't enjoy them, but put up with them every now and then – and do it gracefully! And let her buy all the clothes she wants . . . of course she'll buy far too many, but you can afford it, so why not? In everything that doesn't matter, let her be the boss. But on everything essential' – and the Chief's brow contracted and his voice took on a harder tone – 'over work, travel, pleasure, over all *that* – be like iron! Once she knows you won't budge, she'll stop.' He paused and wagged a finger thoughtfully: 'It's the hope of getting their own way that keeps them nagging. But no hope – no nagging! Finally, my friend, get one thing clear – *we can have no scandal!* I'm in the public limelight. So, to a lesser extent, are both of you – and that means caution. However, we're not, thank God, a censorious society, and one can enjoy life pretty freely without causing scandal.'

Walpole laughed: 'I should say you've caused rather a lot of scandal in your time, Chief.'

'Gossip, my friend, not scandal – a very different thing. Gossip does no harm, it's talk which can't be proved, and on the whole does you good. Keeps you in the public eye and shows you're human . . . the public hates a cold fish. But scandal's different. Scandal's gossip which can be verified, and those whose profession it is to be virtuous – clergy, the law, self-important journalists and so on – have to denounce you, otherwise their position as moral guardians is in question. So keep clear of scandal – for all our sakes!'

'Right, Chief. I'll bear that in mind. . . . By the way, I hear there's some trouble in our region, rioting in country districts and so on. Is the government worried about this?'

The Chief looked at Walpole sharply, and his voice took on a cold, almost angry tone. 'Gossip is one thing, Walpole. Listening to rumours and spreading them is another. I'm surprised you should take part in it. But since you have, let me tell you this. Rumours about trouble in this region are totally unfounded. They're being spread by malicious, disaffected persons – and it's the duty of us all to contradict them wherever we come across them.'

'I'll remember what you say, Chief,' said Walpole and got up to leave.

As he reached the door the Chief – thinking perhaps he had

gone too far with the official line and reluctant to part on such a
note – called after him.

'One more thing, Walpole, to come back to serious – that is
personal – matters.'

'What's that?'

'Find yourself a nice kind girlfriend – that is if you haven't
done so already. . . . There's nothing like it for keeping a man
good-tempered.'

Walpole left with much to think about. He had been
inclined to discount what Stephen told him about trouble
brewing. But the Chief's lack of candour, coupled with a
reproof which was obviously insincere, implied substance in
these stories. In the Chief's final advice too there was
something puzzling, as though there were factors in his
situation with Alicia which the Chief understood, and of
which Walpole was unaware.

Since he had returned Walpole had had no speech with
Kalio, though he had noticed him standing by his outhouse
whenever he drove in or out, as if awaiting a visit from the
master. However he was in no hurry to talk to Kalio and when
he finally went across one evening, carried with him no gin
bottle.

'Master no come spik wid Kalio,' he observed reproach-
fully.

'I've come now, Kalio. Is there something you want to say?'

'Master bin sick.'

'Yes, Kalio. Very sick. Hamisu told you?'

'Not Hamisu. De bones done tell me master sick in sma'-
sma' hut. De bones done tell dat ole man die, an' dis make
master sad.'

'It's true.'

'De ole man dat done die he wantin' give master message by
de bones.'

'What message?'

'If master wish for power an' money – he mus' kip close wid
wife, an' close wid chief. Mus' stay all time here in Lagos.'

Walpole looked at Kalio and saw he was holding something
back. 'And what if I don't want power and money? What did
the old man say about that?'

Kalio lowered his eyes. 'Master wish I roll bones now for
spik wid dis ole man?'

'No, Kalio. I know what the old man would say if he could
speak, so I don't need to ask him anything.'

And Walpole went on into the house.

It was a week later when Walpole set out from home, and he recalled that morning twelve years earlier when he had left Madam Abiose's on his first long drive around his native land. That trip had been meant to pave the way to fame and riches but had ended in break-up and disaster – where would this journey lead, and how would the pattern of his life be altered by it? His talk with the Chief, he could see, conveyed a stern warning beneath the friendliness: 'My daughter's your problem now. You took her on – don't imagine you can unload her back! There can be no break-up between you and her, but then why should there be? Live the life you want, and maintain a suitable façade.' It was advice whose worldy wisdom he could appreciate, or would have done until recently when the idea had started to take shape in his mind that the course the Chief recommended – that of doing one thing while pretending to do another – might lie at the root of his unhappiness.

In fact what he was intending now was just the opposite of what the Chief advised. He meant there to be no façade to his life, no gap between what he meant and what he said. It was duplicity and double dealing which had landed him in marriage with a woman whose aims and view of life were utterly different from his own. The Chief's advice was to make duplicity his guide and ruthlessness a principle. But the death of Mr Ali – and what Walpole felt as his own failure to give comfort to the man to whom he owed so much – had given a deep shock to Walpole's moral nature. From the depths of his being he now longed to be different. Just how different and in what ways he could not yet resolve. But he certainly did not mean to become another Chief Efunshile. Alicia and her friends must accommodate themselves to this, if he was to continue living in their world.

Walpole had set out at dawn, and a couple of hours out of Lagos he was driving through the forest. On either side of the road lay strips of cultivated land beyond which trees closed in, so that it was impossible to see more than thirty yards for the curtain of palm, plantain, cocoa or cassava, above which soared an occasional forest giant whose silvery trunk, supported at the base by buttresses, unfolded to the sky only a ridiculous parasol of leafage. The road passed through no villages, yet was never free of people for more than a few hundred yards, men and women with farm tools on shoulders and bundles on their heads, the children striding on skinny legs to work the family plot beside their parents.

After some hours of forest the road led up into savannahs giving glimpses of blue hills in a rolling landscape, before winding down to the Niger which he crossed on the ferry, among a fleet of buses and mammy-wagons, to reach Enugu after dark. As capital of the Eastern Region, its importance was much greater than its size, so that new buildings were everywhere springing up.

Meaning to gather his own impressions, Walpole had told no one of his coming, so spent the night at a small hotel and was out early next morning at the site of the new barracks. Having made himself known to the manager, he spent the first hours going over plans and quantities and the afternoon with under-managers and foremen. Finally he went to where the ground was being cleared for the new wing. Since this had not been allowed for on the original plan, its introduction meant cutting into the hillside to level space for the foundations, and Walpole watched as a battery of earth-shifters charged one after the other against the slope. The uproar was prodigious but exhilarating, clanking of the monsters' jaws as they bit into the earth, rattling of chains as they raised their scoops, crash of gears and volleying of exhausts as they backed and slewed to spread their spoil evenly at a distance.

Above the noise could be heard the foreman's shout as he called one of the drivers over, bawled him out for not filling the scoop properly, and then jumped up into the cab to demonstrate. He was a heavily built young man in shorts and a yellow helmet, and after watching for a while Walpole went across to make a note of his name for the future, but as he approached the face seemed familiar.

'Hey, man! You know me – Basil Chukuma! What you doing here? Are we behind schedule or something?'

'Good God, Basil, I didn't recognize you. Does your lot always work at this pace?'

'Why yes, man, that's how we make the money. We're on piece work – each of these drivers takes home more than your head clerk.'

'So he should! But you won't be going on all night. . . . See you at the Bristol around six for a drink.'

Washed and dressed, it was a different Basil who called at the hotel, less jovial and more like the Basil whom Walpole

had known in Lagos, but an impression of change remained
and after a while Walpole remarked: 'Something's happened
to you, Basil. You look different – twice the size for one
thing. . . . And the way you had those men working – I was
coming over to take a note of your name for the future. . . . So
what *has* happened?'

Basil smiled. 'You should know, man, you sent me here.
My father wanted me to be a lawyer. My friends thought me
only fit to be a layabout. But here I've found something I can
do.'

'Good! But is that *all* that's happened – finding something
you can do?'

'Finding something I can do – and getting away from Lagos
and my father.'

'Your father's very fond of you,' Walpole insisted.

'Not fond of what I am. Fond of what he'd like me to be – an
imitation of himself!'

'He naturally wants you to get on.'

'And what I want's to be left alone! We had hellish rows
when he was up here a few weeks back. I wish to God he'd stay
away.'

Walpole did not mean to involve himself in a Chukuma
family dispute, so drank for a minute in silence and then asked:
'Where're you living now?'

Basil hesitated, and then asked: 'Doing anything tomorrow
night?'

Walpole shook his head.

'Okay then, come round to my place. . . . You better know
beforehand there are two of us. But Nwanyieke can cook so
you needn't worry. Here, I'll show you how to get there,' and
taking a stub of pencil and an old pay envelope from his coat,
Basil started to rough out a map.

Next evening as he was about to leave, Basil surprised
Walpole by turning up at the hotel and suggesting they had a
drink before starting out. They had more than one or two, and
then Walpole asked: 'Well, Basil, I thought we were going
round to your place?'

'So we are – but there's something you must know first.'

'What's that?'

'Nwanyieke – she's not a been-to or socialite. She's a girl
from the bush.'

'How did you find her?'

'She'd come in to market and couldn't find the right bus

home. She doesn't read, and was shy of asking city people. I saw her wandering about, got the van out and ran her back. Next time she came to market we met again. . . . We've been in this flat now three-four months,'

'Have you met her family?'

Basil laughed. 'About fifty of them so far.'

'Well, if that's all that's keeping us,' said Walpole, 'drink up and let's go.'

Basil drove the short distance to his home, a small flat in a new block. There was no one in the living room, which was sparsely furnished. A bulb in mid-ceiling gave the only light, showing a strip of matting on the floor and some dyed cloth on the wall for decoration. Basil brought out a jug of palm wine strong enough, he claimed, to "knock the tusks off an elephant", and was filling their glasses when the kitchen door opened and a tall, handsome girl came in. She said something to Basil without looking up until he told her to come and meet their guest, when she advanced a couple of paces, raised her eyes, and then looked away.

'Take my friend's hand, Nwanyieke,' Basil ordered, and she touched Walpole's fingers timidly. She wore what was evidently a new robe and he could see she had taken trouble to look her best. Over supper Walpole tried several times to bring her into the talk, but she only smiled politely and said nothing.

'Nwanyieke's shy,' Basil explained. 'We don't see many strangers and she doesn't speak much English. By ourselves we talk Ibo.'

Later as they sat smoking Walpole remarked: 'She's a fine girl, Basil. I see it isn't only work that's happened to you. . . . I suppose like the rest of us you've begun to find out who you really are.'

'That's it, man!' Basil burst out as though some spring inside him was released. 'That's how it *is*! I'm a simple man you see, Walpole, not like my father . . . and not clever and ambitious like you. A man has to find out what he can do . . . what he can really do' – the words came spilling out. 'Well, now I've a job I can handle. It's the same with Nwanyieke, she suits me and we understand each other. . . . My father was always on at me to make what he called "a good marriage" . . . know what I mean? Take some rich girl out and flatter her – pretend you're in love and all that crap. Make up to her family who are looking you up and down, wondering how much your old man will hand over if they have you. . . . Made me sick, man. Used to make me sick. Lies and sham, that's all it was. But with Nwanyieke I don't pretend. She knows what I'm like, and it's enough for her.'

'So you're happy with her?'

'She gives me what I want,' said Basil stoutly.

'What about your father? Has he met Nwanyieke?'

'No. Nor won't if I can help it.'

'How did you manage when he was up here?'

'I went along to his hotel.'

'But didn't he want to see how you were living?'

'He thinks I share a hut with other men on the job – as I did for the first months.'

'You should have brought him here. He's bound to hear about Nwanyieke, so it's better to have it out with him yourself.'

'Listen, Walpole, I've got so much to have out with that man – and one day I'll have the lot out at one blow! I don't want a lot of small rows. Just the one final one.' Seeing that Walpole was about to speak, he continued rapidly: 'Leave him to me, Walpole! Let me handle my father my own way.'

Though far from confident in Basil's ability to 'handle' Mr Chukuma, Walpole said nothing and left soon afterwards. Back in his hotel room he thought the evening over; his too-pliable friend had found something he could do and make others do, even if it was only scraping up the soil. There was also something touching in his relation to Nwanyieke, an Adam and Eve in an Eden of two rooms, an Adam who for the first time had found someone needing his protection, and an Eve happy to prepare his food and 'give him what he wanted'.

All the same there remained something violent and un-predictable in Basil's nature, particularly in relation to his father, which was likely, Walpole thought, to burst out before long. He had been meaning, if he found Basil doing well, to bring him back to head office since he could hardly spend his whole life driving bulldozers. But it might be better, he now thought, to leave Basil where he was for some months longer and then talk over his future with Stephen before taking any step, and meantime he could at least keep a friendly eye on the couple.

38
Trouble Brewing

Six weeks later, following a second fortnight in Enugu, Walpole was on his way home one evening when on approaching the outskirts of Lagos he saw many more people than usual on the streets, and wondered whether there were some big sporting event or celebration going on. However, as he drove further into the city it was evident this was no cheerful celebration but a crowd in angry mood. Hundreds of youths in their uniform of white shirts, short trousers and bare legs were milling about in groups, shouting slogans and waving torches. To either side of the highway lay a stretch of barren ground before any shops or houses were reached, and this normally would have been full of all kinds of petty trading . . . sellers of hot chop and cold drink, peddlers of patent medicines, small gatherings of religious sects and sessions of 'colleges of higher education' with equipment consisting of six benches and a blackboard.

But tonight all these had fled and as Walpole drove on he could see the remaining stalls being broken up and bonfires started with the debris. He put on speed, but quickly reached a traffic jam where angry faces started to peer in and threatening cries assailed him from all sides. Walpole wound his window up quickly and pushed down the locks on all the doors, whose handles were soon being shaken as the youths tried to force their way in. The car ahead of Walpole's was a smaller one, and the crowd had already started rocking to overturn it. His turn would be next, but for the moment the youths round his car had joined the rest in their attack. Glancing round, he saw there was a space between his own car and the one behind, so backing rapidly he swung the wheel over and took off for the waste land with horn blaring. There was a shudder as the back wheels almost stuck in the ditch which separated the road from the dusty strip, and a crash as the wing struck a kerosene drum filled with concrete, but as the car gathered speed the youths sprang aside, contenting themselves with curses and a shower of stones. Turning down the first opening between the houses, then taking a side road parallel to the highway, Walpole was able to get back on course a mile or two further on, having bypassed the milling crowds.

The house was dark when he reached home, Alicia having evidently gone out for the evening, but Kalio was standing by his outhouse.

'I see master's car done bin hit,' Kalio remarked in his usual sardonic manner.

'Yes. How long has all this been going on?'

'Since two-three month de people gettin' mo' an' mo' angry – den las week dey start burnin' cars on Ikorudu Road. Dey burn cars an' buses, an' dey set three-four petrol stations on fire.'

'But what's the good of that? And why here of all places?' The Ikorudu Road was not far off, the main artery to Lagos which Walpole used daily for getting to his office.

'Dey only burnin' big cars,' Kalio reported, as though this explained and justified their action.

'But why big ones?' Walpole asked, conscious of his own imposing American saloon.

'Big cars b'long Ibos, becos Ibos takin' all top jobs.'

'Even if that were true, what good does it do? It won't help Yorubas get the jobs back.'

Kalio spat contemptuously. 'People of dis region bin damfool people. Dey wish for govern country – but Action Group got no place in federal government. Government all only Northerners and Ibos, an' dey fixin' everything de way dey want. . . . So Action Group followers git mad.'

'Well, isn't it natural for them to get angry? So why call them "damfool people"?'

'Master, sah!' Kalio raised his palm as though in protest at having to expound so elementary a lesson. 'No good for git mad when you no have power to strike. Federal government make dis car-burnin' de excuse, an' soon take away sma'-sma' power dat remain. Dey carve new Midwest State out of dis region. Dey take away Lagos for make federal capital. Dey choppin' off mo' an' mo' an' leave dis region like snake wid no head.'

'So what *should* the Yorubas do?'

'Use de wits de devil done give um – an' lie low. When you wish fight man stronger dan yo'self, you 'bliged for bide yo' time.' Kalio paused before adding thoughtfully: 'De lion dat no roar bin de lion dat eat meat.'

'That's all very well for lions – but if the people don't make trouble nothing will get changed.'

'Is one time for make trouble, sah, an' one time for lie low. Dis bin time for lyin' low.'

'And what about the future? When do we stop lying low?'

'I done tell master three-four time,' said Kalio sharply, 'de future kin bring all master want. But master 'bliged for remember what de old men say.'

'What *do* the old men say?'

Kalio held up a forefinger. 'No crack louse wid jus' one finger.' He raised a second finger beside the first in a gesture familiar to Walpole from their talks: 'Master stay close wid Chief – den all go well.'

'Well for me perhaps, but what about this country? What's going to happen here? Will it remain one country – or is it all going to be split apart?'

'I done roll bones many time 'bout future of dis country, but I no see. . . . Too big for bones. . . . Too big for Kalio. . . .'

Next day Walpole spoke of the crowds and excitement to Stephen, who had heard further stories of trouble in Midwestern districts, but had so far seen nothing himself.

'You've been away a fortnight, but you've seen more than I have. You were lucky to get out of that alive.'

'Lucky to get out unhurt – but I don't think there was going to be killing. A few people will have got badly shaken and lost their cars. They certainly took it out on mine – it was hit by half a dozen rocks besides having a wing bashed in. . . . Someone told me later they probably thought it was an Ibo's car. Is that likely?'

'Quite likely. Some Ibo traders on the Ikorodu Road have had their stalls burned. And your big American car could well belong to an Ibo tycoon.'

'Next time I'll take one of the firm's Land-Rovers. . . . But there didn't used to be such hostility to Ibos. Not open, anyway.'

'They moved into key jobs under the British – and into a lot more since Independence. Particularly around the capital. They're in the government with the Northerners, while we Yorubas are left out. The Northerners always concentrate on their own region, and so Ibos get more than their share here.'

'True enough, but that's nothing new. So who's stirring the pot?'

'The politicians. Or some of them.'

'But what are our Action Group politicians after?'

'Power, of course, but they're split over how to get a share. The right wing wants a deal with the emirs and sheikhs, because it believes the Northerners are stronger. The left wing hopes to patch things up with the Ibos because we and they are Southerners with a lot in common.'

'What do you think, Stephen?'

'I wish they'd all just keep quiet for six months.'

'Why for six months.'

'Because Cécile's having a baby, and I don't want her upset.'

Walpole took his friend's hand: 'Wonderful, Stephen. I'm happy for you both.'

A pattern had taken shape whereby Walpole spent a fortnight in Enugu, a day or two in travel and the rest of his time at home. What he looked forward to was the period in Enugu, and the journey there, however hot and dusty, passed pleasantly enough. He was eager to see how the work progressed, glad to keep contact with Basil and Nwanyieke, but above all looked forward to being on his own. At home, mindful of the Chief's advice, he took part in whatever social activities Alicia arranged, but noticed with relief that these had started to become fewer. Sometimes when he returned from the East she would be out, and even while he was at home would go to parties on her own. 'I'm going to drinks at the High Commission – I know you hate that kind of thing. I'm not sure when I'll be back. . . . Kunle will give you your dinner.'

To Walpole it seemed that, having failed as hostess but not lost her appetite for social life, Alicia was settling for the easier alternative of being a guest. Hosts and hostesses are always short of well-dressed guests willing to talk without becoming noisy and swallow drinks without becoming drunk, so she would be welcome everywhere, and as regards entertainment in return, her father entertained lavishly enough for any obligations a whole team of daughters might incur.

One evening when Walpole was sitting at home reading, the telephone rang. He picked up the receiver, but there was no voice, though he could tell someone at the other end was listening.

'Well?' he demanded irritably, anxious to get back to his book. 'Who d'you want? This is Walpole Abiose.'

There was a moment's silence. Then: 'This is Ayoka – Ayoka Fashanu.'

Taken aback, Walpole stammered: 'Oh, yes. . . . Well, Ayoka, I expect you want to speak to Alicia . . . she's out at present.'

'No, Walpole,' said Ayoka cooingly. 'It isn't Alicia I want to speak to – it's you. I know Alicia's out because I've just seen her at a party, so I thought I'd ring you and have a chat. . . .'

She seemed to be waiting for a response, so Walpole pulled himself together. 'Thanks very much, Ayoka. . . . Very good of you. D'you want anything special?'

'Depends what you mean by "special", Walpole. I thought – now that you've so much time on your hands – we might occasionally meet again. We used once to be be good friends, or have you forgotten?'

'Thank you, Ayoka. But I'm not going out at present. I've a lot of work on hand.'

There was silence, and then a reply in icy tones: 'Very well, Walpole, if that's how you feel I won't waste your time. . . . I suppose you know where Alicia is?'

'Yes. She went to a drinks party at the Bakares with a girlfriend.'

'I know that's where she *went*. But the party ended an hour ago. D'you know where she is now?'

'No.'

'She's at flat number ten, Iworan Buildings, just off Montgomery Road in Yaba.'

'What's that got to do with me?'

Ayoka laughed. 'Why – maybe nothing at all, my friend! Depends how much you're interested in your wife. Knowing you, Walpole, I dare say you're not the least bit interested. . . . But in case you are, I tell you she's there with her cousin Wilson. . . . Are you listening?'

Walpole growled in reply.

'Her young cousin Wilson – your predecessor in her affections – if that's what Alicia calls them. So it's only fair he should also be your successor, don't you think? Funny it must be for you, being a sandwich between two Wilsons. Well, I just thought you ought to know. After all, you *are* her husband, aren't you?' And he heard the receiver click.

Walpole knew Wilson Efunshile well enough, having met him a number of times at the Chief's and elsewhere. He was a good-looking youth, a couple of years younger than Alicia, with a taste for loud clothes and pop music, and a talent for dancing High Life that was almost genius. And now, as

Walpole thought of Alicia and her cousin, the whole picture of Alicia and her marriage to him fell into place. He recalled his first sight of her creeping in late on the night of the party for Chief Pontius, fearful of being detected and grateful for his protection. But why had he never asked the obvious question of where she had been? Her father had spoken of his difficulty in controlling her and of her staying out as often as she pleased, and casually Walpole had assumed that she stayed out with some group of friends – assuming this because at the time he just wasn't interested in where she went to or with whom. But now it was plain enough where she had been. Wilson was an ineffective character, living on an allowance from his family, while he claimed to be 'studying' this or 'making a fresh start' in that. It must be his weakness, his dependence, that appealed to Alicia as someone she could manage, someone who looked up to and probably almost adored her in return.

The Chief had shown surprise, he now remembered, at his suggestion of marrying Alicia – but why should a father be surprised at a man wanting to marry his daugher? His surprise must have been that Walpole either did not know about Alicia's affair with her cousin, or was willing to overlook it if he did. At their wedding party too, late in the evening when all the guests were either dancing or rushing about in cars, Alicia had been missing for an hour or more. At the time he had been grateful for the chance of a quiet talk with Stephen, while at that moment Alicia no doubt was saying a tearful goodbye to her young cousin. Later, on coming to their bedroom, he had been relieved to find Alicia already asleep, but why was she asleep – and had she indeed been genuinely asleep at all?

Thinking the marriage over and looking at it from her side as well as his, Walpole was inclined to give Alicia the benefit of much doubt. She had, he believed, honestly intended to settle down and live with him as his wife. She could not marry Wilson who was unable even to support himself, but she wanted to be married and Walpole was a good match and a not ill-looking husband. Had all gone well, she would have kept her cousin in his place and Wilson, by far the weaker personality, would have had no choice but to abide by her decision. It was her discovery that Walpole had married her for business advantage which altered everything. Since he had deceived her, why should she deny herself in order to remain faithful? Inclination and the wish to be revenged must both have urged her to take up the affair again, and one whistle would have been enough to bring Wilson back. When her father urged Walpole to be tolerant and to 'get yourself a nice, kind girlfriend', he was revealing his awareness of what went on, and the reason Alicia had lately given up ambition as a hostess was not because of failure – on the contrary she had just had her first taste of success – but because it involved building her life around her husband. She had taken to being a guest and going around because doing so brought her in contact with her lover.

That Ayoka's information was true Walpole never doubted. It fitted too exactly into the picture, so that he could only be amazed at his obtuseness in not having intuited a lover for Alicia before now. As for what had impelled Ayoka to ring him now, that again was obvious. Seeing Alicia and Wilson everywhere together, she guessed that Walpole would be at a loose end and available. Possibly her own man had dropped her, or perhaps the Chief had passed her on a word since she fitted his idea of what 'a nice kind girlfriend' ought to be. And as he thought over their easy good-humoured relationship in the days before he took up with Bisi, Walpole was tempted to ring Ayoka back, say it was all a mistake and he'd be over to see her in an hour. It was a long time since he had had his arms around a woman, for with Alicia he had had nothing to do since he got back after Mr Ali's death. Abstinence did not come naturally to Walpole, and he could be sure of a welcome with Ayoka, that shoulder for every troubled head, those thighs ever open for a friend with no place to enter. The prospect was tempting, all the more since with Ayoka there would be no need for time-wasting pretence.

But even as he reached for the phone the thought hit him that if he took up with Ayoka now he would merely be climbing back on to the treadmill, the routine of pleasure, money, power which had sickened him, not only with life but with himself and which he had determined to break through. Regretfully he let the receiver slip back. Ayoka was all very well, but to find some purpose in living had come to mean more than an hour's casual enjoyment.

Next morning at breakfast Alicia informed him that she was going to be away for a few weeks, staying with a school friend in Ibadan who required her help. Walpole wished her a happy visit, and was not surprised to learn before long that Wilson Efunshile had left Lagos for a course of study in Ibadan university.

39

Dangerous Influences

On his next visit Walpole reached Enugu a day earlier than he was expected, and having nothing to do in the evening walked round to his friend's flat for a talk and drink. From outside the door he could hear raised voices and on impulse opened it and walked straight in. There was the silence which comes over a group when their discussion is interrupted by a newcomer and Basil, taken aback and looking for a moment almost frightened, jumped up: '*You* here, Walpole? But I wasn't expecting you before tomorrow,' then quickly recovering introduced his two companions – Jackson Apara, a heavily built young man with no neck and a rapacious look, and Chike Ajoku, gaunt and willowy with the stoop of a man who spends his life at desks. Even indoors he was wearing dark glasses, and Walpole took him for a lecturer or scientific worker.

Whatever the subject of their conversation it evidently could not be continued, and after a pause Jackson Apara asked: 'You've just got here, it seems. Where are you from?'

'I drove up from Lagos today.'

'You must have driven hard or started early.'

'As soon as there was light. But I know the road – I come up every month. Basil and I work in the same firm.'

'He's my boss,' Basil put in.

'Well, and how's everything in my home town? All quiet as usual?' As he spoke Jackson shot a half-glance round the others which Walpole interpreted as meaning 'Let's see how he answers this!' and concluded that the talk before he arrived had been political.

'No. Not quiet. I should say your fellow countrymen are getting restless.'

'How do they show that? In the usual way, I suppose, by talk. That's the curse of all Yorubas.'

'Not only by talk. Have you been in Lagos lately?'

'Not for three-four months – much as I wish to. But as a federal official, seconded up here to the Eastern Region, it's not easy to get away.'

'Well, you'll notice a big difference next time you're back.'

'In what way?'

'General unrest. It started in country districts a couple of months ago and everyone said it would soon die down, but it hasn't. Now it's got as far as the suburbs.' Walpole felt all three listening intently.

'Unrest?' put in Basil. 'What sort of unrest, man? You mean meetings?'

'I don't know about meetings – if there are I didn't see them. No. I mean rioting, burning cars, shops, petrol stations. . . .'

'Did you observe any of this yourself?' Chike Ajoku spoke in a high, querulous voice, his manner suggesting a lawyer trying to pin down an evasive witness.

'Not only saw it – I experienced it.'

'What did you experience?'

'I was coming into Lagos down the Ikorudu Road and ran into a mob who were stopping cars and threatening drivers. When they started to turn over the car in front of mine, I managed to drive off the road, bump over the ditch and get down a side turning. But the car's a mess – hit by a lot of rocks. So this time I've come up in a Land-Rover.'

'It's started! It's started!' muttered Jackson excitedly. But Chike, beckoning him to be quiet, asked: 'This rioting you saw – what's behind it? What was the crowd after? Were they shouting slogans? Did they have banners? Or were they just looting?'

Walpole hesitated. 'As a matter of fact, they seemed to be looking for Ibos – wanting to burn their cars. . . . I was told later that might be why I was stopped.'

'But you're not an Ibo?'

'No. But I drive an American car – and big cars are supposed to belong to Ibos.'

'And d'you know why?' demanded Jackson, who could be kept quiet no longer. 'Because they take all the top jobs! That's how I got sent up here – an Ibo got the promotion I should have had. You'd think an Ibo would want to work among his own people, wouldn't you? Not a bit of it! What he wants is the best job going – and to hell with everybody else!'

'You seem to think Ibos are different from us. But isn't every group the same – some good and some bad?' Walpole

felt he sounded pompous, but was determined to protest
at this outburst of tribal feeling.

'It's not a question of good or bad,' Jackson declared
impatiently. 'It's not a question of ethics, or rubbish of that
kind. It's a matter of the way they all hang together to keep
everyone else out. We're supposed to be a united country, no
more tribal discrimination, all brother Nigerians and so on.
But I tell you – and I'm talking of my own experience – allow
one Ibo into a ministry, and you've had it! He brings in a dozen
more, and that dozen each brings in another dozen – brothers,
cousins, nephews. In no time even the messengers have to be
Ibo.'

'It's true, my friend,' remarked Chike, stretching his long
legs. 'We Ibos are known for our strong family feelings. You
should respect us for it!'

But Jackson was not to be diverted by banter. 'It isn't only
the way they cling together – it's their bloody hypocrisy! You
needn't worry about Chike here. He knows what I'm talking
about – he's a victim of it. Every Ibo talks democracy, national
unity and the rest. But if the NCNC★ had any honesty, what
they'd have on their banners would be two words – TRIBALISM
and NEPOTISM! Those are the principles they stand for – and
they should admit it!'

'Sounds as though Ibos are not the only tribalists around,'
said Walpole drily. 'Didn't you say you were a federal official?
Do your colleagues talk like this?'

Once again Chike, despite his casual manner, got his word
in before his friend. 'You mustn't take it out on Jackson! You
can't blame him for being angry.'

'Why can't I blame him? If federal officials don't speak up
for a united country – who will?'

'Apart from the fact that one pinched his job,' said Chike,
'he's got every right as a Yoruba to be angry with us Ibos.
After all we scorned his proffered hand of friendship.'

'When did you scorn our proffered hand?' asked Basil.

'Over the elections before Independence, my dumb friend,'
Chike remarked. 'You naturally concluded that when the
British cleared off and a federal government was formed, our

★National Council for Nigeria and the Cameroons, the predominantly Ibo
party which governed the Eastern Region after Independence and formed
part of the federal government together with the Northern People's
Congress (NPC).

two peoples would be in alliance. We've got everything in common – culture, institutions, religion, a long connection with the outside world. But what connection has either of us with the Northerners – a lot of warlike Moslems whose idea of education is reading the Koran?'

'Then why *aren't* our peoples in alliance?' Basil asked.

'Because the Ibos turned us down in favour of an alliance with the bloody Northerners. That's why!' declared Jackson emphatically. 'They did a deal with them, and pushed us out. So the Northerners, who didn't give a damn about Independence, now have the lion's share of benefit. They provide the army and police. And the Ibos have the top jobs in the professions and civil service, as well as having far more than their share of trade and industry. . . . It's a bloody carve-up!'

'If the Northerners control the army and police,' Walpole put in, 'then in the last resort it's they who have the power. So what happens if they get fed up with all the rioting, and decide to take over?'

Chike cackled. 'No fear of that! The army could never govern the country, and it knows it. It has to take orders from politicians – the only question is from which? At this moment it takes orders from the federal government. But everyone can see this government's a disaster. It doesn't even know what to do about this trouble in the Western Region. All it can think of is to deny it exists and hope it'll go away.'

'What would you do, Chike,' Basil inquired, 'if you had charge of the government?'

'Cut its throat and set up a new one,' Chike answered. 'The only arrangement that makes sense is for Ibos and Yorubas to be in alliance, with Northerners in opposition.'

'So you see this rioting,' Walpole suggested, 'as a first step towards that new alliance?'

'It *could* be,' Chike replied, as though debating some abstract point, 'it could very well be so. A popular uprising by people driven too far *might* well be the first step. . . .'

But Jackson could no longer be repressed: 'Of course it's the first step! Things have begun to move – and once they start there'll be no stopping them!'

'You sound as though you want them to move,' Walpole remarked.

'Of course I do! Don't you? You're a Yoruba like Basil and myself – and Chike here's an honorary Yoruba. D'you accept for our people to be left without a share in power? Without a voice? For all our struggle to have brought us nothing?'

'Of course we should have a share,' Walpole agreed. 'What I'm asking is how car-burning in Lagos will bring about a government of Yorubas and Ibos?'

'What has to be done,' Chike replied, as Jackson buried his face in the palm-wine jug, 'is to break the existing pattern. Bring this lot down. Unrest is only the first step.'

'Then what's the second?'

'More unrest.'

'You mean?'

'What I mean,' Chike expounded patiently, 'is that one thing leads to another. Looting and burning leads to more looting and burning. Paralysis of government. Then come assassinations. Seizure of power by those who've made preparations to seize power. In effect – armed revolution.'

The contrast between the programme Chike reeled off and his querulous voice and scholarly manner struck chill into Walpole's heart. He sounded as though for him 'insurrection', 'death', 'assassination' were words in a history book corresponding to no grim reality. Such men, he thought, are the most dangerous of all since they play with ideas without visualizing consequences.

On Jackson, who had been hammering the palm wine all evening, the effect was dramatic. Springing to his feet and knocking glasses over, he shouted: 'Roll on the revolution! Roll on the assassinations! As for this government – herd the lot into their own parliamentary buildings – and blow the place up! That's the way to solve *their* problem!'

'Stop fooling, Jackson!' said Chike sharply. 'Walpole may not understand your sense of humour.'

'Humour be damned! . . . ' But before he could say any more, Chike had pulled him to his feet. 'Come on – you've had too much palm wine. Pack it in, Jackson, before you say something indiscreet!'

'What d'you think of them?' Basil asked when the sounds of his two visitors arguing had faded into the night.

'What *you* think of them is what matters?'

'Oh I like both! They're the most interesting men I see up here. In fact they're my only friends – apart from you, and you're usually away. Jackson's a bit wild, of course. You mustn't take what he says seriously – he's angry because he missed that job. But Chike's a thinker – he's got a first-class mind. You must have seen that yourself.'

'What is he? A college lecturer?'

'No – a journalist. At least he was. But he got turned out of his job for criticizing government policy. He's an Ibo who's anti-Ibo, and I can tell you that takes some courage. Above all up here.'

'He may be brave – but he's certainly reckless. You should think twice, Basil, before getting involved with men like those two. You may find yourself drawn in a lot further than you want.'

'But what's wrong with being interested in politics, man? Haven't you always been interested in them yourself? And having a couple of hours' talk and a few drinks doesn't mean I'm 'involved'. You make it sound like some sort of conspiracy.'

'Your word, Basil, not mine. But I mean what I say – those two and the way they talk can land you in a heap of trouble. Do they often hold meetings here?'

'They come along two or three times a week, I suppose. But only to talk – you can't call that a meeting.'

'The government would,' Walpole replied, 'and you must stop it. Let them hold their discussions somewhere else. I'm advising you, Basil, as a friend. If Jackson and Chike want to play at revolutions, that's their look-out. But it's no business of yours, and I'm not having the firm involved in political disputes. Is that clear?'

'Why yes, man. If you say so, man, then that's how it has to be. But I must say you're making a great deal out of very little. People should be able to talk about anything they please. After all, it's a free country, isn't it?'

40
River Crossing

A couple of days later, before returning to Lagos, Walpole went round to Basil's flat to leave instructions on the work to be done over the next fortnight. Basil was not at home, but Nwanyieke let him in, explained haltingly that her man would be back soon and then withdrew into the kitchen. Lying on the table among newspapers and correspondence was a leaflet, the cover of which bore a palm tree, symbol of the Action Group, and the words ACTION SOON! Supposing it to be some piece of propaganda left over from an earlier election, Walpole picked it up and began reading.

TO ALL YORUBA PEOPLE

Cast your mind back only one and a half years – you stand at history's most glorious moment, the birth of our independent state! In October 1960, out of all runners in the race to African freedom, Nigeria was poised to move first into a true democratic system for in Nigeria political power was broad-based. It did not stand on one leg only, but chieflike sat upon a stool. Each of the three parties was lord of its own region, but none by itself could form a Federal Government and rule the nation. So the pleasing prospect before our country was of a true broad-based democracy.

THE PSALMIST'S PROPHECY

But what did the psalmist say? 'Every prospect pleases and only man is vile.' The psalmist foretold truth, because already that pleasing prospect has faded into mirage through vileness of man.

In the 1959 elections which heralded independence, the Northern People's Congress (NPC), a party concentrated only within Northern Region, gained 134 seats in the Federal Parliament, because of that region's huge population. The National Council for Nigeria and the Cameroons (NCNC), party of Ibos and the Eastern Region, gained itself 89 seats. But the Action Group of the Yorubas, which bravely contested seats throughout the whole of Nigeria, gained only 73 seats.

At that moment good sense dictated either coalition of all parties, or else alliance between NCNC and Action Group, with NPC in opposition. No party could govern alone, and this offered the most even balance. Also the Yoruba and Ibo peoples are closer in culture, religion and political experience than either is with the North.

HOW A MONSTER WAS BORN

But see how the psalmist's words came true! Because man is vile, he is able even to divert history out of its appointed channel. So what did we see? Alliance between NPC and NCNC – an unnatural union, for NPC is not a political party of the modern world but a bossdom of Emirs and Sheikhs. No wonder the government born of such union is a monster – and no wonder its actions are monstrous!

Just one year ago these partners in crime resolved to carve a

Midwest Region out of our Western area – but not to create any new states in the Northern and Eastern Regions which they govern themselves. Lately two further stages in their cruel plottings have been revealed:

1. To extend the boundaries of the Federal Capital, Lagos, so as to take in areas carved from Western Region territory.
2. To dissolve our Western Legislature and set up a so-called 'caretaker government' in place.

For Yoruba peoples this would be the end – our future stolen before we enjoy the present. And even before these latest actions, what do we see around us? Everywhere top jobs filled by Ibo persons brought in with Northerners' support – while our own qualified citizens are thrust aside, only for the crime of being Yoruba! Thus fighters for freedom are excluded from fair share, while those who risked nothing during independence struggle grow fat and rich!

FREEDOM BATTLE ALREADY JOINED

Today reactionary forces exult they have control over armed forces and police. But though progressive elements seem dead, they are only living underground. In early part of this year have been many disturbances throughout Western and Midwest Regions. In Ibadan area in a single week, thug hirelings employed by reactionary chiefs were attacked by enraged populace and eighteen of them killed! Numbers of such chiefs have been forced to flee! Of our own people more than forty have sacrificed their most valuable possession – breath of life – in freedom struggle.

JUSTICE – BARE-HANDED IF NEED BE

From this moment, these riotings will increase! To achieve Yoruba freedom, our people are ready to do battle with bare hands. But bare-hand fight will not be needed. Plans are on foot, men trained, arms secreted. When the day dawns our traditional leaders will be at the head. You are chosen to receive this message because those who watch know you to be honest, patriotic citizen! Before long a LEADER will visit this area, and you will be called to hear him speak. Talk of this to no one but friends. ACTION DAY approaches. BE READY WHEN IT COMES!

Walpole read the leaflet through twice, then looked to see if any organization claimed responsibility or if the cover carried a printer's name, but there was none. Evidently it was an illicit publication to be passed from hand to hand. When Basil got home Walpole exchanged news with him and then asked: 'Where on earth did you get this?'

'What? Oh, that man? Just a leaflet. Must have been pushed under my door.'

'Any idea who wrote it?'

'No . . . but I might guess.'

'Who then?'

'Could have been Chike Ajoku. . . . It's the way he talks. And it's the line he takes. . . . You know, that the Yorubas have been let down because the NCNC sided with the Northerners.'

'How did it get under your door?'

Basil hesitated. 'It's possible Jackson and a few friends may be distributing it . . . but only to people they know support them.'

'Which evidently includes you. D'you realize what you're doing, Basil? Just possessing this leaflet can land you in the shit.'

'How could it? I can't stop things being pushed under my door!'

'But this "thing's" treasonable. It talks about uprisings planned and arms secreted for a coup. If you have this in your house and do nothing, the police will say you're implicated – otherwise you'd have reported it to them.'

'But I knew nothing about it!'

'You'd have a job convincing them of that. It says it's only issued to "chosen" people.'

'But I haven't conspired against anyone. I don't believe they've really got arms – or a plan for using them. There's no harm in having an opinion. That's not illegal, is it?'

'Look, Basil, I haven't come round for a chat on political theory. Two days ago when I met Jackson and Chike here, I advised you as a friend to see less of them and make them hold meetings somewhere else. Now I'm not advising you – I'm telling you! Either you stop seeing these two men and cut all connections with their group – or else. . . .'

'Or else what?'

'Or else I go straight to your father.'

'God, Walpole, you couldn't do that! He'd be up here in a flash. He'll take me away from the work, my friends, Nwanyieke. . . . He'd have me back in his office before you could turn round. That would be the finish, Walpole, you *can't* do that to me!'

'You just see if I can't, Basil! I'd have to tell him the whole story anyway.'

'Why on earth?'

'To explain why I'm throwing his son out of the firm –

although he knows I like you, and I've told him what a good job you're doing.'

Basil thought in silence for a moment, and then: 'Okay, man. . . . You win. What d'you want?'

'Your promise to take no part in any political activity. You're to destroy this leaflet – and if you get more, destroy them too! And from now on, stop seeing Jackson and Chike! I don't care what the hell you tell them – blame it on me, the firm, your father, anyone. But you *must* stop seeing them. Promise me that – and I'll say nothing to your father.'

'That's a deal, man – and thanks!' said Basil, holding out his hand a shade too readily – as Walpole thought even while taking it.

For hours after he returned to his room Walpole was unable to sleep. It seemed the whole familiar world was starting to crack under his feet. His marriage was sliding to disaster, and if his marriage went, so would his 'special relationship' with the Chief, his father-in-law, and with that would go the mainstay of the firm's prosperity. Stephen and Mr Chukuma must face heavy losses, but both had ample funds and property to live on, while he, with much less behind him, could find himself back almost at the beginning. And now there was Basil who – through inability to say 'No', and a confusion of feelings towards his dominating father – seemed bent on landing himself in trouble, and could very well land the firm in serious trouble too. The conspiracy, if there were one, looked too naïve and amateurish to threaten danger to the government, but it could well be fatal to those involved. Whichever way he looked, Walpole could see only difficulty and danger for the country, the firm, his friends and for himself, and when at last he fell asleep it was to be dragged through forests full of murdered men, to cross oceans in howling tempests, and finally to be locked in the cell of a desolate prison whose walls and corridors were patrolled by crocodiles.

Anxious to reach the ferry before the volume of traffic built up, Walpole rose with daylight and was quickly on his way. He loved driving, and the empty roads, the freshness of early morning, the flights of white cattle herons sailing out into the fields and the occasional hornbill arrowing across from tree to tree gave him a sense of oneness with the natural world before it hardened into another working day. His forebodings had not diminished and the journey home was to tension and conflict, but he felt confident that his difficulties would somehow be resolved and that even if everything he had were lost, he would survive in the future as he had done in the past. As he drew near to the landing place of the Onitsha ferry numbers of people were pouring down both sides of the road and a young girl in her hurry to get on stepped into the road, causing him to swerve. She looked so slim and elegant in a flowery dress and stepped with such vitality that it gave him a moment's joy just to have seen her, and he wished he had passed her half an hour earlier so that he could have offered her a lift. But she had already been swallowed into the flow of walkers and it was not long before he reached the ramp leading to the ferry. Having driven the Land-Rover on board, Walpole climbed out and started to wander round the deck, already full of a motley crowd. Here were imposing citizens on business between the two cities, most of whom remained standing by their large cars – not only as symbols of prestige but as refuge from the throng. There were local traders in loose robes, chatting about their deals; workers with the cares of families and poverty around their shoulders, crossing dejected to their daily toil; and there was a horde of youths in white shirts and shorts – standard uniform of schoolboys, small-time clerks and messengers – jabbering and excited as a flock of noisy birds.

Walpole took in the scene idly, enjoying the drama as the boat pushed off, with last-minute travellers pleading to be taken on and some great man's car arriving late, the angry sounding of its horn, with jeers and answering whistles from the schoolboys. A quarter of an hour later, leaning on his elbows, he was watching the boat's sideways struggle in face of the river's force, when his eye was caught by a swirl of movement among the crowd in the forepart of the boat, and he drew nearer to see what was going on. Half a dozen of the youths were scuffling around tormenting, he supposed, one of their own number. But the other passengers began to move away as though not wanting to be involved, and Walpole was about to do the same when he saw it was not one of themselves they were tormenting, but a girl. She was standing helpless but defiant with her back to one of the ship's girders while the youths danced mockingly around, and he at once recognized her as the girl he had passed earlier on his way down to the ferry. Suddenly one of the bigger youths ran forward and gave her a shove, half playful but half vicious, so that she stumbled to her knees, dropping her coat and the case she was holding, and at this the youths instantly closed in. Not waiting to see what they intended, Walpole dashed into them shouting to let her go. None took any notice so, doubly furious at their disregard, he fell on the two nearest, grabbed their shirts and dragged them backwards, half tearing the garments off them. At this the remainder turned on him and six or seven were more than he could handle, so pouncing on the smallest youth, he carried him bodily to the ship's side, swung his legs over and held him above the racing flood. The boy, terrified, clung to Walpole's neck.

'Leave her alone!' Walpole bellowed at the others. 'Get away from her – or I throw him in!'

After a moment's doubt the youths fell back and Walpole dragged the boy inboard and flung him down heavily at his companions' feet.

'Get out!' he shouted, glaring fiercely round. 'Get the hell out – or I throw the lot of you in – one by one!'

Intimidated by his passion more than his threats the youths backed off, complaining that he was a madman, that they'd done no harm, he'd torn their clothes and ought to pay for them. But the by-standers who had taken no part in the action, now that it was over rounded on the youths who quickly slunk back into the crowd. Walpole went over to the girl who was sitting shaken and distressed, helped her to her feet, then looking round picked up one of her shoes, a small cardboard suitcase, one or two books and a hair ribbon. A long scratch over one eye had begun to bleed and Walpole took out his handkerchief and began to mop it.

'You're hurt. Come and sit in the car while I get some water.'

She looked up, crying and smiling at the same time. 'Thank you . . . you came just in time.'

Taking her by the elbow, he started to guide her through the crowd towards the Land-Rover, but felt her suddenly lean against him and, looking down, saw she was about to faint, so put his arm round her and holding her close made his way to the car, the crowd opening up and looking curiously on. He pulled the door open, lifted her in and laid her along the seat, then folded his coat and slid it underneath her head. She would be safe here while he went to find some water. This, however, took longer than he intended and when he got back with a glass she was already sitting up.

'How d'you find water on a boat like this?'

'The captain gave it me.'

'That was kind.'

'Not really. When I asked for water he laughed and pointed to the river. So I told him a federal minister's daughter had been hurt in a scuffle on his boat. If she didn't get water right away, the minister would send men later to find out why not – so he sent for it at once.'

'But that wasn't true.'

'No. But it got the water.'

The girl laughed. Then, after a moment: 'I don't think they really meant to hurt me. . . . They got carried away.'

'If they weren't trying, they'd at least made a good start.'

As she sipped, the girl gazed at him over the glass and he gazed back, taking each other in. She seemed no more than a child. Her cheeks were smooth as a fruit and he put her age down as thirteen. While he was searching for the water she had put back the ribbon in her mass of close black curls and tidied her dress as best she could.

'You can take the glass back now – I'm all right.'

Walpole set it down in an angle of one of the boat's steel ribs. 'The captain can look for it. It'll help him to be more friendly next time.'

But now the boat was sliding crabwise in towards the landing place and the girl gathered herself and her few belongings together. 'Thank you for helping me. But now I must go and try to find a bus.'

'Where are you going?'

'Lagos.'

'Good. Then I can take you with me, so you needn't look for any bus.'

As they drove on Walpole questioned the girl as to where she came from and why she was going to Lagos by herself. Her name, she said, was Nana Oredola and she thought her parents, whom she did not know, had come from Ghana. She had been at a missionary school and was being sent to Lagos to learn to take care of small children. Was she going to a family, Walpole asked.

'No. I'm going to a "Refuge", a place homeless children are taken to, to be looked after. It's run by the same people as the school I've been at.'

Had he been alone Walpole would have driven through to Lagos without a break, but Nana kept falling asleep and it was evident she had had more than enough for one day. He decided therefore to pull in at a rest house for the night. They left early next morning but travelling was slow, so that it was mid-afternoon before they reached the city. It then took Walpole quite a while to find the Refuge whose address Nana carried in her case, though it had also been pinned to her coat by the nuns or whoever it was who ran the missionary centre she had left.

But at last he arrived at the door and rang the bell. After a pause footsteps sounded along the passage, a bolt was drawn bac¹·, the door opened – and Walpole found himself face to face with Regina.

41

Reunited

As they faced each other in the doorway, the flash through Walpole's mind was not so much of recognition as bewilderment. 'Regina! But why d'you look so different? How d'you come to be here?'

After he had handed Nana over, explaining how he happened to have brought her, Regina showed him into a waiting room, saying she'd be back before long. As Walpole sat in the nondescript room taking in nothing of his surroundings, deaf to voices in the corridor and the cries of children playing in the yard, he realized his whole existence had gone back into the melting pot. Regina – here in Lagos and having, it seemed, broken with her old life – made anything possible, anything except a return to the sham of his former existence.

Hardly two years had gone by since Regina and he had parted, but in that time had had learned the folly of pursuing money and power – a pursuit in which failure brings distress, but success freezes the heart. The solitary death of his oldest friend and benefactor had given Walpole a shock from which he could only recover by finding a different way of life, which meant becoming different in himself. Had some similar change been happening to Regina? Regina, the most extravagant fashion queen in Lagos, had stood in the doorway simply dressed and with little make-up. Nothing could make her less than beautiful – the change, apparent at a glance, was that she no longer seemed absorbed in her own beauty.

A thousand times Walpole had gone over in his mind what he would say and how act if ever the two of them should meet again. What he had never bargained for was their meeting not at the point at which they had parted but somewhere further along the road, at which – as if by mutual complicity – they had arrived together. Regina had given him a look of delighted recognition which told everything. His own look would have said to her: 'I've loved you ever since we parted. A moment ago I didn't know it. Now I know!'

And now Regina had come back into the room and Walpole sprang to his feet. He did not take her in his arms but put his hands on her shoulders and stood gazing into her eyes while the tears gathered in his own and began rolling down his cheeks. It was Regina who, unable to bear it any longer, flung her arms round him.

For an hour and more they sat in gathering darkness while the children's voices fell silent and lights in the outside world came on, talking in turn and sometimes both at once. Regina had gone back to Duke's flat after leaving Walpole to find herself already being watched by two of Duke's bullies, who later took her to the airport. She was still hoping to get away, but they stood there while she phoned and even walked out with her to the plane. When she arrived in Paris Duke was waiting. . . .

'While we were travelling around he swore a dozen times that if I tried to contact you he'd kill you – or have you killed. Later I managed to phone Cécile and from time to time she'd tell me what she could of you, which wasn't much. I felt you'd lost all feeling for me. And I didn't blame you. I saw it was all my fault, my weakness. . . .'

'No! It wasn't,' Walpole broke in. 'It was *mine*. After you phoned I should have gone straight to the airport, found what flight you were on and followed next day. Duke's not inconspicuous! Within a week I'd have been bound to find you – in Paris or wherever you were. But how *did* you get away?'

'Duke was talking to one of his associates about some business deal. When I saw them deep in argument I just ran out of the hotel with nothing. . . . Then I went to a fashion house I'd worked for before and got a modelling job.'

'But how d'you come to be in this place?'

Regina hesitated. 'One day when I rang Cécile she told me you were marrying Alicia Efunshile, and I thought – that's what I've done to Walpole. He's bound to be miserable and I caused it. . . . I knew then I couldn't go on any longer the way I had been doing. I was sick of dressing up and showing myself off – and sick of being exploited. . . . I decided I'd change my way of life . . . start to live differently . . . become different in myself. I couldn't live differently in Paris, so I came back here.'

'Then what?'

'I lived by myself in a rented room. One day I saw a girl I'd known when we were children and asked what she was doing. She said she worked here and I came a couple of times to visit her. Then one day I said I'd like to help. They give me a room and food . . . and plenty to do.'

And so, talking and holding hands, each blaming the self and not the other, all lingering resentment over the past dissolved away and confidence in the future opened out.

'Well, Walpole, what about *your* life?'

'I've finished with it. I was going to get out of it even before we met . . . but *now*!'

'Now what?'

'Now I'm going to get free of all my ties and marry you. I'm going to do that whatever it costs and whatever I have to go through.'

And in the darkness which had now fallen they kissed and said good night.

Next morning Walpole went round to see Stephen and Cécile before going to work.

Cécile was delighted with his news: 'You and Regina were always meant for one another. I can't wait to go and see her.'

'Be careful!' Stephen urged. 'You know Duke – especially where his vanity's concerned. If Regina starts coming out into the world and he hears of it, nothing'll stop him trying to get hold of her.'

'I'll be careful,' Cécile assured them both. 'I'll only see her at the Refuge.'

But Stephen was still far from happy. 'I'm truly glad you and Regina have found each other – you've both been through enough. But when you talk of "marrying" that means divorcing Alicia. *Can* you? Will she give you a divorce? I doubt it. And Efunshile will go up the wall! As for what'll happen to the firm. . . . Just one thing, Walpole!'

'What's that?'

'Say nothing to Chukuma for the moment. You're going to have to tell him before long. But at least delay it all for a few weeks.

Some ten days later when Walpole repaired to Enugu, he arrived on a Sunday evening and went directly round to Basil's flat. Once again he was out, and when Walpole asked Nwanyieke where he was, she first in her hesitant English inquired if he were 'one of them'. When Walpole, not fully understanding her question, answered that he was, she showed him a piece of paper with a pencilled message: 'In the Hall. Science Lecture Room. 7.15.' Walpole knew the place referred to and had no doubt this must be a meeting of the group, and possibly that appearance of 'a leader' forecast in the leaflet. Despite his promise, Basil had told him nothing, which proved how deeply he must be involved, so obviously the best thing was to go along and find out all he could.

The Hall, which in fact was a technical college, stood on a hill at the edge of the town, and on driving up to the gateway and finding no one on guard, Walpole switched off his lights and drove quietly into the car park. One room on the ground floor was lit up and might well be guarded, so he entered from the back and on making his way towards the front of the building caught the raised tones of someone addressing an audience. Peering round a buttress, Walpole could see a thickset man, presumably a bodyguard, lounging in the doorway, so waited until the man started to pace down the corridor away from him, then followed softly, tried the handle of the door next to the one where the meeting was being held, and slipped inside. Had he been stopped he would say he was looking for the principal with an urgent message.

Connecting doors showed a gleam of light and Walpole tiptoed towards the crack, through which he could see the audience but not the speaker. Basil was there with Chike and Jackson, but he recognized no one else. They looked, he thought, like a bunch of intellectuals, men of thought perhaps, but hardly men of action – 'the only one I'd go hunting with is that thug outside the door. . .' . Though the speaker was not in view, his voice sounded vaguely familiar and as clear as though they were both in the same room. It was a cultivated voice and whoever it belonged to spoke with the flow of a practised orator.

What he was detailing were the sums stowed away by leading members of the government through corruption. He spoke precisely, naming contracts and percentages, with the amounts taken out of the country into Swiss and German hideouts, denouncing particularly those Ibo leaders who '. . .out of rivalry and hostility, not least against members of my own family, have entered into shameful alliance with emirs and sheikhs knighted by the British – who always have a weakness for desert dwellers in Nigeria as elsewhere.

'Together these two parties have followed that familiar precept: "Pluck the chicken while it is fat – good times do not last for ever!" I am telling these leaders and their parties here and now that they are right! The "good times" of evil men are coming to an end. Those uprisings you hear of are only the beginning. I tell you from my own knowledge that the alliance between North and East on which this whole government depends is far less strong than it appears. Many Ibos distrust the Northerners and have secretly set their hopes on an independent state – you, who live here in Enugu, must be aware of this. But such division, even if for a moment it succeeds, means the downfall of our nation and the end of all hopes for a great Nigeria.

'You will be told – I can hear the cynical voices now – "no action can succeed because army and police support the government". You should hear, as I often do, what these say among themselves! I tell you both are disaffected, eager for change. To the rank and file Independence has been a fraud, since their chances of promotion are just what they always were – *nil*! Among officers, the young and idealistic – of whom there are many – detest the corruption they are forced to protect. While the men at the top are angry for the opposite reason – that they get no share of the spoils. Today this government, which looks so secure, is cracking inwardly and can be overthrown with one strong push. But that push must be given by devoted, idealistic persons who will replace corruption with honesty, and substitute service for exploitation. A push, my friends, *is going to be given*! *Soon*! Make your minds up now, here together in this room – are you the men to give it?'

Walpole had guessed by now whose voice he had been listening to. This must be Richard Olakunle, and his presence here meant that the conspiracy had secured the vital support it needed, that of Action Group leaders, and above all – it would seem – of Richard's uncle, the great Chief Olakunle, revered throughout the whole Western Region simply as 'The Chief', who, being a hereditary ruler as well as renowned politician, could count on a huge following. Richard Olakunle was an orator and political figure in his own right, but volatile and unstable and had been rescued from more than one reckless escapade by his uncle's influence. But it was what his presence tonight implied that counted, not the man himself. Now, having finished his speech, he moved down from the platform – and therefore into Walpole's view – and walked round among the audience to receive congratulations and pledges of support: 'We're with you, Richard!' 'Count on us!' 'Just tell us what to do!'

Having remounted the platform, passing out of Walpole's vision, Olakunle asked if there were any man present not a hundred per cent in support of change. No voice was raised. When he asked whether silence meant they were all one hundred per cent determined on action to bring down the government, there was a roar of assent. The speaker then said that before 'Colonel X' set before them the plan of action, every man in the room must swear a double oath – first to maintain absolute secrecy over everything they heard or would hear; secondly to carry out whatever orders would be given 'by your own local leaders Chike Ajoku and Jackson Apara'. There was a bustle while they all took the two oaths, and then the invisible Colonel X began to talk, in a hush which grew more intense with the mounting concentration of his listeners. He spoke in the clipped tones of the parade ground, unlike Richard Olakunle's political oratory, and far more menacing.

'We Yorubas appear weak, but we have one weapon which the government forgets. The Federal Parliament meets in Lagos. It does not meet in Kano, Kaduna or Benin – but in Lagos, among the people who have most cause to hate it. Fortunate too, because nowhere except Lagos would the plan we will put into action be possible. As it is, that plan, framed for its situation, is certain of success.' There was a deeper hush as Colonel X slowly enunciated: 'We shall take over the capital by night with a small force, cutting it off from the remainder of the country. Since the heart of the city is an island connected to the mainland only by Carter Bridge, this is a task not only possible but easy for determined men. At the same time we shall also seize the two bridges to Ikoyi, thus sealing off the police barracks, also the bridge to Victoria Island. This completes the iron circle. The night chosen will be a big public occasion when the Prime Minister and most of his colleagues are obliged to be in Lagos. The actual night has already been decided, and it will be the last function these politicians will ever attend. We have reconnoitred all key points, and each man knows what action he must take. We shall seize the power station at Ijora, throw the main switch – and the whole capital will be in darkness. This will take place at two a.m. and our men, already in position, will allow no one in or out. Armed with automatic pistols and carrying powerful torches, they will be the only ones with sight in a country of the blind. During the blackout small hand-picked groups will surround State House and move in to capture the Prime Minister and all other ministers we can lay hands on. Similar trained groups will have taken over the Apapa naval base, the control tower at Ikeja airport and Lagos radio. No one will be able to leave the country, and no help from outside can come in.

'The instant this is achieved, our leader will go to the radio station at Ikoyi to announce he has assumed power and is now Prime Minister of the Federation of Nigeria. He will call upon army and police throughout the country to remain in barracks and await orders. The revolution will be over.'

He ended as abruptly as he had begun, and Richard Olakunle again took charge, thanking Colonel X for his 'convincing explanation' and added: 'We have only to follow this simple but brilliant manoeuvre – and in the course of a single night history will have been rewritten. The wrongs done to our people will be righted – and Nigeria restored to true democracy. But before we talk of your part in this coming triumph, have any of you any questions about the plan you have just heard? If you have doubts or hesitations, state them freely! If you see some weak point now is the time to clear this up!'

From the darkness and isolation of his room Walpole was half expecting the whole audience to rise as one man and shout objections, but the few tentative queries on side issues seemed to be raised more to show interest than out of horror or bewilderment. 'Have the new ministers who will take over been appointed yet?' 'Have arrangements been made for recognition of the new regime by foreign countries?' 'About

finance – are there sufficient funds in hand to cover costs?' To
such inquiries Richard Olakunle gave reassuring answers, and
then declared: 'If there are no further questions, we will turn to
your own share in the task. I leave this to your leader – Chike
Ajoku.'

Walpole could see Chike step out of the audience and after a
few moments heard his sarcastic tones: 'That moment when
our new Prime Minister – whose name must be familiar to
each of one of us – the moment he broadcasts from Ikoyi is the
moment we all await, for then we shall spring to life, as will
many other groups throughout the country. That will be the
moment of truth! And of surprise for many persons who now
think themselves secure! By then each man present here will
have been assigned his task – and the tools to complete it.
These tools will be brought to us shortly by one of our number
well accustomed to handling heavy vehicles. They will be
stored in a place already prepared, known only to myself and
Jackson Apara.

'What will our long-awaited task consist of? We shall kill or
capture those political leaders in our region who support the
present regime, and are therefore partners in its crimes. There
are certain others it would be dangerous to leave alive – who
will therefore *not* be left alive. We shall seize the radio station in
the town and declare support for the new leaders. We shall
place our own men in charge of government offices and
printing presses. Being by then the legal government, the
police will come at once under our control and take instructions from us. You have all sworn to carry out the orders given
by myself and Jackson, and so one – or at most two – days
before action starts I shall contact each man, allot your
assignments and hand over your weapons. You will not wait
long before using them! One final order – and it's crucial! GIVE
NO PRIVATE WARNINGS! Let fall no hints. Do not take any
precautions or make special preparations. Our families and
friends must take their chance – as *we* all have to do. That is all!'

Walpole was watching Basil's face during Chike's talk, and
it was clear from his glance of recognition at the mention of
'heavy vehicles' that he had been flattered or cajoled into
accepting the most dangerous assignment – that of conveying
the group's supply of weapons, either from a central dump or
from some frontier post where they would be handed over.

The meeting was now breaking up, and Walpole waited
until the last footsteps died away down the corridor before

slipping out and walking over to the car park. For an hour he sat there, appalled by what he had heard. It seemed inconceivable that grown men, many with political and a few with military experience, should have entered upon so reckless a conspiracy. Equally astounding was its acceptance by an audience who, if not practical men were at least intelligent, yet were ready to hazard their lives and freedom without asking even one of the obvious questions. These men who were to cut off the capital by seizing bridges, power stations and the rest – how many would be needed? A minimum surely, of three or four hundred. But how could so many men have been found and trained, even in a neighbouring country, without the authorities getting wind of it? Without their families talking of where they had gone? Without one or two dissatisfied recruits betraying the plot to the authorities? How, when the day came, were the men to be armed, brought into Lagos, concealed and put into position at the right moment? Yet even if all went well and the hand-picked group – 'the only men with sight in the country of the blind' – *did* actually kidnap or kill the Prime Minister and his colleagues, where did that leave the plotters? By daybreak they would be tired, unfed, their torches and pistols useless if the army moved in with tanks and motorized vehicles.

Could it be that the conspirators had already secured the backing of army and police? Evidently not, since if the army supported them they could seize the capital direct without any of these extravagant manoeuvres. And even if, which seemed unthinkable, the tiny force held Lagos for a few days, they would still be doomed, since the only support they could count on in the region would be of groups like the one that had just dispersed, committing murders and attempting to seize key points. . . . How many of them, Walpole wondered, even knew how to handle the weapons they would be given?

The more he thought over details of the scheme, and the more clearly he recalled the chief speaker's words, the more certain he felt that voluble, genial Richard Olakunle ought to have been certified years ago. . . . 'The address the new Prime Minister will speak is already written. Once that has been delivered the army and police will owe allegiance to him alone'. . . . 'Recognition of the new regime abroad? We have friends in half a dozen embassies who will see to that'. . . 'Money? I assure you it is in good supply. It would never do to go broke just when all the action starts!'

Such statements and answers to questions should have been enough to freeze the blood of the most ardent conspirator, and certainly, thought Walpole, they freeze mine. But if the conspirators are crazy and Richard Olakunle round the bend, then maddest of all must be the one on whom they are all relying, the great man in the background, 'the Chief' himself. He must be familiar with his nephew's character, can hardly help knowing what he is up to now. Yet he is staking his position, prestige and the lives of followers, by backing a scheme as surely doomed to failure as any in the history of conspiracy.

42
Confrontations

Walpole thought long and hard about what he should do after learning the conspirators' plans. If he went to the police Basil would be arrested along with the others, and he thought it likely he might himself be detained and cross-questioned. So far as the ministers were concerned, they were in no immediate danger since the Federal Parliament was not in session and they were dispersed about the country. The nearest occasion for which they seemed likely to reassemble and a coup to become possible was a visit by Pandit Nehru still some little while ahead.

Meanwhile there was no one with whom he could discuss the situation. The first person he would have gone to would have been Mr Chukuma, who was the last he could talk to in the present case. Nor could he tell Stephen, since this would only put his friend into the same uncomfortable position as himself, that of possessing a dangerous secret and not knowing what to do about it. As for trying yet again to persuade Basil to extricate himself, he dismissed the idea as impracticable. Committed as he was, he would certainly pass on to fellow conspirators any warnings Walpole gave – the consequence of which might be to precipitate violent action, since if the conspirators were incompetent they were also ruthless. In the end he simply wrote a note and pushed it under Basil's door, saying he presumed Basil was keeping his side of their agreement, but that if he should find himself in unexpected difficulty he could contact him at his home phone number, which he gave. If Basil rang there, he should be extremely careful what he said, and must on no account ring the office on anything but the firm's business. He urged him to memorize the number and immediately destroy the note.

Meantime Walpole had other matters to worry about closer home. When Alicia returned he meant to face her and her father with his determination to divorce or be divorced by Alicia and in due course marry Regina. He would, he knew, be met by a blank refusal. Alicia was not going to surrender her status as married woman: Wilson might be well enough as lover, but as a husband his rating among her friends would not be high. Efunshile, having so recently – and so expensively – got Alicia off his hands, would assent to no arrangement which would hand her back. Genial as friend, as an opponent he would be ruthless. All that could be hoped for was that in time Alicia would become sick of a marriage which all her friends would know to be a sham, and that either Wilson or someone else would then seem preferable.

Difficult as his situation was, there was one aspect which afforded hope. Walpole's value, both as husband and son-in-law, derived from his success; he was well-off, almost rich, and the director of a fast-growing enterprise. But if he dropped out of the firm, or if the firm without the Chief's support started to crumble, a new situation would arise. Walpole poor and jobless would offer a very different prospect to them both. Until Alicia returned he could take no action, but with Chukuma, he felt, he must have the matter out without delay. Once he had spoken to Alicia and she told her father, the news might quickly spread. A partner had the right to be informed by him and not to hear it from someone else as rumour. Accordingly, a day or two later, having informed Stephen of his intention, he called a meeting in the board-room.

'Well,' Mr Chukuma began, 'I see there's no regular agenda. But it's you, Walpole, who brought us here – so suppose you get on with it.'

'I've bad news for you,' Walpole said. 'Alicia gets back next week. When she does I shall ask for a divorce. She'll take this badly, and it's bound to infuriate her father. The Chief can't prevent our working out existing contracts – but when they're done, we'll get no more. And if he's bloody-minded he may make things difficult with other government departments too.'

'Hey – not so fast!' said Mr Chukuma. 'One thing at a time. What's this about divorce? I don't think either of us supposed your marriage was a grand romantic passion – any more than any other marriage. But it was a practical arrangement with solid advantages for both sides. Why are you wanting to break all that up?'

'For me our "practical arrangement" has been a disaster – which is why I've been spending so much time in Enugu. But I put up with it for all our sakes. Now someone has come back into my life whom I want to marry. So despite those "solid advantages", I intend to leave Alicia. She will, of course, tell Efunshile – with consequences we can all anticipate.'

'Someone in your life?' said Mr Chukuma meditatively. 'Someone you love and want to marry? . . . Well, I'm sure we're both glad a new happiness has come into your life. But I suggest we keep our heads on, all the same. Love can be important, I'm aware, when one is young – but how does divorce come into the picture? Won't this woman of yours live with you unless you marry her? I should think that rather unlikely, Walpole.'

'No,' said Walpole, 'it isn't a case of what she won't do for me. It's what I mean to do for her.'

'A noble sentiment – which does credit to your heart at least. You've "fallen in love" – if you don't mind the ridiculous cliché – so you want to give her everything you've got. But let's think the position out a little, in her interest as well as yours.'

'Go ahead!'

'If you get divorced from Alicia in the way you propose, "everything you've got" will amount to very little. D'you mind my referring in front of Stephen to your marriage contract?'

'Not a bit.'

'As you know, I drew that document up on your behalf – and though I did the best for you I could, Efunshile's terms were extremely tough. You had to settle pretty well all you possess on Alicia. Consequently, if the marriage ends without further bargaining, you've got damn little to offer this young woman except your heart of gold and your two strong arms. Is that really what you want – and what will make her happy?'

'Yes. I realize that by ending my marriage I become a poor man – or very nearly.'

'A fine gesture too, my friend! What I'm saying is that it's needless. Even harmful.'

'What's the alternative?'

'Don't be in such a hurry! Your wife, by all accounts, has a romantic interest of her own. Don't rush in and beg her to divorce you, play it the other way round. Keep cool and keep your eyes open – before very long Alicia may be the one who wants the marriage ended. . . . You won't get back all you've signed away, but you could certainly expect to get something back. Then too, instead of breaking with Efunshile – and landing us all in a very tight spot – you'll be doing him a favour, covering up for his daughter while she transfers her affections to . . . wherever else she is transferring them. Isn't that a more rewarding proposition all round than the one you outlined? Be patient, Walpole, that's all I'm suggesting – and everything can work out as you want.'

'I appreciate your advice,' Walpole answered. 'And if my life were a business deal, I'd act as you say. But it isn't. I've met someone I love. I want to marry and take care of her. I value my property since I worked hard to get it – but if I could save the lot by staying married to Alicia for another year, I'd still walk out of the house tomorrow morning.'

Mr Chukuma scratched his grey and curly head. 'I have to say this, Walpole, and I trust you won't take offence – but these naïve ideas about life you're putting forward don't sound like you at all. They sound like something out of a girl's love story or as though you've been seeing too many romantic films. . . .'

'What d'you mean?'

'In the past – if rumour's correct – there's been no lack of what's called "love interest" in your life. I dare say you've had as many affairs as three normal men such as Stephen and myself, but you've never allowed your interest in a woman to cut across your career. In fact I've admired the way you secured the best of both worlds. But what you're telling us contradicts all this. You say you've met someone for whom you'll throw up *everything* – including the firm's success and the interests of your friends? To me, Walpole, this is a transformation – and an unwelcome one. May I inquire who *is* this person to whom everything has to be sacrificed?'

'You know her and have met her. Though not recently – Regina.'

Mr Chukuma started visibly. 'You mean Regina the show girl who used to live with Duke Ombo?'

'Yes.'

'Regina? Duke Ombo's Regina?' Mr Chukuma repeated, peering closely into Walpole's face as though for symptoms of mental deterioration. 'And it's because of *her* you're planning this wholesale upheaval of your life? Have I got this right?'

'You have.'

'And in order to marry this woman – a beautiful and talented woman, but a woman of the world and not a simple schoolgirl – you're prepared, even determined, to destroy your career and ruin this firm in which your friends are involved?'

'I am. But I haven't called this meeting to get advice about my personal life, I've called it to let you know what to expect – so that we can plan how to meet a business difficulty.'

This mild rebuff did not go down well with Mr Chukuma. 'And what I'm trying to tell *you*, my friend, though I seem to have wasted my time, is that the difficulty itself can be avoided. I'm telling you that, if you only exercise a little restraint, you can get what you want without blowing the place up. And I must add that, if you refuse to wait, say six months or a year, to see how things work out, then you'll be acting in a way that's both irresponsible and selfish.'

But at this Stephen, who had kept silent rather than interrupt the others, broke in: 'That's not true of Walpole. It's a setback for the firm if he ends his marriage. But we can't expect him to go on with it, even for six months, just to help us maintain profits. And in a time like this to want to look after the woman he means to marry isn't irresponsible or selfish. On the contrary – I admire him for it.'

'Well, I don't,' Mr Chukuma answered roundly. 'To be prepared to break up a business on which a lot of people's living depends for the sake of an emotional satisfaction, is just what I've said it is – selfish and irresponsible! Besides being unnecessary.'

'I'm sorry you see it that way,' said Walpole. 'But I shall not change my mind.'

'And *I'm* not asking you to change it,' said Stephen firmly.

'I see I'm up against you both,' Mr Chukuma replied. 'Two romantics who consider "love" must carry all before it, against one sane man who believes emotions should be kept under control. My advice to you, Walpole, is to take a holiday – go off somewhere by yourself, and when you come back we'll talk about this again. But as regards the business of the firm, I'm saying – as chairman, that I accept nothing that's been said here today as final.'

'And what I'm telling you,' said Walpole, 'is that it *is* final! And I didn't expect to have to tell you, Chukuma, of all people, that it's better to face a situation squarely than to sit back and hope it'll vanish over the next six months.'

Mr Chukuma had been controlling his mounting exasperation with difficulty for the last half-hour, and this was more than he could take. 'And I didn't expect to have to tell you, Walpole, of all people, not to act like a complete bloody fool! As a man, you ought to have more sense – to say nothing of what you owe your friends!'

And gathering his papers together, Mr Chukuma stormed out of the room.

On the evening Alicia returned, Walpole said nothing to her immediately. She was tired and visibly depressed, probably because an enjoyable holiday was over and the future looked uncertain. But next morning he asked for an hour's talk before she went out.

'All right then - talk if you must! But if it's about your having met up with your old flame Regina, you can save your breath. I know all about her – kind friends kept me informed about all you've been up to.'

'Just as they did for me about you and your cousin Wilson.'

Alicia gasped. 'When? What d'you mean?'

'Months ago. Long before you went to join him at Ibadan.'

'You never said anything to me!'

'Why should I? It was your affair. I don't want to talk about him now. It's you and me we must discuss.'

'About you and me there's nothing to discuss.'

'Oh yes, there is.'

'Say what you want to say then. I haven't got all day.'

'I want to end our marriage – but I'd like it to end by agreement if we can.'

Alicia laughed. 'Of course you would! That would make things nice and easy for you, wouldn't it?'

'They can't be easy, but they needn't be worse than they have to be. Tell me honestly – d'you want to marry your cousin? Or is that just an affair?'

'What's it got to do with you? If you're imagining some kind of cosy deal – you go off with Regina because I want to marry someone else – you can think again. Ours was a business arrangement from the start – and it still is. So keep to your agreement like a man and don't bother me with your emotional hang-ups.'

'It's true our marriage has been pretty much of a business arrangement,' Walpole replied. 'What I'm telling you now is that I want to end it.'

'*You* want to end it – that's rich! It's for me to say whether it'll end or not – and what I'm telling you, Walpole, is that it won't. You're not much of a husband, but you're better than no husband at all. And we don't have much of a life, but it's better than the one I was leading with my father. As for wanting to marry Wilson – that's a matter for him and me. If we decide one day we want to marry, I'll let you know.'

'In that case, Alicia, I'm getting out.'

She looked at him with horror. 'You mean you'll leave this house? You couldn't do that – even *you* couldn't. Take all the freedom you want – I've never tried to stop you – but you *must* go on living here. . . . There has to be some show of decency, some proper appearance – for both our sakes.'

'Our marriage is over, Alicia. I'm not staying on.'

Alicia glared at him and then burst out: 'That bitch! I suppose she'll take nothing less – and you're so infatuated you must give her what she wants. Well, she may injure me – but she's finished you! You realize what this means?'

'What *what* means?'

'You'll get no more contracts from my father – don't think it! And it isn't just his own board, he knows how to spread the poison – haven't I seen him do it? Your firm'll be finished for government work in every region. You'll be bankrupt before long, my friend, have you thought of that? And what's your whore going to say when she's got a down-and-out on her hands hunting for a job, instead of a rich man paying her bills and buying presents?'

'That won't be your worry, Alicia.'

'Think again, Walpole, think again! We all get into states at times, but there's no need to make a fool of yourself publicly – no need to destroy your firm. Tell the girl a lie or two – you've

told a few in your day when it suited you. Tell her you'll
marry her when you can, but ask if meantime she wants to see
you ruined? Exercise that Walpole self-protection we all know
about – and come in out of the rain!'

'Yes. I'm sorry about damaging the firm. I've spoken to
them already.'

'And what did they say?'

'They're upset, naturally. But I haven't told them the whole
story.'

'Of course you haven't, Walpole! Trust you! Always keep
something up your sleeve. . . . Well, what haven't you told
them? Or aren't you going to tell me either?'

'What I haven't told them is that if my staying on harms the
firm, I shall resign.'

'Resign?' She looked at him with incredulity. 'You mean
give up your job – your directorship? But that's your whole
income?'

'Yes.'

'How *dare* you resign?' Alicia's disbelief turned into blazing
rage. 'How dare you put a stop to my income without
consulting me? You've no right to do this on your own! I'm
your wife – you can't just walk out of your job and leave me
penniless! It isn't even legal. You're compelled to support me
properly!'

'Stop being hysterical, Alicia! You're not being left penniless. You know I settled pretty well everything I had on you
when we got married. You can keep this house too – provided
you agree to divorce me.'

'And if I don't?'

'I leave at once. You can go on living here. I'll give you a
reasonable allowance out of my income as long as I have one.
And I shall consult my lawyers about the prospects of
divorcing *you*. You've given me quite as much cause as I've
given you.'

'You'll get no divorce out of me, Walpole, so you can tell
that to Regina. You're going to wish you'd never met this
woman, and she's going to wish she'd never set eyes on you –
and before long she'll be telling you so!'

The storm raged on until Alicia, looking at her watch, said she
had to get dressed and go out. 'But you're to do nothing before
the weekend! That's the least you owe me. You'll come with me
to see my father – I look forward to *that* interview – and you'll go
on living here until we've talked to him. Is that understood?'

'Stop giving orders! If you want me to come to see your father with you, I will. And if you ask me not to leave this house before the weekend, I agree. I don't promise one day longer.'

When she came back in the afternoon having seen her father, Alicia was a good deal calmer. He could not see Walpole until the weekend, she said, being heavily involved with work heaped on him by the Prime Minister in connection with the coming visit of Pandit Nehru. But it emerged that the Chief had spoken sharply to his daughter, ordering her not to fuss. He had also, it seemed, warned her that her affair with Wilson was common knowledge and her position a lot less secure than she supposed. He would speak to Walpole by himself and later, if necessary, Alicia and he could come along together, the implication being that this was something the two men could settle if she would only give them the opportunity.

Alicia ended by saying: 'I was told to give you a message – a piece of advice.'

'What was that?'

'We should neither of us leave the house for the next three days.'

'Why ever not?'

'Something's happening in the political world. I don't know what, and he wouldn't tell me – perhaps to do with all these rumours of a plot. Anyway, the government intends to act – there'll be a round-up of suspects and the police will be out in force. Some people may resist, so there's likely to be shooting, and for a day or two we'll be safer indoors. That's his warning anyway. I mean to act on it. What you do's your affair.'

'Thanks,' said Walpole. 'It's good of your father to let me know.'

Next day, despite the warning, Walpole went to work as usual. He did not see Mr Chukuma but had a talk with Stephen, told him of his conversation with Alicia and ended: 'I also said something to her which I didn't say in the boardroom the other day.'

'What's that?'

'If the Chief turns nasty, and it's going to help things, I'm ready to leave the firm.'

'Leave the firm? But without you there wouldn't *be* a firm!'

'Oh yes, there would – and it may well be better off. You and Chukuma can run the financial side perfectly well, and you can always hire a man with know-how to drive the construction work along.'

'I can't speak for Chukuma,' said Stephen, 'but for myself, rather than lose you, I'd give up "political business" altogether and cut the firm back to what it used to be. We'd make enough to live on without all the anxiety.'

'Would Chukuma agree? I doubt it.'

'I don't know. But if he doesn't, let him take the political business and set up on his own. Form a new company – we can make an amicable split. But let you and me stick together, even if it means going back to where we started.'

Later that evening Walpole went round to see Regina. He told her what had happened and said he was sure that if they held on to one another, all would work out in the end. He repeated what Efunshile had said about a possible political coup, and begged her on no account to go out for the next few days.

'I won't go out if you won't,' Regina told him. 'I've a lot more cause to be anxious about you than you have to worry over me.'

43
Behind Bars

Soon after Walpole first started visiting Enugu, there had occurred a riotous session of the Western Region parliament in Ibadan which the federal government had used as excuse to declare a State of Emergency, suspend parliamentary government throughout the region, confine party leaders to their homes and replace them by an Administrator with special powers. So much was official and generally known, but everything else was a mass of rumour which varied from day to day, though it was common knowledge that the burnings and overturnings of vehicles continued in some towns, and that attacks on government-appointed chiefs and their paid bodyguards were increasing in country areas. Everywhere there was tension as men waited, with anxiety or hope, to see whether the federal government or its opponents would act first. To Walpole, the Chief's warning that Alicia and he should stay indoors over the next few days made it apparent that the government was taking the initiative, and as he sat in his study on what he expected to be the final weekend in his home, he spent much time listening to the radio. The Chief had arranged to see him on Wednesday morning, so between now and then whatever was due to happen would take place.

Monday was the nation's Independence Day, and on the Sunday evening Walpole heard a dramatic broadcast by the Prime Minister in which he claimed the police had uncovered a plot to overthrow the federal government by force, that three of those most deeply involved had fled the country, and that other guilty men were at the moment being rounded up. The army and the police remained completely loyal, the situation was in hand, and all good citizens should be on their guard against the enemies of the state and rally to the support of their democratically-elected government.

Walpole rang Stephen and Mr Chukuma, who had both heard the broadcast but knew no more than he did, apart from the fact that police and troops were everywhere in the city, and that posters denouncing political leaders who had fled their homes were already going up in the streets. Since Monday was a holiday the directors would in any case not be going to the office, but agreed to meet as usual on Tuesday unless anything happened in the meantime.

Anxious and uneasy, Walpole did not feel like sleep and was sitting in his armchair trying to focus his mind on reading when the phone in the study half-rang and then stopped. He picked up the receiver but could hear no voice. A couple of minutes later the same thing happened again, and when he raised the receiver there was only silence, so that he asked angrily: 'Who's there? What d'you want? If you don't want anything, ring off!'

'Is that you, Walpole?'

'Of course it is – who's that?'

'Someone you told to ring if I need help. I do.'

'Where are you?'

'Not far off. Can I come and see you?'

'Are you being followed?'

'Not as far as I know.'

Walpole considered. There was no reason why his house should be being watched.

'If you're not being followed, come here. If you are, I'll meet you somewhere outside.'

'No. I don't think so. See you soon.'

A quarter of an hour later Basil came to the door and Walpole, on the watch to let him in without anyone noticing, led him to the study.

'I must get out – out of the country. You *have* to help me, Walpole.'

'If I can – but start at the beginning. Why're you here?'

'I was in the plot with Chike and the rest. I lied to you about it . . . no good going into all that now . . . yesterday I was sent to the border, to Idiroko, with a lorry to collect a load of arms.'

'Where's it now? The lorry?'

'Up the road, man. Out of sight – I put it in some trees.'

'Where're you supposed to take it?'

'Enugu. But I spotted all the cops about so I stopped and phoned Chike. He ordered me not to bring the stuff there or they'd all be dished. They got a tip-off in the afternoon that they were to be picked up. Jackson's gone and Chike was just getting out – he didn't say where to. Just told me to do the best for myself and slammed the receiver down. I didn't know what the hell to do, then I remembered your saying I might call you if I had to – so here I am.'

'Sure you weren't followed from Idiroko?'

Basil swallowed. 'Pretty sure, man. Not a hundred per cent – but I think not.'

A frightening thought struck Walpole: 'You're not using one of our firm's vehicles, are you?'

Basil shook his head. 'It's hired.'

'Will the police have the number?'

'No reason why they should.'

'Is there much stuff on board?'

'A good bit – she handles heavy.'

'How's it labelled?'

'Holy Bibles – addressed to one of the churches in a suburb.'

'Okay then, Basil. Here's what you do. Take my car, drive *back* to Idiroko and put it in a garage – there can't be many, and I'll find out tomorrow where it is. Don't let them think you're dropping it. Complain about the brakes – say they aren't handling properly. Say you're staying the night in Idiroko but *must* have the car in the morning to come back into Lagos. Make a fuss! Have you got that?'

Basil nodded and Walpole went on: 'Idiroko's a turning point. Lots of lorries from Ghana and up-coast bring stuff in, unload and push off back. Get talking to the drivers in the chop bars round the square. Will the man who brought your load in still be there?'

'He might. If not I'll find someone else. I know these drivers and their ways – I've been one. If I had money there's no problem.'

'Good. Then get one of them to hide you in his load and take you to Accra. I'll give you money, but from Accra you're on your own. Before you leave, phone your father and tell him the truth. In twenty-four hours he'll know everything – he'd best hear it from you.'

Ever since the rumours started Walpole had taken two precautions, to keep the car full of petrol and to have a good sum of money in the house. He took £200 out of his desk, meaning to give it all to Basil, but instead, acting on impulse, divided it into halves and handed him one.

'There's a hundred. That should see you through.'

'Thanks, man. It will.' Basil put a couple of notes into his pocket and then, taking off his shoes, stowed the rest inside his socks.

'Can't be too careful! Don't want to waste your cash.'

Following Basil's example, Walpole did the same and hid his share.

'Surely you're not coming too, man? You've got no cause to clear out.'

'No. But I have to shift that lorry.'

'Where you taking it?'

'Can't be left here – right on my doorstep. I suppose it's an Enugu registration. It's known I go to and from there all the time.'

'Christ, man! I hadn't thought of that. What'll you do?'

'Run it part way into town and ditch it on waste land. If there's no one about I'll strip off number plates and licence and bury them.'

'You're taking a chance, Walpole – you know that?'

'Don't waste time talking, Basil. D'you need a drink – or do we go?'

The two men drove up the road to near the trees in which Basil had left the lorry, got out and approached the place on foot – but there was no one around and after they had gone over the controls together, Basil took the car and set off for

Idiroko. Once he was out of hearing, Walpole started the engine, switched on the lights and drove the lorry back on to the road. All went well until he got out on to the main airport road, where there appeared to be police every hundred yards. Never mind, he thought, I'll take the first turning off, dump this lot and walk home. I can be back in my study in a couple of hours.

Ahead of him in the road a light was waving, probably some crazy cyclist, and he pulled out to pass. But now he saw it was police and they waved him down.

'Where you from?'

Walpole hadn't thought this one out, but answered quickly: 'Airport dee-po.'

'What you carryin' back in there?'

'Bibles.'

'Bibles, man. What de hell. . . .'

'Bibles. Holy Bibles. Done you never hear of de good book – dey's for a bishop an' his flock.'

'Where you go for take dese Holy Bibles?'

'Mornin' I take dem for Enugu. But now I go git myself one big drink.'

'Okay. If dese bin Holy Bibles, you free go piss yo'self,' said one, while the other went round to the back and climbed in over the tailboard. Walpole could hear him moving around, muttering: 'Dese bin de damn heavies' Bibles – ' then suddenly a shout. Walpole made a move to thrust the lever into gear but the cop had already drawn his pistol: 'You stayin' still, my frien'.'

A few minutes later Walpole was in the back of a police car speeding into Lagos with siren blaring. He had handcuffs on his wrists and swelling bruises on his head.

The interrogation centre appeared to be in a school, a range of low buildings enclosed by a high barbed-wire fence and the whole area lit by arc lights strung on wires. There were troops on guard at the entrance through which lorries and cars were pouring in, stopping for recognition or papers to be examined, and then driving on up to the main buildings to disgorge bedraggled prisoners. The hot night air was full of uproar, revving of engines, hooting, shouting of orders, cries and pleadings . . . blinding light and deafening noise. Walpole was hauled out of the car and pushed through into an entrance hall where police officers at half a dozen desks were taking down particulars. Once his name, address, details of the lorry and its contents had been recorded, with the names of those who arrested him, they were sent back to carry on searching and Walpole was taken down a corridor and thrust through a door which was double locked behind him.

The room in which he found himself was large, completely devoid even of a bench, and the windows had been newly bricked up almost to the top. There were about twenty people in the room, all men, and the stench hit him like a blow in the face. It was mainly the smell of sweat, not the sweat due to exertion but the unforgettable acrid smell of sweat wrung out of men by terror. Mingled with it were the stinks of diarrhoea and vomit, for the men were locked in and the only provision for their bodily functions were a couple of overflowing buckets in a corner.

On entering the room Walpole wondered for a moment whether its occupants were still alive. None of them looked up or moved. They crouched or lay around, not close together but dotted around the room as though they were pawns or counters in some dreadful game, or as though each had marked himself off a tiny space to sit enclosed in private suffering. They did not look as though they had sat down but as though they had collapsed, leaning forward with bent heads on outstretched arms, or curled up on their sides like question marks or unborn babies. Around some the boards were dark and damp with urine, blood or both, and of the faces he glimpsed as he moved across the room most were battered and blood-stained. Walpole found a square yard as close to a window as he could and sat down. Apart from the noise from outside, there was silence broken by an occasional whimper and one voice which every minute or so muttered: 'Jesus Christ Almighty, Jesus Christ Almighty . . .' in a tone which might either have been prayer or agonized denunciation. Walpole tried to think and frame up a story of some kind, but the stench and a sense of the violence pervading the whole building made coherent thoughts impossible. There was only one shared thought in every mind – when would he be sent for and what would happen to him when he was?

Walpole had not long to wait. A lorry load of arms was a prize catch, and news of it must have quickly reached the officers in charge, for within half an hour his name was bellowed from the door and he was pushed down the corridor to a smaller room, in which two senior officers and a man in civilian clothes sat at a desk. Once again particulars were taken down and then the questioning began.

Where had the arms come from?

Who handed them over to him?

Where was he taking them?

Who were his accomplices?

Who were the leaders who had given him his orders?

Walpole replied that the lorry had been dumped on him by a man who had absconded. He had only been driving it for ten minutes when he was picked up. He had been told the cargo was Holy Bibles, which he had undertaken to deliver for a friend.

Who then was the friend?

Where were the Bibles to be delivered?

When he refused to answer the first and had no satisfactory answer to the second, he was struck a heavy blow on the head from the police standing behind him and further blows for each refusal.

After a minute the officer in charge said: 'I advise you to tell me what you know. This is only the beginning. We have plenty of time. Yours is an important case. What you've said so far is nonsense. You'd better now start telling us the truth.'

'I believe the lorry was going to Enugu,' Walpole managed to get out. 'Who it was going to I don't know, nor where it came from. But it wasn't I who brought it. You can prove I was at home till half an hour before I was picked up. The houseboys saw me. They know I've been at home all the last day or two. The directors in my office know I was in Lagos yesterday – we talked over business on the phone. I know nothing of any conspiracy, apart from what the Prime Minister said on the radio.'

The officers were about to resume their questions when the man in plain clothes looked closely at Walpole.

'What you say your name is?'

'Walpole Abiose.'

'What's the name of your firm?'

'Balogun and Abiose.'

'What was your wife's name before you married?'

'Alicia Efunshile.'

'Chief Efunshile's daughter?'

'Yes.'

The man in plain clothes looked at the other two and shook his head. He whispered to them for a moment and then went out, obviously to check up. When he returned in a few minutes, he asked Walpole how long he had been married, where the marriage took place, how long since he had last spoken to Chief Efunshile, what were the names of the directors of his firm and what business they had in Enugu. The answers evidently corresponded to his notes, because he asked again: 'Who was this man from whom you took the lorry?'

'I can't answer that.'

'Where did he hand it over to you?'

'In a clump of trees not far from my home. There must be wheeltracks on the ground.'

'Why did you take it from him?'

'I wanted to help him.'

'But if it contained Holy Bibles, what cause had he to worry?'

'He told me his load was Bibles – but I guessed it wasn't. I didn't want the lorry left near my house. I was going to dump it somewhere in the city on waste ground.'

'The lorry has an Enugu registration. Did it come from there?'

'I don't know. It may have done.'

'Did this man who left the lorry come from Enugu?'

'He may have done.'

'Your firm does a lot of business in Enugu?'

'Yes.'

'This man who left the lorry – does he work for your firm in Enugu?'

Silence.

The officers clearly did not like having the inquiry taken out of their hands in this way, and Walpole could hear one of them object that time was being wasted when the lives of ministers might be at stake. Driving a lorry full of arms proved this man a conspirator and they should get all he knew out of him without delay. The plain-clothes man pointed to the dial of his watch, spoke inaudibly for a minute or two to the officers, and went out. From his action Walpole guessed the sense of what he had said. The prisoner had important friends. His story might be true. It would not do to knock him about too badly until more was known. He himself was going to leave the room for a short period during which they could try whatever they liked. But when he came back the prisoner had better not have been injured beyond recognition or repair.

Walpole set his teeth to endure what he reckoned could hardly last more than half an hour.

It was a tiny cell in which he found himself a few hours later, about the smallest space into which a man can be fitted, he thought, before his final fitting-out of wood. He had no idea of the time, since his watch and other personal belongings had been taken from him, but he reckoned it might be between three and five in the morning. Where he was he did not know, but could remember being taken from the interrogation centre in a van, lying on the floor with others in the same state as himself. After a short journey they were hauled out again and dragged down corridors. On the way, the others seemed to disappear, and Walpole, the last of all, was thrust into this cell. Inside was nothing put a pallet of planks and a bucket. There was one small window high up in the wall. A low-power bulb shed a dim light from behind thick glass, and the heavy black-painted door was reinforced by bars. Whatever time it was the prison continued to be full of noise. Doors clanged, locks were turned, bolts shot and orders shouted; there were also continual yells and moaning. After a while there began a subdued tapping from the cells on either side which Walpole, not yet having learned the language common to all prisons, could not interpret, but tapped back as a sign of comrade-ship. . . .

After perhaps half an hour Walpole, who had been leaning against the wall in one corner of his cell, expecting to be kept awake all night by the noise and the pain all over his head and body, sat down on the pallet, keeled over and dropped instantly into a stunned sleep as though he had fallen down a well.

44
Treasonable but Insane

Throughout the whole of the next day Walpole sat or lay in a stunned daze. The cell door was opened only twice, once for a bowl of some greasy fluid to be pushed in and once for a mug of what might have been either tea or soup with a hunk of greyish bread. None of it could he touch, but towards evening his requests for water were answered with a jugful. The noise by now was dying down, there was less shouting, less trampling along corridors and a sense that prison life was coming back to normal, whatever that might be. On his second night Walpole slept and woke and slept again fitfully. The tea he was given next morning looked less greasy and he drank some of it but his teeth ached too much for him to eat the bread. Not long afterwards the lock was turned again.

'Git' yo'self ready for questions. Dey fetchin' you one-time,' the prison officer ordered, and Walpole supposed the whole dreadful process of interrogation was to be repeated. However when he was summoned after a further hour it was by a different officer who advised: 'Make yo'self clean. De guv'nor done send for you.'

There was no mirror in the cell, no soap or towel, but Walpole did what he could to make himself presentable with a bowl of water and a rag brought by the officer, and was then led out of the great central hall with its landings, staircases, and rows of cells like a gigantic honeycomb, and on down yet another of the many corridors he had followed in the last forty-eight hours, to a room with a table and a chair on either side, where he found, not the governor nor the interrogating panel he was dreading, but the welcome face of Mr Chukuma. The officer indicated that Walpole should sit on one side of the table and Mr Chukuma on the other, but Mr Chukuma rushed towards Walpole to embrace him. Then noticing his swollen lips and discoloured cheeks, he burst out: 'Oh God, Walpole, what's happened to you?'

'Another time,' said Walpole with a glance at the prison officer, who motioned them to sit on opposite sides of the table, and then, impressed by the lawyer's air of riches and importance, took his stand at a discreet distance by the door.

'What brought you here?' Walpole went on. 'I suppose Basil phoned?'

'He did indeed – a few hours ago. But it wasn't that which brought me at this hour. It was Regina.'

'Regina? Not in this place, for God's sake?'

'No. She's outside in the car. My wife's with her.'

'Is she all right?'

'Of course she is – only distracted till she knows you're

safe. . . .' and he went on to describe how very early that same morning, Stephen and Cécile, hearing knocking and a cry, had found Regina on their doorstep. . . . 'Ever since the Prime Minister's broadcast she'd worried about you and listened to all the radio bulletins. For the first twenty-four hours there were only accounts of round-ups, movements of troops into Lagos and so on – but from yesterday evening they started giving lists of names, and in one of them around midnight Regina heard yours. She tried to phone Cécile, but all the phones had been cut off, so she walked out into the street and set off for the middle of town to find a taxi. She was lucky indeed to find an honest man who brought her to Cécile and Stephen. Of course they took her in and looked after her, but what she wanted was to get hold of me to do something for you. With the phones cut I couldn't be contacted, but at daybreak Stephen brought her round. She wasted no time in giving me my orders – to find out where you were, go there right away – and get you out!'

Walpole laughed as well as his swollen face allowed: 'You said that might be difficult?'

'Worse, my friend, much worse. . . . I'm ashamed to remember it. I did indeed say it would be impossible to do anything quickly. But I added that if you'd been such a fool as to involve yourself in political trouble, then either you or your father-in-law must get you out of it. . . . It was cruel and thoughtless. But I was still angry with you – and not very sympathetic to Regina whom I saw as the cause of all the trouble. Please forgive me!'

'How did Regina take this?'

'She said: "As Walpole's friend I counted on you to help him. But if you won't, then get me a car or taxi. I shall go to the Prime Minister's office. I shall see him if I have to stand outside his door all day. I'm not leaving Walpole inside there!" '

'Did she go?'

'No, because while I was still raising objections the phone rang – and it was Basil!'

'Is he safe?'

'Indeed he is – thanks to you. Because if you hadn't. . . .'

'Where is he?' Walpole interposed.

'Safe in Accra, just as you planned. But he got there a day later than you both expected.'

'How was that?'

'When he got to Idiroko he found the driver who had brought his load. But the man wasn't going back to Ghana till next day. Basil suggested finding another driver, but the man warned him not to speak to anyone he didn't know, as the place was full of police spies. However he knew a house where Basil could lie up next day, and at night he'd smuggle him out in a load of household goods. Provided, of course, Basil could pay – which thanks to you he could. But for the hold-up, Basil said, he'd have phoned twenty-four hours earlier – and I'd have been round to see you yesterday.'

'It was Basil's name they were trying to get out of me . . . I was afraid he might have been held up – which is why I wouldn't give it.'

Mr Chukuma took Walpole's hand across the table, but for a moment could not speak. Then: 'We'll talk about Basil later. . . . It's you we're concerned with now, and how to get you out.'

'Not easy, I imagine.'

'Not at once. The first thing is to show the authorities that you've got influential friends, and a case which is going to be fought. Of course if your father-in-law speaks up too, that'll help the situation.'

'I'm sure he won't. And he's got enough explaining to do on his own account – having his son-in-law involved in . . . in what?'

' "Treasonable felony" would be the charge – if it ever came to trial, which I intend to see it doesn't. But we're not dependent on Efunshile. When I get to the office I shall call one or two legal friends in high places and set things moving. We shall maintain your hundred per cent innocence of any connection with the plot.' He paused and lowered his voice to a whisper: 'I suppose we *can* maintain that, can't we?'

'One hundred per cent. I'm no conspirator at any time – but I detest inept conspiracies!'

'I was sure of it!' Mr Chukuma said with a relief that belied his words. 'As your legal adviser I'll be seeing you regularly and you can tell me the whole story bit by bit. . . . In the long run there's no cause to worry. The more inquiries they make, the more they'll find you in the clear. And now that Basil's abroad, we can use the fact of his involvement – for which he must carry responsibility himself. The immediate thing is for me to see the governor. I shall let him know who he's dealing with, have you examined by a doctor, and of course arrange to have food and anything you need sent in. I anticipate no problem there. Now – is there anything I can do for you outside?'

'Only take care of Regina – particularly on account of Duke. If he knows she's about he'll send some of his thugs after her. If she's with you though, even he'll think twice.'

'He had better,' said Mr Chukuma grimly. 'She will be with my wife and me while you're inside. Have you any message for her?'

'Yes. Tell her I'm always with her, just as she is always with me. And if I had to go through it all over again to be with her in the end, I'd do it gladly.'

Mr Chukuma said nothing for a moment, and then a voice that was almost tender, asked: 'Anything else?'

'Yes. Have a man fetch my car from Idiroko where Basil left it in some garage.'

An hour later a doctor visited Walpole in his cell. He asked no questions, but bandaged him where the skin was broken, gave him ointments and sleeping pills, and sent for the chief prison officer. He instructed him that Walpole was to be given a mattress and blanket. He was to be allowed special food which was being sent in for him, and he must have clean water to take the medicines given him. 'I shall be seeing this man again in two days' time,' he said warningly, and went out leaving Walpole a great deal happier, and grateful for that combination of financial reward with intimidation which Mr Chukuma knew so well how to apply.

Towards evening came an important change. Walpole was taken out of solitary confinement and put into a large cell with several other prisoners. This was something he had dreaded, disliking the idea of intimate contact with strangers and afraid he would find them hostile. To his surprise, however, he was made welcome and even treated with respect. Two of his cellmates were 'politicals' pulled in on the same night as himself. They were small fish who had joined the conspiracy for what they could get, hand-outs of cash, the loan of a car, a few weeks in Ghana for so-called 'military training', and they looked on Walpole as one who had supported the same cause but at the risk of wealth and position. His refusal to give away names was already known, as all such knowledge quickly becomes known in prison, marking him out as a courageous character. Before long too the supplies of food promised by

Mr Chukuma started to come in on a generous scale, and were freely shared with his companions.

But if respect surprised him, something he had expected less was a kind of liveliness and at times even gaiety about the place, which he now knew to be the celebrated Kiri-Kiri prison. Once the upheaval caused by the new arrests had died down, the newcomers been absorbed into the community and the prison officers were less under pressure, this liveliness soon reappeared. Its leading spirit was a tubby, vivacious man in his late thirties, that same Freddie Fagbemi whom Walpole had known as a night-club owner and leader of his own 'High Life' band, and who had now been in Kiri-Kiri for more than a year. Naturally reckless and extravagant, when his club got into difficulties he had attempted to solve them by writing cheques with signatures that were not always his own. Following his conviction he had rechristened himself 'Mr Fraudulent Conversion', and was known throughout the prison as 'Fraudie'. He at once recognized Walpole and, having learned of the charge he expected to face, gave him the name of 'Mr Treasonable Felon, or 'Felon' for short.

Freddie enlivened prison life with mock trials, debates and clowning performances of all kinds, but his most popular activity was the prison orchestra, carefully trained and re-hearsed by himself. This gave performances after the last meal of the day – with squeezebox, mouth organ, whistles, spoons played as castanets and the rhythmical drumming of wrists and elbows on wooden tables – which officers from all over the prison found excuses to attend. Once established as general entertainer, Freddie enjoyed the run of the prison looking for new talent and, knowledgeable in the by-ways of prison life, he soon initiated Walpole into many small ways of making life more comfortable.

'Anything's possible in prison,' he explained, 'provided you have the one thing needful – money. So it's really just like life outside.'

Walpole thought gratefully that as long as he had the contents of his socks, life would be bearable. Having expected to find prison gloomy and depressing, he found in Kiri-Kiri a boisterous communal life more appropriate to an army on the march than to a bunch of outcasts guilty over the past and with nothing to hope for in the future.

Mr Chukuma's next visit took place a couple of weeks after Walpole's change of cell and they met in the same room as

before. He had been seeing much of Regina meantime and
while Walpole was eager to learn how she was, Mr Chukuma
kept repeating: 'A lovely girl! A truly lovely girl! My friend,
you are fortunate indeed! I wonder if you appreciate your own
good fortune!'

'I know! I know – but tell me, how *is* she?'

Mr Chukuma sighed. 'How I wish I were thirty years
younger! I would have been a very different man.'

'Yes, yes. But is she happy? Is she well?'

'She thinks you are a hero! What more can you ask? She's
distressed to think of you in prison – but she's happier to know
you're noble than miserable over your sufferings.'

'Noble? Me? Why the whole thing was accidental. . . . If I'd
known I was going to be arrested, I'd never have offered to
move the lorry. Anyway, it was as much to protect myself as
Basil that I shifted it.'

'Possibly, my friend. But it wasn't to protect yourself that
you remained silent under a heavy beating – was it? You're
noble in Regina's eyes, and you're noble to my wife and
myself, and to Stephen and Cécile.'

'Well, I won't argue against being thought well of by
Regina – or by you. But tell me, how's everything on the legal
side?'

'Nothing definite yet. But a situation which may be very
helpful is starting to build up. One of my contacts is a civil
servant in the Ministry of Justice who's under an obligation to
me. He tells me that at this moment the government is
extremely worried as to how to play the situation.'

'What d'you mean – how to "play" it?'

'At first they simply rounded everyone up and questioned
them. The idea was to lay on "Show Trials", convict as many
as they could on the most serious charges possible – then sit
back and congratulate themselves on having crushed the plot
and warned off others who might be thinking the same way.'

'Well? *Why* don't they do this?'

'Because the more they inquire, the further they find the
conspiracy had spread. There's talk of "sleeping partners"
inside the federal government itself ! And it's been admitted that
no conspiracy – above all a crackbrained one like this – could
have gone so far without collusion from high up in the army
and police. What's making them sweat is the thought of what
will come out if they launch public trials. They must produce
hard evidence to justify the arrests and the alarming statements

they've put out. But if the trials give the impression that half the country's disaffected, the whole thing must recoil on their own heads.'

Walpole laughed. 'They want to frighten off those tempted to conspire, not encourage them to make a better job next time.'

'Exactly – and the line isn't easy to draw. At the moment the legal advisers are split. Some argue it would have been wiser if the whole thing had been more or less hushed up from the beginning.'

'How does this affect me?'

'I don't know yet – but I shall do before long,' and he went on to report that he had been over to Ghana to see Basil and discuss his future. They had agreed that Basil should go abroad for a year or two, probably to London to study civil engineering, and when he had acquired qualifications – and the political storm died down – he might possibly come back into the firm. Nwanyieke might either join him in London or go back to her village, as the two of them decided.

'Basil also asked how he could help you. I told him the best thing he could do was write a full record of his own involvement, come with me to a commissioner for oaths and swear an affidavit. So I have brought back a statement covering all his Enugu activities, ending with his bringing the arms in and dumping them on you. He declares you warned him more than once to have nothing to do with the plotters – and had actually made him promise to give it all up. His friend, Jackson Apara – *not* a man I took to warmly – was also in Accra and short of funds. So he too was glad to write an affidavit – not as useful as Basil's and a lot more expensive. But it provides reinforcement, and I've given copies of both to my civil servant friend.'

A further fortnight passed before Walpole saw Mr Chukuma again, and he could tell from his expression he had something on his mind. He had been summoned to see one of the government's chief legal advisers. After the usual compliments, this man explained that the government was anxious not to extend the number of those held under Emergency Regulations beyond the absolute minimum, and that he had been given the task of going through the list and making recommendations for release. Among those under consideration was Walpole Abiose '. . . and he asked if I could provide any special reasons for making such a recommendation in your case. Well, of course,' Mr Chukuma went on, 'I covered the familiar ground of your having taken little part in political life, and none at all in the conspiracy. I also took a chance and said they must have corroboration of this from the fact that your name cannot ever have been mentioned by persons they interrogated. Naturally he wasn't going to confirm this to me, but I saw from his face that it was true. I went on to tell him we have conceded your having driven a vehicle containing arms, but it was evident you had little idea of the contents and no intention of delivering them to the conspirators – from whom indeed you were actually taking them *away*. The most you could properly be charged with therefore, was a quite minor offence such as hindering the police in the execution of their duties, despite which you had already been more than a month in prison without any charges being brought. He answered that the case involved much more than a minor offence, as would be clear if it ever came to court. But he went on to suggest that this might be avoided providing a satisfactory formula could be found for your release.'

'What did you say to that?'

'I nodded sagely and waited to hear what he proposed.'

'What *did* he propose?'

'It's a suggestion you may not altogether like, Walpole. It seems reasonable to me, but whether we avail ourselves of it or not is entirely up to you. Their problem,' Mr Chukuma explained, 'is that the formula must be special to yourself. It must not apply to other cases or establish any kind of precedent.'

'Sounds a tall order. What's their suggestion?'

'The authorities might consider releasing you if it can be shown that at the time of the offence you were not fully responsible for your actions. . . . You were under great stress . . . the business facing difficulties . . . your marriage breaking up . . . and then suddenly you found your best friend in danger. Emotionally and mentally you'd reached breaking point and were guilty of an action quite out of character – an action reckless almost to insanity.'

'Insanity? You mean I should be certified?'

'No, no, no! No one's suggesting anything of the kind, and if they were I should no more consent to it than you would. But there's a gap between normal behaviour and actual insanity – and in law that gap can prove useful. As it happens, there's at present in the University of Nsukka an American

Professor of Psychology personally known to the Minister of Justice. Someone from that ministry has already spoken to this professor, who has expressed interest in your case. He would constitute an expert opinion, and is also someone in whom the government feels confidence. So the suggestion is simply that this professor comes to see you.'

'Whose suggestion is it?'

'The government's But the formal approach must come from our side. In other words I make application to the authorities for the professor to visit you as part of the preparation of your defence.'

'Then what happens?'

'The government gives permission and he sees you. Then, if he writes a report saying in effect that you're a well-behaved citizen who acted as you did in a moment of aberration due to stress, the way is open for you to be released into the care of some even more well-behaved and responsible citizen – who in this case would be myself. It gets you out, but provides no precedent for the plotters. What d'you think of the idea?'

'Think? I don't need to think – I jump at it! I don't fancy being let out of here in order to be shut up in an asylum. But released on grounds of "diminished responsibility", "exceptional stress" or whatever, into the care of my old friend Chukuma – why, what more could I ask?'

'That's how I hoped you'd feel. . . . So you're willing to see the prof?'

'Just wheel him in, and "the sooner the quicker" as my father-in-law says.'

Professor Willard W. Gompertz, seconded from the University of Abilene to the University of Nsukka to assist in setting up its new Department of Applied Psychology, Business Psychiatry and Financial Reintegration, was a grey man of indeterminate age whose gold-rimmed spectacles protected watery blue eyes. He spoke rapidly in a high fluting voice as though lecturing in church, and throughout several hours with Walpole nothing resembling a smile disturbed the flatness of his features. The first half-hour was spent by the professor on the subject of his own qualifications, outlining his academic history, listing his degrees, mentioning articles which had appeared in learned journals with a short résumé of their contents. He stressed that his temporary absence from Abilene was not due to lack of enthusiasm for him on the part of colleagues, students or administration, but on the contrary. . . . 'They are anxious for me to bring my powers of identifying with students and motivating them positively, to bear in the challenge of a "developing country situation".'

When the professor paused, Walpole asked politely whether he had found scope at Nsukka for such identifying and motivation, and the professor replied that there had at first been opposition due to misunderstanding, but that this had quickly been resolved. '. . . and it is in consequence of my experience in handling conflict situations that the government has consulted me over its current dilemma, in which authority has to be preserved while at the same time individual liberty must be respected. You will appreciate,' he went on, 'my obligation to make my qualifications clear before asking you to reply to a number of questions, some concerned with your early life and others related to recent activities.' Walpole, who had begun to think the professor would continue to talk throughout the interview, and that the most asked of him would be to fill in a printed form, soon found himself answering questions which were often difficult. But he replied as honestly as he could and the professor took down his replies in shortened form.

After more than two hours of this, the professor asked if there were any further points Walpole wished to make. Cooperation over the task had produced a dry camaraderie between them and this – coupled with the fact that the professor had taken off his glasses and without them looked oddly defenceless – caused Walpole to reply: 'I'll be glad if your visit leads to my release, but whether it does or not, thank you for coming here. I hope from your point of view it hasn't been a waste of time.'

The professor put his glasses back on. 'For me, Mr Abiose, *no* new experience is a waste of time.'

'But I'm pretty sure his new experience was a waste of time for me,' Walpole told Mr Chukuma when he called a week later to discuss the interview.

'You're mistaken, Walpole. Look at this' – and he handed over the carbon of a couple of typed sheets.

In compliance with instructions I interviewed Mr Walpole Abiose in Kiri-Kiri prison.

Mr Abiose conveys the overall impression of a balanced citizen, lacking symptoms of serious deviation from accepted behavioral patterns. Certain negative factors resulting from parental deprivation and scholastic inadequacy had been overcome by early adulthood and a more than adequate record of business achievement attained. Two principal partners, both of whom were also interviewed, commented on the subject's capacity to isolate relevant factors and extrapolate appropriate solutions to industrial and constructional problems of challenging complexity.

Politically he does not appear to have been excessively, perhaps not even adequately, involved in the current situation patterns of a developing state, and there are no indications of the 'rebellion syndrome' which seldom fails to manifest itself to a qualified inquirer within the interviewal timespan. Recently it appears that exceptional circumstances and in particular problems connected with his marriage had led to a loosening of the subject's grip on reality factors. His readiness to renounce a valuable directorial position for reasons of a purely emotional nature is a significant indicator of that weakening of financial stimulus which not infrequently proves the precursor to a loss of sense of values and a general personality breakdown. As of now, the subject is tending to react with criticism to the normal stratification of any ongoing materially-oriented society such as ours, and seeking solutions to problems personal in origin through notions of community service which derive from an association emotional in character with a young woman with whom he is involved. It must be emphasized that such notions, albeit impeding to the success-drive of the subject himself, are of a kind to preclude and not induce any form of violent action or hostile manifestation of a socio-political nature.

As a result of conflicts on a variety of levels, the subject was under intense strain during the weeks immediately preceding his arrest, so that emotional and idealistic fantasies were tending to obscure the dictates of natural self-interest.

It is the opinion of this interviewer, having given full weight to all relevant factors, that if the decision is taken to release this subject no dangerous consequence of a political or social nature need be anticipated. But at this moment in time and while a measurable degree of personality disturbance may be assumed to continue in operation, it would be advisable that release should take place within the parameters of a familiar, stabilized environment and into the care of some trusted associate, preferably senior in age, who would be in a position on the one hand to regulate any tendency to idealistic excess and on the other to guard against decline into self-generating inertia with consequent debilitation of the decision-making process. Particular consideration has been given to possible consequences of the subject's release, both as establishing precedent and as providing excuse for criticism media-wise, but from the available feedback it does not appear that either of these possibilities need serve as an inhibiting factor in arriving at any early decision.

>*Signed*: Willard A. Gompertz
>Professor of Psychological Assessment in the University of Abilene
>Visiting Professor of Applied Psychology, Business Psychiatry and Financial Reintegration in the University of Nsukka

Walpole read the document through twice before handing it back to Mr Chukuma. 'I can't see that getting me out of here, can you?'

'Indeed I *can*! And if I understand the official who talked to me, it's exactly what the government requires to get you off its hands.'

'But it doesn't mean anything at all.'

'*Precisely* – but it says it in the accepted terms and the appropriate tone of voice. So it won't be easy for opponents to criticize.'

'*When* might it get me out of here?'

'In two or three weeks, I hope, once all the right people have initialled it.'

Walpole seized Mr Chukuma's hand: 'D'you mean I might see Regina *in three weeks*?'

'See her, my friend? I hope you'll be with her for good.'

'You've done wonders – as always! And there's no trusted associate, senior in age and of exceptional stability, into whose care I'd sooner be released. And if you're right about the professor, he's certainly earned his fee.'

'Wait,' grunted Mr Chukuma, 'till you hear how much he charges.'

Back in his cell Walpole found Fraudie instructing his 'secretary' to make out invitations on sheets of toilet paper to be sent to a chosen list of inmates.

'What's going on?' he asked.

'We're having a debate tonight – just twenty or thirty friends and a little liquor. You're down as one of the speakers.'

'What's the subject?'

'Is Life a Rat Race, or a Search for God?'

'But I can't speak on either side.'

'Why not?'

'Because I think it's both.'

'Good!' said Fraudie. 'That means we have speakers of equal weight and calibre. Put down well-known businessman

Walpole Abiose to propose the Rat Race, and our friend
Treasonable Felon to reply for God.'

45
Liberation

While Walpole was still awaiting the result of the professor's
intervention, an envelope was brought him in his cell. It came
from a firm of solicitors.

Dear Sir,
This is to inform you that we have been instructed by our client Mrs
Alicia Abiose to initiate proceedings for divorce. You will be aware
you have afforded ample grounds for such proceedings and the fact that
you have allowed yourself to become associated with a treasonable
conspiracy makes it essential in the interest of her family as well as of
herself that the case proceed with the minimum of delay. We shall be
glad to receive notice from your solicitors as to whether you intend to
defend the case or not, also as to the financial provision you propose
making for our client.
*　　Yours etc.*

Walpole gazed at the letter with amazement. That he would
one day come out of prison he had assumed, all he need do was
to be patient, and sooner or later he would be free. But that he
might be freed from his marriage without years of delay and
endless negotiation was something that had hardly crossed his
mind. There was for the moment no one else in the cell, and he
leaned back on his pallet and closed his eyes while a sense of
thankfulness spread over him like the warm water of a bath.
But to whom or what was he thankful? To help a friend he had
done a disinterested action, and the consequence had been
what was to be expected – beating-up, imprisonment,
disgrace. But this further, utterly unexpected, consequence
was a boon which far outweighed those sufferings, a liberation
much greater than the confinement of his weeks in prison.
Was this mere accident, a chance coincidence? Or was it some

kind of reward? But if reward, where had it come from?

It seemed in a strange way logical – a gift of freedom for an acceptance of confinement. But what did such logic imply? Is there in the seeming confusion of life an underlying pattern, based on the fact that at some invisible level all human beings are united? If so, then by helping another we must always in some way help ourselves, and shall equally incur suffering for every injury we do. But since we do not relate cause with its effect, both good and bad fortune come as 'bolts from the blue' which we feel we have done nothing to deserve. Yet if there is indeed such a pattern, a justice and a logic in seeming chaos, by what unseen powers is it maintained? Where are the judge and jury? Are these the ancestors, the once embodied now disembodied wisdom of past ages, its possessors having moved on into a world from which they keep watch over their children, rewarding us lovingly and beyond expectation for any generous act, and not so much punishing us for meanness, dishonesty, cowardice, as allowing us to meet their inevitable consequences in the knowledge that one day we are bound to learn?

Or is this logic and justice – whereby the good tend to become happy despite seeming misfortune and the self-interested miserable in spite of all their gains – maintained by what men call 'God', a universal spirit pervading all creation in its endless task of evolution, but affecting us humans in a special sense because we possess consciousness and hence the capacity to grow in understanding.

Ancestors or God, Walpole felt he had had a glimpse of their influence at work, and as he lay with eyes closed he seemed, as if from some tower or point of vantage, to view the prison and its inmates, prisoners and guards alike, busy at their various tasks but all connected without knowing it. And now, floating higher, he could see far over the country in villages and towns the dependents of these prisoners and guards, the families they loved, and these too all united with each other and himself as part of a network reaching out to cover the whole world. He could see this network like some shining web, and the thought came to him that if ever the peoples of the world should look up and perceive it only just above their heads, the whole nature of life would be transformed, and everyday relationships would take on the blissful aspect of his own with Regina.

And as he thought of Regina and that before very long they would be married, he took in for the first time what this was

going to mean. Every relationship in the past he had looked on
as a bonus, an addition to life in which he would remain the
same as before while something extra – sexual pleasure,
companionship, money, access to influence and power –
would be added to what he already had.

But marrying Regina would not be like that at all. It would
be more like a dive into a lake, with the certainty that whatever
its surface hid he would no more emerge unchanged than she
would. For both it would be a total relationship into which
their whole natures would be drawn and altered, perhaps
almost out of recognition, losing much but gaining infinitely
more, until over the years they grew into a blissful oneness
which he could actually feel, as he stretched himself on the
planks, pervading his whole being.

From his reverie Walpole was distracted by voices outside
the cell door, implying that the inmates were coming back
from exercise.

'Dey say dis Walpole Abiose goin' be set free 'cos he bin
mad when he done take dat mammy-wagon full o' guns?'

'Is so, my frien', I hearin' dis same t'ing.'

'I got noth'n 'gainst dis Walpole, noth'n 't all, but I myself
bin madder dan dis man. So why dey settin' um free, not me?'

'De *gov'ment* say dis Walpole mad. Gov'ment no say you bin
mad – only you yo'self sayin' dat. If you kin make gov'ment
sign paper sayin' you bin mad den you goin' free same like dis
Walpole. But how you git yo'self dis piece of paper? Dat what
I askin' you, my frien'.'

A day or two later, when Mr Chukuma came to see him
with the news that the government accepted the report of Mr
Willard Gompertz and were proposing shortly to release him,
Walpole handed him the letter he had received.

'Ha! We've got them there!' Mr Chukuma chuckled,
punching his fist into his open hand. 'When you wanted a
divorce there was nothing doing. Now *they're* asking for it,
not you. Your wife has given just as much grounds for divorce
as you have – more, since it's very doubtful if she ever broke
off her association with her cousin. You could bring proceedings yourself and not have to pay a penny. But if they want it
this way – which is obviously better for Efunshile's position
and Alicia's future prospects – they can have it. But in that
case, no financial provision. Oh, no, no!'

'But I'm prepared to make financial provision,' Walpole
objected.

'Why on earth should you? Damn it – it's not as if the woman were hard up.'

'Because I told Alicia I would, and anyway I owe her something for having married her at all! I'd have given every penny I possess to get free from this marriage, so if it's handed to me on a plate I should be willing to pay reasonably.'

'Reasonably perhaps – but not ridiculously. Whatever you said to Alicia was said under quite different circumstances – circumstances in which she was refusing what she's now trying to obtain. I'm your legal adviser, Walpole, and I mean this to be handled practically. They can keep most, but not all, of your marriage settlement. But you're going to keep the house, and there can be no question of your having to pay alimony.'

'But. . . .'

'No more, Walpole! Leave this to me to handle as I think best, or I throw up the work and you find yourself another lawyer.'

Walpole laughed. 'I *could* find myself another lawyer – there are several inside this prison if it comes to that. But where could I find myself another Chukuma?'

Mr Chukuma smiled agreement. 'Of course you couldn't, Walpole, no such creature exists. And you couldn't go to another lawyer anyway even if you wanted to, because in three days' time you'll be released into my care and supervision. So you're wise to make the best of what you've got. The day after tomorrow, my friend, I shall be calling for you here. Regina is already with us, and I shall take you straight back to my home where you'll both stay as long as you please – and it can't possibly be long enough for my wife and myself.'

When Fraudie came back to the cell, Walpole told him the glad news – tomorrow was to be his final day in prison.

'Is there anything left in that sock of yours, Felon?'

'There is.'

'Then hand it over.'

Walpole passed over all that remained and the next evening after the prison meal ended, Mr Fraudulent Conversion stood up and silence fell.

'Inmates and members of the Kiri-Kiri Club – the easiest to join and the hardest to resign from in Nigeria – I've an announcement to make. A member of our company, Mr Walpole Abiose, is leaving us. During his stay he has made many friends and we would gladly keep him longer if he cared to stay. He has also made national and legal history – he is the first Insane Treasonable Felon our country has produced.

Whatever position he may take up after leaving our establish-
ment, this marks him as a man of promise. We shall follow his
progress with interest – so far as it is possible to do so from
inside these walls.

'Here in these buckets beside me I have what appears to be
dishwater, but it is not dishwater – it is very good palm wine
which Mr Abiose has provided. How did it get here? In the
same way we all did – being carried in bodily by our good
friends the prison officers. If you will pass up your mugs, and
then wait till all customers are served, we will drink together
to our friend's happiness. After that the musicians have an
entertainment for us.'

When each mug had rejoined its owner, Mr Fraudulent
Conversion stood up and raised his to Walpole. There was an
outburst of applause and then every prisoner raised his too and
either drained or sipped, swallowed or spun out the contents
according to his nature.

'And now,' cried Fraudie, 'I want silence for the new High
Life written in our friend's honour. We shall play and sing two
verses to give you the theme – then you can all take it away!'

He looked round at his orchestra, raised a spoon as baton,
and launched away:

> Insane pris'ners bin de happies' pris'ners
> Dat plain for all to see
> Insane pris'ners bin de happies' pris'ners
> Dat go for you 'n' me.

> Insane pris'ners bin de happies' pris'ners
> Dat what de records show
> Insane pris'ners bin de happies' pris'ners
> Dat cos dey lett'n um go.

The tune was catchy and the beat potent and familiar, so that in
no time many of the prisoners were on their feet, jiving,
twisting, rocking, threading their way in and out of tables and
trucking off into the open spaces of the hall, while the rest
hammered the rhythm out with spoons on plates or with their
knuckles on the wooden tables, just as though it were their
own release they were celebrating.

> Insane pris'ners bin de happies' pris'ners
> In all Kirree-Kirree
> Insane pris'ners bin de happies' pris'ners
> Dat cos dey sett'n um free.